1

Dick o' the Fens: A Tale of the Great East Swamp

by George Manville Fenn

Copyright © 10/15/2015
Jefferson Publication

ISBN-13: 978-1518641305

Printed in the United States of America

Table of Contents

Chapter One.

In the Fen.

Dick Winthorpe—christened Richard by order of his father at the Hall—sat on the top of the big post by the wheelwright's door.

It was not a comfortable seat, and he could only keep his place by twisting his legs round and holding on; but as there was a spice of difficulty in the task, Dick chose it, and sat there opposite Tom Tallington—christened Thomas at the wish of his mother, Farmer Tallington's wife, of Grimsey, the fen island under the old dyke.

Tom Tallington was seated upon one side of a rough punt, turned up to keep the rain from filling it, and as he was not obliged to hold on with his legs he kept swinging them to and fro.

It was not a pleasant place for either of the lads, for in front of them was a ring of fire where, upon the ground, burned and crackled and fumed a quantity of short wood, which was replenished from time to time by Mark Hickathrift, the wheelwright, and his lad Jacob.

At the first glance it seemed as if the wheelwright was amusing himself by making a round bonfire of scraps, whose blue reek rose in the country air, and was driven every now and then by the wind over the boys, who coughed and sneezed and grumbled, but did not attempt to move, for there was, to them, an interesting feat about to be performed by the wheelwright—to wit, the fitting of the red-hot roughly-made iron tire in the wood fire upon the still more roughly-made wheel, which had been fitted with a few new spokes and a fresh felloe, while Farmer Tallington's heavy tumbril-cart stood close by, like a cripple supported on a crutch, waiting for its iron-shod circular limb.

"Come, I say, Mark, stick it on," cried Dick Winthorpe; "we want to go."

"'Tarn't hot enough, my lad," said the great burly wheelwright, rolling his shirt sleeves a little higher up his brown arms.

"Yes, it is," said Tom Tallington. "You can see it all red. Why don't you put it on cold, instead of burning the wood?"

"'Cause he can't make one fit, and has to burn it on," said Dick.

The wheelwright chuckled and put on some more wood, which crackled and roared as the wind came with a rush off the great fen, making the scattered patches of dry reeds bend and whisper and rustle, and rise and fall, looking in the distance of the grey, black, solemn expanse like the waves of the sea on a breezy day.

"Oh! I say, isn't it choky!" cried Tom.

"Thou shouldstna sit that side then," said the wheelwright.

"Hoy, Dave!" shouted Dick Winthorpe. "Hi, there: Chip, Chip, Chip!" he cried, trying to pat his leg with one hand, the consequence being that he overbalanced himself and dropped off the post, but only to stay down and caress a little black-and-white dog, which trotted up wagging its stump of a tail, and then beginning to growl and snarl, twitching its ears, as another dog appeared on the scene—a long, lank, rough-haired, steely-grey fellow, with a pointed nose, which, with his lean flanks, gave him the aspect of an animal of a vain disposition, who had tried to look like a greyhound, and failed.

This dog trotted out of the wheelwright's workshop, with his coat full of shavings and sawdust, and lay down a short distance from the fire, while the little black-and-white fellow rushed at him, leaped up, and laid hold of his ear.

"Ha, ha! look at old Grip!" cried Tom Tallington, kicking his heels together as the big dog gave his ears a shake, and lay down with his head between his paws, blinking at the fire, while his little assailant uttered a snarl, which seemed to mean "Oh you coward!" and trotted away to meet a tall rugged-looking man, who came slouching up, with long strides, his head bent, his shoulders up, a long heavy gun over his shoulder, and a bundle of wild-fowl in his left hand, the birds banging against his leather legging as he walked, and covering it with feathers.

He was a curious, furtive-looking man, with quick, small eyes, a smooth brown face, and crisp, grizzly hair, surmounted by a roughly-made cap of fox-skin.

He came straight up to the fire on the windy side, nodded and scowled at the wheelwright as the latter gave him a friendly smile, and then turned slowly to the two boys, when his visage relaxed a little, and there was the dawning of a smile for each.

"What have you got, Dave?" cried Dick, laying hold of the bunch of birds, and turning them over, so as to examine their heads and feet; and, without waiting for an answer, he went on—"Three curlews, two pie-wipes, and a—and a—I say, Tom, what's this?"

Tom Tallington looked eagerly at the straight-billed, long-legged, black-and-white bird, but shook his head, while Chip, the dog, who had seated himself with his nose close to the bunch, uttered one short sharp bark.

"I say, Dave, what's this bird?" said Dick.

The man did not turn his head, but stood staring at the fire, and said, in a husky voice, what sounded like "Scatcher!"

"Oh!" said Dick; and there was a pause, during which the fire roared, and the smoke flew over the wheelwright's long, low house at the edge of the fen. "I say," cried Dick, "you don't set oyster-catchers in the 'coy."

"Yow don't know what you're talking about," growled the man addressed.

"Why, of course he didn't," cried Tom Tallington, a stoutly-built lad of sixteen or seventeen, very much like his companion Dick, only a little fairer and plumper in the face. "They ain't swimmers."

"No, of course, not," said Dick. "Kill 'em all at one shot, Dave?"

The man made no answer, but his little dog uttered another short bark as if in assent.

"Wish I'd been there," said Dick, and the dog barked once more, after which the new-comer seemed to go off like a piece of machinery, for he made a sound like the word "kitch," threw the bunch of birds to the wheelwright, who caught them, and dropped them in through the open window of the workshop on to his bench, while Dave jerked his gun off his shoulder, and let the butt fall between his feet.

Just then the wheelwright roared out, with one hand to his cheek:

"Sair—rah! Ale. Here you, Jake, go and fetch it."

The short thickset lad of nineteen, who now came from behind the house with a fagot of wood, threw it down, and went in, to come back in a few moments with a large brown jug, at the top of which was some froth, which the wind blew off as the vessel was handed to the wheelwright.

"She's about ready now," said the latter. "You may as well lend a hand, Dave."

As he spoke, he held out the jug to the donor of the birds, who only nodded, and said, as if he had gone off again, "Drink;" and propping the gun up against the crippled cart, he took off his rough jacket and hung it over the muzzle.

In kindly obedience to the uttered command, the big wheelwright raised the brown vessel, and took a long draught, while Dave, after hanging up his jacket, stood and looked on, deeply interested apparently, watching the action of the drinker's throat as the ale went down.

Jacob, the wheelwright's 'prentice, looked at the ale-jug with one eye and went on placing a piece of wood here and another there to keep up the blaze, while Dick went and leaned up against the cart by the gun.

Then the jug was passed, after a deep sigh, to Dave, who also took a long draught, which made Jacob sigh as he turned to go for some more wood, when he was checked by a hollow growl from Dave, which came out of the pot.

But Jacob knew what it meant, and stopped, waiting patiently till Dave took the brown jug from his lips, and passed it to the apprentice, letting off the words now:

"Finish it."

Jacob was a most obedient apprentice, so he proceeded to "finish it," while the wheelwright and Dave went to the workshop, and as he was raising the vessel high Tom Tallington stooped, picked up a chip of wood from a heap, gave Dick a sharp look, and pitched it with so good an aim that it hit the jug, and before the drinker could lower it, Tom had hopped back against the cart, striking against the gun, and nearly knocking it down.

"I see yow, Masr' Dick," said Jacob, grinning; "but yow don't get none. Ale arn't good for boys."

"Get out!" cried Dick; "why, you're only a boy yourself. 'Prentice, 'prentice!"

"Not good for boys," said Jacob again as he finished the last drop perseveringly, so that there should be none left; and then went indoors with the jug.

"Dick—I say," whispered Tom as, after slipping one band into the big open pocket of the hanging coat, he drew out a well scraped and polished cow-horn with a cork in the thin end.

Chip, the dog, who was watching, uttered a remonstrant bark, but the boys paid no heed, being too intent upon the plan that now occurred to one, and was flashed instantaneously to the other.

"Yes, do," whispered Dick. "How much is there in it?"

"Don't know; can't see."

"Never mind, pitch it in and let's go, only don't run."

"It would be too bad," said Tom, laughing.

"Never mind—we'll buy him some more powder. In with it."

"No," said Tom, hesitating, though the trick was his suggestion.

Dick snatched the powder-horn from his companion, gave a hasty glance at the workshop, from which came the clink of pincers, and pitched the horn right into the middle of the blaze.

Chip gave a sharp bark, and dashed after it, but stopped short, growling as he felt the heat, and then went on barking furiously, while the two boys walked off toward the rough road as fast as they could, soon to be beyond the reach of the wheelwright's explosion of anger, for they regretted not being able to stop and see the blow-up.

"What's your Chip barking at?" said the wheelwright, as the two men walked out, armed with great iron pincers, the wheelwright holding a pair in each hand. "What is it, Chip?"

The dog kept on barking furiously, and making little charges at the fire.

"There's summat there," said Dave in a low harsh voice. "Where's they boys?"

"Yonder they go," said the wheelwright.

"Then there's summat wrong," said Dave, taking off his fox-skin cap and scratching his head.

An idea occurred to him, and he ran to his coat.

"Hah!" he ejaculated in a voice that sounded like a saw cutting wood and coming upon a nail; "keep back, Chip! Here, Chip, boy; Chip! They've throwed in my powder-horn."

"Eh!" cried the wheelwright.

Pop! went the horn with a feeble report, consequent upon there being only about a couple of charges of powder left; but it was enough to scatter the embers in all directions, and for a few moments all stood staring at the smoking wood in the midst of which lay the great iron tire, rapidly turning black.

Dave was the first to recover himself.

"Come on," he shouted, and, pincers in hand, he seized the heated ring, the wheelwright followed suit, the apprentice joined, and lifting the glowing iron it was soon being hammered into its place round the smoking wheel, the soft metal bending and yielding, and burning its way till, amidst the blinding smoke, it was well home and cooling and shrinking, this part of the business being rapidly concluded by means of buckets of water brought by Jacob, and passed along the edge of the wheel.

"I say, Tom, it wasn't half a bang," said Dick as the two lads ran towards home with the wind whistling by their ears.

"No," was the panted-out reply; "but I say, what will old Dave say?"

"I don't care what he says. I shall give him a shilling to buy some more powder, and he can soon make himself another horn."

Chapter Two.

The Great Fen Drain.

"Yes, it's all right, Master Winthorpe," said Farmer Tallington; "but what will the folks say?"

"Say! What have they got to do with it?" cried Squire Winthorpe. "You boys don't make so much noise. I can't hear myself speak."

"Do you hear, Tom, howd thy row, or I'll send thee home," said the farmer; "recollect where you be."

"Yes, father," said, the lad.

"It wasn't Tom; it was me," said Dick quietly.

"Then hold your tongue, sir," cried the squire. "Now look here, Master Tallington. If a big drain is cut right through the low fen, it will carry off all the water; and where now there's nothing but peat, we can get acres and acres of good dry land that will graze beasts or grow corn."

"Yes, that's fine enough, squire," said Tom's father; "but what will the fen-men say?"

"I don't care what they say," cried the squire hotly. "There are about fifty of us, and we're going to do it. Will you join?"

"Hum!" said Tom Tallington's father, taking his long clay-pipe from his lips and scratching his head with the end. "What about the money?"

"You'll have to be answerable for a hundred pounds, and it means your own farm worth twice as much, and perhaps a score of acres of good land for yourself."

"But it can't be good land, squire. There be twenty foot right down o' black peat, and nowt under that but clay."

"I tell you that when the water's out of it, James Tallington, all that will be good valuable land. Now, then, will you join the adventurers?"

"Look here, squire, we've known each other twenty year, and I ask thee as a man, will it be all right?"

"And I tell you, man, that I'm putting all I've got into it. If it were not right, I wouldn't ask you to join."

"Nay, that you wouldn't, squire," said Farmer Tallington, taking a good draught from his ale. "I'm saäving a few pounds for that young dog, and I believe in you. I'll be two hundred, and that means—"

"Twice as much land," said the squire, holding out his hand. "Spoken like a man, Master Tallington; and if the draining fails, which it can't do, I'll pay you two hundred myself."

"Nay, thou weänt," said Farmer Tallington stoutly. "Nay, squire, I'll tak' my risk of it, and if it turns out bad, Tom will have to tak' his chance like his father before him. I had no two hundred or five hundred pounds to start me."

"Nor I," said the squire.

"May we talk now, father?" said Dick.

"Yes, if you like."

"Then," cried Dick, "I wish you wouldn't do it. Why, it'll spoil all the fishing and the 'coy, and we shall get no ice for our pattens, and there'll be no water for the punt, and no wild swans or geese or duck, and no peat to cut or reeds to slash. Oh, I say, father, don't drain the fen."

"Why, you ignorant young cub," cried the squire, "do you suppose you are always to be running over the ice in pattens, and fishing and shooting?"

"Well, no, not always," said Dick, "but—"

"But—get out with your buts, sir. Won't it be better to have solid land about us instead of marsh, and beef and mutton instead of birds, and wheat instead of fish?"

"No, I don't think so, father."

"Well, then, sir, I do," said the squire. "I suppose you wouldn't like the ague driven away?"

"I don't mind, father," said Dick laughing. "I never get it."

"No, but others do, and pains in their joints, and rheumatics. I say, Tallington, when they get as old as we are, eh?"

"Yes, they'll find out the difference, squire; but do you know, that's how all the fen-men'll talk."

"Let 'em," said the squire; "we've got leave from the king's magistrates to do it; and as for the fen-men, because they want to live like frogs all their lives, is that any reason why honest men shouldn't live like honest men should. There, fill up your pipe again; and as for the fen-men, I'll talk to them."

There was a bonny fire in the great open fireplace, for winter was fast coming on, and the wind that had been rushing across the fen-land and making the reeds rustle, now howled round the great ivy-clad chimney of the Hall, and made the flame and smoke eddy in the wide opening, and threaten every now and then to rush out into the low-ceiled homely room, whose well-polished oak furniture reflected the light.

The two lads sat listening to the talk of their elders, and after a time took up the work that had been lying beside them—to wit, some netting; but before Dick had formed many meshes he stopped to replenish the fire, taking some awkward-looking pieces of split root which were as red as mahogany, and placing them upon the top, where they began to blaze with a brilliant light which told tales of how they were the roots of turpentine-filled pines, which had been growing in the ancient forest that existed before the fen; and then taking from a basket half a dozen dark thick squares of dried peat and placing them round the flaming embers to keep up the heat.

"I say, Tom," said Dick in a low voice, "I don't think I should care to live here if the fen was drained."

"No," replied Tom in the same tone, "it would be a miserable place."

"Now, Tom, lad, home!" said the farmer, getting up. "Good-night, squire!"

"Nay, I won't say good-night yet," cried the squire. "Hats and sticks, Dick, and we'll walk part of the way home with them."

As they left the glowing room with its cosy fire, and opened the hall door to gaze out upon the night, the wind swept over the house and plunged into the clump of pines, which nourished and waved upon the Toft, as if it would root them up. The house was built upon a rounded knoll by the side of the embanked winding river, which ran sluggishly along the edge of the fen; and as the party looked out over the garden and across the fen upon that November night, they seemed to be ashore in the midst of a sea of desolation, which spread beneath the night sky away and away into the gloom.

From the sea, four miles distant, came a low angry roar, which seemed to rouse the wind to shout and shriek back defiance, as it plunged into the pines again, and shook and worried them till it passed on with an angry hiss.

"High-tide, and a big sea yonder," said the squire. "River must be full up. Hope she won't come over and wash us away."

"Wesh me away, you mean," said Farmer Tallington. "You're all right up on the Toft. 'Member the big flood, squire?"

"Ay, fifteen years ago, Tallington, when I came down to you in Hickathrift's duck-punt, and we fetched you and Tom's mother out of the top window."

"Ay, but it weer a bad time, and it's a good job we don't hev such floods o' watter now."

"Ay 'tis," said the squire. "My word, but the sea must bite to-night. Dick here wanted to be a sailor. Better be a farmer a night like this, eh, Tallington?"

"Deal better at home," was the reply, as the door was closed behind them, shutting out the warmth and light; and the little party went down a path leading through the clump of firs which formed a landmark for miles in the great level fen, and then down the slope on the far side, and on to the rough road which ran past Farmer Tallington's little homestead.

The two elder friends went on first, and the lads, who had been together at Lincoln Grammar-School, hung behind.

To some people a walk of two miles through the fen in the stormy darkness of the wintry night would have seemed fraught with danger, the more so that it was along no high-road, but merely a rugged track made by the horses and tumbrils in use at the Toft and at Tallington's Fen farm, Grimsey, a track often quite impassable after heavy rains. There was neither hedge nor ditch to act as guide, no hard white or drab road; nothing but old usage and instinctive habit kept those who traversed the way from going off it to right or left into the oozy fen with its black soft peat, amber-coloured bog water, and patches of bog-moss, green in summer, creamy white and pink in winter; while here and there amongst the harder portions, where heath and broom and furze, whose roots were matted with green and grey coral moss, found congenial soil, were long holes full of deep clear water—some a few yards across, others long zigzag channels like water-filled cracks in the earth, and others forming lanes and ponds and lakes that were of sizes varying from a quarter of a mile to two or three in circumference.

Woe betide the stranger who attempted the journey in the dark, the track once missed there was death threatening him on every hand; while his cries for help would have been unheard as he struggled in the deep black mire, or swam for life in the clear water to find no hold at the side but the whispering reeds, from which, with splashings and whistling of wings, the wild-fowl would rise up, to speed quacking and shrieking away.

But no thoughts of danger troubled the lads as they trudged on slowly and moodily, the deep murmur of their elders' voices being heard from the darkness far ahead.

"Wonder what old Dave said about his powder-flask?" said Tom, suddenly breaking the silence.

"Don't know and don't care," said Dick gruffly.

There was a pause.

"I should like to have been there and heard Old Hicky," said Tom, again breaking the silence.

"Yah! He'd only laugh," said Dick. "He likes a bit of fun as well as we do."

"I should have liked to see the fire fly about."

"So should I, if he'd thought it was Jacob, and given him what he calls a blob," said Dick; "but it wasn't half a bang."

"Well, I wish now we hadn't done it," said Tom.

"Why?"

"Because Dave will be so savage. Next time we go over to his place he'll send us back, and then there'll be no more fun at the duck 'coy, and no netting and shooting."

"Oh, I say, Tom, what a fellow you are! Now is Dave Gittan the man to look sour at anybody who takes him half a pound of powder? Why, he'll smile till his mouth's open and his eyes shut, and take us anywhere."

"Well, half a pound of powder will make a difference," said Tom thoughtfully.

"I'll take him a pound," said Dick magnificently.

"How are you going to get it?"

"How am I going to get it!" said Dick. "Why, let Sam Farles bring it from Spalding; and I tell you what, I won't give him the pound. I'll give him half a pound, and you shall give him the other."

"Ah!" cried Tom eagerly; "and I tell you what, Dick—you know that old lead?"

"What! that they dug up when they made the new cow-house?"

"Yes, give him a lump of that, and we'll help him melt it down some night, and cast bullets and slugs."

"Seems so nasty. Father said it was part of an old lead coffin that one of the monks was buried in."

"Well, what does that matter? It was hundreds of years ago. Dave wouldn't know."

"And if he did he wouldn't mind," said Dick. "All right! we'll take him the lead to-morrow."

"But you haven't got the powder."

"No, but Hicky goes to Ealand to-morrow, and he can take the money to the carrier, and we can tell Dave we've sent for it, and he knows he can believe us, and that'll be all right."

There was another pause, during which the wind shrieked, and far overhead there came a confused gabbling noise, accompanied by the whistling of wings, a strange eerie sound in the darkness that would have startled a stranger. But the boys only stood still and listened.

"There they go, a regular flight!" said Dick. "If Dave hears them won't he wish he'd got plenty of powder and lead!"

7

"Think the old monks'll mind?" said Tom.

"What! that flock of wild-geese going over?"

"No-o-o! Our taking the lead."

"Oh! I say, Tom, you are a chap," cried his companion. "I know you believe in ghosts."

"No, I don't," said Tom stoutly; "but I shouldn't like to live in your old place all the same."

"What! because it's part of the old monastery?"

"Yes. The old fellows were all killed when the Danes came up the river in their boats and burned the place."

"Well, father and I aren't Danes, and we didn't kill them. What stuff!"

"No, but it's not nice all the same to live in a place where lots of people were murdered."

"Tchah! who cares! I don't. It's a capital old place, and you never dig anywhere without finding something."

"Yes," said Tom solemnly, "something that isn't always nice."

"Well, you do sometimes," said Dick, "but not often. But I wouldn't leave the old place for thousands of pounds. Why, where would you get another like it with its old walls, and vaults, and cellars, and thick walls, and the monks' fish-ponds, and all right up on a high toft with the river on one side, and the fen for miles on the other. Look at the fish."

"Yes; it's all capital," said Tom. "I like it ever so; but it is precious monky."

"Well, so are you! Who cares about its being monky! The old monks were jolly old chaps, I know."

"How do you know? Sh! what's that?"

"Fox. Listen."

There was a rush, a splash, a loud cackling noise, and then silence save for the wind.

"He's got him," cried Tom. "I wish we had Hicky's Grip here; he'd make him scuffle and run."

"Think it was a fox?" said Tom.

"Sure of it; and it was one of those old mallards he has got. Come on. Why shouldn't the fox have duck for supper as well as other people?"

"Ah, why not?" said Tom. "But how do you know the monks were jolly old chaps?"

"How do I know! why, weren't they fond of fishing, and didn't they make my ponds? I say, let's have a try for the big pike to-morrow. I saw him fly right out of the water day before yesterday, when it rained. Oh, I say, it is a shame!"

"What's a shame?" said Tom.

"Why, to do all this draining. What's the good of it?"

"To make dry fields."

"But I don't want any more dry fields. Here have I been thinking for years how nice it would be, when we'd done school to have all the run of the fen, and do what we liked, netting, and fishing and shooting, and helping Dave at the 'coy, and John Warren among the rabbits."

"And getting a hare sometimes with Hicky's Grip," put in, Tom.

"Yes; and now all the place is going to be spoiled. I say, are we going right home with you?"

"I suppose so," said Tom. "There's the light. Old Boggy'll hear us directly. I thought so. Here he comes."

There was a deep angry bark at a distance, and this sounded nearer, and was followed by the rustling of feet, ending in a joyous whining and panting as a great sheep-dog raced up to the boys, and began to leap and fawn upon them, but only to stop suddenly, stand sniffing the air in the direction of the old priory, and utter an uneasy whine.

"Hey, boy! what's the matter?" said Tom.

"He smells that fox," said Dick triumphantly. "I say, I wish we'd had him with us. There! he's got wind of him. I wish it wasn't so dark, and we'd go back and have a run."

"Have a run! have a swim, you mean," said Tom. "Why, that was in one of the wettest places between here and your house. I say, how plainly you can hear the sea!"

"Of course you can, when the wind blows off it," said Dick, as he listened for a moment to the dull low rushing sound. "Your mother has put two candles in the window."

"She always does when father's out. She's afraid he might get lost in the bog."

"So did my mother once; but it made father cross, and he said, next time he went out she was to tie a bit of thread to his arm, and hold the end, and then he would be sure to get home all right. Why, there's a jack-o'-lantern on the road."

"That isn't a jacky-lantern," replied Tom, looking steadfastly first at the two lights shining out in the distance, and then at a dim kind of star which seemed to be jerking up and down.

"Tell you it is," said Dick shortly.

"Tell you it isn't," cried Tom. "Jacky-lanterns are never lame. They never hop up and down like that, but seem to glide here and there like a honey-bee. It's our Joe come to meet us with the horn lantern. It's his game leg makes it go up and down."

"Dick!" came from ahead.

"Yes, father," shouted the lad; and they ran on to where the squire and Farmer Tallington were awaiting them.

"We'll say 'good-night' now," said the squire. "Here, Dick, Farmer's Joe is coming on with the lantern. Shall we let him light us home?"

"Why, we should have to see him home afterwards, father," said Dick merrily.

"Right, my lad! Good-night, Tallington! You are in for your two hundred, mind."

"Yes, and may it bring good luck to us!" said the fanner. "Good-night to both of you!"

"Good-night!"

Dick supplemented his "good-night" with a pat on the head of the great sheep-dog, which stood staring along the track, and snuffing the wind; and then he and his father started homeward.

"I shall come over directly after breakfast, Dick," shouted Tom.

"All right!" replied Dick as he looked back, to see that the lantern had now become stationary, and then it once more began to dance up and down, while the two lights shone out like tiny stars a few hundred yards away.

"They've got the best of it, Dick," said the squire. "Why, we were nearly there. Let's make haste or your mother will be uneasy. Phew! the wind's getting high!"

Chapter Three.

A Stormy Night.

It was a tremendous blast which came sweeping over the sea, and quite checked the progress of the travellers for the moment, but they pressed on, seeming to go right through the squall, and trudging along sturdily towards home.

"I begin to wish someone had put a light in the window for us, Dick," said the squire at the end of a few minutes' walking. "It's getting terribly dark."

Dick said, "Yes," and thought of the thread, but he made no allusion to it, only laughed to himself and tramped on.

"By the way, how uneasy that dog seemed!" said the squire as they trudged on with heads bent, for they were facing the blast now.

"Yes, father; we passed a fox."

"Passed a fox! Why, you couldn't see a fox a dark night like this."

"No, but I could smell him, father, and we heard him catch a duck."

"Ah! I see. And did the dog scent out the fox?"

"Yes, I think so, and that made him whine."

"Come along, my lad. Let's get on as fast as we can. It's growing blacker, and I'm afraid we shall have some rain."

No rain fell, but the sky was completely clouded over and the darkness seemed to grow more and more intense. The wind kept increasing in violence and then dying out, as if it came in huge waves which swept over them and had a great interval between, while as the rush and roar of the gusts passed there came the deep hoarse murmur of the distant sea.

"Dick," said the squire suddenly, "you are so young that you can hardly feel with me, but I want someone to talk to now, and I may as well tell you that I am going to risk a great deal of money over the draining of the fen."

"Are you, father?"

"Yes, my lad, and I have been feeling a natural shrinking from the risk. To-night sweeps all that away, for in spite of having lived here so many years as I have, I never before felt how needful it all was."

"Do you think so, father?"

"Indeed I do, my lad, for anything more risky than our walk to-night I hardly know. What's that?"

The squire stopped short and grasped his son's arm, as, after a furious gust of wind, the distant murmur of the sea seemed to have been overborne by something different—a confused lapping, trickling, and rushing noise that seemed to come from all parts at once.

"I don't know, father," said Dick, who was slightly startled by his father's manner. "Shall we go on?"

"Yes," said the squire hoarsely. "Let's get home quick."

They started on again, walking fast, but at the end of a minute Dick uttered a cry.

"We're off the road, father. Water!"

As he spoke he was ankle-deep, and in taking a step to catch his son's arm, Squire Winthorpe felt the water splash up around him.

"Can you see the lights at the Priory, Dick?" he said sharply.

"No, father."

"We can't be off the path," said the squire. "Is it boggy and soft under you?"

"No, father—hard; but I'm in the water."

"It's hard here too," said the squire, trying the ground with his feet; "and yet we must be off the road. Stand fast, my boy; don't move."

"Are you going away, father?" said Dick.

"No, only a few yards, boy. I want to see where we got off the track, whether it's to the right or left."

"It's so dark," said Dick, "I can hardly see my hand. Mind how you go, father; there are some deep bog-holes about here."

"Then you stand fast, my boy."

"Hadn't you better stand fast too, father?"

"And both perish in the wet and cold, my boy! No. I'll soon find the road. It must be close by."

Not a tree or post to guide him, nothing but the thick darkness on all sides, as Squire Winthorpe cautiously moved one foot before the other, keeping one upon solid ground while he searched about with the other, and as he moved *splash—splish—splash*, the water flew, striking cold to his legs, and sending a chill of dread to his very heart.

"It's very strange," he cried; "but don't be frightened, Dick. We shall be all right directly."

"I'm not frightened, father," replied the boy. "I'm puzzled."

"And so am I, my lad, for I did not know we could find such solid bottom off the road. Ah!"

"What's the matter, father?"

"I told you not to move, sir," roared the squire, for he had heard a slight splash on his right.

"I couldn't help it, father; my foot seemed to slip, and—why, here's the road!"

"There?" cried the squire eagerly.

"Yes, father, and my foot's slipped down into a big rut."

"Are you sure, boy?"

"Sure! Yes, father, it *is* the road. I say, what does it mean?"

The answer was a quick splashing sound, as Squire Winthorpe hurried to his son's side and gripped his arm, to stand there for a few moments listening and thinking as he realised the meaning of the strange rushing, plashing noise that came from all round.

"I know," cried Dick suddenly; "the sea-bank's broke, and we're going to have a flood."

"Yes," said the squire hoarsely; "the bank has gone, my boy."

"Hadn't we better push on, father, before it gets any deeper?"

"Stop a moment, Dick," said the squire, "and let me try to think. Home's safe, because the Priory's on the Toft; but there's Tallington and his wife and boy. We must try and help them."

"Come on, then, father!" cried Dick excitedly.

"No, Dick, that will not do; we shall only be shutting ourselves up too and frightening your mother to death. We must get home and then on to Hickathrift's. He has a big punt there."

"Yes, father, but it hasn't been mended. I saw it this afternoon."

"Then he has wood, and we must make a raft. Come on. Here: your hand."

For a few minutes there was nothing heard but the rushing of the wind and the *splash, splash* of the water, as they pressed on, the squire cautiously trying to keep one foot by the rut which had guided his son, and, when it became intangible, seeking for some other means to keep them from straying from the submerged road in the darkness, and going off to right or left into the bog.

It was a terrible walk, for they had a full mile to go; and to the squire's horror, he found that it was not only against the wind but also against the sharply running water, which was flowing in from the sea and growing deeper inch by inch.

As if to comfort each other father and son kept on making cheery remarks apropos of their rough journey. Now it was Dick, who declared that the water felt warmer than the air; now it was the squire, who laughingly said that he should believe now in blind men being able to find their way by the touch.

"For I'm feeling my way along here famously, Dick."

"Yes, father, only it seems such a long way—ugh!"

"What is it, boy?"

"One foot went down deep. Yes, I know where we are."

"Yes, close home, my boy," cried the squire.

"No, no; half a mile away by the sharp turn, father; and I nearly went right down. We must keep more this way."

The squire drew his breath hard, for he knew his son was right, as the road proved when they turned almost at right angles and plashed on through the water.

Half a mile farther to go and the current rushing on! It had been only over their ankles, now it was above their knees, and both knew that at this rate it would be waist-deep, if not deeper, before they could reach the high ground at home.

"It is very horrible, Dick, my lad," cried the squire at last as they kept on, with the water steadily and surely growing deeper.

"Oh, I don't mind, father! We shall get on so far before it's over our heads that we shall be able to swim the rest of the way. You can swim, father?"

"I used to, my lad; perhaps I have not forgotten how. But I am thinking of the people about. I wonder whether Hickathrift has found it out."

"I dare say he's in bed, father," said Dick.

"That's what I fear, my boy; and then there's John Warren."

"He'll get up the sand-hills, father."

"If he knows in time, my boy; but Dave Gittan has no place to flee to."

"He has his little boat, father; and Chip would warn him if he has gone to bed. I know what he'd do then."

"What, my lad?"

"Pole himself along to John Warren and fetch him off, and come on to the Toft."

"Mind, take care, we're going wrong," cried the squire excitedly, as he slipped and went in right up to his waist, but Dick clung to his hand, threw himself back, and with a heavy splash the squire managed to regain the hard road off whose edge he had slipped.

"We must go slower, father," said Dick coolly. "You pull me back if I go wrong this way and I'll pull you. I say, isn't it getting dark!"

The squire made no answer, but feeling that their case was growing desperate, and if they did not progress more rapidly they would be in such deep water before they could reach the Priory that it would be impossible to keep the track, and they would be swept away, he pushed on, with the result that in a few minutes Dick had a narrow escape, slipping right in and coming up panting, to be dragged back, and stand still quite confused by his total immersion.

"We must get on, Dick, my boy," said his father; "the water's growing terribly deep, and it presses against us like a torrent. Forward!"

They recommenced their journey, wading on slowly over what seemed to be an interminable distance; but no sign of the dark village or of the island-farm in the fen appeared, and at last the water deepened so that a chilly feeling of despair began slowly to unnerve the squire and set him thinking that theirs was a hopeless case.

"Be ready, Dick," he whispered, as, after a tremendous puff of wind which stopped them for the moment, he once more pressed on.

"Ready, father?" panted Dick. "What for?"

"We may have to swim directly. If it gets much deeper we cannot force our way."

"Oh, we shall do it!" cried the boy; "we must be close there now."

"I fear not," said the squire to himself. "Hold on, boy!" he cried aloud. "What is it?"

"Water's—up to my—chest," panted Dick; "and it comes so fast here—it's—it's too strong for me."

SQUIRE WINTHORPE AND HIS SON SAVED FROM THE FLOOD

Page 11

"Dick!" cried the squire in agony.

"I must swim, father," cried Dick.

"And be swept away!" cried the squire hoarsely. "Heaven help me! what shall I do?"

He had gripped his son tightly in his agony, and they stood together for a few moments, nearly swept off their feet by the swirling current, when a bright idea flashed across the squire's mind.

"Quick, Dick! don't speak. Climb on my back."

"But, father—"

"Do as I bid you," roared the squire, stooping a little, and bending down he made of one hand a stirrup for his son's foot, who, the next moment, was well up on his back.

"That's better, boy," panted the squire. "You are safe, and your weight steadies me. I can get on now; it can't be far."

As he spoke a light suddenly flashed up a couple of hundred yards ahead, and gleamed strangely over the water like a blood-red stain.

Then it died out, but flashed up again and increased till there was a ruddy path of light before them, and behind the glow stood up the trees, the long, low Priory and the out-buildings, while figures could be seen moving here and there.

"I know," cried Dick. "I see, father. They've lit a bonfire to show us which way to go. Ahoy!"

"Ahoy!" came back in a stentorian shout, and something was thrown upon the fire which dulled it for the moment, but only for it to flash up in a tremendous blaze, with the sparks and flames of fire rushing towards them.

11

"Ahoy!" came the shout again.

"Ahoy!" answered Dick.

"That will do, my boy," panted the squire. "The water's getting horribly deep, but I can manage now, for I can tell which way to go."

"Little more to the left, father," cried Dick.

"Right, boy!"

"No, no, father," shrieked Dick; "left!"

"I meant you are right, my lad," said the squire, moving on, with the water growing deeper still, while the stentorian voice kept uttering cheering shouts to them, which they answered till they were only about fifty yards away, when it became plain that someone was coming to meet them, splash, splash, through the water, with a pole in his hand.

The figure, though only head and half his body were visible above the plashing water, looked large, and for a few moments in his confusion Dick was puzzled; but he realised who it was at last, and cried:

"Why, it's old Hicky!"

He was right; and just in the veriest time of need the great blacksmith reached the fainting squire, and grasping his arm breasted the water with him; and in another minute they were ascending the slope, with the water shallowing, till they reached a blazing fire, where Mrs Winthorpe clasped husband and son to her breast!

"All right, wife!" cried the squire. "Glad you are here, Hickathrift! All your people too?"

"Yes, squire, all safe here; but we're uneasy like about Dave o' the 'Coy and John Warren."

"But they've got the boat," cried Dick.

"Yes; I hope they're safe," said the squire. "Hickathrift, my lad, that was a brave thought of yours to light that fire. It saved our lives."

"Nay, squire," said the big fellow; "it was no thowt o' mine—it was thy missus put it into my yead."

The squire gave his wife a look as she stood there in the midst of a group of shivering farm-servants, and then turned to the wheelwright.

"The boat," he said—"did you come in the boat?"

"Ay, squire. She leaks a deal, but I thrust an owd pillow in the hole. But I nigh upon lost her. My Grip woke me howling, for we were abed. I jumped out and ran down, thinking it was the foxes after the chickens, and walked right into the water. I knowed what it meant, and got over to the saw-pit, and just caught hold of the boat in the dark as it was floating away. Then I got my leaping-pole and run her under the window, and made my missus give me a pillow to stop the leak 'fore I could bale her out. Then Jacob come, and we got the missus down and poled her along here, but was nearly swept by."

"You're a good fellow, Hickathrift," cried the squire. "Wife, get out some hollands; we're perished. Have a glass, my man; and then we must go in the punt to Grimsey and get the Tallingtons out. We're all right here, but Grimsey Farm will soon be flooded to the bed-room windows. Light a lanthorn, some one, and put in a spare candle. You'll go with me, Hickathrift?"

"Ay, squire, to the end of the world, if thou bids me; but I tell ye—"

He stopped short.

"Well, what, man? Here, drink!"

"Efter yow, squire," said the big fellow sturdily. "I tell ye that no mortal man, nor no two men, couldn't take that punt across to Grimsey in the dark to-night. We should be swept no one knows wheer, and do no good to them as wants the help."

"But we can't leave them to drown, man!" cried the squire.

"No; we can't do that, and we wean't," cried Hickathrift. "They'll get right on the roof if the bed-rooms gets full; and while we're waiting for day we'll have the punt hauled up. Jacob'll howd the light, and I'll see if I can't mend the hole. You've got a hammer and some nails in the big barn?"

"Yes," said the squire; "yes, you are right, my man—you are right. Come, Dick: dry clothes."

There was nothing else to be done; and as the bonfire was kept blazing the punt was hauled up, and in the midst of the howling wind and the rush of the water Dick stood looking on, his heart full as he thought of Tom Tallington asking his help away there in the darkness; while tap, tap, tap went the wheelwright's hammer, after his saw had rasped off a thin piece of board.

"That'll do it," he cried at last; and the punt was placed ready for launching when the day showed.

Meanwhile the squire gave orders for the fire to be kept well alight; and fagots of wood and straw trusses were piled on, with the odds and ends of broken farming implements and worn-out wooden shedding that had been the accumulation of years.

The result was that the flames rose high over the wild weird scene, gilding the wind-tossed pines and staining the flood for far, while there was so much excitement in thus sitting up and keeping the fire blazing that it would have been real enjoyment to Dick had he not been in a constant state of fret and anxiety about his friends.

For, living as he did in that island of good elevated land in the great wild fen where inhabitants were scarce, everybody was looked upon as an intimate friend, and half the lad's time was spent at the bottom of the slope beyond the ruinous walls of the old Priory, watching the water to see how much higher it had risen, and to gaze out afar and watch for the coming of boat or punt.

In truth, though, there was only one vessel likely to come, and that was the flat-bottomed punt belonging to Dave, who worked the duck-decoy far out in the fen. The people on the sea-bank had a boat; but they were five miles away at least, and would not venture on such a night.

"What should I do?" thought Dick as he walked down to the edge of the water again and again. "If Tom is drowned, and Dave, and John Warren, they may drain the fen as soon as they like, for the place will not be the same."

The night wore on; and Mrs Winthorpe made the people in turn partake of a meal, half supper, half breakfast, and, beyond obeying his father's orders regarding dry clothes, Dick could go no further. He revolted against food, and, feeling heartsick and enraged against the wheelwright for eating a tremendous meal, he once more ran down to the water's edge, to find his father watching a stick or two he had thrust in.

"Tide has turned, Dick," he said quietly; "the water will not rise any higher."

"And will it all run off now, father?"

The squire shook his head.

"Some will," he replied; "but the fen will be a regular lake till the sea-bank has been mended. It must have been rough and the tide very high to beat that down."

"Will it come in again, then?" asked Dick.

"Perhaps: perhaps not. It's a lucky thing that I had no stock down at the corner field by the fish-stews. If they had not been up here in the home close, every head must have been drowned."

"Do you think the fish-ponds are covered, father?"

"Five or six feet deep, my boy."

"Then the fish will get out."

"Very likely Dick; but we've something more important to think about than fish. Hark! what's that?" and he listened.

"Ahoy!" roared Hickathrift from just behind them. "Hear that, squire?"

"Yes, my lad, I heard a cry from off the water."

Just then came another faint hail from a distance.

"That's Dave," said Hickathrift, smiling all over his broad face; "any one could tell his hail: it's something between a wild-goose cry and the squeak of a cart-wheel that wants some grease."

The hailing brought out everybody from the house, Mrs Winthorpe's first inquiry being whether it was the Tallingtons.

"Pitch on a bit more straw, Dick," cried the squire; and the lad seized a fork and tossed a quantity on the fire, while the wheelwright stirred up the embers with a pole, the result being that the flames roared up tremendously, sending out a golden shower of sparks which were swept away before the wind, fortunately in the opposite direction to the house, towards which the squire darted one uneasy glance.

"Ahoy!" shouted the wheelwright, and there was a fresh response which sounded weird and strange, coming as it did from out of the black wall of darkness seen beyond the ring of ruddy light which gleamed upon the water.

"They'll get here easily now," said the squire from the very edge of the flood, as he tossed out a piece of wood, and saw that it was floated steadily away. "The current is slack."

He could not avoid shuddering as he thought of the way in which it had pressed upon him as he waded toward the island with Dick upon his back; but the memory passed away directly as a fresh hail came from off the water; and as the group looked out anxiously and listened for the splash of the pole, they at last saw the fire-light shining upon a figure which gradually came gliding out of the darkness. At first it seemed strange, and almost ghastly; but in a few more moments those who watched could see that it was Dave o' the 'Coy in his fox-skin cap standing up in his little white punt and thrusting it along by means of a long pole, while a man sat in the stern.

"Yon's John Warren along wi' him," cried Hickathrift. "I thowt they'd be all right. Come on, lads, clost in here," he shouted; and without making any reply, the strange-looking man in the bows of the boat pulled her along till the prow struck upon the flooded grass, and he threw a rope to the wheelwright.

"Got your gun, Dave?" cried Dick eagerly.

The man turned his head slowly to the speaker, laid the pole across the boat, which was aground a dozen feet from the dry land, stooped, picked up his long gun, and uttered a harsh—

"Kitch!"

As he spoke he threw the gun to the wheelwright, who caught it and passed it to Dick, while the second man handed Dave another gun, which was sent ashore in the same way. Then, taking up the pole, Dave placed it a little way before him, and leaped ashore as actively as a boy, while the second man now advanced to the front, caught the pole as it was thrown back, and in turn cleared the water and landed upon the dry ground.

"Glad to see you safe, Dave," said the squire, holding out his hand. "Glad to see you, too, John Warren. You are heartily welcome."

The two men took the squire's hand in a limp, shrinking manner; and instead of giving it a hearty grip, lifted it up once, looking at it all the time as if it were something curious, and then let it fall, and shuffled aside, giving a furtive kind of nod to every one in turn who offered a congratulation.

They were the actions of men who led a solitary life among the birds and four-footed animals of the great wild fen, and to be made the heroes of an escape seemed to be irksome.

Just then there was a diversion which took off people's attention, and seemed to place them more at ease. A sharp quick yelp came from the boat, followed by a bark, and, plainly seen in the fire-light, a couple of dogs placed their paws on the edge of the little vessel, raised their heads to the full stretch of their necks, and with cocked-up ears seemed to ask, "What's to be done with us?"

"Hi! Chip, Chip! Snig, Snig! Come, boys," shouted Dick, patting his leg; and the dogs barked loudly, but did not stir.

"Come on, you cowards!" cried Dick. "You won't get any wetter than I did."

"Here!" said Dave; and Chip leaped over and swam ashore, gave himself a shake, and then performed a joy dance about Dick's legs.

This time there was a dismal howl from the punt, where the second dog was waiting for permission to land.

13

"Come on!" said the second man, a frowning, thoughtful-looking fellow of about fifty, the lower part of whose face was hidden by a thick beard—a great rarity a hundred years ago—and the other dog leaped into the water with a tremendous splash, swam ashore, rushed at Chip, and there was a general worry, half angry, half playful, for a few moments before the pair settled down close to the fire, as if enjoying its warmth.

"This is a terrible misfortune, Dave," said the squire.

"Ay; the water's out, mester," said the man in a low husky way.

"How did you escape?"

"Escape?" said Dave, taking off his fox-skin cap and rubbing his head.

"Seed the watter coming, and poonted ower to the Warren," said the second man, thrusting something in his mouth which he took out of a brass box, and then handing the latter to Dave, who helped himself to a piece of dark-brown clayey-looking stuff which seemed like a thick paste made of brown flour and treacle.

"I wish you men would break yourselves of this habit," said the squire. "You'll be worse for it some day."

"Keeps out the cold and ager, mester," said the second man, thrusting the box back in his pocket.

"Then you've been waiting at the Warren?"

"Ay, mester. Me an' him waited till we see the fire, and thowt the house hed kitched, and then we come."

"It was very good of you, my lads," said the squire warmly. "There, get in, and the mistress will give you some bread and cheese and ale."

"Arn't hungry," growled the second man. "Can'st ta yeat, Dave, man?"

"Ah!" growled Dave, and he slouched round, looking at the ground, and turned to go. "Gimme mai goon," he added.

"The guns are all right, Dave," cried Dick. "I've got 'em. I say, John Warren, will the rabbits be all drowned?"

"Drowned, young mester! Nay, not they. Plenty o' room for em up in the runs where the watter won't come."

"But the foxes, and hares, and things?" cried Dick.

"Them as has got wings is flied awayer," growled the second man; "them as has got paddles is swimmed; and them as can't find the dry patches is gone down."

After this oracular utterance John o' the Warren, who took his popular name from the rabbit homes, to the exclusion of his proper surname of Searby, tramped heavily after his companion to the Priory kitchen, where they both worried a certain amount of bread and cheese, and muttered to one another over some ale, save when Dick spoke to them and told them of his anxieties, when each man gave him a cheery smile.

"Don't yow fret, lad," said Dave. "Bahds is all reight. They wean't hoort. Wait till watter goos down a bit and you an' me'll have rare sport."

"Ay, and rabbuds is all reight too, young mester," added John Warren. "They knows the gainest way to get up stairs. They're all happed up warm in their roons, ready to come out as soon as the watter goos down."

"But how did it happen?"

"Happen, lad!" said the two men in a breath.

"Yes; what caused the flood?"

"Oh, I d'n'know," growled Dave slowly. "Happen sea-bank broke to show folk as fen warn't niver meant to be drained, eh, John Warren?"

"Ay, that's it, lad. Folk talks o' draäning fen, and such blather. Can't be done."

"I say, John, I don't want the fen drained," whispered Dick.

"Good lad!" growled John Warren; and then Dave shook his head at the ale-mug, sighed, and drank.

"But don't let father hear what you say, because he won't like it."

"Nay, I sha'n't say nowt," said Dave.

"Nay, nor me neither, only natur's natur, and floods is floods," added John Warren; and he too shook his head at the ale-mug, and drank.

"Now, then," cried the squire, coming quickly to the door, "Hickathrift and I are going in the big punt to see if we can help the Tallingtons; the stream isn't so strong now. Are you men going to try to help us?"

"Get Farmer Tallington out?" said Dave. "Ay, we are coming."

"Let me come too, father," cried Dick.

"No, my lad, I'm afraid I—"

"Don't say that, father; let me go."

"No no, Dick," cried Mrs Winthorpe, entering the kitchen, for she had been upon the alert. "You have run risks enough to-night."

"Yes; stay and take care of the women, Dick," said his father.

Dick gave an angry stamp on the floor.

"Mother wants me to grow up a coward," he cried. "Oh, mother, it's too bad!"

"But, Dick, my boy," faltered the poor woman.

"Let the boy come, wife," said the squire quietly; "I'll take care of him."

"Yes, and I'll take care of father," cried Dick, rushing at his mother to give her a sounding kiss, and with a sigh she gave way, and followed the party down to the water's edge.

Chapter Four.

A Journey by Punt.

There was still a furious current running on the far side of the Toft, as, well provided with lanterns, the two punts pushed off. On the side where the two last comers landed it had seemed sluggish, for an eddy had helped them in; but as soon as they were all well out beyond the pines the stream caught them, the wind helped it, and their task was not to get towards Grimsey, but to retard their vessels, and mind that they were not capsized by running upon a pollard willow, whose thin bare boughs rose up out of the water now and then, like the horrent hair of some marine monster which had come in with the flood from the sea.

"We've done wrong, Hickathrift," said the squire after they had been borne along by the current for some distance; "and I don't understand all this. I thought that when the tide had turned, the water would have flowed back again through the gap it must have broken, instead of still sweeping on."

"Ay," said the great wheelwright, who was standing in the bows with his long leaping-pole in his hand; "I do puzzle, squire. I've been looking out for a light to show where Grimsey lies, for here, in the dark, it's watter, watter, watter, and I can't see the big poplar by Tallington's. Hi! Dave, where's Grimsey, thinks ta?" he shouted.

"Nay, I don't know."

"Can you make it out, John Warren?"

"Nay, lad, I'm 'bout bet."

"Then, squire, if they can't say, I can't. What shall we do?"

"We must wait for daylight," said the squire, after peering into the darkness ahead for some time. "We shall be swept far past it if we go on. Can you hold the punt with your pole?"

"Nay, no more'n you could a bull with a bit o' tar band, mester. We mun keep a sharp look-out for the next tree, and lay hold of the branches and stop there. D'ye hear, lads?"

"Aye, what is it?" came from the other boat.

"Look out for the next tree, and hing on till daylight."

Dave uttered a grunt, and they floated on and on for nearly a quarter of an hour before Dick uttered a loud "Look out!"

"I see her, my lad," cried Hickathrift; and he tried to give the boat a good thrust by means of his pole; but though he touched bottom it was soft peat, and his pole went down, and the next moment they were crashing through the top of a willow, with the boat tilting up on one side and threatening to fill; but just as the water began to pour in, there was a whishing and crackling noise as it passed over the obstacle and swung clear, with Hickathrift holding on to a branch with all his might.

"Look out! Can you tek howd, lad?" came from the other boat, which came gliding out of the darkness, just clear of the tree.

As it came on, Dick caught the pole Dave held out to him and checked the progress of the little punt; but he had miscalculated his strength as opposed to the force of the current, and after a jerk, which seemed to be tearing his arms out of their sockets, he was being dragged out of the boat, and half over, when his father seized him round the hips.

"Can you hold on, Dick?" cried the squire.

"A—a little while," panted the lad.

"Get howd o' the pole, mester," shouted Warren from the other boat.

"I can't, man, without loosing the boy. We shall have to let you go."

"Let go, then," growled Dave; "we can find our way somehow."

"Nay," shouted Hickathrift. "Howd hard a minute till I've made fast here. I'm coming."

As he spoke he was busy holding on to the elastic willow branch with one hand, while with the other he drew the rope out of the boat's head, and, with a good deal of labour, managed to pass it round the bough and make it fast.

"There, she's all right," he cried, stepping aft carefully, the boat swaying beneath his huge weight. "Now, squire, I mun lean ower thee to get howd o' the pole. Eh! but it's a long way to reach, and—"

"Mind, man, mind!" cried the squire, "or we shall fill with water; we're within an inch now."

"Nay, we sha'n't go down," cried Hickathrift, straining right over the squire and Dick, and sinking the stern of the boat so far that his face kept touching the water, and he had to wrench his head round to speak. "There, I've got howd o' the pole, and one leg hooked under the thwart. Let go, Mester Dick; and you haul him aboard, squire, and get to the other end."

It needed cautious movement, for the boat was now so low that the water rushed over; but by exerting his strength the squire dragged Dick away, and together they relieved the stern of the pressure and crept forward.

"Now Dave, lad, haul alongside, and make your rope fast to the ring-bolt," cried Hickathrift; and this was done, the punt swung behind, and the great Saxon-like fellow sat up laughing.

"Is it all safe?" cried the squire.

"Ay, mester, so long as that bough don't part; but I've got my owd ear full o' watter, and it's a-roonning down my neck. But say, mester, it's a rum un."

15

"What is, my lad?"

"Why, it wur ony yesday I wur saying to my Jacob as we'd get the poont mended, and come out here with the handbills and brattle (lop) all the willows anywhere nigh, so as to hev a lot to throost down about our plaääce to grow. Now, if we'd done that there'd ha' been no branch to lay hold on here, and we might ha' gone on to Spalding afore we'd stopped. Eh, but howding on theer made me keb."

(Keb: pant for breath.)

"Are you hurt, Dick?" said the squire.

"N–no, I don't think I'm hurt, father," replied Dick, hesitatingly; "only I feel—"

"Well, speak, my lad; don't keep anything back."

"Oh, no, I won't keep anything back, father!" said Dick, laughing; "but I felt as if I'd been one of those poor fellows in the Tower that they used to put on the rack—all stretchy like."

"Mak' you grow, Mester Dick," said Hickathrift, "mak' you grow into a great long chap like me—six foot four."

"I hope not," said the squire, laughing. "Draw the line this side of the six feet, Dick. There: the stiffness will soon pass off."

They sat talking for a time, but words soon grew few and far between. The two fen-men swinging in their boat behind had recourse to the brass box again, each partaking of a rolled-up quid of opium, and afterwards crouched there in a half drowsy state, careless of their peril, while the squire and his companions passed their time listening to the rush of the water and the creaking of the willow bough as it rubbed against the side of the boat, and wondered, as from time to time the wheelwright examined the rope and made it more secure, whether the branch would give way at its intersection with the trunk.

The darkness seemed as if it would never pass, whilst the cold now became painful; and as he heard Dick's teeth begin to chatter, the wheelwright exclaimed:

"Look here, young mester, I ain't hot, but there's a lot o' warmth comes out o' me. You come and sit close up, and you come t'other side, squire. It'll waärm him."

This was done, and with good effect, for the lad's teeth ceased their castanet-like action as he sat waiting for the daylight.

No word was spoken by the men in the little punt, and those uttered in the other grew fewer, as its occupants sat listening to the various sounds that came from a distance. For the flood had sent the non-swimming birds wheeling round in the darkness, and every now and then the whistling of wings was quite startling. The ducks of all kinds were in a high state of excitement, and passed over in nights or settled down in the water with a tremendous outcry, while ever and again a peculiar clanging from high overhead gave warning that the wild-geese were on the move, either fleeing or attracted by some strange instinct to the watery waste.

But morning seemed as if it would never come, and it was not until hours upon hours had passed that there was a cessation of the high wind, and a faint line of light just over the water, seaward, proclaimed that the dawn could not be far away.

"Can you see where we are?" said the squire, as it began to grow lighter.

"Ay, it's plain enough now, mester," was the reply; "and yonder's Grimsey."

"I can see Tom," said Dick just then; "and there's Farmer Tallington, and all the rest, right on the top of the roof."

In a few minutes more all was plain enough, and the reason apparent why the people at Tallington had not shown a light in the course of the night or done anything else to indicate their position, for it was evident that they had been driven from below stairs to the floor above, and from thence to the roof, where they must have sat out the evening hours, perhaps doubtful of how long the place would last before it was swept away.

So intent had the squire and Dick been in watching for the dawn, that the gradual cessation of the flowing water had passed unnoticed; but it was plain now that the surface of the wide expanse out of which the Toft rose, with the old Priory buildings a couple of miles away, was now unruffled by the wind, and that the current had ceased to flow.

But for this the party of rescue in the two punts would not have been able to reach the inundated farm, for it was only here and there that a firm place could be found for the poles, which generally sank deeply in the peat covered by the water to an average depth of about eight feet.

In the course of half an hour the boats were close up to the reed thatch of the great farm-house, a rope made fast to the chimney-stack, and Mrs Tallington, the farmer, Tom, a couple of maids and three men were transferred to the boats, all stiff and helpless with the cold.

"I don't mind now," said Tom, shivering as he spoke. "A boat isn't much of a thing, but it will float, and all last night it seemed as if the old house was going to be swept away."

"Are these your horses?" said Dick, pointing to a group of dejected-looking animals standing knee-deep in company with some cattle, about a quarter of a mile away.

"Yes, and our cows," replied Tom, shivering. "Oh, I say, don't talk; I'm so cold and hungry!"

All this time Hickathrift was diligently using the pole in the larger boat, and Dave leading the way in the other, both being well laden now, and progressing fairly fast toward the Toft, which stood up like an island of refuge in the midst of the vast lake, dotted here and there with the tops of trees. At times the poles touched a good firm tuft of heath or a patch of gravel, and the boat received a good thrust forward; at other times, when the bottom was soft, Hickathrift struck the water with it right and left as he stood up in the prow, using it as a kind of paddle.

Before they were half-way on their journey the sun came out from a cloud, just at the edge of the inundation; and with it and the prospect of warmth and food at the Priory, everybody's spirits began to rise.

"Might have been worse, neighbour," shouted the squire. "You sold all your sheep last week."

"Ay," said the farmer from Dave's punt; "and we might all have been drowned. It's a sore piece of business; but it shows a man what his neighbours are, and I won't murmur, only say as you do, it might have been worse."

16

"And thank God for sparing all our lives!" said the squire, taking off his hat.

"Amen!" said Farmer Tallington, and for a time there was nothing heard but a sob from Mrs Tallington and the splashing of the poles.

But two boys could not keep silence long with the sun shining and the place around wearing so novel a guise; and Dick soon burst out with:

"Look, Tom; look at the teal!"

He pointed to a flock forming quite a patch upon the water some hundreds of yards away.

"Ay," said the squire; "it's good for the wild-fowl, but bad for us. The sooner the place is drained now, neighbour, the better, eh?"

"Ay, squire, you're right; but how are we to get rid of all this watter?"

"Ah, we must see," said the squire; and Dave and John Warren exchanged glances and shook their heads. "The sooner the draining works are commenced the better."

"Toft Fen wean't niver be drained, mester," said Dave in a low voice, as he rested his pole in the punt and stood there looking as if he believed himself to be a prophet.

"Oh, you think so, do you, Dave?" said the squire quietly. "I daresay hundreds of years ago, before the sea-wall was made, some men said that no farming could be done in the fen, but the sea has been kept out for all these years."

"Ay, but it's come through at last in its natural way, mester," said John Warren.

"Yes, John," said the squire; "but we men who think how to live, make nature work for us, and don't work for nature. So we're going to turn the sea off the land again, and drain the fresh water off as well, so as to turn this wild waste into fertile land. Do you hear, Dick?"

"Yes, father, I hear," said the lad; and he looked at Dave and John Warren, in whose boat he was, and read incredulity there; and as he gazed over the inundated fen, and thought of fishing, and shooting, and boating there, he felt himself thoroughly on the fen-men's side, while, feeling ashamed of this, he bent over the boat side, scooped up some water in his hand and drank, but only to exclaim, "Ugh!"

"Ah! what does it taste like, Dick?" said the squire.

"Half salt, father."

"Then it is the sea broke in," said the squire. "Ahoy! all right!" he shouted, standing up and waving his cap. "Shout, Dick, and let your mother see you're here. Come, cheer up, Mrs Tallington; there's a warm welcome for you yonder from the wife; the water will soon go down, and we're going to try and protect ourselves from such mischief coming again."

The squire was right; there was a warm welcome waiting for the homeless neighbours, to whom, after a good, snug, and hearty breakfast, everything looked very different from what it had seemed during the long dark stormy watches of the night.

(Wall, in fen-lands, the artificial bank or ridge of clay raised to keep back river, drain, or sea.)

Chapter Five.

The Roman Bank.

It was like standing on a very long low narrow island, with the peculiarity that one side was sea, the other inland lake. The sun shone brilliantly, and the punt in which the squire, Farmer Tallington, Dave, Warren, Hickathrift, and the two lads had come was lying on the inner side of the sandy ridge covered with thin, wiry, harsh grass.

This ridge formed the island upon which they stood, in company with some sheep and cattle which had instinctively made their way to the high ground as the water rose.

The tide was down now; a great deal of the water had drained away, and the party were standing by a great breach in the bank through which at high-tide during the storm the sea had made its way.

"I can't quite understand how it could have broken through here," said the squire; "but I suppose it was quite a small crack at first, and the water soon washed it bigger."

There was a great channel at their feet, cut clean through the embankment; and though the party were standing amongst the sand, they could see that the bank which protected the fen from the sea, and ran up alongside of the river, running inland, was formed of thick clay, matted with the long roots of the grass.

"Who was it made this great bank, father?" said Dick.

"Your old friends you read about at school, they say, the Romans, first; but of course it has been added to since. Well, neighbour, we can do no good by ourselves. We must call together the adventurers, and it can soon be mended and made stronger than it was at first. Let's go back. Unless we have a gale, no more water will come through this. It's years since I've been here. If one had taken a look round one would have seen the weak spot."

They re-entered the punt, and Hickathrift poled them back, being relieved in turn by Dave and Warren, by whose solitary cottage they paused—a mere hut upon a sandy patch, standing like an island out of the watery waste, and here he elected to stay with the rabbits which frisked about and showed their cottony tuft tails as they darted down into their holes.

"How about your cottage, Dave?" said the squire, shading his eyes as he looked across the flooded fen.

"Wet," said Dave laconically.

"Yes, there are four feet of water yonder, I should say. You will have to stop at the Toft for the present."

"Not I, mester," said the rough fellow. "I don't mind a drop o' watter."

"Not to wade through, perhaps, my man; but you can't sleep there."

"Sleep in my boat," said Dave laconically. "Won't be the first time."

"Do as you please," said the squire quietly; and he turned to talk to Farmer Tallington.

"I say, Dave," whispered Dick, "you're just like an old goose."

"Eh?" said the man with his eyes flashing.

"I mean being able to sleep on the water floating," said Dick, laughing, and the angry look died out.

It was plain enough that the water had sunk a good deal already, but the farmers had to face the fact that it would be weeks before the fen was in its old state, and that if the breach in the sea-wall were not soon repaired, they might at any time be afflicted with a similar peril.

But notice was sent to those interested, while the farmers here and there who held the patches of raised land round the borders of the fen obeyed the summons, and for about a month there was busy work going on at the sea-wall with spade and basket, clay being brought from pits beneath the sand upon the sea-shore, carried up to the breach, and trampled down, till at last, without further mishap, the gap in the embankment was filled up strongly, and the place declared to be safe.

Of those who toiled hard none showed so well in the front as Dave o' the 'Coy, and John Warren, and the squire was not stinted in his praise one day toward the end of the task.

"Wuck hard, mester!" said Dave. "Enough to mak' a man wuck. John Warren here don't want all his rabbits weshed away; and how am I to manage my 'coy if it's all under watter."

"Ah, how indeed!" said the squire, and he went away; but Dick stayed behind with Tom Tallington, and sat upon the top of the embankment, laughing, till the rough fen-man stood resting on his spade.

"Now then, what are yow gimbling (grinning) at, young mester?" he said.

"At yow, Dave," said Dick, imitating his broad speech.

"Then it arn't manners, lad. Thowt you'd been to school up to town yonder to larn manners both on you?"

"So we did, Dave, and a lot more things," cried Dick. "How to know when anyone's gammoning."

"Gammoning, lad?" said Dave uneasily.

"Yes, gammoning. You don't want the flood done away with."

"Not want the flood done away wi'!"

"No; and you don't want the fen drained and turned into fields."

"Do yow?" said Dave fiercely, and he took a step nearer to the lad.

"No, of course not," cried Dick. "It would spoil all the fun."

"Hah!" ejaculated Dave, as his yellow face puckered up with a dry smile, and in a furtive way which fitted with his fox-skin cap he turned and gave John Warren a peculiar look.

"When may we come over to the 'coy, Dave?"

"When you like, lads. Soon as the watter's down low enough for us to work it."

"It's sinking fast, Dave," said Tom. "It's all gone from our garden now, and the rooms are getting dry."

"Ay, but my pipes are covered still, and it'll be a good month, my lads, 'fore we can do any good. But I might ha' took you both out in the punt for a bit o' shooting if you hadn't played that game on me, and spoiled my horn and wasted all my powder."

"Ah, it was too bad, Dave; but there are a couple of fine large horns at home I've saved for you, and we've bought you a pound of powder."

"Nay, I sha'n't believe it till I see 'em," said Dave. "I did mean to hev asked you lads to come netting, but I can't ask them as plays tricks."

"Netting! What, the ruffs?"

"Ay, I weer thinking about heving a try for 'em. But I shall give it up."

"Dave, you promised me a year ago that you'd take us with you some time, and you never have," cried Dick.

"Nay, did I though?"

"Yes; didn't he, Tom?"

"Nay, yow needn't ask him; he'll be sewer to say yes," said Dave, grinning.

"Look here," cried Dick, "I'm not going to argue with you, Dave. Are you going to take us?"

"Some day, lad, when the watter's down, if my live birds aren't all drownded and my stales (stuffed decoys) spoiled."

"Oh, they won't be!" cried Dick. "When will you go?"

"When the watter's down, my lad."

"It's low enough now. There are plenty of places where you can spread your nets."

"Ay, but plenty of places don't suit me, my lad. You wait a bit and we'll see. Get John Warren to tek you ferreting."

"Yes, that will do," cried Tom. "When are you going, John?"

The man addressed shook his head.

"Rabbuds don't want no killing off. Plenty on 'em drownded."

"Why," cried Dick, "it was only the other day you said that none were hurt by the flood."

"Did I, Mester Dick? Ah, yow mustn't tek no notice o' what I say."

"But we shall take notice of what you say," cried Tom. "I don't believe he has any ferrets left."

"Ay, bud I hev. Theer I'll tek you, lads. Why don't thou tek 'em wi' you, Dave, man? Let un see the netting."

Dave smiled in a curious way, and then his eyes twinkled as he looked from one to the other.

"Well, you wait a week, lads, and then I'll fetch you."

"To see the netting?"

"Ay. In another week there'll be a deal more dry land, and the ruffs and reeves'll be ower in flocks, I dessay. If they aren't, we'll try for something else."

"Hooray!" cried Dick; and that evening there was nothing talked of but the projected trip.

Chapter Six.

The Departing Flood.

The water sank slowly and steadily, leaving dry patches here and there all over the fen; but the lake-like parts far exceeded the dry land, and two or three fields still contained so much water that the squire set men to work to cut a drain to carry it away.

"Kill two birds with one stone, Dick," he said. "It will be useful by and by."

At the time Dick did not understand what his father meant; but it was soon evident when all hands were hard at work cutting down through the peat to make the dyke. For, instead of digging in the ordinary way, the men carefully cut down through what was not earth, but thick well-compressed black peat, each piece, about ten inches square and three or four thick, to be carefully laid up like so much open brickwork to drain and dry.

Good store for the next winter's fuel, for it was peat of fine quality stored up by nature ages before, and not the soft brown mossy stuff found in many places, stuff that burns rapidly away and gives out hardly any heat. This peat about the Toft was coal's young relative, and burned slowly into a beautiful creamy ash, giving out a glow of warmth that was wanted there when the wind blew from the northern sea.

The two lads watched the process with interest—not that it was anything new, for they had seen it done a hundred times; but they had nothing else to do that morning, having tired themselves of gazing at the flocks of birds which passed over to the feeding grounds laid bare by the sinking water. It had been interesting to watch them, but Dave had not kept his word about the netting; the decoy had not been worked; and gunning was reserved for those of elder growth. So that morning, though the great lakes and canals among the reeds were dotted with birds, the lads were patiently watching the cutting of the little drain.

Six men were busy, and making steady progress, for the peat cut easily, the sharp-edged tools going through it like knives, while the leader of the gang busied himself from time to time by thrusting down a sharp-pointed iron rod, which always came in contact with sand and gravel a few feet down.

"No roots, my lad?" said the squire, coming up.

"No, mester," said the labourer. "I don't think—well, now, only think of that!"

He was thrusting down the iron rod as he spoke, and the point stuck into something that was not sand or gravel, while upon its being thrust down again with more force it stuck fast, and required a heavy jerk to drag it out.

"That seems to be a good one," said the squire, as the lads watched the process with interest.

"Shall we hev it out, mester?"

"Have it out! Oh, yes!" said the squire; and a couple of hours were spent widening the drain at that part, so as to give the men room to work round what was the root of an old tree, just as it had been growing in the far-distant ages, before the peat began to rise over it to nine or ten feet in thickness.

It was a long job, and after the great stump had been laid bare, axes had to be used to divide some of the outlying roots before it was finally dragged out by the whole force that could be collected by the hole, and finally lay upon the side.

"Just like the others, Dick. There must have been a tremendous fire here at one time."

"And burned the whole forest down?"

"Burned the whole of the trees down to the stumps, my lad, and then the peat gradually formed over the roots, and they've lain there till we come and dig them out for firewood."

"And they haven't rotted, father, although they have been under the peat and water all this time."

"No, my boy; the peat is a preservative. Nothing seems to decay under the peat. Why, you ought to have known that by now."

"I suppose I ought," said Dick rather dolefully, for he was beginning to wake up to the fact of what an enormous deal there was in the world that he did not know.

As he spoke, he picked up some of the red chips of the pine-root which had been sent flying by the strokes of the axe, to find that they were full of resin, smelling strongly of turpentine.

"Yes, it's full of it," said the squire; "that's one reason why the wood has kept without rotting. Here you two boys may as well do something for your bread and butter."

Dick said something to himself answering to nineteenth-century Bother! and awaited his father's orders.

"You can drag that root up to the yard. Get a rope round it and haul. Humph, no! it will be too heavy for you alone. Leave it."

"Yes, father," said Dick with a sigh of relief, for it was more pleasant to stand watching the men cutting the peat and the birds flying over, or to idle about the place, than to be dragging along a great sodden mass of pine-root.

19

"Stop!" cried the squire. "I don't want the men to leave their work. Go and fetch the ass, and harness him to it. You three donkeys can drag it up between you."

The boys laughed.

"I'm going up the river bank. Get it done before I get back."

"Yes, father," cried Dick. "Come along, Tom."

The task was now undertaken with alacrity, for there was somehow a suggestion to both of the lads of something in the nature of fun, in connection with getting the ass to drag that great root.

The companions ran along by the boggy field toward the farm buildings on the Toft, to seek out the old grey donkey, who was at that moment contemplatively munching some hay in a corner of the big yard, in whose stone walls, were traces of carving and pillar with groin and arch.

Now some people once started the idea that a donkey is a very stupid animal; and, like many more such theories, that one has been handed down to posterity, and believed in as a natural history fact, while donkey or ass has become a term of reproach for those not blessed with too much brain.

Winthorpe's donkey was by no means a stupid beast, and being thoroughly imbued with the idea that it was a slave's duty to do as little work as he possibly could for those who held him in bonds, he made a point of getting out of the way whenever he scented work upon the wind.

He was a grey old gentleman, whose years were looked upon as tremendous; and as he stood in the corner of the yard munching hay, he now and then scratched his head against an elaborately carved stone bracket in the wall which took the form of a grotesque face.

Then his jaws stopped, and it was evident that he scented something, for he raised his head slightly. Then he swung one great ear round, and then brought up the other with a sharp swing till they were both cocked forward and he listened attentively.

A minute before, and he was a very statue of a donkey, but after a few moments' attentive listening he suddenly became full of action, and setting up his tail he trotted round the yard over the rotten peat and ling that had been cut and tossed in, to be well trampled before mixing with straw and ploughing into the ground. He changed his pace to a gallop, and then, still growing more excited, he made straight for the rough gate so as to escape.

But the gate was fastened, though not so securely but that it entered into a donkey's brain that he might undo that fastening, as he had often undone it before, and then deliberately walked off into the fen, where succulent thistles grew.

This time, however, in spite of the earnest way in which he applied his teeth, he could not get that fastening undone; and, after striking at it viciously with his unshod hoof, he reared up, as if to leap over, but contented himself with resting his fore-legs on the rough top rail, and looking over at the free land he could not reach; and he was in this attitude when the two lads came up.

"Hullo, Solomon!" cried Dick. "Poor old fellow, then! Did you know we'd come for you?"

The donkey uttered a discordant bray which sounded like the blowing badly of a trumpet of defiance, and backing away, he trotted to the far end of the yard, and thrust his head into a corner.

"Where's the harness?" said Tom.

"In the stone barn," was the reply; and together the lads fetched the rough harness of old leather and rope, with an extra piece for fastening about the root.

"I say, Dick, he won't kick that root to pieces like he did the little tumbril," said Tom, who for convenience had placed the collar over his own head.

"Nor yet knock one side off like he did with the sled," replied Dick with a very vivid recollection of one of Solomon's feats. "Now, then, open the gate and let's pop the harness on. Stop a minute till I get a stick."

"Get a thick one," said Tom.

"Pooh! he don't mind a thick stick; he rather likes it. Hicky says it loosens his skin and makes him feel comfortable. Here, this will do. Must have a long one because of his heels."

"Oh, I say, Dick, look at the old rascal; he's laughing at us!"

It really seemed as if this were the case, for as the lads entered the yard Solomon lowered his head still more in its corner, and looked at them between his legs, baring his gums the while and showing his white teeth.

"Ah, I'll make him laugh—*gimble*, as old Dave calls it—if he gives us any of his nonsense! Now, you, sir, come out of that corner. Give me the collar, Tom."

As Dick relieved his friend of the collar, and held it ready to put over the donkey's head, though they were at least a dozen yards away, Solomon began to kick, throwing out his heels with tremendous force and then stamping with his fore-feet.

"Isn't he a pretty creature, Tom? He grows worse. Father won't sell him, because, he says, he's an old friend. He has always been my enemy."

"You always whacked him so," cried Tom.

"No, I didn't; I never touched him till he began it. Of course I wanted to ride him and make him pull the sled, and you know how he ran after me and bit me on the back."

"Yes, I know that somebody must have ill-used him first."

"I tell you they didn't. He's always been petted and spoiled. Why, that day when he kicked me and sent me flying into the straw I'd gone to give him some carrots."

"But didn't you tickle him or something?"

"No, I tell you. A nasty ungrateful brute! I've given him apples and turnips and bread; one Christmas I gave him a lump of cake; but no matter what you do, the worse he is. He's a natural savage, father says; and it isn't safe to go near him without a stick."

"Well, you've told me all that a dozen times," said Tom maliciously. "It's only an excuse for ill-using the poor thing."

"Say that again and I'll hit you," cried Dick.

"No, you won't. Here, give me the harness again and I'll put it on, only keep back with that stick. That's what makes him vicious."

"How clever we are!" cried Dick, handing back the collar. "There: go and try."

"Ah, I'll show you!" said Tom, taking the collar with its hames and traces attached, and going up toward the donkey, while Dick stood back, laughing.

"Take care, Tom; mind he don't bite!"

"He can't bite with his hind-legs, can he?" replied Tom. "I'll mind. Now, then, old fellow, turn round; I won't hurt you."

Solomon raised his tail to a horizontal position and held it out stiffly.

"Don't be a stupid," cried Tom; "I want your head, not your tail."

Dick burst into a roar of laughter, but Tom was not going to be beaten.

"You leave off laughing," he said, "and go farther back with that stick. That's right. Now, then, old boy, come on; turn round then."

Whack!

Poor Tom went backwards and came down a couple of yards away in a sitting position, with the collar in his lap and an astonished look in his countenance.

"Oh, I am sorry, Tom!" cried Dick, running up. "You, Solomon, I'll half kill you. Are you hurt, Tom?"

"I don't know yet," said the lad, struggling up.

"Where did he kick you?" cried Dick, full of sympathy now for his friend.

"He didn't kick me at all," said Tom dolefully. "I was holding the collar right out and he kicked that, but it hit me bang in the front and hurt ever so."

"Let me take the harness; I'll get it on him."

"No, I won't," cried Tom viciously. "I will do it now. Here, give me that stick."

"Why, I thought you said I ill-used him!"

"And I'll ill-use him too," said Tom savagely, "if he doesn't come and have on his collar. Now, then, you, sir, come here," cried Tom sharply.

By this time the donkey had trotted to another corner of the yard, where he stood with his heels presented to his pursuers, and as first one and then the other made a dash at his head he slewed himself round and kicked out fiercely.

"This is a nice game," cried Dick at last, when they were both getting hot with the exercise of hunting the animal from corner to corner, and then leaping backward or sidewise to avoid his heels, "Now, just you tell me this, who could help walloping such a brute? Hold still will you!"

But Solomon—a name, by the way, which was given him originally from its resemblance to "Solemn-un," the latter having been applied to him by Hickathrift—refused to hold still. In fact he grew more energetic and playful every minute, cantering round the yard and dodging his pursuers in a way which would have done credit to a well-bred pony, and the chances of getting the collar on or bit into his mouth grew more and more remote.

"I tell you what let's do," cried Dick at last; "I'm not going to run myself off my legs to please him. I've got it!"

"I wish you'd got the donkey," grumbled Tom. "I don't see any fun in hunting him and nearly getting kicked over the wall."

"Well, don't be in a hurry," said Dick; "I know how to manage him. Here, catch hold of this harness. I know."

"You know!" grumbled Tom, whose side was sore from the donkey's kick upon the collar. "What are you going to do?"

"You shall see," cried Dick, busying himself with the wagon rope he had brought, and making a loop at one end, and then putting the other through it, so as to produce an easily running noose.

"What are you going to do with that?" asked Tom.

"Hold your noise," whispered Dick; "he's such an artful old wretch I don't know that he wouldn't understand us. I'm going to make you drive him round by me, and then I'm going to throw this over his head and catch him."

"I don't believe you can," cried Tom.

"Well, you'll see. There, that'll do. I'm ready; take the stick and make a rush at him. That will drive him round near me, and then we'll try."

Tom laid down the harness, took the stick and made the rush at Solomon. The latter kicked out his heels and cantered round by Dick, who threw his noose, but failed to lasso the donkey, who took refuge in another corner.

"Never mind," cried Dick, gathering up the rope, "I shall do it next time. Now, then—I'm ready. Drive him back again."

Tom made another rush at the obstinate animal, which cantered off again, working considerably harder than it would if it had submitted patiently to being bitted. This time he gave Dick a better chance, and the boy threw the rope so well that it seemed as if it must go over the creature's head. But Solomon was too sharp. He shied at the rope and tossed his head aside; but though he avoided the noose and escaped it so far, as he plunged he stepped right into it, tightened it round his fore-legs, and the next instant fell over at one end of the rope, kicking and plunging as he lay upon his side, while at the other end of the rope there lay Dick upon his chest. For he had been jerked off his feet, but held on to the rope in spite of the donkey's struggles.

21

"I've got him, Tom; come and lay hold," panted Dick as the donkey made a desperate plunge, got upon his legs, and then fell down again upon the loose ling and straw, kicking out as if galloping.

This gave Dick time to rise, and, seeing his opportunity, he ran to the gate and passed the slack rope round, drew it tight, and shouted to Tom to come and hold on.

Just as Tom caught hold of the rope the donkey rose again and made a plunge or two, but only to fall once more, slacking the rope to such an extent that the boys were able to haul in a couple of yards more and hold on, stretching Solomon's legs out and drawing them so tightly that he uttered a piteous cry like the beginning of a bray chopped off short.

"Do you give in, then?" cried Dick.

The donkey raised his head slightly and let it fall again, gazing wildly at his captors, one of whom rushed round, avoided a feeble kick, and sat down upon the helpless animal's head.

"Now," cried Dick, "we've got him, Tom; and I've a good mind to play the drum on his old ribs till he begins to sing!"

"Don't hit him when he's down," said Tom. "It isn't English."

"I wasn't going to hit him," said Dick. "He's a prisoner and has given in. Bring me the bit."

Solomon opened his mouth to utter a bray; but Dick put the stick between his teeth, and he only uttered a loud sigh.

"Ah! now you're sorry for being such a brute, are you?" cried Dick. "Come along, Tom."

"I'm coming, only the things have got all mixed," was the reply.

"Give 'em to me," cried Dick. "That's it. Now, then, you sit on his neck, Tom, and then I'll get up. And look here, you, sir," he added to the donkey, "you come any more of your games, and I'll knock your head off!"

Solomon's flanks heaved, but he lay quite still, and did not resent Tom's rather rough treatment as he bestrode his neck and sat down. On the contrary, he half-raised his head at his master's command, suffered the bit to be thrust between his teeth and the head-stall to be buckled on, after which Tom leaped up.

"Take the rope from about his legs now, Tom," cried Dick.

"Suppose he kicks!"

"He won't kick now," cried Dick. "He'd better! Here, you hold the rein and I'll take it off."

"No, I'll do it," said Tom sturdily; and going cautiously to work he unknotted the rope and drew it away, the donkey lying quite motionless.

"Now, then, Sol, get up!" cried Tom.

The donkey drew his legs together, leaped to his feet, shook himself till his ears seemed to rattle, and uttered a sound like a groan.

"He is beaten now," said Dick. "Come and put on the pad and we'll go. That's right; buckle it on."

Tom obeyed, and the rough scrappy harness was fixed in its place, while Solomon twitched his ears and rolled them round as if trying to pick up news in any direction.

"He won't kick now, will he?" said Tom.

"Not unless he feels a fly on his back, and then he'll try to kick it off."

"Why, he couldn't kick a fly off his back if he tried," said Tom.

"No, but he'd try all the same. Look out!—there he goes!"

Tom leaped aside, for the donkey kicked out fiercely for a few moments.

"Why, there are no flies now!" said Tom.

"Must be. Look out!—he's going to kick again!"

The donkey's heels flew out, and Tom made a feint of punching his companion's head.

"How clever we are!" he cried. "Just as if I didn't see you tickling him to make him kick!"

"Tickle him!" said Dick laughing. "Why, I wasn't tickling him when he kicked up in the corner there. But come along or we shall never get that log up to the yard, and father won't like it. Now, Sol! Open the gate, Tom."

Tom opened the gate, and with Dick holding the rein the donkey walked along by his side as meekly as if he had never kicked or shown his teeth with the intention of biting in his life. The rope was doubled up and thrown over his back; and when they had gone a few yards Dick, without pausing, made a bit of a jump and struggled on to the animal's back, getting himself right aft, as a sailor would say, so that it seemed as if at any moment he might slip off behind.

But Solomon made no objection; he just twitched and wagged his tail for a moment or two, and then put it away out of sight. For the donkey chained, or rather harnessed, became an obedient slave—a very different creature from the donkey free.

When they reached the dyke where the men were standing delving out the peat, it was to find a group of three fresh arrivals in the persons of Hickathrift the wheelwright, Dave, and John Warren, and all in earnest converse upon some subject.

"Yow may say what yow like," cried Dave, "but fen-land's fen-land, and meant for the wild birds."

"And rabbuds," put in John Warren.

"Ay, lad, and rabbuds," assented Dave; "and it weer nivver meant to grow corn and grass. Yow can't do it, and yow'll nivver make fen-land fields. It's agen natur."

"So it is to ride in a cart or on a sled, lad," said Hickathrift good-humouredly; "but I make 'em, and folk rides in 'em and carries things to market."

"Ay, but that's different," said Dave. "Fen-land's fen-land; and you can't dree-ern that."

"You can't dree-ern that," said John Warren, nodding his head in assent.

"Well, they'll drain these fields, at all events," said Hickathrift. "Yow can't say they weant do that."

"I say fen-land's fen-land," reiterated Dave, taking off his fox-skin cap and rubbing his ear viciously; "and it can't be dree-ernt."

"Ah! you two are scarred about your 'coy and your rabbud-warren," cried Hickathrift good-humouredly. "I wish they'd dree-ern the whole place and have roads all over it, so as to want carts and wains."

"Nay, they nivver will," said Dave sourly. "Tek to makkin' boats and punts, mun. Them's best."

"Hullo, Dave!" cried Dick; "how about the ruffs and reeves? You said you'd take me to the netting."

"Well, haven't I come for you, lad?" said Dave quietly.

"Have you? Oh, Tom, and we've got this old stump to draw away! I can't go now, Dave."

"There's plenty o' time, lad. I'm not going back yet Hicky's got to put a bit o' plank in my boat 'fore I go back."

"Come on, Tom, and let's get it done," cried Dick. "Here, give us the rope."

He took the rope, fastened it to one of the roots, and then joined the traces together, and tied the rope about them.

After this the donkey was turned so that his head was toward the sharp slope, leading to the Priory on the Toft, and a start was made. That is to say, the donkey tightened the traces, stuck his hoofs into the ground, tugged for a minute without moving the stump, and then gave up.

"Why, Mester Dick, yow'll have to get root on a sled or she weant move."

"Oh, we'll do it directly!" cried Dick. "Here, Tom, you give a good shove behind. Now, then, pull up!"

Tom thrust with all his might, while Dick dragged at the donkey's head-stall, and once more, after offering a few objections, Solomon tightened the traces and rope, and tugged with all his might, but the root did not move.

"Yow weant move her like that, I tell you, lad," said Hickathrift.

"Won't I!" cried Dick angrily; "but I just will. You Tom, you didn't half push."

"Shall I give her a throost?" said the wheelwright, smiling.

That smile annoyed Dick, who read in it contempt, when it was only prompted by good temper.

"We can do it, thank you," cried Dick. "Now, Tom, boy, give it a heave. Pull up, Solomon."

Tom heaved, but Solomon refused to "pull up;" and after his late disappointments, and his discovery that the root was heavier than he, it took a great deal of coaxing to get him to stir. At last, though, just as Hickathrift was coming up good-temperedly to lend his aid, it seemed as if the donkey anticipated a tremendous blow from the long staff the wheelwright carried, for he made a plunge, Dick took tightly hold of the rein and gave it a drag, and Tom sat down on the great root, to follow Hickathrift's example and roar with laughter, in which the men who were delving peat joined, while Dave and John Warren, men who took life in a very solemn manner, actually smiled.

For Solomon's sudden plunge, joined to Dick's drag at the head-stall, showed that it was quite time a new fit out of harness was provided, inasmuch as the old leather gave way in two or three places, and the donkey, with nothing on but his collar, was off full gallop, feeling himself a slave no longer, while Dick, after staggering backwards for a yard or two, came down heavily in a sitting position, and in a very wet place.

"Yes, it's all very well to laugh," said Dick, getting up and looking ruefully at the broken bridle and bit which he held in his hand; "but see how cross father will be."

"And look where old Solomon has gone!" cried Tom. "I say, how are we to catch him? Ha! ha! ha! Only look!"

Everyone but Dick joined in the laugh, for Solomon was rejoicing in his liberty, and galloping away toward the fen, shaking his head, and kicking out his heels; while every now and then he stretched out his neck, grinned, and bit at the wind, for there was nothing else to bite.

"Nice job we shall have!" grumbled Dick. "Oh, I say, Tom, we are in a mess."

"Oh, there's nowt the matter, Mester Dick!" said Hickathrift good-temperedly, as he picked up the broken harness and examined it. "Why, I could mend all this in less than an hour with some wax-ends and a brad-awl."

"Yes, but will you, Hicky?"

"Of course I will, my lad. Theer, don't look that how. Go and catch the Solemn-un, and me, and Dave, and John Warren'll get the root up to the yard for you."

"Will you, Hicky?" cried the boys joyfully. "Oh, you are a good old fellow! Come on, Tom, and let's catch Solomon."

The harness was thrust aside by the wheelwright, ready to take home, and then at a word the two fen-men came forward, and together they rolled the awkwardly-shaped root over and over toward the farm; while, once satisfied that the pine-root was on its way, Dick gave his companion a slap on the shoulder, and moistened his hand to get a better grip of his stick.

"Get a stick, Tom," he said. "I don't want to drum old Solomon's ribs; but I'm just in the humour to give it him if he plays any of his tricks."

That was just what the donkey seemed determined upon. He had been shut up for a fortnight in the yard, and hardly knew how to contain himself, as he bounded along in a way he never attempted when he was not free. There were spots which he knew of where succulent thistles and water plants grew, and after a long course of dry food he meant to enjoy a feast.

The boys shouted as they ran, and tried to get ahead; but the more they shouted the more Solomon kicked up his heels and ran, performing a series of capers that suggested youth instead of extreme old age.

"We shall never get him," cried Tom as he panted along.

"We must catch him," cried Dick, making a furious rush to head off the frolicsome animal, which seemed as if he thoroughly enjoyed teasing his pursuers.

Dick was successful in turning the donkey, but not homeward, and he stopped short unwillingly as he saw the course taken.

"I say, Dick, isn't it soft out there?"

"Soft! Yes. Mind how you go!"

This advice would have been thrown away upon Solomon, though, had he comprehended it, the effect might have been beneficial. For, whatever knowledge the donkey might have possessed about the flood, he did not realise the fact that since he last tickled his palate with the spinous thistle—an herb which probably assumed to his throat the flavour that pepper does to ours—there had been a considerable depth of water over the fen, and that it was very soft. The result was, that while the lads stopped short, and then began to pick their way from tussock to tussock, and heather patch to patch, Solomon blundered on, made a splash here, a bit of a wallow there, and then a bound, which took him in half-way up his back; and as he plunged and struck out with fore-legs and heels, he churned up the soft bog and made it softer, so that he sank in and in, till only his spine was visible with, at the end, his long neck and great grey head, upon which the ears were cocked out forward, while an expression of the most intense astonishment shone out of his eyes.

"Oh, Tom, what shall we do?"

He-haw—he-yaw—he-yaw!

Solomon burst out into the most dismal bray ever heard—a long-drawn misery-haunted appeal for help, which was prolonged in the most astounding way till it seemed to be a shrill cry.

"I don't know," responded Tom, wiping the tears out of his eyes.

"Oh, come, I say," said Dick, "it isn't anything to laugh at!"

"I know it isn't," cried Tom; "but I can't help it. I feel as if I must laugh, and—Ha! ha! ha!"

He burst into a tremendous peal, in which his companion joined, for anything more comic than the aspect of the "Solemn-un" up to his neck in the bog it would be hard to conceive.

"Here, this won't do," cried Dick at last, as he too stood wiping his eyes. "Poor old Sol, we mustn't let you drown. Come on, Tom, and let's help him out."

How Dick expected that he was going to help the donkey out he did not say; but he began to pick his way from tuft to tuft, avoiding the soft places, till he was within twenty feet of the nearly submerged animal, and then he had to stop or share his fate.

"I say, Tom, I can't get any farther," he cried. "What shall we do?"

"I don't know."

"What a fellow you are!" was the angry reply. "You never do know. Old Sol will be drowned if we don't look sharp. The bog is twenty feet deep here."

"Can't he swim out?"

"Can't you swim out!" cried Dick. "What's the good of talking like that? You couldn't swim if you were up to the neck in sand."

"But he isn't up to his neck in sand."

"But he's up to his neck in bog, and it's all the same."

"Ahoy! what's matter?" came from a couple of hundred yards away; and the lads turned, to see that it was Hickathrift shouting, he and the others having just succeeded in taking up the root to its destination.

"Ahoy! Bring the rope," shouted Dick.

"He-haw—haw—haw—haw!" shouted the Solemn one dismally, as if to emphasise his young master's order.

"Why, how came he in there?" cried Hickathrift, trotting up with the rope, but picking his way carefully, for the peat shook beneath his feet.

"He went in himself," cried Dick. "Oh, do get him out before he sinks! Make a noose, and let's throw it over his head."

"We shall pull his head right off if we do," said Hickathrift, but busily making the noose the while.

"Oh, no, I don't believe you would!" cried Tom. "He has got an awfully strong neck."

"It won't hurt him," said Dave, who came up slowly with the rest.

"Well, there's no getting it under him," said the wheelwright; "he'd kick us to pieces if we tried."

"I'll try," said Dick eagerly.

"Nay, I weant let you," said Hickathrift. "I'll go my sen."

"It weant bear thee, neighbour," said John Warren warningly.

"Eh? weant it? Well, I can but try, mun. Let's see."

The good-natured wheelwright went cautiously towards where Dick was standing waiting for the rope; but at the third step he was up to his middle and had to scramble out and back as fast as he could.

"I'm too heavy," he said; "but I'll try again. All right, I'm coming soon!" he added as the donkey uttered another dismal bray.

But his efforts were vain. Each time he tried he sank in, and at last, giving up to what was forced upon him as an impossibility, he coiled up the rope to throw.

"Thou mun heave it over his head, my lad. Don't go no nigher to him; it isn't safe."

He threw the rope, and Dick caught the end and recoiled it preparatory to making a start over the moss.

"Nay, nay, stop!" shouted Hickathrift.

"I must go and try if I can't put it round him, Hicky," cried Dick.

"Come back, thou'lt drown thysen," shouted Dave excitedly.

"No, I won't," said Dick; and picking his steps with the greatest care, he succeeded in stepping within ten yards of the donkey, which made a desperate struggle now to get out and reach him, but without success; all he did was to change his position, his hind-quarters going down lower, while his fore-legs struck out into the daylight once or twice in his hard fight for liberty.

"Now, my lad, heave the rope over his head, and we'll haul him out," cried Hickathrift.

But Dick paid no heed. He saw in imagination the poor animal strangled by the noose; and with the idea that he could somehow get alongside, he struck out to the left, but had to give up, for the bog was more fluid there.

On the other side it was even worse, and Dick was about to turn and shout to the men to try if they could not get the punt up alongside, when a fresh struggle from Solomon plainly showed him that the animal must be rescued at once or all would be over.

Dick made one more trial to get nearer, in spite of the cries and adjurations of those upon the firmer ground; but it was useless, and struggling to a tuft of dry reed, he balanced himself there and gathered up the rope, so as to try and throw the loop over the donkey's head.

As he held it ready there was another miserable bray, and the lad hesitated.

"It means killing him," he muttered. "Poor old Solomon! I never liked him, but we've had so many runs together."

His hand dropped to his side with the rope, and he tottered, for the reed tuft seemed to be sinking.

Solomon brayed again and fought desperately to free himself, but sank lower.

"Heave, Dick, heave!" shouted Tom.

"Throw it over, my lad! throw it over, or thou'lt be too late!" cried the wheelwright; but Dick did not move. His eyes were fixed upon the donkey's head, but his thoughts were far back in the past, in sunny days when he had been riding by the edge of the fen to the town, or down to the firm sand by the sea, where Solomon always managed to throw him and then gallop off. Then there were the wintry times, when the donkey's hoofs used to patter so loudly over the frozen ground, while now—

Perhaps it was very childish, for Dick was a strongly built lad of sixteen, and had his memory served him truly it would have reminded him of that terrible kick in the leg which lamed him for a month—of the black-and-yellow bruise upon his arm made by the vicious animal's jaws one day when he bit fiercely—of that day when he was pitched over Solomon's head into the black bog ditch, and had to swim out—of a dozen mishaps and injuries received from the obstinate beast. But Dick thought of none of these, only of the pleasant days he had had with the animal he had known ever since he could run; and, whether it were childish or not, the tears rose and dimmed his eyes as he stood there gazing at what seemed to be the animal's dying struggles, and thinking that it would be kinder to let him drown than to strangle him, as he felt sure they would.

"Why don't you throw, Dick?" cried Tom again in an excited yell that was half drowned by Solomon's discordant bray, though it was growing more feeble as the struggles were certainly more weak.

All at once Dick started and his eyes grew more clear. It was not at the warning shout of the wheelwright, nor the yell uttered by the other men, but at the action of the sufferer in the bog. For, feeling himself surely and certainly sinking lower, the donkey made one more tremendous effort, extricating his fore-legs and beating the fluid peat with them till it grew thinner, and with neck outstretched and mouth open it sank more and more back, till head and legs only could be seen.

Dick did it unconsciously. His eyes were fixed upon the struggling beast, but his ears were deaf to the shouts behind him. All he heard was the dismal bray enfeebled to a groan so full of despair that the lad threw the rope, and in throwing lost his balance, fell, and the next moment was struggling in the mire.

He tried to rise, but it was impossible, and as he fought and struggled for a few moments it was to find that the bog was growing thinner and that the patches about him, which looked firm, were beginning to sink.

Was he too going to drown? he asked himself, and something of the sensation he had felt on the night of the flood came over him.

Then he felt a snatch, and a voice like thunder brought him to himself.

"Howd tight, lad!"

The next moment Dick felt himself gliding over the soft bog, and directly after Dave had hold of one of his hands and drew him to a place of safety before running back to the rope.

"All together, lads! Haul!"

There was a shout and a tremendous splashing, and Dick Winthorpe struggled to his feet, wiping the black fluid bog from his eyes, to see Solomon hauled right out, slowly at first, then faster and faster, till he was literally run over the slippery surface to where there was firm ground.

"I got it over his head, then?" said Dick huskily.

"Ay, lad, and over his legs too," cried Hickathrift, as he bent down and loosened the noose. "Eh, bud it's tight. That's it!"

He dragged the rope off, and the donkey lay perfectly motionless for a few moments, but not with his eyes closed, for he seemed to be glowering round.

"Is he dying, Hicky?" said Dick.

"Nay, lad; yow can't kill an ass so easy. Seems aw reight. There!"

The last word was uttered as the donkey suddenly struggled up, gave himself a tremendous shake, till his ears rattled again as the bog water flew; and then stretching out his neck as if he were about to bray, he bared his teeth and made a fierce run at the wheelwright.

But Hickathrift struck at him with the rope, and to avoid that, Solomon worked round, made a bite at Dick, which took effect on his wet coat, tearing a piece right out. Then he swerved round like lightning and threw out his heels at Tom, tossed up his head, and then cantered off, braying as he went, as if nothing had been the matter, and making straight for the yard.

25

"Well, of all the ungrateful brutes!" cried Tom.

"Ay, we might just as well hev let him get smothered," said the wheelwright, joining in the laughter of the others. "Didn't hurt you, did he, Mester Dick?"

"No, Hicky. Only tore my coat," replied Dick, turning reluctantly up to the house, for he was wet and now felt cold.

"I say, Dick, what about the netting?" cried Tom.

The lad looked piteously at Dave and his companion of the rabbit warren—two inseparable friends—and felt that his chance of seeing the ruffs and reeves captured was very small.

"Are you going—to-day, Dave?" he faltered.

"Nay, lad," said Dave dryly, "yow've had enough o' the bog for one day. Go and dry thysen. I'll coom and fetch thee to-morrow."

So the lads went up to the house, the men returned to their draining, and the wheelwright walked slowly away with Dave and John Warren.

"Let's run, Dick," said Tom, who was carrying the rope; "then you won't catch cold."

"Oh, I sha'n't hurt," said Dick, running all the same; and in passing the yard they closed the gate, for Solomon was safe inside; but as they reached the house, where Mrs Winthorpe stood staring aghast at her son's plight, Solomon burst forth with another dismal, loud complaining: "*He-haw*!"

Chapter Seven.

The Fen-man's Wages.

Dave did not keep his promise the next day, nor the next; but Dick Winthorpe had his attention taken up by other matters, for a party of men arrived and stopped with their leaders at the Toft, where they were refreshed with ale and bread and cheese, previous to continuing their journey down to the seaside.

The squire and Farmer Tallington accompanied them down to their quarters, which were to be at a disused farm-house close to the mouth of the little river; and incidentally Dick learned that this was the first party of labourers who were to cut the new lode or drain from near the river mouth right across the fen; that there was to be a lock with gates at the river end, to let the drain-water out at low tide, and that the banks of the drain were to be raised so as to protect the land at the sides from being flooded.

Fen people from far and wide collected to see the gang, and to watch the surveyors, who, with measuring chain and staves and instruments, busied themselves marking out the direction in which the men were to cut; and these fen people shook their heads and shrugged their shoulders, while more than once, when Squire Winthorpe addressed one or the other, Dick noticed that they were always surly, and that some turned away without making any answer.

"Never mind, Dick," said the squire laughing. "Some day when we've given them smiling pastures and corn-fields, instead of water and bog and ague, they will be ashamed of themselves."

"But—"

"Well, but what, sir?" said the squire as the lad hesitated.

"I was only going to say, father, isn't it a pity to spoil the fen?"

The squire did not answer for a few moments, but stood frowning. The severe look passed off directly though, and he smiled.

"Dick," he said gravely, "all those years at a good school, to come back as full of ignorance and prejudice as the fen-men! Shame!"

He walked away, leaving Dick with his companion Tom Tallington.

"I say," said the latter, "you caught it."

"Well, I can't help it," said Dick, who felt irritated and ashamed. "It does seem a pity to spoil all the beautiful pools and fishing places, and instead of having beds of reeds full of birds, for there to be nothing but fields and a great ugly drain. Why, the flowers, and butterflies, and nesting places will all be swept away. What do we care for fields of corn!"

"My father cares for them, and he says it will be the making of this part of the country."

"Unmaking, he means," said Dick; and they went on to watch the proceedings of the strange men who had come—big, strong, good-tempered-looking fellows, armed with sharp cutting spades, and for whose use the lads found that a brig had come into the little river, and was landing barrows, planks, and baskets, with a variety of other articles to be used in the making of the drain.

"I'm afraid we shall have some trouble over this business, Tallington," said the squire as they went back.

"Well, we sha'n't be the only sufferers," said the farmer good-humouredly. "I suppose all we who have adventured our few pounds will be in the people's black books. But we must go on—we can't stop now."

The next day Tom came over, and the lads went down towards the far-stretching fen, now once more losing a great deal of the water of the flood.

They passed the Solemn one apparently none the worse for his bath, for he trotted away from the gate to thrust his head in the favourite corner by the old corbel in the wall, and look back at them, as if as ready to kick as ever.

"Poor old Solomon!" said Dick laughing, "I should have been sorry if he had been lost."

"Oh, never mind him," cried Tom; "is old Dave coming over to fetch us? Why, Dick, look!"

"I can't see anything," said Dick.

"Because you're not looking the right way. There! Now he's behind that bed of reeds a mile away."

"I see!" cried Dick. "Why, it is Dave, and he's coming."

The lads ran down to the edge of the fen, and made their way to the end of a long, open, river-like stretch of water, which was now perfectly clear, so that everything could be clearly distinguished at the bottom; and before long, as they walked to and fro, they caught sight of a little shoal of small fish, and soon after of a young pike, with his protruding lower jaw, waiting for his opportunity to make a dash at some unfortunate rudd, whose orange fins and faintly-gilded sides made him a delectable-looking morsel for his olive-green and gold excellency the tyrant of the river.

"He's coming here, isn't he?" said Tom, gazing out anxiously over the reedy waste.

"Yes; I can see his old fox-skin cap. He's coming safe enough."

"Oh, Dick!" cried his companion.

"Well! What?"

"The powder. You've never given him the powder, and he'll be as gruff as can be. Has he had the horn?"

"Had two," said Dick, watching the approaching punt, which was still half a mile away, and being poled steadily in and out of the winding water-lane, now hidden by the dry rustling reeds which stood covered with strands of filmy conferva or fen scum.

"But he hasn't had the powder we promised him."

"No," said Dick loftily; "not yet."

"Why, you haven't brought it, Dick!"

"Haven't brought it, indeed! Why, what's this, then?"

He drew a bottle from his pocket, took out the cork, and poured a little of its contents into his hand—dry, black grains, like so much sable sand, and then poured it back and corked it tightly.

"You are a good fellow, Dick; but I haven't paid my share."

"I don't want your share," said Dick loftily. "Father gave me half-a-crown the other day."

"I wish my father gave me half-crowns sometimes," sighed Tom; "but he isn't so rich as yours."

"There, don't bother about money!" cried Dick. "Let's think about the birds. Hooray! here he comes! Hi, Dave!"

Sound travels easily over water, and the decoy-man must have heard the hail, but he paid no heed, only kept on poling his punt along, thrusting down the long ash sapling, which the fen-men used as punt-pole, staff, and leaping-pole in turn; and then as the boat glided on, standing erect in her bows like some statue.

"Now, what a dried-up old yellow mummy he is!" cried Dick. "He can see us, but he's pretending he can't, on purpose to tease us. Look at that! He needn't have gone behind that great reed patch. It's to make us think he is going down to your place."

"Let's run down and meet him," said Tom eagerly.

"No, no; stop where you are. If he sees us go down there he'll double back directly and come here. He's just like an old fox. I know. Come along!"

Dick started up and ran in the same direction as Dave had taken with the punt before he disappeared behind the reed-bed. Tom followed, and they raced on along the edge till a clump of alders was reached.

"Pst! Tom, round here," whispered Dick; and leading the way he doubled back, following the long low bed of swamp-loving wood, and keeping in its shelter till they were once more opposite to the spot where Dave should have landed.

There, still hid among the trees, Dick stooped down in a thick bed of dry reeds, pretty close to the water, and in full view of the rough winding canal leading far and wide.

"Let's hide for a few minutes," said Dick chuckling. "You'll see he'll come here after all."

The lad had a good idea of Dave's ways, for before they had been watching many minutes there was the splashing of the pole heard in the water, and the rustling of the reeds, but nothing was visible, and Tom began to be of opinion that his companion had been wrong, when all at once the reeds began to sway and crackle right before them, and before Tom recovered from his surprise the punt shot right out of the middle of the long low wall of dried growth, and in answer to a vigorous thrust or two from the pole, glided across to within a dozen yards of where the lads crouched.

"Come on, Tom!" said Dick, and they stepped out at once so suddenly that the decoy-man, in spite of his self-control, started. A curious smile puckered his face directly and he stood staring at them.

"Why, you have been a long time, Dave," cried Dick.

"Long, boy?"

"Yes, long. You asked us to come over and see the netting."

"Ay, so I did, boy; but there soon wean't be no netting."

"Then come on and let's see it while there is some," cried Dick. "When we used to be home from school you always said we were too young. You can't say that now."

"Ay, bud I can," said the man with a dry chuckle.

"Then don't," said Dick. "You've brought your gun there!" he cried joyfully.

"Ay, I've brote my gun," said Dave; "but I hevven't any powder."

"Yes, you have, Dave," cried Dick, tugging the wine-bottle from his pocket. "Here's some."

"Eh? Is that powder or drink?" said the man, taking the bottle and giving it a shake. "It arn't full, though."

27

"No, it isn't full," said Dick in a disappointed tone; "but there's a whole pound, and it's the best."

DAVE AND THE BOYS AT THE DECOY

Page 28

"Ah, well, I daresay it'll do," said Dave slowly.

"Load the gun, then, and let's have a shot at the snipes as we go," said Tom.

"Nay, she wean't go off till she has had a new flint in. I'm going to knap one when I get back."

"Jump in, then," cried Dick. "I'm going to pole her across."

"Nay, I don't think it's any use to-day."

"Why, Dave, this is just the sort of day you said was a good one for netting."

"Did I, lad?"

"Yes; didn't he, Tom? And what's that wisp of birds going over the water, yonder?"

"Quick, in wi' ye, lads!" cried the decoy-man, with his whole manner changed. "The right sort. Look, lads, another wisp! See how low they fly. They mean feeding."

The boys leaped into the punt, and Dick was about to seize the pole, but Dave stopped him.

"Nay, lad, let me send her across. Save time."

"Then may I have a shot at the first heron I see?"

"Nay, nay; don't let's scar' the birds, lad. It's netting to-day. We'll shute another time when they wean't come near the net."

Dick gave way, and Dave took the pole, to send the light punt skimming over the water, and in and out among the reed-beds through which, puzzling as they would have been to a stranger, he thrust the vessel rapidly. They were full of devious channels, and Dave seemed to prefer these, for even when there was a broad open piece of water in front he avoided it, to take his way through some zigzag lane with the reeds brushing the boat on either side, and often opening for himself a way where there was none.

The man worked hard, but it seemed to have no effect upon him; and when the lads were not watching him and his energetic action, there was always something to take up their attention. Now a heron would rise out of one of the watery lanes, gaunt, grey, and with his long legs stretched out behind to look like a tail as his great flap wings beat the air and carried him slowly away.

28

Then with a loud splash and cackling, up would spring a knot of ducks, their wings whirring as they rapidly beat the air in a flight wonderful for such a heavy bird. Again a little farther and first one and then another snipe would dart away in zigzag flight, uttering their strange *scape, scape*. And all tempting to a lad who sat there within touch of a long heavy-looking gun, which had been cleaned and polished till every part was worn.

But he had been told that it was not charged and that the flint-lock was in a failing condition; and besides, Dick felt that it would be dishonourable to touch the gun now that it was almost trusted to his care.

In spite of Dave's ability and knowledge of the short cuts to the part of the fen where he lived, it took him nearly three-quarters of an hour to punt across, where the lads landed upon what was really an island in the fen, though one side ran pretty close up to some fairly dry land full of narrow water-lanes and pools, all favourite breeding ground for the wild-fowl.

The boys leaped out while Dave fastened the punt to an old willow trunk, and, quite at home in the place, went on first to a rough-looking house nearly hidden among alders and willows, all of which showed traces of the flood having been right up, submerging everything to a depth of three to four feet.

"Hullo, Chip! Chip! Chip!" cried Tom, and the decoy-man's little sharp-looking dog came bounding to them, to leap up, and fawn and whine, full of delight at seeing human faces again.

There was the twittering and piping of birds, and the scuffling, scratching noise made by animals in a cage, as they reached the roughly-fenced yard, more than garden, about Dave's cottage, the boys eager to inspect the birds, the ferrets, the eel-spear leaning against the reed thatch, and the brown nets hung over poles, stretching from post to post, as if to dry.

"Why, it's months sin' you've been to see me," said Dave.

"Well, whose fault's that?" said Dick sharply. "I say, Dave, these nets are new."

"Ay, every one of 'em. Made 'em all this summer."

"Didn't you get lots of things spoiled when the flood came?" cried Tom.

"N–no, lad, no. Nearly had my birds drownded, but I got 'em atop of the thack yonder."

"But hasn't your cottage been dreadfully wet?" asked Dick, who was poking his finger in a cage full of ferrets. "I say, what are John Warren's ferrets doing here?"

"Doin' nothing, and waiting to be took out, that's all, lad."

"But wasn't your place horribly wet?"

"What care I for a drop o' watter?" said Dave contemptuously.

"Look here, Dick, at the decoys," cried Tom running to a large wicker cage in which were four of the curious long-legged birds known as ruffs and reeves.

"Was six," said Dave. "I lost two."

"How?"

"Fightin', lad. I niver see such bonds to fight. Gamecocks is babies to 'em. I'm going to try a new improved way of ketching of 'em by challenging the wild ones to fight."

"Never mind about them," said Dick eagerly; "are you going to start now?"

"Ah! you're so precious eager to begin, lad," said Dave; "but when you've been sitting out there on the boat for about a couple of hours you'll be glad to get back."

"Oh, no, we sha'n't!" cried Dick. "Now, then, let's start."

"Ay, but we've got to get ready first."

"Well, that's soon done. Shall I carry the birds down to the boat?"

"Nay; we wean't take them to-day. I've sin more pie-wipes than ruffs, so let's try for them."

He went round to the back of the hovel and took from the roof a cage which the lads had not yet seen, containing seven green plovers, and this was carried to the boat, where the frightened birds ran to and fro, thrusting their necks between the wicker bars in a vain attempt to escape.

This done, a bundle of net, some long stout cord, and poles were carefully placed in the stern, after which Dave went into his cottage to bring out a mysterious-looking basket, which was also placed in the stern of the boat.

"That's about all," said the man, after a moment's thought; and unfastening the punt after the boys were in, he pushed off, but only to turn back directly and secure the boat again.

"Why, what now, Dave?" cried Dick. "Aren't you going?"

"Going, lad! yes; but I thowt if we caught no bohds you might like me to shute one or two."

"Well, we've got the gun and plenty of powder."

"Ay, lad; but I've lost my last flint, and I've got to knap one."

The boys followed him ashore, leaving the plovers fluttering in the cage, and Dave went inside his cottage, and returned directly with a hammer and a piece of flint, which he turned over two or three times so as to get the stone in the right position, as, taught by long experience, he struck a sharp blow.

Now Dave, the duck-decoy-man of the fens, knew nothing about lines of fracture or bulbs of percussion as taught by mineralogists, but he knew exactly where to hit that piece of flint so as to cause a nice sharp-edged flake to fly off, and he knew how and where to hit that flake so as to chip it into a neat oblong, ready for his gun, those present being ignorant of the fact that they were watching workmanship such as was in vogue among the men who lived and hunted in England in the far-distant ages of which we have no history but what they have left us in these works. Dave Gittan chipped away at the flint just as the ancient hunters toiled to make the arrow-heads with which they shot the animals which supplied them with food and clothing, the flint-knives with which they skinned and cut up the beasts, and the round sharp-edged scrapers with which they removed the fat and adhering flesh as they dressed and tanned the skins to make them fit to wear.

Dave chipped one gun-flint very accurately, failed to make a second, but was triumphant with the third attempt, and fitting it exactly in the lock of his piece with a piece of leather at top and bottom, he loaded the gun with a great deal of ceremony, measuring the powder with a tiny cup which fitted over the top of his powder-horn, and his shot with the same vessel, so many times filled.

These rammed down in place with some rough paper on the top, and the ramrod measured to see whether it stood out the right distance from the barrel, the pan was primed and closed, and the gun carefully laid ready for use.

"There," cried Dave in an ill-used tone, "I don't know why I'm tekkin' all this trouble for such a pair o' young shacks as you; but come along."

"It's because he likes us, Dick," said Tom merrily.

"Nay, that I don't," cried Dave. "I hate the lot of you. Not one of you'll be satisfied till you've spoiled all my fen-land, and made it a place where nivver a bird will come."

"Why, I wouldn't have it touched if I could help it—St! Dave, what bird's that?" said Dick.

"Curlew," replied Dave in a low voice, whose tones were imitated by the lads as the boat was softly punted along. "See them, boys!"

He nodded in the direction they were going, towards where a number of birds were flying about over some patches of land which stood just over the level of the water. Now they looked dark against the sky, now they displayed feathers of the purest white, for their flight with their blunted wings was a clumsy flapping very different to the quiver and skim of a couple of wild ducks which came by directly after and dropped into the water a quarter of a mile ahead.

"You come and see me next spring, my lads, and I'll show you where there's more pie-wipes' eggs than ever you found before in your lives."

"But you'll take us one day to the 'coy, Dave?" said Dick.

"Nay, I don't think I can," said Dave.

"But it's my father's 'coy," said Dick.

"Ay, I know all about that," said the man harshly; "but it wean't be much good to him if he dree-erns the fen."

Dave's voice was growing loud and excited, but he dropped it directly and thrust away without making the slightest splash with his iron-shod pole.

As they came near one bed of reeds several coots began to paddle away, jerking their bald heads as they went, while a couple of moor-hens, which as likely as not were both cocks, swam as fast as their long thin unwebbed toes would allow them, twitching their black-barred white tails in unison with the jerking of their scarlet-fronted little heads, and then taking flight upon their rounded wings, dragging their long thin toes along the top of the water, and shrieking with fear, till they dropped into the sheltering cover ahead.

Snipes flew up from time to time, and more curlews and green plovers were seen, offering plenty of opportunities for the use of the gun, as the punt progressed till a long low spit of heathery gravel, about forty feet in length and five wide, was reached, with a patch of reeds across the water about a couple of hundred yards away.

"Is this the place?" cried Dick excitedly; and upon being answered in the affirmative—"Now, then, what shall we do first?"

"Sit still, and I'll tell you, lads," was the stern reply, as Dave, now all eagerness, secured the boat and landed his net and poles.

"Don't tread on her, my lads," he said. "Now help me spread her out."

He showed them how to proceed, and the net, about a dozen yards in length, was spread along the narrow spit of land, which was only about a foot wider than the net, at whose two ends was fixed a pole as spreader, to which lines were attached.

The net spread, the side nearest to the water was fastened down with pegs, so adjusted as to act as hinges upon which the apparatus would turn, while as soon as this was done Dave called for the mysterious-looking basket.

This being produced from the punt and opened was found to contain about a dozen stuffed peewits, which, though rough in their feathers, were very fair imitations of the real things.

These were stuck along the edge of the net outside and at either end.

"Now for the 'coys," cried Dave, and Tom brought the cage of unfortunate peewits, who had a painful duty to perform, that of helping to lead their free brethren into the trap that was being laid for them.

Each of these decoy-birds was quickly and cleverly tethered to a peg along the edge of the net upon the narrow strip of clear land, a string being attached to one leg so long as to give them enough freedom to flutter a little among the stuffed birds, which seemed to be feeding.

"There!" cried Dave, when all was ready; and at a short distance nothing was visible but the group of birds fluttering or quiescent, for the net was wonderfully like the ground in colour. "There, she's ready now, my lads, so come along."

He bade Dick thrust the punt along to the bed of reeds; and as the lad deftly handled the pole, Dave let out the line, which was so attached to the ends of the poles that a vigorous pull would drag the net right over.

It was quite a couple of hundred yards to the reeds, through which the punt was pushed till it and its occupants were hidden, when, having thrust down the pole as an anchor to steady the little vessel, the line was drawn tight so as to try whether it would act, and then kept just so tense as to be invisible beneath the water, and secured to the edge of the punt.

"That ought to bring them, lads," said Dave, with his eyes twinkling beneath his fox-skin cap, after beating a few reeds aside so that they could have a good view of where the unfortunate peewits fluttered at the pegs.

"But suppose they don't come?" said Tom. "I know if I was a piewipe I wouldn't be cheated by a few dummies and some pegged-down birds."

"But then you are not a piewipe, only a goose," said Dick.

"Hist!" whispered Dave, and placing his fingers to his mouth he sent out over the grey water so exact an imitation of the green plover's cry that Dick looked at him in wonder, for this was something entirely new.

Pee-eugh, pee-eugh, pee-eugh! And the querulous cry was answered from a distance by a solitary lapwing, which came flapping along in a great hurry, sailed round and round, and finally dropped upon the little narrow island and began to run about.

"You won't pull for him, will you, Dave?" whispered Dick.

Dave shook his head, and the boys watched as from time to time the man uttered the low mournful cry.

"Wonder what that chap thinks of the stuffed ones?" whispered Dick.

"Why don't the live ones tell him it isn't safe?" said Tom.

"Don't know; perhaps they're like old Tom Tallington," said Dick: "whenever they get into a mess they like to get some one else in it too."

"You say that again and I'll hit you," whispered Tom, holding up his fist menacingly.

"Hist!" came from Dave, who uttered the imitation of the peewit's whistle again, and a couple more of the flap-winged birds came slowly over the grey-looking water, which to anyone else, with its patches of drab dry weeds and bared patches of black bog, would have seemed to be a terrible scene of desolation, whereas it was a place of enchantment to the boys.

"They come precious slowly," said Dick at last. "I thought that there would have been quite a crowd of birds, like you see them sometimes. Look at the old bald-heads, Tom."

He pointed to a party of about half a dozen coots which came slowly out of the reeds and then sailed on again as if suspicious of all being not quite right.

Then there was another little flock of ducks streaming over the fen in the distance, and their cries came faintly as they dashed into the water, as if returning home after a long absence.

"There goes a her'n," whispered Tom, who was not very good at seeing birds and worse at telling what they were.

"'Tisn't," cried Dick; "it's only a grey crow."

"If you two go on chattering like that we shall get no birds," said Dave sharply. "What a pair o' ruck-a-toongues you are; just like two owd women!"

"Well, but the birds are so long coming," said Dick; "I'm getting the cramp. I say, Dave, are there any butterbumps (bitterns) close here?"

"Plenty; only they wean't show theirsens. Hah!"

They had been waiting a couple of hours, and the peewit's cry had been uttered from time to time, but only a straggler or two had landed upon the strip of land. Dick had been eager to capture these, but Dave shook his head. It wasn't worth while to set the net and peg out decoys and stales, he said, to catch two pie-wipes that weren't enough for a man's dinner.

So they crouched there in the punt, waiting and growing more cold and cramped, fidgeting and changing their positions, and making waves seem to rise from under the boat to go whispering among the reeds.

Every now and then Tom uttered a sigh and Dick an impatient grunt, while at these movements Dave smiled but made no other sign, merely watching patiently. His eyes glittered, and their lids passed over them rapidly from time to time; otherwise he was as motionless as if carved out of old brown boxwood, an idea suggested by the colour of his skin.

"I say," said Dick at last, as there were tokens in the distance of the day coming to an end with mist and fine rain, "I am getting so hungry! Got anything to eat, Dave?"

"When we've done, lads."

"But haven't we done? No birds will come to-day."

Dave did not answer, only smiled very faintly; and it seemed as if the lad was right, for the sky and water grew more grey, and though the stuffed birds appeared to be diligently feeding, and those which were tethered hopped about and fluttered their wings, while the two free ones ran here and there, flew away and returned, as if exceedingly mystified at the state of affairs on that long, narrow strip of land, Dave's calls seemed to be as vain as the snares he had made.

"I wonder whether these birds break their shins in running over the meshes of the net!" said Dick after a long yawn. "Oh, I say, Dave, there's no fun in this; let's go!"

"Hist! pee-eugh, pee-eugh!" whistled Dave loudly, and then in quite a low tone that sounded distant, and this he kept up incessantly and with a strange ventriloquial effect.

The boys were all excitement now, for they grasped at once the cause of their companion's rapid change of manner. For there in the distance, coming down with the wind in scattered flight and as if labouring heavily to keep themselves up, appeared a flock of lapwings pretty well a hundred strong.

"Hooray! At last, Tom!" cried Dick. "Will they come and settle on the net, Dave?"

"Not a bird of 'em if thou keeps up that ruck," whispered the man excitedly.

The next minute he was imitating the cry of the peewit, and it was answered from the distance by the birds coming along, while the two stragglers which had been hanging about so long now rose up, circled round, and settled again.

"Look at them!" whispered Dick. "Lie low, Tom; they're coming."

31

Both lads were on the tiptoe of expectation, but it seemed as if they were to be disappointed, for the flock came on slowly, uttering its querulous cries, and circled round as if to pass over, but they were evidently still attracted by the decoy-birds, and hesitated and flew to and fro.

"Oh, if they don't light now!" said Dick to himself. "They're going," he sighed half aloud, and then he seized Tom's arm in his excitement, and gripped it so hard that the boy nearly cried out, and would have done so but for the state of eagerness he too was in.

For after farther signs of hesitation and doubt, all of which were in favour of the flock going right away, one of them seemed to give a regular tumble over in the air, as if it were shot, and alighted. Another followed, and another, and another, till, to the intense excitement of the occupants of the boat among the reeds, the long, low spit of gravel, almost level with the water, became alive with birds running here and there.

It was on Dick's lips to cry, "Now, Dave, pull!" but he could not speak, only watch the thin, keen, yellow man, whose eye glittered beneath his rough hairy cap as he slowly tightened the line, drawing it up till it was above the surface of the water, which began to ripple and play about it in long waves running off in different directions. There was so great a length that it was impossible to draw it tight without moving the spreader poles; and as the lads both thought of what the consequences would be if the line broke, the movement at the ends of the long net spread the alarm.

There was a curious effect caused by the spreading of the wings of the birds, and the whole island seemed to be slowly rising in the air; but at that moment the water hissed from the punt right away to where the flock was taking flight, and as the line tightened, a long filmy wave seemed to curve over towards them. By one rapid practice-learned drag, the net was snatched over and fell on to the water, while a great flock of green plovers took flight in alarm and went flapping over reed-bed and mere.

"Oh, what a pity!" cried Dick, jumping up in the boat and stamping his foot with rage.

"And so near, too!" cried Tom.

"Sit down, lads," roared Dave, who was dragging the pole out of the ground, and the next moment he was thrusting the light boat along over the intervening space, and the more readily that the bottom there was only three or four feet below the surface, and for the most part firm.

"Why, have you caught some?" cried Dick.

The answer was given in front, for it was evident that the net had entangled several of the unfortunate birds, which were flapping the water and struggling vainly to get through the meshes, but drowning themselves in the effort.

The scene increased in excitement as the boat neared, for the birds renewed their struggles to escape, and the decoys tethered on the island to their pegs leaped and fluttered.

In an incredibly short time the skilful puntsman had his boat alongside the net, and then began the final struggle.

It was a vain one, for one by one the plovers were dragged from beneath and thrust into a large basket, till the net lay half-sunk beneath the surface, and the feeble flapping of a wing or two was all that could be heard.

The boat was dripping with water and specked with wet feathers, and a solitary straggler of the plover flock flew to and fro screaming as if reproaching the murderers of its companions; otherwise all was still as Dave stood up and grinned, and showed his yellow teeth.

"There!" he cried triumphantly; "yow didn't expect such a treat as that!"

"Treat!" said Dick, looking at his wet hands and picking some feathers from his vest, for he and Tom after the first minute had plunged excitedly into the bird slaughter and dragged many a luckless bird out of the net.

"Ay, lad, treat!—why, there's nigh upon fourscore, I know."

Dick's features had a peculiar look of disgust upon them and his brow wrinkled up.

"Seems so precious cruel," he said.

Dave, who was rapidly freeing his decoy-birds and transferring them to the cage, stood up with a fluttering plover in one hand.

"Cruel!" he cried.

"Yes, and treacherous," replied Dick.

"Deal more cruel for me to be found starved to death in my place some day," said Dave. "Pie-wipes eats the beedles and wains, don't they? Well, we eats the pie-wipes, or sells 'em, and buys flour and bacon. Get out wi' ye! Cruel! Yow don't like piewipe pie!"

"I did, and roast piewipe too," cried Dick; "but I don't think I shall ever eat any again."

"Hark at him!" cried Dave, going on rapidly with his task and packing up his stuffed birds neatly in their basket, drawing out his pegs, and then rolling up and wringing the wet net before placing it in the punt, and winding in the dripping line which he drew through the water from the reed-bed. "Hark at him, young Tom Tallington!"—and he uttered now a peculiarly ugly harsh laugh—"young squire ar'n't going to eat any more bacon, 'cause it's cruel to kill the pigs; nor no eels, because they has to be caught; and he wean't catch no more jacks, nor eel-pouts, nor yet eat any rabbud-pie! Ha—ha—ha—ha—ha!"

"Look here, Dave!" cried Dick passionately, "if you laugh at me I'll shy something at you! No, I won't," he shouted, seizing the cage; "I'll drown all your decoys!"

"Ay, do!" said Dave, beginning to use the pole. "You're such a particular young gentleman! Only, wouldn't it be cruel?"

"Ha—ha—ha!" laughed Tom.

"Do you want me to punch your head, Tom?" roared Dick, turning scarlet.

"Nay, lads, don't spyle a nice bit o' sport by quarrelling," said Dave, sending the boat rapidly homeward. "I wean't laugh at you no more, Mester Dick. I like you for it, lad. It do seem cruel; and sometimes when I weer younger, and a bud looked up at me with its pretty eyes, as much as to say, 'don't kill me!' I would let it go."

"Ah!" ejaculated Dick with a sigh of relief.

"But what did that bud do, lad? If it was a piewipe, go and kill hundreds o' worms, and snails, and young frogs; if it was a heron, spear fish and pick the wriggling young eels out of the mud. No, lad, it wean't do; buds is the cruellest things there is, pretty as they are—all except them as only eats seeds. Everything 'most is cruel; but if they wasn't the world would get so full that everything would starve. We've got say fourscore pie-wipes—not for fun, but for wittles—and what's fourscore when there's thousands upon thousands all about?"

"Why, Dave, you're a philosopher!" said Dick, who felt relieved.

"Yes," said Dave complacently, but with a very foggy idea of the meaning of the word; "it's being out so much upon the water. Now, there's a nice couple o' ducks swimming just the other side o' them reeds, as a lad might hit just as they rose from the water when we come round the corner; and I'd say hev a shot at 'em, Mester Dick—on'y, if I did, it would hurt your feelings."

Dick was silent for a moment or two as he tried to keep down his human nature. Then he spoke out:

"I beg your pardon, Dave, after what you did for us. May I take up the gun?"

"Ay. Steady, lad!—keep her head over the stem, and I'll turn the boat round and send you along gently. Now you lie down on your chesty and rest the barr'l on the net, for she's too heavy for you to handle. Then wait till the ducks rise, and let go at 'em."

There was another interval full of excitement; the punt was sent quietly toward the end of the reed-bed; and in obedience to his instructions Dick knelt ready to fire—Tom watching him enviously, and wishing it were his turn.

Nearer, nearer, with the punt allowed to go on now by the force of the last thrust given to it, till the last patch of reed was cleared; and there, not twenty yards away, swam a fine shieldrake and four ducks.

As the punt glided into sight there was a splashing and whirring of wings, a great outcry, and away went the birds.

"Now, lad!" cried Dave; and the gun was fired with a deafening report. But no feathers flew—no unfortunate duck or drake dropped, broken-winged, into the water. The only living being injured was Dick, who sat up rubbing his shoulder softly.

"I say," he said, "how that gun kicks!"

"Yes," said Dave dryly, "I put a big charge in her, my lad; but it was a pity to waste it."

"I couldn't help missing," said Dick. "They were so quick."

"Nay, you wouldn't try to hit 'em, lad, because you thought you'd hot 'em," said Dave, chuckling; and Tom laughed, while Dick sat and nursed the gun in silence, till the punt was poled ashore and its contents landed.

"Now," said Dave, "I've got a rabbud-pie as I made mysen. Come and hev a bit, lads; and then you shall take home a dozen pie-wipes apiece. It'll be moonlight, and I'll soon punt you across."

That pie, in spite of the rough surroundings, was delicious; and Dick forgot to pity the poor rabbits, and he did not refuse to take his dozen lapwings home for a welcome addition to the next day's dinner.

"You see, Tom," he whispered, "I think I was a little too particular. Good-night, Dave, and thank you!" he shouted.

"Good-night, lads—good-night!" came off the water. Then there was a splash of the pole, and Dave disappeared in the moonlit mist which silvered the reeds, while the boys trudged the rest of their way home.

Chapter Eight.

The Drain Progresses.

The number of workers increased at the sea-bank, quite a colony growing up, and Dick paid several visits to the place with his father to see how busily the men were delving, while others built up what was termed a *gowt*—a flood-gate arrangement for keeping out the sea at high water, and opening it at low, so as to give egress to the drain-water collected from the fen-land.

Both lads were eager enough to be there to witness the progress of the works at first; but after going again and again, they voted the whole thing to be uninteresting, and no more worth seeing than the digging of one of the ditches on the farms at home.

And certainly there was no more difference than in the fact that the ditches at home were five or six feet wide, while the one the adventurers were having cut through the fen-land would be forty feet, and proportionately deep.

So the big drain progressed foot by foot, creeping on as it were from the sea-shore, an innocent-looking channel that seemed valueless, but which would, when finished, rid the land of its stagnant water, and turn the boggy, peaty soil of the fen into rich pasture and corn-land, whereas its finest produce now was wild-fowl and a harvest of reeds.

"We're getting on, neighbour," said the squire to Farmer Tallington one evening.

"Ay, but it's slow work," said Tom's father. "It'll be years before that lode is cooten."

"Yes, it will be years before it is finished," said the squire, "certainly."

"Then, what's the good of us putting our money in it, eh? It'll do us no good, and be robbing our boys."

"Then why don't you leave off, father?" said Tom stoutly. "Dick Winthorpe and I don't want the fen to be drained, and we don't want to be robbed. Do we, Dick?"

The two elders laughed heartily, and the squire was silent for a few minutes before he began to speak.

"The drain's right, neighbour," he said gravely. "Perhaps you and I will reap no great benefit from it; though, if we live, we shall; but instead of leaving to our boys, when they take up our work, neighbour, either because we are called away to our rest or because we have grown old, these farms with so much good land and so much watery bog, we shall leave them acre upon acre of good solid land, that has been useless to us, but which will bear them crops and feed their beasts."

"Yes," said Farmer Tallington, "there's something in that, but—"

"Come, neighbour, look ahead. Every foot that drain comes into the fen it will lower the level, and we shall see—and before long—our farm land grow, and the water sink."

"Ye–es; but it's so like working for other people!"

"Well," said the squire laughing, "what have you been doing in that half acre of close beside your house?"

"That! Oh, only planted it with pear-trees so as to make a bit of an orchard!"

"Are you going to pick a crop of pears next year, neighbour?"

"Next year! Bah! They'll be ten years before they come well into bearing." (This was the case with the old-fashioned grafting.)

"So will the acres laid bare by the draining," said the squire smiling, "and I hope we shall live to see our boys eating the bread made from corn grown on that patch of water and reeds, along with the pears from your trees."

"That's a clincher," said the farmer. "You've coot the ground from under me, neighbour, and I wean't grudge the money any more."

"I wish father wouldn't say *coot* and *wean't*!" whispered Tom, whose school teaching made some of the homely expressions and bits of dialect of the fen-land jar.

"Why not? What does it matter?" said Dick, who was busy twisting the long hairs from a sorrel nag's tail into a fishing-line.

"Sounds so broad. Remember how the doctor switched Bob Robinson for saying he'd been *agate* early."

"Yes, I recollect," said Dick, tying a knot to keep the hairs from untwisting; "and father said he ought to have been ashamed of himself, for *agate* was good old Saxon, and so were all the words our people use down here in the fen. I say, what are they talking about now?"

"Well, for my part," said the squire rather hotly, in reply to some communication his visitor had made, "so long as I feel that I'm doing what is right, no threats shall ever stop me from going forward."

"But they seem to think it arn't right," said the farmer. "Those in the fen say it will ruin them."

"Ruin! Nonsense!" cried the squire. "They'll have plenty of good land to grow potatoes, and oats, instead of water, which produces them a precarious living from wild-fowl and fish, and ruins no end of them with rheumatism and fever."

"Yes, but—"

"But what, man? The fen-men who don't cultivate the soil are very few compared to those who do, and the case is this. The fen-land is growing about here, and good land being swallowed up by the water. Five acres of my farm, which used to be firm and dry, have in my time become water-logged and useless. Now, are the few to give way to the many, or the many to give way to the few?"

"Well, squire, the few think we ought to give way to them."

"Then we will not," said the squire hotly; "and if they don't know what's for their good, they must be taught. You know how they will stick to old things and refuse to see how they can be improved."

"Ay, it's their nature, I suppose. All I want is peace and quietness."

"And you'll have it. Let them threaten. The law is on our side. They will not dare."

"I don't know," said Farmer Tallington, scratching his head as they walked out into the home close. "You see, squire, it wean't be open enemies we shall have to fear—"

"The Winthorpes never feared their enemies since they settled in these parts in the days of King Alfred," said Dick grandly.

"Hear, hear, Dick!" cried his father, laughing.

"No more did the Tallingtons," said Tom, plucking up, so as not to be behindhand.

"Nay, Tom, my lad," said the farmer, "Tallingtons was never fighting men. Well, squire, I thought I'd warn you."

"Of course, of course, neighbour. But look here, whoever sent you that cowardly bit of scribble thought that because you lived out here in this lonely place you would be easily frightened. Look here," he continued, taking a scrap of dirty paper out of his old pocket-book; "that bit of rubbish was stuck on one of the tines of a hay-fork, and the shaft driven into the ground in front of my door. I said nothing about it to you, but you see I've been threatened too."

He handed the paper to Farmer Tallington, who read it slowly and passed it back.

"Same man writ both, I should say."

"So should I—a rascal!" said the squire. "Here, Dick, don't say a word to your mother; it may alarm her."

"No, father, I sha'n't say anything; but—"

"But what? Speak out."

"May I read it—and Tom?" he added, for he saw his companion's eager looks.

"Well, yes, you've heard what we've been talking about—what neighbour Tallington came over for."

"Yes, father," said Dick, taking the piece of paper, and feeling very serious, since he knew that it contained a threat. But as soon as he grasped its contents—looking at them as a well-educated lad for his days, fresh from the big town grammar-school—he slapped his thigh with one hand, and burst into a roar of laughter, while his father looked on with a grim smile.

"What is it, Dick?" cried Tom eagerly.

"Here's a game!" cried Dick. "Just look!"

There was not much on the paper, and that was written in a clumsy printing-letter fashion, beneath a rough sketch, and with another to finish.

"Why, here's a hollow turnip and two sticks!" cried Dick aloud; "and—and what is it, Tom?"

'stope the dyke

or yow hev 2

   dighe'

"Stop the dyke or you'll have to dig," said Tom eagerly. "You'll have to dig! Does he mean dig the ditch?"

"No!" roared Dick; "that's the way he spells die, and that long square thing's meant for a coffin."

"Yes, Dick, and that's the spirit in which to take such a cowardly threat—laugh at it," said the squire, replacing the letter in his pocket-book. "I only wish I knew who sent it. Who's this coming?"

"Why, it's Dave!" cried Tom eagerly, as the man came slowly along one of the winding lanes of water in his punt.

"Oh, yes, I remember!" said the squire; "he was here yesterday and said he would come and fetch you, Dick, if you liked to go, over to the decoy."

"And you never said a word about it, father! Here, come along, Tom."

The latter glanced at his father, but read consent in his eyes, and the two lads dashed off together.

"Seems to be letting him idle a deal," said Farmer Tallington thoughtfully.

"Not it," said the squire. "They're both very young and growing. Let them enjoy themselves and grow strong and hearty. They've had a long turn at school, and all this will do them good."

"Ay, it'll mak 'em grow strong and lusty if it does nowt else," said the farmer.

"And as to the big drain," said the squire; "we're farmers, neighbour, even if I do work my land as much for pleasure as for profit."

"Ay, but what's that to do with it?"

"This," said the squire, smiling; "a man who puts his hand to the plough should not look back."

"That's true," said Farmer Tallington; "but when he gets a letter to say some one's going to kill him, and draws coffins on the paper, it's enough to mak' him look back."

"It's all stuff, neighbour! Treat it as I do—with contempt."

"Ah! you see you're a gentleman, squire, and a bit of a scholar, and I'm only a plain man."

"A good neighbour and a true Englishman, Tallington; and I'm glad my son has so good and frank a companion as your boy. There, take my advice: treat all this opposition with contempt."

"Theer's my hand, squire," said Farmer Tallington. "You nivver gave me a bad bit of advice yet, and I'll stick to what you say—but on one condition."

"What's that?" said the squire, smiling.

"You'll let me grumble now and then."

Long before Farmer Tallington had parted from the squire at the beginning of the rough track which led from the Priory to Grimsey, Dick and Tom were down by the water's edge waiting for Dave, who came up with a dry-looking smile upon his face—a smile which looked as if it were the withered remains of a last year's laugh.

"How are you, Dave?" cried Dick. "We only just knew you were coming. Are there plenty of ducks?"

"Mebbe. Few like," said Dave in the slow way of a man who seldom speaks.

"*Wuph! wuph!*" came from the boat.

"What! Chip, boy! how are you?" cried Dick, patting the dog, which seemed to go half mad with delight at having someone to make a fuss over him, and then rushed to Tom to collect a few more friendly pats and words.

"Shall we get in, Dave?" cried Tom.

"Get in, lad! Why, what for?"

"Now, Dave, don't go on like that," cried Dick impatiently. "Let's get on, there's a good fellow. I do want to see you work the decoy."

"Oh, you don't care for that! 'Sides, I want to go to Hickathrift's to see his dunky pigs."

"Nonsense! What do you want to see the dunks for?"

"Thinking o' keeping a pig o' my own out thar, lads. It's rayther lonesome at times; and," he added quite seriously, "a pig would be company."

The boys looked at one another and smothered a laugh for fear of giving offence.

"What, with a place like a jolly island all to yourself, where you live like a Robinson Crusoe and can keep tame magpies and anything you like, and your boat, and your dog, and eel-spear?"

"And nets," put in Tom.

"And fishing-lines," said Dick.

"And gun," said Tom.

"Ay, lads," said Dave gravely; "seems aw reight to you, but it be lonesome sometimes when the bootherboomps get running out o' the reeds in the dark evenings and then go sailing high up and round and round."

"Oh, I should like that!" said Dick.

"Nay, lad, yow wouldn't. It would scar yow. Then o' soft warm nights sometimes the frogs begins, and they go on crying and piping all round you for hours."

"Pooh!" said Tom; "who'd mind a few frogs?"

"And then o' still nights theer's the will o' the wipses going about and dancing over the holes in the bog."

"I say, Dave, what is a will o' the wisp really like?"

"What! heven't you niver seen one, lad?" said Dave, as he seated himself on the edge of the boat.

"No; you see we've always been away at school. I can remember one of our men—Diggles it was—pointing out one on a dark night when I was quite young, and I saw some kind of light, and I was such a little fellow then that I ran in—frightened."

"Ay, they do frecken folk," said Dave, putting a piece of brown gum in his mouth; "only you must be careful which way you run or you may go right into the bog and be smothered, and that's what the wills like."

"Like! why, they're only lights," said Tom.

"They'm seem to you like lights, but they be kind o' spirits," said Dave solemnly; "and they wants you to be spirits, too, and come and play with 'em, I s'pose."

"But, Dave, never mind the will o' the wisps. Come on to the 'coy."

"Nay, it's no use to go there; the nets that goes over the pipes has been charmed (gnawed) by the rats."

"Yes, I know," cried Dick, laughing; "and you've put all new ones. I heard you tell father so, and he paid you ever so much money. He's only playing with us, Tom."

Dave laughed like a watchman's rattle, whose wooden spring had grown very weak.

"Look here, Dave, now no nonsense! Want some more powder?"

"Nay, I don't want no poother," said Dave.

"Do you want some lead to melt down? I'll give you a big lump."

"Nay, I don't want no poother, and I don't want no lead," said Dave in an ill-used tone. "I can buy what I want."

"He does want it, Dick."

"Nay, I don't, lad; and things a man do want nobody asks him to hev."

"Why, what do you want, Dave?"

"Oh, nowt! I don't want nowt. But there is times when a man's a bit ill out there in the fen, and he gets thinking as a drop o' sperrits 'd do him good. But I d'n know."

"All right, Dave! I won't forget," said Dick. "Jump in, Tom."

"Nay, what's the good?" said Dave.

"All right, Tom! He's going to take us to the 'coy."

Tom followed his companion into the boat, the dog leaped in after them, whining with pleasure; and shaking his head and talking to himself, Dave followed, seized the pole, giving a grunt at Dick, who wanted to preside over the locomotion, and then, with a tremendous thrust, he sent the punt surging through the water.

"Nay, I'll pole," he said. "Get us over sooner, and we can begin work."

Dick exchanged glances with his companion, and they sat playing with the dog and watching the birds that rose from the reeds or swept by in little flocks in the distance, till, after about half an hour's poling, Dave ran the boat into a narrow lane among the uncut reeds, after a warning to be quite still, which the lads observed and the dog understood, going forward and crouching down in front of his master, with his eyes glittering and ears quivering with the intense way in which he was listening.

The way through the reeds was long, and in spite of the stealthy way in which the boat was propelled, several birds were startled, and flew up quacking loudly, and went away.

At last, though, they emerged from the dry growth into a little open pool, and crossing this, landed by a low house thatched with reeds and hidden in a thick grove of alders.

"Now, lads," said Dave in a whisper, "not a word. Stay here while I go and look. I wean't be long."

He secured the boat to a stump of wood, and landed, leaving the lads seated in the punt, and gazing about them. But there was very little to see, for, save in the direction of the patch of reeds through which they had passed, there was a low dense growth of alders and willows running up to the height of twelve or fifteen feet; and it was beyond this that the sport was to be had.

They had not very long to wait before Dave returned, with Chip the piper at his heels—not that the dog had any musical gifts, but that he was clever in doing certain duties in connection with a pipe, as will be seen, and to perform these adequately utter silence was required.

Dave seemed quite transformed. His yellow face, instead of being dull and heavy, was full of anxious lines, his eyes twinkled, his mouth twitched and worked, and his brown wiry hands were fidgeting about his chin.

As he came up he held a finger in the air to command silence, and with stooping body and quick alert way he paused till he was close to the boys, and then whispered:

"You couldn't hev come better, lads; there's a boat load of 'em in the pond."

"What sort?" whispered Dick excitedly.

"All sorts, lad: widgeons, teal, mallards, and some pochards. Only mind, if you say a word aloud, or let that theer dog bark, we sha'n't get a duck."

Dick clapped his hand over his mouth, as if to ensure silence, and Tom compressed his lips.

"Come along, then, boys, and I'll set yow wheer yow can look through a hole in one o' the screens and see all the fun."

"But can't we help, Dave?" asked Tom.

"Help, lad! no, not till the ducks are in the net. Then you may. Now, not a word, and come on."

Dave led the way to the little house, where he filled his pockets with barley and oats mixed, out of a rough box, and as he did so he pointed to one corner which had been gnawed.

"Been charming of it," he whispered. "Eats! Now come, quiet-like;" and he stepped out and into a narrow path leading through the dense alder wood, and in and out over patches of soft earth which quivered and felt like sponges beneath their feet.

Dave glanced back at them sharply two or three times when a rustling sound was made, and signed to them to be careful. Then once he stopped in a wider opening and tossed up a feather or two, as if to make sure of the way the wind blew. Apparently satisfied, he bent towards the two lads and whispered:

"I'm going to the second pipe. Come quiet. Not a word, and when I mak' room for you, peep through the screen for a minute, and then come away."

The boys nodded, and followed in silence through a part of the alder wood which was not quite so dense, for here and there patches of tall reeds had grown out of a watery bed, and now stood up seven or eight feet high and dry and brown.

Then all at once Dave stopped and looked back at them with a sly kind of grin upon his face, as he pointed down to a strong net stretched loosely over some half hoops of ash, whose ends were stuck down tightly in the soft ground so as to form a tunnel about two feet wide.

This was over the soft earth, upon which lay the end of the net, tied round with a piece of cord. A few yards farther on, however, this first net was joined to another, and the tunnel of network was arched over a narrow ditch full of water, and this ditch gradually increased in width as the man led on, and ran in a curve, along whose outer or convex side they were proceeding.

Before long, as the bent-over willows spanned the ditch or "pipe," as it was called, the net ceased to come down quite to the ground, its place being occupied by screens made of reeds and stakes, and all so placed that there was room to go round them.

The boys now noted that the dog was following close behind in a way as furtive as his master, and apparently quite as much interested as he in what was to take place.

The water ditch increased in width rapidly now till the net tunnel became six feet, twelve feet, twenty feet, and, close to the mouth, twenty-four feet wide, while the light ash-poles, bent over and tied in the middle, were quite twelve feet above the water.

They were now near the mouth of the curved ditch, whose narrow portion bent round quite out of sight among the trees, while at a signal from Dave they went to a broad reed screen in front, and gazed through an opening, to see stretching out before them, calm and smooth beneath the soft grey wintry sky, a large pool of about a couple of acres in extent, surrounded by closely growing trees similar to those through which they had passed, while at stated intervals were openings similar to that by which they stood, in all five in number, making a rough star whose arms or points were ditches or pipes some five-and-twenty feet wide, and curving off, to end, as above told, sixty or seventy yards from the mouth, only two feet wide, and covered right along with net.

All this was well-known to them before, and they hardly gave it a second glance. What took their attention were some half dozen flocks of water-fowl seated calmly on the smooth surface of the pool and a couple of herons standing in the shallow water on the other side, one so hitched up that he seemed to have no neck, the other at his full height, and with bill poised ready to dart down at some unfortunate fish.

Here and there a moor-hen or two swam quietly about flicking its black-barred white tail. There were some coots by a bed of reeds, and a couple of divers, one of which disappeared from time to time in the most business-like manner, and came up at the end of a long line of bubbles many yards away.

Nearest to them was a large flock of quite a hundred ordinary wild ducks, for the most part asleep, while the others sat motionless upon the water or swam idly about, all waiting patiently in the secluded pool, which seemed to them a sanctuary, for nightfall, when slugs and snails would be out and other things in motion, ready to supply them with a banquet on some of their far-off feeding grounds. The drakes were already distinct enough from the sober-feathered ducks, but the former were not in their spring plumage, when they would put on their brightest colours and their heads glisten in green and gold.

Away to the left were a number of flat-looking squatty-shaped pochards with their brown heads and soft grey backs, while to the right were plenty of widgeons and another little flock of teal, those pretty miniature ducks, with here and there a rarer specimen, among which were pintails, drakes with the centre feathers of the tail produced like those of a parroquet.

The lads could have stopped for an hour gazing at the manners and customs of the wild-fowl dotting the lake in happy unconsciousness of the enemies so near; but, just as Dick had fixed his eyes upon a solitary group of about a couple of dozen ducks nearly across the pond, he felt a tug behind him, and turning, there was Dave signing to him to come away.

Dave made the lads follow him till he could place them in among the trees with a tuft of reeds before them, which proved sufficient screen and yet gave them a view of part of the pool, and the entrance to the pipe upon whose bank they had been standing.

"Now, look here, bairns," he whispered; "if you move or says a word, there'll be no ducks."

The lads nodded and crouched in their places, while Dave disappeared behind them, but appeared again close to the screen of reed which hid him from the birds in the pool.

Matters were so exciting now as the watchers looked on that Dick relieved his feelings by pinching Tom's leg, and then holding up his fist, as if in promise of what was to follow if he made a sound.

Meanwhile, with Chip close at his heels, Dave went to the farthest screen and peered through the opening, and after satisfying himself they saw him thrust one hand into his pocket and make a sign to Chip, while almost simultaneously he scattered a handful of the oats and barley right over the water, the grain falling through the meshes of the outspread net.

Just then Chip, in the most quiet matter-of-fact way, made his appearance on the fore-shore of the pool, and, without barking or taking notice of the ducks, trotted slowly along toward the entrance to the pipe, leaped over a low piece of wood, and disappeared from sight to join his master behind the screen, when the dog was rewarded for what he had done with a piece of cheese.

The coming of the dog, however, had created quite a commotion upon the lake, for the knot of two dozen ducks on the other side no sooner caught sight of him than, uttering a prodigious quacking, they came swimming and half flying as rapidly as they could toward the mouth of the pipe, to begin feeding upon the oats scattered upon the water.

"Look at the decoy-ducks," whispered Dick, and then he watched in silence, for these two dozen were regularly fed wild-fowl which had become so far half tame that, knowing the appearance of the dog to be associated with corn and other seeds at the mouth of the pipe, they came at once.

This was too much for the strangers, which followed them, mingled with them, and began to feed as well.

Dave was at this time behind the second screen waiting for Chip, who showed himself for a moment or two at the edge of the long water ditch, trotted on towards the second screen, leaped over a low wood bar at the end, and joined his master, to receive a second piece of cheese.

That white dog was a wonder to the wild ducks, which left off eating directly and began to swim slowly and cautiously up the netted tunnel to try and find out what he was doing.

Had Chip stopped and looked at them, and barked, they would all have taken flight, but the dog was too well taught. He was a piper of the highest quality, and knew his business, which was to show himself for a short time and then trot on to the next screen and leap over and disappear just as if he were engaged in some mysterious business of his own.

This was too much for the ducks, which cackled and bobbed their heads up and down and swam on, moved by an intense curiosity to find out what was Chip's particular game.

But Chip's proceedings were stale to the decoy-ducks, who had seen him so often that they cared nothing, but stopped behind to partake of the food, while quite a hundred followed their leaders up the pipe in happy ignorance of the meaning of a net. What was more, the decoy-ducks often found food at the mouths of the pipes when their wild relatives were off feeding, and hence they troubled themselves no more. All that was impressed upon their small brains was that the appearance of Chip meant food, and they stayed behind to feed.

Chip was invisible eating a piece of cheese. Then he appeared again higher up, trotted on, leaped over the low wood bar, and joined his master for more cheese.

And so it went on, Dave going higher and higher from screen to screen, and the dog slowly following and alternately appearing to and disappearing from the sight of the ducks, which never of course caught sight of Dave, who was too well hidden behind the screens.

At last they were lured on and on so far by the dog that they were where the ditch began to bend round more sharply and the pipe was narrowing. This was the time for a fresh proceeding.

Dave had gone on right up to the farthest screen, and suddenly dived into a narrow path through the trees which led him, quite concealed from view, round and back to the first screen. He passed the boys, making them a sign to be silent, and then went right round that first screen just as Chip was appearing far up by the side of the pipe—and the flock of ducks were following—and quickly now showed himself at the mouth of the trap.

The ducks saw him instantly, and there was a slight commotion as he took off and held up his hat; but there was no attempt at flight, the birds merely swam on rapidly farther toward the end and disappeared round the curve.

Dave went quickly on past a screen or two and showed himself again, the curve of the pipe bringing him once more into view. He held up his hat and the ducks swam on, out of sight once more.

This was continued again and again, till the ducks were driven by degrees from where the ditch and its arching of net decreased from eight feet wide to six feet, to four feet, to two feet, and the flock was huddled together, and safe in the trap that had been prepared for them.

All at once, while the two lads were watching all these proceedings, Dave came into sight for a moment and waved his hand for them to come, but signed to them at the same time to be quiet.

It was as well that he did, for otherwise they would have uttered a shout of triumph.

"We've got 'em, lads," he said, with his yellow face puckered up with satisfaction; "but don't make a noise. I like to keep the 'coy quiet. Come along!"

"Is there any fear of their getting away now, Dave?" whispered Dick as he followed.

"Yes, to market," said Dave grimly.

As they neared the end of the pipe there was a loud cackling and fluttering heard, and the ducks were disposed to make a rush back, but the sight of the man sent them all onward once more to the end of the pipe, where they were driven to leave the water for the dry land, over which the net was spread for the last few yards, forming a gigantic purse or stocking.

And now a tremendous fluttering and excitement ensued, for as, in obedience to their leader's sign, the lads stopped once more, Dave stepped forward rapidly, detached the final portion of the net which formed the bag or purse from the bent-over ash stick, and twisted it together and tied it round, with the result that the birds were all shut up in the long purse and at his mercy.

Just then Chip performed a kind of triumphal dance, and leaped up at Dick and again at Tom before becoming quiescent, and looking up at all in turn, giving his little stumpy tail a few wags, while his whole aspect seemed to say:

"Didn't we do that well?"

"That's a fine take, my lads," said Dave in congratulatory tones.

"Yes," said Dick, looking down at the frightened birds scuffling over each other; "but—"

"Nay! don't, man, say that!" cried Dave. "I know, my lad. But wild duck's good to yeat; and they've got to be killed and go to market. Yow wanted to see me ketch the duck, and theer they are. Going to help me kill 'em?"

"No!" cried Dick in a voice full of disgust. But he helped carry the capture to the boat after the slaying was at an end and the empty short net replaced, ready distended at the end of the tunnel or pipe.

"There we are!" said Dave. "Ready for another flock?"

"And are you going to try for another in one of the pipes over the other side?"

"Nay, not to-day, my lad," was the reply. "The 'coy-ducks wean't be hungry and come for their food, so we'll wait for another time."

"Don't the 'coy-ducks ever go right away, Dave?" asked Tom, as the boat was being quietly poled back.

"Sometimes; but not often, and if they do some others taks their places, and stops. They get fed reg'lar, and that's what a duck likes. Good uns to eat, ducks. They mak' nests and bring off broods of young ones, and keep to the pool year after year, and seem to know me a bit; but if Chip here went barking among 'em, or I was to go shooting, they'd soon be driven away."

"But do they know that they are leading the wild ducks into the pipe?" said Dick eagerly.

"*Not* they. Ducks can't think like you and me. They come to be fed, and the others follow 'em, and then get thinking about Chip and follow him."

"Does Chip know?" said Tom.

"Ask him," said Dave, laughing in his grim, silent way. "I think he doos, but he never said so. Hello!"

They were passing the edge of a great bed of reeds, and rounding a corner, when they came in sight of three or four teal, and no sooner did the birds catch sight of them than they began to scurry along the water preparatory to taking flight, but all at once there was a rush and a splash, and the party in the boat saw a huge fish half throw itself out of the water, fall back, and disappear.

"He caught him," said Dave grimly. "You see, lad, other things 'sides me ketches the ducks."

"A great pike!" cried Dick, standing up to try and catch sight of the tyrant of the waters.

"Ay! One as likes duck for dinner. He'll eat him without picking his feathers off."

"Wasn't it a very big one, Dave?" cried Tom.

"Ay, lad, a thirty-pounder like enew," said Dave, working his pole.

"Dave, shall you know this place again?" cried Dick.

"Should I know my own hand!"

"Then let's come over and try for that fellow to-morrow or next day."

"Right, lad! I'll come. We'll set some liggers, and I dessay we can get hold of him. If we can't theer's plenty more."

"To-morrow, Dave?"

"Nay, I shall be getting off my ducks. Two hundred wants some seeing to."

"Next day, then?"

"Say Saturday, my lads. That'll give me time to get a few baits."

So Saturday was appointed for the day with the pike, and the ducks and the boys were duly landed, the latter to go homeward with four couples each, and Dick with strict orders to ask the squire whether he wanted any more, before they were sent off in Hickathrift's car to the town.

Chapter Nine.

Dick is called early.

It was Friday night. Dick had been over with the squire and two or three gentlemen interested in the great drain, to see how it progressed; and the lad had found the young engineer in charge of the works ready to ask him plenty of questions, such as one who had a keen love of the natural objects of the country would be likely to put.

The result was that Squire Winthorpe invited him over to the old Priory to come and make a fishing, shooting, or collecting trip whenever he liked.

"You are very hospitable, Mr Winthorpe," he said.

"Oh, nonsense! Shame if we who bring you people down from London to do us good here in the fens, could not be a little civil."

This was after the inspection was over, the young engineer at liberty, and he was walking part of the way back with Dick.

"Well, I must frankly say, Mr—ought I to say Squire Winthorpe?"

"No, no, Mr Marston," was the laughing reply, "I am only a plain farmer. It is the fashion down here to call a man with a few acres of his own a squire. I'm squire, you see, of a lot of bog."

"Which we shall make good land, Mr Winthorpe," said the engineer. "But I was going to say it will be a treat to come over from my lonely lodgings to some one who will make me welcome, for I must say the common people here are rather ill-disposed."

"Only snarling," said the squire. "They daren't bite. They don't like any alterations made. Take no notice of their surly ways. The soreness will soon wear off. Cruel thing to do, Mr Marston, turn a piece of swamp into a wholesome field!"

They both laughed, and soon after parted.

"I rather like that young fellow, Dick," said the squire. "Knows a deal about antiquities. Little too old for a companion for you, but people who collect butterflies and nettles and flowers generally mix regardless of age."

"Do you think the people about will interfere with the works, father?" said Dick, as they trudged along homeward.

"No, I don't, Dick," said the squire. "I should like to catch them at it."

Dick went to bed that night very tired, and dropped asleep directly, thinking of Dave and the expedition to set trimmers, or "liggers" as they called them, and he was soon in imagination afloat upon the lanes and pools of water among the reeds, with Dave softly thrusting down his pole in search of hard places, where the point would not sink in. Then he dreamed that he had baited hook after hook, attached the line to a blown-out bladder, and sent it sailing away to attract the notice of some sharking pike lurking at the edge of one of the beds of reeds.

Then he dreamed that the sun was in his eyes as it went down in a rich glow far away over the wide expanse of water and rustling dried reed, where the starlings roosted and came and went in well-marshalled clouds, all moving as if carefully drilled to keep at an exact distance one from the other, ready to wheel and turn or swoop up or down with the greatest exactness in the world.

That dreamy imagination passed away, and he became conscious that he was having his morning call, as he termed it, and for which he always prepared when going to bed by pulling up the blind and drawing aside the white curtains, so that the sun who called him should shine right in upon his face.

For the sun called Dick Winthorpe when he shone, and as the lad lay upon his side with his face toward the window the sun seemed to be doing his morning duty so well that Dick yawned, stretched, and lay with his eyes closed while the glow of red light flooded his room.

"Only seem to have just lain down," he grumbled, keeping his eyes more tightly shut than ever. "Bother! I wish I wasn't so drowsy when it's time to get up!"

At last he opened his eyes, to stare hard at the light, and then with a cry full of excitement, he threw off the clothes and leaped out of bed, to rush to the window.

"Oh!" he ejaculated; and darting back to the bed-side he hurried on his trousers, opened his door, and the next moment his bare feet padded over the polished oak floor as he made for his father's room and thumped at the door.

"Father, quick!—father!"

"Hallo! Any one ill?" cried the squire, for thieves and burglars were known only by repute out there in the fen.

"Tallington's farm's in a blaze!" cried Dick, hoarsely.

He heard a thump on the floor, a hasty ejaculation from his mother, and then ran back to his own room to finish dressing, gazing out of his window the while, to see that the bright glow about Grimsey was increasing, and that a golden cloud seemed to be slowly rising up through the still air.

"Now, Dick!" shouted his father, "run down and rouse up the people at the cottages."

Dick ran out, and down past the old Priory ruins, to where a cluster of cottages, half-way to Hickathrift's, were occupied by the people who worked upon the farm; and, distant as the fire was, he could yet see the ruddy glow upon the water before him.

Half-way there, he heard a shout:

"Who's there!"

It was in a big bluff voice, which Dick recognised at once.

"That you, Hicky? Fire! fire!"

"Ay, my lad, I was coming to rouse up the folk. You go that end, I'll do this. Hey! Fire! Fire!"

He battered cottage door after cottage door, Dick following his example, with the result that in their alarm the people came hurrying out like bees whose hive has been disturbed by a heavy blow.

There was no need to ask questions. Every man, while the women began to wail and cry, started for the Tallingtons' farm; but they were brought up by a shout from the squire.

"What are you going to do, men?" he cried.

"The fire!"—"help!"—"water!"—rose in a confused babble.

"Back, every one of you, and get a bucket!" cried the squire. "You, Hickathrift, run into the wood-house and bring an axe."

"Aw, reight, squire!" cried the wheelwright, and in another minute every man was off at a trot following Dick's father, and all armed with a weapon likely to be of service against the enemy which was rapidly conquering the prosperous little farm at Grimsey.

Two miles form a long distance in a case of emergency, and before the party were half-way there they began to grow breathless, and there was a disposition evinced to drop into a walk. One or two of those in advance checked their rate, others followed, and for the next two or three hundred yards the rescuers kept to a foot-pace, breathing heavily the while, and speaking in snatches.

"Which is it, Dick—the house or the great stack?"

"I can't see, father," panted the lad; "sometimes it seems one, sometimes both."

"Stacks, squire, I think," cried Hickathrift. "I don't think house is afire yet, but it must catch the thack before long."

The faint sound of a dog barking at a distance now reached their ears, but it was evidently not from the direction of the farm, and the squire's thoughts were put into words by Dick, who, as he looked on now between his father and the wheelwright, exclaimed in a hoarse voice:

"Why, father, don't they know that the place is on fire?"

"Nay, that they don't," cried the wheelwright excitedly. "They're all asleep."

"Let's run faster," cried Dick.

"No. We have a long way to go yet," cried the squire, "and if we run faster we shall be too much exhausted to help."

"But, father—oh, it is so dreadful!" cried Dick, as in imagination he pictured horror after horror.

"Can you run, Dick—faster?"

"Yes, father, yes."

"I can't," panted Hickathrift; "I've growed too heavy."

"Run on, then, and shout and batter the door. We'll get up as quickly as we can."

"Ay, roon, Master Dick, roon!" cried the wheelwright. "Fire's ketched the thack."

Dick doubled his fists, drew a long breath, and made a rush, which took him fifty yards in advance. Then he trotted on at the same pace as the others; rushed again; and so on at intervals, getting well ahead of the rest. But never, in the many times he had been to and fro, had he so thoroughly realised how rough and awkward was the track, and how long it took to get to Grimsey farm.

As he ran on, it was with the fire glowing more brightly in his face, and the various objects growing more distinct, while there was something awful in the terrible silence that seemed to prevail, in the midst of which a great body of fire steadily rose, in company with a cloud of smoke, which was spangled with tiny flakes that seemed to be of gold. Tree, shed, barn, and chimney-stack, too, seemed to have been turned to the brilliant metal; but to the lad's great relief he saw that the wheelwright was wrong, the "thack" had not caught, and so far the house was safe, though the burning stacks were so near that at any moment the roof of the reed-thatched house might begin to blaze.

At last there was a sound—one that might have been going on before, but kept by the distance from reaching Dick's ear—a cock crowed loudly, and there was a loud cackling from the barn where the fowls roosted.

Then came the lowing of a cow; but all was perfectly still at the house, and it seemed astounding that no one should have been alarmed.

Only another hundred yards or so and the farm would be reached. Dick had settled down to a much slower speed. There was a sensation as if the fire that shone in his face had made his breath scorching, so that it burned his chest, while his feet were being weighted with lead.

"Tom!" he tried to shout as he drew near; but his voice was a hoarse whisper, and it seemed to be drowned by the steady beat of the feet behind upon the road.

"Tom!" he cried again, but with no better result, as he staggered on by the wide drain which ran right up to the farm buildings from the big pool in the fen where the reeds were cut.

And now that full drain and the pool gleamed golden, as if they too were turned to fire, as Dick pushed by, realising that the hay-stack, the great seed-stack, and the little stack of oats were blazing together, not furiously, but with the flame rising up in a steady silent manner which was awful.

There was a rough piece of stone in the way, against which Dick caught his foot and nearly fell; but he saved himself, stooped, and picked up the stone; and as he panted up to the long low red-brick farm, he hurled it through a window on his left, and then fell up against, more than stopped at, the door, against which he beat and kicked with all his might.

The crashing in of the leaded pane casement had, however, acted like the key which had unlocked the silent farmstead.

Tom Tallington rushed to the window.

"Who's—"

He would probably have said "that," but he turned his sentence into the cry of "Fire! fire!"

The alarm spread in an instant. Farmer Tallington's window was thrown open; and as he realised all, he dashed back, and then the rest of the party came panting up, and Hickathrift cried, "Stand clear, Mester Dick!"

He threw himself against the door, to burst it open, just as the farmer came down, half carrying his wife wrapped in a blanket, and Tom ran out, to dart down to the end of the long low building where a second tenement formed the sleeping-place of the two men and a big lad who worked upon the farm.

They were already aroused, and came out hurrying on their clothes, while the squire and Hickathrift got out the women, who, with Mrs Tallington, were hurried into a cart-shed.

"Why, neighbour, you'd have been burned in your bed!" cried the squire. "Now, lads, all of you form line."

"She's caught now!" shouted Hickathrift, who had been round to the back.

"Then we must put it out," said the squire, as he busily ranged his men, and those of Farmer Tallington, so that they reached from the nearest point of the big drain to the corner of the farm, and in a double line, so that full buckets of water could be passed along one and returned empty along the other.

"Hickathrift, you go and dip."

"Ay, ay, squire!" roared the great fellow, and he rushed down to the water's edge like a bull, while the squire went to the other end.

"Neighbour," cried Farmer Tallington excitedly, "you'll go on, wean't you? I must get in and bring out a few writings and things I'd like to save."

"Here, Tom, let's you and me get out the clothes and things."

"Yes, and the small bits of furniture, boys," cried the squire. "Now, my lads, ready!"

There was a general shout from the men, who fell into their places with the promptitude that always follows when they have a good leader.

"Get all you can out in case," shouted the squire; "but we're going to save the house."

"Hurrah!" shouted the men as they heard this bold assertion, which the squire supplemented by saying between his teeth, "Please God!"

41

"Bring up that ladder," cried the squire—"two of them."

These were planted against the end of the house, and none too soon, for the corner nearest the burning stacks was beginning to blaze furiously, and the fire steadily running up, while a peculiar popping and crackling began to be heard as the flames attacked the abundant ivy which mounted quite to the chimney-stack.

"Ho! ho! ho! ho!" came now from the front of the cart-shed in a regular bellowing cry.

"What is it, wench—what is it?" cried Farmer Tallington, as he hurried out of the burning house, laden with valuables, which he handed to his quiet business-like wife.

"My best Sunday frock! Oh, my best Sunday frock!" sobbed the red-faced servant lass.

"Yes, and oh my stacks! and oh my farm!" cried her master, as he ran back into the house after a glance at the squire, who, in the midst of a loud cheering, stood right up with one foot on the ladder, one on the thatched roof, and sent the first bucket of water, with a good spreading movement, as far as he could throw it, and handed back the bucket.

The flames hissed and danced, and there was a rush of steam all along the ridge, but the water seemed to be licked up directly.

Another was dashed on and the bucket passed back, and another, and another; but the effect produced was so little that, after distributing about a dozen which the wheelwright sent along the line, making the men work eagerly, as he plunged the buckets into the drain and brought them dripping out, the squire shouted, "Hold hard!" and descended to change the position of the long ladder he was on by dragging out the foot till it was at such an angle that the implement now lay flat upon the thatch, so that anyone could walk right up to the chimney-stack.

"Now, then!" cried the squire, mounting once more. "We want another flood just now, my lads, but as there isn't one we must make it."

"It arn't safe," muttered one of the men. "See theer, lad!"

The others needed no telling, as the speaker, who had followed the squire on to the roof so as to be within reach, now felt the flames scorch him, though what he had alluded to was the top of the ladder which was beginning to burn where it lay on the burning thatch, and crackling and blazing out furiously.

Whizz-hizz rose from the water as the first bucket was thrown with such effect that the ladder ceased to burn, and, undismayed by the smoke and flame that floated towards him, the latter in separated patches with a strange fluttering noise, the squire scattered the water from his advantageous position, and with good effect, though that part of the house was now burning fast, the fire having eaten its way through the thatch into the room below.

Meanwhile, as the burning stacks made the whole place light as day, Dick and Tom rushed in and out of the house, bringing everything of value upon which they could lay their hands, to pass their salvage to Mrs Tallington and the women, who stored them in a heap where they seemed safe from the flames.

"Look at that, Tom!" cried Dick, as he paused for a few moments to get breath, and watch his father where he stood high up on the burning roof, like some hero battling with a fiery dragon.

"Yes, I see," said Tom in an ill-used tone.

"Isn't it grand?" cried Dick. "I wish I was up there. Don't it make one proud of one's father?"

"I don't see any more to be proud of in your father than in mine," said Tom stoutly. "Your father wouldn't dare to go into that burning house like mine does. See there!"

This was as Farmer Tallington rushed into the house again.

Dick turned sharply upon his companion.

"There isn't time to have it out now, Tom," he said in a whisper; "but I mean to punch your head for this, you ungrateful beggar. Afraid to go into the house! Why, I'm not afraid to do that. Come on!"

He ran into the house and Tom followed, for them both to come out again bearing the old eight-day clock.

"Its easy, that's what it is," said Dick. "Hooray, father!" he shouted, "you'll win!"

It did not seem as if the squire would win, for though he was gradually being successful in extinguishing the burning thatch, the great waves of fire which came floating from the blazing stacks licked up the moisture and compelled him from time to time to retreat.

Fortunately, however, the supply of water was ample, and, thanks to the way in which Hickathrift dipped the buckets and encouraged the men as he passed them along, the thatch became so saturated that by the time quite a stack had been made of the indoor valuables there seemed to be a chance to leave the steaming roof and attack the burning stacks.

This was done, the ladder being left ready in case of the thatch catching fire again; and soon the squire was standing as close as he could get to the nearest stack, and sending in the contents of the buckets.

There was no hope of saving this, but every bucket of water promised to keep down the great flashes of fire which floated off and licked at the farm-house roof as they passed slowly on.

It was a glorious sight. Everything glowed in the golden light, and a fiery snowstorm seemed to be sweeping over the farm buildings, as the excited people worked, each dash of water producing a cloud of steam over which roared up, as it were, a discharge of fireworks.

For some time no impression whatever appeared to be made, but no one thought of leaving his position; the squire and those nearest to him were black and covered with perspiration, their faces shining in the brilliant light, and the leader was still emptying the buckets of water, when Farmer Tallington ran up to him.

"Let me give you a rest now," he cried.

"Nay, neighbour, I'll go on."

The friendly altercation seemed to be about to result in a struggle for the bucket, when Dick, who had been in one of the back rooms, came running out of the house shouting:—

"The stable—the stable is on fire!"

This caused a rush in the direction of the long low-thatched building on the other side of the house, one of a range about a yard.

There was no false alarm, for the thatch was blazing so furiously, that at a glance the lookers-on saw that the stable and the cart lodge adjoining were doomed.

"Did any one get out the horses?" roared Farmer Tallington.

There was no answer, and the farmer rushed on up to the burning building through tiny patches of fire where the dry mouldering straw was set alight by the falling flakes.

The squire followed him, and, seeing them enter the dark doorway, Dick and Tom followed.

It was a long low building with room for a dozen horses; but only two were there, standing right at the end, where they were haltered to the rough mangers, and snorted and whinnied with fear.

Each man ran to the head of a horse, and cut the halters, lit by the glow that came through a great hole burned in the thatched roof, from which flakes of fire kept falling, while the smoke curled round and up the walls and beneath the roof in a silent threatening way.

HICKATHRIFT SAVES THE SQUIRE FROM THE FIRE AT
FARMER TALLINGTON'S

It was easy enough to unloose the trembling beasts; but that was all that could be done, for the horses shivered and snorted, and refused to stir.

Both shouted and dragged at the halters; but the poor beasts seemed to be paralysed with fear; and as the moments glided by, the hole in the roof was being eaten out larger and larger, the great flakes of burning thatch falling faster, and a pile of blazing rafter and straw beginning to cut off retreat from the burning place.

"It's of no use," cried Farmer Tallington, after trying coaxing, main force, and then blows. "The roof will be down directly. Run, boys, run!"

"You are coming too, father?" cried Tom.

"Yes, and you, father?" cried Dick.

43

"Yes, my lads; out with you!"

"Try once more, father," said Dick. "The poor old horses!"

"Yes, but run!" cried the squire. "I must run too. Off!"

There was a rush made through the burning mass fallen from the roof; and, scorched and half-blind, they reached the door half-blocked by the anxious men.

"Safe!" cried the farmer. "Here: where's squire?"

As the words left his mouth there was a fierce snorting and trampling, and those at the door had only just time to draw back, as the two horses dashed frantically out, and then tore off at full gallop across the yard.

"Winthorpe!" cried Farmer Tallington. "This way!"

"Father!" cried Dick in an agonised voice, following the farmer into the burning building; but only to be literally carried out by his companion, as they were driven back by a tremendous gush of burning thatch and wood which roared out of the great doorway consequent upon a mass of the roof falling in.

As soon as he could recover himself, Dick turned to rush in again; but he was checked by Hickathrift.

"Stand back, bairn! art mad?" he cried. "Not that way."

Dick staggered away, and nearly fell from the tremendous thrust given to him by the big wheelwright, and as he regained his equilibrium, it was to see Hickathrift with something flashing in his hand, making for the other end of the stable, which was as yet untouched.

A few blows from the axe he carried made the rough mud wall collapse, and, without a moment's hesitation Hickathrift forced his way through the hole he had broken, and from which a great volume of smoke began to curl.

Dick would have followed; but Tom clung to his arm, and before he could get free, during what seemed to be a terribly long period of suspense, the wheelwright appeared again, and staggered out, bearing the insensible body of the squire.

For a few minutes there was a terrible silence, and Hickathrift tottered from the man he had left where he had dragged him on the ground.

For the wheelwright was blinded and half strangled by the smoke, and reeled like a drunken man.

He recovered though, directly, and seized a bucket of water from one of the men. With this he liberally dashed the squire's face, as Dick knelt beside him in speechless agony, and grasped his hand.

For a few minutes there was no sign. Then the prostrate man uttered a low sigh, and opened his eyes.

"Dick!" he said, as he struggled up.

"Yes, father. Are you much hurt?"

"No, only—nearly—suffocated, my boy; but—but—Oh, I remember! The horses?"

"They're safe, neighbour," cried Farmer Tallington, taking his hand.

"Mind the knife!" cried the squire. "I remember now. I was obliged to be very brutal to them to make them stir."

He looked down at the small blade of the pocket-knife he held, closed it with a snap, and then stared about him at the people in a vacant confused way.

Several of the men, led by Hickathrift, began to carry pails of water to the burning stable, and this building being so low, they were not long in extinguishing the flames.

Hardly had they succeeded in this before the shrieks of the women gathered together in a low shed drew their attention to the fact that the roof of the house was once more blazing, and this seemed to rouse the squire again to action, for, in spite of Hickathrift wanting to take his place, he insisted upon re-climbing the ladder when the buckets of water were once more passed along till all further danger had ceased, and the farm-house escaped with one room seriously damaged and one side of the thatched roof burned away.

The men still plied the buckets on the burning stacks, but only with the idea of keeping the flames within bounds, for there was nothing else to be done. One rick was completely destroyed; the others were fiery cores, which glowed in the darkness, and at every puff of wind sent up a cloud of glittering, golden sparks, whose course had to be watched lest a fresh fire should be started.

And now the excitement and confusion died out as the fire sank lower. The women returned to the house, and the men, under the farmer's direction, carried back the household treasures, while Mrs Tallington, with the common sense of an old-fashioned farmer's wife, spread a good breakfast in the kitchen for the refreshment of all.

It was a desolate scene at daybreak upon which all gazed. The half-burned roof of the farm-house, the three smoking heaps where the three stacks had stood, and the stable roofless and blackened, while the place all about the house was muddy with the water and trampling.

"Yes," said Farmer Tallington ruefully, "it'll tak' some time to set all this straight; but I've got my house safe, so mustn't complain."

"Yes; might have been worse," said the squire quietly.

"Ay, neighbour, I began to think at one time," said Farmer Tallington, "that it was going to be very much worse, and that I was going to have to bear sad news across to the Toft; but we're spared that, squire, and I'm truly thankful. Feel better?"

"Better! oh yes, I am not hurt!"

Just then Dick asked a question:

"I say, Mr Tallington, wasn't it strange that you didn't know of the fire till I came?"

"I suppose we were all too soundly asleep, my lad. Lucky you saw it, or we might have been burned to death."

"But how did the place catch fire?"

"Ah!" said Farmer Tallington, "that's just what I should like to know.—Were you out there last night, Tom?" he added after a pause.

"No, father, I wasn't near the stacks yesterday."

"Had you been round there at all?" said the squire.

"No, not for a day or two, neighbour. It's a puzzler."

"It is very strange!" said the squire thoughtfully; and he and Farmer Tallington looked hard at each other. "You have had no quarrel with your men?"

"Quarrel! No. Got as good labourers as a man could wish for. So have you."

"Yes, I have," said the squire; "but those stacks could not catch fire by accident. Has anybody threatened you?"

"No," replied the farmer thoughtfully. "No! Say, neighbour—no, they wouldn't do that."

The wheelwright had come up, and stood listening to what was said.

"What do you mean?" said the squire.

"Oh! nothing. 'Tisn't fair to think such things."

"Never mind! Speak out, man, speak out!"

"Well, I was wondering whether some one had done this, just as a hint that we were giving offence by joining in the drain business."

"No, no!" cried the squire indignantly. "People may grumble and be dissatisfied; but, thank Heaven, we haven't any one in these parts bad enough to do such a thing as that, eh, Hickathrift?"

"I dunno 'bout bad enew," said the big wheelwright; "but strikes me Farmer Tallington's right. That stack couldn't set itself afire, and get bont up wi'out some one striking a light!"

"No, no!" said the squire. "I will not think such a thing of any neighbour for twenty miles round. Now, Mr Tallington, come over to my place and have a comfortable meal; Mrs Tallington will come too."

"Nay, we'll stop and try to put things right."

"Shall I lend you a couple of men?"

"Nay, we'll wuck it oot oursens, and thank you all hearty for what you've done. If your farm gets alight, neighbour, we'll come over as you have to us."

"May the demand never arise!" said the squire to himself, as he and his party trudged away, all looking as blackened and disreputable a set as ever walked homeward on an early winter's morn.

Dick had made a good meal, and removed the black from his face after deciding that it would not be worth while to go to bed, when, as he went down the yard and caught sight of Solomon, he stopped to stare at the cunning animal, who seemed to be working about his ears like semaphores.

"I've a good mind to make him take me for a long ride!" said Dick to himself. "No, I haven't. Somehow a lad doesn't care for riding a donkey when he gets as old as I am."

He walked away, feeling stiff, chilly, and uncomfortable from the effects of his previous night's work, while his eyes smarted and ached.

"I'll go over and see how old Tom's getting on," he said as he looked across the cheerless fen in the direction of Grimsey, where a faint line of smoke rose up toward the sky. "Wonder who did it!"

Plash! *plash*! *plash*! *plash*!

He turned sharply, to see, about a hundred yards away, the figure of gaunt, grim-looking Dave standing up in his punt, and poling himself along by the dry rustling reeds, a grey-drab looking object in a grey-drab landscape.

Then, like a flash, came to the lad's memory the engagement made to go liggering that day, and he wondered why it was that he did not feel more eager to have a day's fishing for the pike.

Pee-wit! *pee-wit*! came from off the water in a low plaintive whistle, which Dick answered, and in a minute or two the decoy-man poled his boat ashore, smiling in his tight, dry way.

"Now, then, young mester," he said, "I've got a straänge nice lot o' bait and plenty o' hooks and band, and it's about as good a day for fishing as yow could have. Wheer's young Tom o' Grimsey?"

"At home, of course!" said Dick in a snappish way, which he wondered at himself.

"At home, o' course?" said Dave quietly as he stood up in the boat resting upon the pole. "Why, he were to be here, ready."

"How could he be ready after last night?" said Dick sharply.

Dave took off his fox-skin cap after letting his pole fall into the hollow of his arm, and scratched his head before uttering a low cachinnatory laugh that was not pleasant to the ear.

"Yow seem straänge and popped (put out of temper) this morning, young mester. Young Tom o' Grimsey and you been hewing a bit of a fight?"

"Fight! no, Dave; the fire!"

"Eh?" said the man, staring.

"The fire! Don't you know that Grimsey was nearly all burned down last night?"

Dave loosened his hold of his pole, which fell into the water with a splash.

"Grimsey! bont down!" he exclaimed, and his lower jaw dropped and showed his yellow teeth, but only to recover himself directly and pick up the pole. "Yah!" he snarled; "what's the good o' saying such a word as that? He's a hidin' behind them reeds. Now, then, lad, days is short! Coom out! I can see you!"

He looked in the direction of a patch of reeds and alders as he spoke, and helped himself to a pill of opium from his box.

"Tom Tallington isn't there, Dave!" cried Dick. "I tell you there was a bad fire at Grimsey last night!"

"Nay, lad, you don't mean it!" cried Dave, impressed now by the boy's earnestness.

"There was! Look! you can see the smoke rising now."

Dave looked as the lad pointed, and then said softly:

"Hey! bud theer is the roke (smoke or vapour) sewer enough!"

"Didn't you see it last night?"

"Nay, lad; I fished till I couldn't see, for the baits, and then went home and fitted the hooks on to the bands and see to the blethers, and then I happed mysen oop and went to sleep."

"And heard and saw nothing of the fire?"

"Nay, I see nowt, lad. Two mile to my plaäce from here and two mile from here to Grimsey, mak's four mile. Nay, I heered nowt!"

"Of course you wouldn't, Dave! The light shone in at my window and woke me up, and we were all there working with buckets to put it out!"

"Wucking wi' boockets!" said Dave slowly as he stared in the direction of Tallington's farm. "Hey, but I wish I'd been theer!"

"I wish you had, Dave!"

"Did she blaäze much, mun?"

"Blaze! why, everything was lit up, and the smoke and sparks flew in clouds!"

"Did it, though?" said Dave thoughtfully. "Now, look here, lad," he continued, taking out his tobacco-box; "some on 'em says a man shouldn't tak' his bit o' opium, and that he should smoke 'bacco. I say it's wrong. If I smoked 'bacco some night I should set my plaäce afire, 'stead o' just rolling up a bit o' stoof and clapping it in my mooth."

"I don't know what you mean, Dave," cried Dick.

"Then I'll tell'ee, lad. Some un got smoking his pipe in one of they stables, and set it afire."

"No, no; some one must have set fire to the stacks."

"Nay!" cried Dave, staring in the lad's face with his jaw dropped.

"Yes; that was it, and father thinks it was."

"Not one o' the men, lad; nay, not one o' the men!" cried Dave.

"No, but some one who doesn't like the drain made, and that it was done out of spite."

Dave whisked up his pole and struck with it at the water, sending it flying in all directions, and then made a stab with it as if to strike some one in the chest and drive him under water.

"Nay, nay, nay," he cried, "no one would do owt o' the soort, lad. Nay, nay, nay."

"Ah, well, I don't know!" cried Dick. "All I know is that the stacks were burnt."

"Weer they, lad?"

"Yes, and the stables."

Dave made a clucking noise with his tongue.

"And the house had a narrow escape."

"Hey, bud it's straänge; and will Tallington hev to flit (move, change residence) then?"

"No; the house is right all but one room."

"Eh, bud I'm straänge and glad o' that, lad. Well, we can't goo liggering to-day, lad. It wouldn't be neighbourly."

"No, I shouldn't care to go to-day, Dave, and without Tom. What are you going to do?"

"Throost the punt along as far as I can, and when I've gotten to the end o' the watter tie her oop to the pole, and walk over to see the plaäce."

"I'll come with you, Dave."

"Hey, do, lad, and you can tell me all about it as we go. Jump in."

Dick wanted no second invitation, and the decoy-man sent the punt along rapidly, and by following one of the lanes of water pursued a devious course toward Grimsey, whose blackened ruins now began to come into sight.

Dick talked away about the events of the night, but Dave became more and more silent as they landed and approached the farm where people were moving about busily.

"Nay," he said at last, "it weer some one smoking. Nobody would hev set fire to the plaäce. Why, they might hev been all bont in their beds."

Tom Tallington saw them coming and ran out.

"Why, Dave," he cried, "I'd forgotten all about the fishing, but we can't go now."

"Nay, we couldn't go now," said the man severely. "'Twouldn't be neighbourly."

Tom played the part of showman, and took them round the place, which looked very muddy and desolate by day.

"I say, Dick, do you know how your father made the horses come out?" he said, as they approached the barn, which had been turned into a stable.

"Hit 'em, I suppose, the stupid, cowardly brutes!"

"No; hitting them wouldn't have made them move. He pricked them with the point of his knife."

"Did he, though?" said Dave, who manifested all the interest of one who had not been present.

At last he took his departure.

"Soon as you like, lads," he said; "soon as it's a fine day. I'll save the baits, and get some frogs too. Big pike like frogs. Theer's another girt one lies off a reed patch I know on. I shall be ashore every day till you're ready."

He nodded to them, and pushed off.

"You won't go without us, Dave?" said Dick, as the boat glided away.

"Nay, not I," was the reply; and the boys watched him till he poled in among the thin dry winter reeds, through which he seemed to pass in a shadowy way, and then disappear.

Chapter Ten.

A Trimmering Expedition.

A stormy time ensued, lasting about a fortnight, during which the draining business was hindered; but, upon the whole, the progress made was steady, for a number of men were now employed, and the fen people, who visited the outfall now and then, began to realise what kind of dyke it was that would run across the great swamp.

At last one evening, as the lads had wandered down to Hickathrift's, and were talking to the great bluff wheelwright as he worked away with his axe at roughly shaping the shaft of a sledge, Dave came silently up, followed by the little decoy-dog; and the first knowledge of his presence was given by an attack made upon Hickathrift's big lurcher, which, after showing its teeth angrily, settled down, and seemed to look scornfully at the little animal, before closing its eyes as if to go to sleep.

"Hallo, Dave!" cried the lads together; "want us?"

"Nay, I don't want you, my lads."

"Well, then, we want you," cried Tom.

"Eh?"

"To take us out after the pike, as you promised."

"Nay, it would be too cold, and you wouldn't like it."

"How do you know, Dave?" cried Dick. "Come, when shall we start?"

"Well," said Dave, looking about him as if in search of a good piece of wood which might prove useful, "I dunno. You lads do as you likes; but if I wanted to go, I sud say as the weather was nicely sattled, and start to-morrow morning."

The hour was settled, as well as the weather, and after obtaining the requisite permission the lads were punctual to their time, and found Dave waiting in his punt, upon whose thwart he was seated gravely tying a hook on to a stout piece of twisted horse-hair.

"Got everything ready, Dave?" cried Dick.

"Ay, lad; all ready."

"So are we. Look, Dave," cried Dick, swinging up the big basket he carried, "pork-pie, bread and cheese, and a lump of bacon, and—"

Dave's face twitched as he listened, but he did not speak, only waited; till, after waiting awhile to whet the man's anxiety, Dick added:

"And a big bottle of beer."

"Oh, I don't want no beer!" grumbled Dave. "Watter's good enough for me."

"Let's leave it behind, Tom," said Dick archly. "It will only be heavy in the boat."

"Nay, put it in," said the man with a dry look. "Mebbe the fish would like a drop. Mak' 'em bite."

The boys laughed, and stepped into the punt, which was soon gliding over the dark waters that lay in pools and winding lane-like canals, Dave, in his fox-skin cap, standing up in front and handling the pole, the boys carefully examining the contents of the boat.

"What's in that bucket, Dave?"

"Never mind; you let it alone," said Dave gruffly; and Dick dropped the net he was raising from the pail.

"Well, let's look at the basket, Dave."

"Nay; I wean't hev my hooks and lines tangled up just after I've laid 'em ready. Yow two wait and see when we get acrost to wheer the pike lays."

"Oh, very well!" said Dick in a disappointed tone. "I would have shown you what we've got in our basket."

"I know what you've got yow telled me," retorted Dave. "I don't want to look at vittles; I want to taste 'em."

There was a pause, while Dave worked steadily away with his pole.

"I shall be glad when the summer comes again," said Tom.

"So shall I," cried Dick.

"Theer, I towd you so," cried Dave. "I knowed you'd find it ower cowd. Let's go back."

"Go on with you!" cried Dick; "who said it was cold? I want the summer, because of the sunshine, and the reeds and rushes turning green again, and the birds."

"There's plenty o' birds," said Dave.

"Yes, but I mean singing birds, and nesting, and flowers, and the warmth."

"Theer, I towd you so. You are cowd," cried Dave.

"When I'm cold I'm going to use the pole," said Dick. "I say isn't it deep here, Dave?"

"Ay, theer's some deep holes hereabouts," said the man, trying in vain to reach the bottom with his long pole. "They wean't dree-ern they in a hurry, Mester Dick."

"Good job too, Dave! We don't want our fishing spoiled. Now, then, how much further are you going?"

"Strite across to wheer we saw that big pike rise, my lad."

"Shall we catch him, Dave?"

"Mebbe yes; mebbe no, my lad. If he wants his dinner, and we sets it down by his door stoop, he'll tek it. If he's hed his dinner he wean't touch it."

"Then let's make haste and get there before dinnertime," cried Tom. "Pole away, Dave."

"Nay, we've got to go quiet-like, my lad. We don't want to scare the fish, and send 'em to the bottom to lie sulky. Nice wisp o' duck yon."

He nodded to a long string of wild-fowl flying low over the melancholy-looking water, and they were watched till they disappeared.

"Caught any more in the 'coy, Dave?" asked Dick.

"Few, lad, few. Not enew to tek' to market. Me and John Warren sent 'em wi' the rabbits."

"Ah! he promised us a day with the ferrets. Let's stir him up, Tom. Now, Dave, do let's begin."

The man shook his head and smiled as if he were enjoying the tantalising process he put the boys through, and kept on poling till they were quite a couple of miles from the Toft, when he suddenly laid down his long pole, and seated himself in the boat by the big basket.

"Now," he said, "if you want to see you shall see;" and he began to take out carefully so many short fishing-lines, the hook in each case being carefully stuck in between the osiers so as not to catch. To every one of these lines was attached a bladder, save and except four, which were bound to as many black and compressed pieces of cork, which looked as if they had been washed ashore after doing duty as buoys to some fishermen's nets.

"Theer we are: ten of 'em," said Dave smiling as if he were anticipating the pleasure he would feel in getting some monster tyrant pike upon the hook. "You, young Tom Tallington, pass me that theer boocket."

Tom lifted the bucket, which stood at the side, covered over with some old pieces of netting, and placed it between Dave's knees in the spot from which he removed the basket.

"Now you can both hev a look," he said with a sly glance from one to the other. "Hey, little boys, then; hey, little boys: back yow go!"

This was to a couple of frogs, which had been in the water the bucket contained, but had climbed up the side, to try and get through the meshes of the net, but only to force their heads through and hold on with their claws.

Dave poked one of the frogs with his finger, but the little reptile swelled itself out, and took hold more tightly of the net.

"Here, let go, will you!" cried Dick, taking the frog between his fingers gently enough; but the little creature clung more tightly, and began to squeal loudly, till it was dislodged and dropped into the pail, the other being shaken free, and falling with a splash beside his fellow, when there was a tremendous commotion in the pail; for, beside a couple more frogs, there were about a dozen small fishes scurrying about in the water.

"Theer," cried Dave, looking up; "what do you say to them for bait, eh?"

"Why, they're gudgeons, Dave!" cried Dick.

"Ay, lad, gudgeons."

"Where did you get them?" asked Tom. "There are no gudgeons in the fen waters."

"Not as I iver see," said Dave with his quiet laugh. "I went right across to Ealand, and then walked four mile with my net and that boocket to Brader's Mill on little Norley stream and ketched 'em theer, and carried 'em all the way back to the boat—four mile. For, I says, I should like they boys to ketch a big pike or two, and gudgeons is best baits I know."

"Better than roach and rudd, Dave?"

"Ay, or perch, or tench, or anything. Carp's a good bait; but you can't always ketch carps."

"You are a good chap, Dave!" cried Tom.

"Ay, that I am, lads. I say, though, talk 'bout ketching; hev the squire and Farmer Tallington ketched the chap as sat fire to Grimsey stables?"

"Nobody set fire to Grimsey stables," said Tom. "It was to the stacks."

"Nay, lad, I knows better than that," cried Dave, shaking his head. "Why, didn't I see with my own eyes as roof weer all bont off the top o' stable, and doors gone."

"Yes; but the stable caught fire from the stacks," said Dick.

"Yah! how could it? Why, it's reight the other side o' the house."

"Well, couldn't the sparks and flames of fire float over and set light to the thatch?" cried Dick.

"Set fire to the thack!" said Dave. "Ah, well, I warn't theer! But hev they ketched him?"

"No, and not likely to. There, never mind Tallington's stacks; let's try for the pike."

"Ay, lads, we will," said Dave, and, plunging his hand into the bucket, he took out a transparent gudgeon, whose soft backbone was faintly visible against the light; then carefully passing the hook through its tough upper lip, he dropped it over the side of the boat into the water directly.

"Theer, lads," he said; "now over with that blether."

Dick seized the line, and as the gudgeon swam off he dropped the bladder over the side, and it was slowly towed away.

"I wish fishing wasn't so precious cruel," said Tom, as he watched the bladder dance upon the surface, while the punt was slowly thrust away from the neighbourhood of the reed-bed, where the big pike was supposed to lie.

"'Tisn't cruel," said Dick.

"'Tis. How should you like to be that gudgeon with a hook in your mouth, or the pike when he's caught?"

"Sarve him right for killing all the little fishes," growled Dave, punting gently along.

"Why did you come fishing?" said Dick sharply.

"'Cause I like it," said Tom frankly; "but it's cruel all the same. Oh, look! Look!"

They were about fifty yards from where the line with its buoy had been put over the side, and as Tom had casually looked back he had seen the bladder give a bob, and then begin to skim along the surface.

"Well, I can see," said Dick, "it's the gudgeon swimming fast."

"Nay," said Dave, ceasing to pull; "something's got it. I shouldn't wonder if it's the big pike."

The lads breathlessly watched the bladder go skimming along. Every now and then it gave a bob or two, and then on it went farther and farther from them toward a patch of reeds all broken down and shattered by the wind and lying by itself quite a hundred yards from where the bait had been dropped in.

"Is it the big pike, Dave?" said Dick eagerly.

"Dunno," was the laconic reply. "Mebbe 'tis, mebbe 'tisn't."

"You'll give it time, Dave," cried Tom excitedly, forgetting all his previous qualms.

"Ay, we'll give him time," said Dave with his face tightened so that the ruddy portion of his lips had disappeared, and his mouth was represented by what seemed to be a scar extending right across the lower portion of his countenance. "Who's going to hook him out?"

"I will," cried Dick quickly. "No, you shall have first go, Tom."

"May I?" cried the lad, flushing.

"Yes; go on. Where's the big hook, Dave?"

"Why, s'pose I forgot it," said Dave slowly.

"You haven't," said Dick. "There's the stick," and he picked up a short staff.

"Ay, lad, bud there be no hook."

"Now, none of your old games, Dave," cried Dick; "just as if we didn't know! Come, out with it! You've got it in your pocket."

Dave chuckled, and produced a hook made by bending round a piece of thin iron rod and sharpening the point.

This hook he inserted in the staff and handed to Dick, who immediately passed it to Tom, the latter standing up ready to hook the line when the time should come.

But that was not yet, for the floating bladder was more than a hundred yards away, and still skimming along.

"Be a long time making up his mind to swallow it," said Dave, slowly and softly reducing the distance between them and the buoy, and then pausing while they were still fifty yards away.

"He has stopped now," said Dick in a hoarse whisper as the bladder gleamed quite white a few yards away from the reeds, and gently rose and fell in the ripple caused by the wind.

"Why, he's gone!" said Tom in a disappointed tone.

Bob went the bladder as if to contradict him, giving one sharp movement, and then remaining still once more.

"Nay, he hasn't gone," said Dave. "Give him a bit more time. We'll set another while we're waiting."

As he spoke he laid the pole across the head of the punt, and quickly baiting another of his hooks, dropped it over the boat side away from the direction in which they had to go; and after checking it once or twice till the bait took the right course, he let it go.

Meanwhile, the lads were impatiently watching the bladder, which now remained perfectly still; and in imagination they saw a monstrous pike swallowing the unfortunate gudgeon which bore the hook.

"Theer!" said Dave, rising and taking up his pole. "He've hed plenty time now. Get the basket ready, young squire Dick. Think it'll hold him?"

"If it won't we'll curl him round, Dave," said the lad, laughing. "Now Tom, don't miss."

The boat approached slowly, and Tom was awkwardly placed; but Dave was prepared for this, and after giving the little vessel a sharp impulse he thrust down the pole to the bottom, and checked the head, so that the stern swung round and gave Tom a fair chance, which he stood ready to seize as the boat drew nearer.

They were soon only about ten yards away, and the bladder remained so motionless that the lads' hearts sank with disappointment, for it seemed as if the bait had been left.

"Look out, lad!" said Dave, however, for his quick eyes had detected what was about to happen, and he gave the boat a tremendous thrust just as the bladder glided rapidly away.

Tom bent down and made a dart with his hook, and so earnestly that he would have gone overboard had not Dick caught him in the nick of time.

"Missed him," he cried.

49

"Here, this awayer," cried Dave. "You was a chap!" and he held up his pole with the line over it. For when Tom missed, his opportunity came, the boat gliding so near that he dropped the pole down over the line, and a tremendous disturbance of the water began.

Tom rushed forward, leaned over the side, and deftly hooked the line which ran through to the bladder as Dave drew away his pole.

"It's a monster! Oh Dick!" cried Tom, as he drew the bladder in. "Now, then, catch hold of the line as I draw it in."

"Yah! Why yow make as much on it as if it weer one o' they long studggins, or a big porpus pig," growled Dave, laughing, as Dick secured the line. "Haul him in."

"I say! 'Tisn't a very big one, Tom; but he's strong," said Dick, pulling the captive to the side, for his companion to gaff and lift into the boat. "Why, it's a perch!"

A perch it was—a fine one with ruddy fins and boldly-barred sides, and, though fine for his kind, less than three pounds in weight.

"I thowt that was what he was," said Dave, laughing, "when I sin him skim that theer blether along. Pop him in the basket, lads, and let's get all the rest of the liggers out, or we shall make a poor time of it."

He plied the pole vigorously and soon stopped to let the boat glide towards an opening in the reeds, where a long water-way ran in. Here another buoyed bait was left, and then they went on to lay another and another, the old decoy-man, with the knowledge bought by very long experience, selecting choice spots till the whole set were disposed of in the course of an hour, over a space far exceeding a mile.

"We shall never recollect where they were all set, Dave," said Dick at last, as he stood up looking back along the side of one of the big pools to which they had made their way through what resembled a little river running among the reeds and joining two great pools together.

"You wouldn't," grumbled the man; "but p'raps I may. Now let's go reight back, and see if theer's any on, or—don't you think, lads, it's 'bout time to try and ketch me?"

Dick stared.

"He means he wants you to try if he'd take a corner of the pie, Dick, if you offered it to him as a bait," cried Tom laughing, while Dave's yellow visage developed into something like a grin.

"Ay, that's it, lad—I feel as if I could coot a loaf in two, and eat half wi'out winking. Nay, wait and I'll throost the boat up to yon trees. Hey, look at that!"

He shaded his eyes, and gazed at a large flock of birds flying as closely together, apparently, as starlings, and hundreds upon hundreds in number. They were flying swiftly at a good height, when all at once, as if by a signal, they changed their direction, and, with the accuracy of drilling, darted down in a great bird stream straight for the earth, disappearing behind a low patch of willows.

"Golden plovers!" cried Dick, excitedly. "Oh, Dave, if you were there with a gun!"

"Ay, lad, and I'm here wi' a pole," said Dave. "Niver mind, I may get a few perhaps wi' my net. Now, then, never mind the pie-wipes; let's wipe that theer pie."

He rapidly thrust the boat along till it was close to the side of the mere, where he anchored it with his pole and then leaned over and washed his hands, which he dried upon a piece of rag.

"Are your hands fishy, Tom?" said Dick.

"No—I washed them."

"Well, then, cut some bread."

The next minute the pie was falling to pieces, the bread undergoing a change, and the ale sinking rapidly in the stone bottle. After which the basket was found to contain a certain number of apples, which were converted into support for the active human beings in the boat, with the result that the basket was tapped upside down on the edge to get rid of a few crumbs before the empty pie-dish and stone bottle were replaced, and the whole tucked away so as to leave all clear.

"Now, lads, I think we ought to do some wuck," cried Dave, seizing the pole. "I thought so," he added; "I knowed there'd be something here."

"Eh!" cried Tom.

"Don't you see?" said Dick. "There, that bladder's fifty yards from where it was laid down."

"Hundered," said Dave, plying his pole. "'Fraid it's another peerch."

Dave was wrong, for as they approached the bladder it went off with a swift dart, and there was a swirl in the water which indicated that a big fish must be on.

A good ten minutes' chase ensued before Dick was able to hook the line.

"I've got him," he cried: "a monster!"

It certainly was a large pike of probably ten or twelve pounds, but in spite of its struggles it was drawn close in, with Dave smiling tightly the while, and ending with a broad grin, for as, in the midst of the intense excitement connected with their capture, Tom took the line and Dick leaned forward to gaff the pike, there was a struggle, a splash, the fish leaped right out of the water, and was gone.

"Hey, but why didn't thou whip the hook into him?" cried Dave.

"I was trying to," said Dick ruefully; "but just as I touched his side he wagged his tail and went off!"

"Niver mind, lad," cried Dave. "Let's look at the line. Ah, I thowt as much! Hook's broke."

"Any chance of catching him if we threw in again?" said Tom.

"Nay, he isn't worth trying for. Mebbe he'd bite; mebbe he wouldn't. He's gone the gainest (nearest) way to his hole. Let's try the next."

The buoy attached to this was not in the place where it had been left, and for a few minutes the lads looked round in a puzzled way, till, with a grim smile, Dave thrust the boat close up to a reed patch, when, just as the punt began to rustle against the long crisp water-grass, a splashing was heard inside somewhere, and after parting the growth with his pole Dave stood aside for his companions to see that the bladder attached to the line had been drawn in for some little distance, and then caught in the midst of a dense tangle, beyond which a good-sized fish was tugging to get away.

It needed some effort to force the boat to where the fish was churning up the water; but at last this was effected, and this time, by leaning forward and holding Tom's hand as a stay, Dick managed to gaff the captive and lift it into the boat.

"A beauty!" said Tom, as they gazed at the bronze, green-spotted sides of the ferocious fish, whose fang-armed jaws closed with a snap upon the handle of the gaff, from which a strong shake was needed to detach it.

"Yes, but not a quarter as big as the one which got away."

"Nay," growled Dave, "there weren't much differ, lads."

Whatever its size, the pike, a fish of several pounds weight, was placed alongside of the perch, upon which, by hazard or natural ferocity, it at once fastened its peculiarly hooked back-teeth, making it almost impossible to loosen its hold when once its jaws were closed; but the discussion which followed upon this was interrupted by the sight of the next bladder sailing away into the broadest part of the pool which they now entered.

"There's a big one howd o' that bait, my lads," said Dave, "and he'll give us a race. Shall we leave him?"

"Leave him! no," cried the lads together.

"Ah, you heven't got to pole!" said Dave thoughtfully, as he gazed at the bladder skimming along a couple of hundred yards away.

"Then let me do the poling," cried Dick eagerly, "I'm not tired."

"Nay," said Dave quietly, "neither you nor me can't do no poling theer. Watter's nigh upon twenty foot deep, and a soft bottom. Pole's no use theer."

"What shall we do then?"

"I weer thinking, lad," said Dave, following the direction taken by the bladder. "He's a makkin for yon way through the reeds into next pool."

"Then let's go there and stop him, Dave," cried Dick.

"Ay, lad, we will. Round here by the side. Longest way's sometimes gainest way."

Dick looked blank upon seeing the boat's head turned right away from the fish that was caught. Dave saw it, and handed him the pole.

"Give her a few throosts, lad," he said.

Dick seized the pole and thrust it down into the water lower and lower till his hands touched the surface.

He tried again and again, but there was no bottom within reach, and the lad handed back the pole.

"Why, you knew it was too deep here!" he cried.

"Ay, I knowed, lad," said Dave, taking the pole; "but yow wouldn't hev been saddisfied wi'out trying yoursen."

He proceeded to row the punt now for a few yards, till, apparently knowing by experience where he could find bottom, he thrust down the pole again, gave a few vigorous pushes, and was soon in shallow water.

It was a bit of a race for the river-like opening, but Dave sent the punt along pretty merrily now, while the bladder came slowly along from the other direction till it was only about fifty yards away, when there was a series of bobs and then one big one, the bladder which gleamed whitely on the grey water going down out of sight.

Dave ceased poling, and all watched the surface for the return of the bladder, as whale-fishers wait for the rising of the great mammal that has thrown his flukes upward and dived down toward the bottom of the sea; but they watched in vain.

A minute, two minutes, five minutes, then quite a quarter of an hour, but no sign of the submerged buoy.

"Yow two look over the sides," said Dave. "I'll run her right over where the blether was took down."

Dave sent the punt along slowly, and the lads peered down into the dark water, but could see no bladder.

"She'll come up somewheers," said Dave at last, sweeping the surface with his keen eyes, and then smiling in his hard, dry, uncomfortable way, as he looked right back over the way by which they had come, and nodding his head, "There she is!" he said.

Sure enough there lay the bladder on the surface forty yards behind them perfectly motionless.

"Yow take howd o' this one, young Tom Tallington," said Dave; and the lad prepared to hook the line as the punt was carefully urged forward.

"Take care, Tom!" whispered Dick excitedly. "Now, now! Oh, what a fellow you are!"

Tom did not dash in the hook when his companion bade him, but all the same he managed to do it at the right time, catching the line just below the bladder, and then stooping to seize it with his hand ready for the struggle which was to ensue.

Both boys were flushed with excitement, and paid no heed to the grim smile upon their companion's face—a smile which expanded into a grin as the line came in without the slightest resistance, and the lads looked at each other with blank dismay.

"Clap the line in the basket, Mester Dick," said Dave; "he's took the bait and gone."

"Why, what a big one he must have been!" cried Tom.

"Ah, he would be a big one!" said Dave with a chuckle, as he urged the punt rapidly on; "them as gets away mostlings is."

"Didn't you feel him a bit, Tom?" asked Dick.

"No, he had gone before I touched the line," was the reply.

It was very disappointing; but there were the other trimmers to be examined, and though it would have puzzled a stranger, Dave went back with unerring accuracy to the next one that had been laid down.

This did not seem to have moved; and as it was drawn in, the bait was swimming strongly and well.

"Let him go, Dick," said Tom.

"Well, I was going to, wasn't I?" was the reply. "There you are, old chap, only got a hole in your gristly lip."

He dropped the gudgeon into the water, and it lay motionless for a moment or two, and then darted downward as the punt glided on.

Another trimmer, and another, and another, was taken up as it was reached, all these with the baits untouched, and the disappointed look grew upon the boys' faces.

"I thought we should get one on every hook," said Tom. "Ar'n't we going to catch any more?"

"Why, you've got two," said Dave.

"Well, what are two, Dave?" cried Dick.

"More'n I've got many a day," said the man. "I often think I'd like a pike to stuff and bake; but lots o' times I come and I never get one. There's one for you yonder."

"Is there—where?" cried Tom.

Dave nodded in the direction of the little bay they were approaching, and it was plain to see that the bladder had been drawn close in to the boggy shore.

"Oh, he's gone!" cried Tom. "I don't believe there's one on."

Tom was wrong, for upon the spot being reached the bladder suddenly became, as it were, animated, and went sailing along bobbing about on the surface, then plunging down out of sight, to come up yards away.

"There's a niste one on theer, lads," said Dave. "Yow be ready with the hook, Mester Dick, and yow kneel down ready to ketch the line, young Tom Tallington."

It was quite a long chase; the bladder bobbing and dancing away till Dave forced the punt pretty near, and by a back stroke Dick caught the line, drew it near enough for Tom to seize, when there was a tremendous splash and plunge, and Tom fell backwards.

"Gone!" cried Dick in a passion of angry disappointment.

"Gone!" said Tom dolefully, "and I'd nearly got him over the side!"

"Ay, that's the way they gooes sometimes," said Dave, sending on the boat. "Put the band in the basket, lads. Better luck next time."

"Why, the line's broken!" cried Dick, handing it to its owner.

"Sawed off agen his teeth," said Dave, after a glance. "Theer, put 'em away, lad. He's theer waiting to be ketched again some day. Theer's another yonder. Nay, he hesn't moved."

This one was taken up, and then others, till only two remained, one of which was set where the great pike had been seen which took down the duck. One had not been touched, but had had the bait seized and gnawed into a miserable state; another bait was bitten right off cleanly close to the head; while another had been taken off the hook; and one bait had probably been swallowed, and the line bitten in two.

"We are having bad luck," cried Dick dolefully. "I thought we should get a basket full."

"I didn't," said Dave. "Nivver did but once. Here, we'll tak' yon last one up first, and come back along here and tak' up the big one, and go thruff yon reed-bed home."

"Big one!" said Tom.

"You don't think he's on, do you?" cried Dick.

"Hey, lad, how do I know! Mebbe he is."

"Then let's go at once," cried Dick excitedly.

"Nay, nay, we'll try yon one first," said Dave, for both the remaining trimmers were in sight, and though not where they had been laid down, they seemed to be no farther off than a lively bait and the wind might have taken them.

"Theer, lads, yow'll hev to be saddisfied wi' what yow've got. No more to-day."

"Oh, very well!" said Dick; "but I wish we'd got something more to eat."

"There's one on," said Tom excitedly, as they neared the most remote of the two trimmers.

"How do you know?"

"Saw it bob."

"Yah! It doan't move."

Dick glanced at Dave, whose face was inscrutable, and then the bladder seemed to be motionless, and as if Tom's "bob" was all imagination. Once more it seemed to move slightly, but it was nothing more than the bait would cause.

"In wi' it, lads," cried Dave. "You, young Tom. I wean't stop. Ketch it as we go by."

Tom reached over and thrust in the hook, just catching the line as the trimmer seemed to be gliding away.

"Something on," he shouted, as he got hold of the line with his hands, and threw down the hook into the boat. For there was a strong sturdy strain upon the cord; and but for the progress of the boat being checked, either the line would have been broken, or Tom would have had to let go.

"Why, you've got hold of a stump!" cried Dick. "What shall we do, Dave—cat the line?"

"Howd on, lads, steady! Ah, that's moved him!"

For just then, in place of the steady strain, there were a series of short sharp snatches.

"Eel, eel!" cried Dick; and at the end of a few minutes' exciting play, a huge eel was drawn over the side of the boat, tied up in quite a knot, into which it had thrown itself just at the last.

"Coot the band close to his neb," (mouth or beak) said Dave, and this being done, and the line saved from tangling, the captive untwisted itself, and began to explore the bottom of the boat, a fine thick fellow nearly thirty inches long, and the possibility was that it might escape over the stern, till Dave put a stop to the prospect by catching it quickly, and before it could glide out of his hand, throwing it into the basket, where the pike resented its coming by an angry flapping of the tail.

"That's better," said Dick, placing the trimmer in the other basket. "I say, Dave, would a fellow like that bite?"

"Nigh tak' your finger off: they're as strong as strong. Say, lads, shall we go home now, or try the other ligger?"

"Oh, let's get the last!" cried Dick; "there may be something on it."

Dave nodded, and poled steadily over to where the last trimmer lay off the reedy point, and perfectly motionless, till they were within ten yards, when there was a heavy swirl on the water, and the bladder dived under, reappeared a couple of dozen yards away, and went off rapidly along beside the reed-bed.

"Is that another perch?" cried Tom, as Dave began to ply his pole rapidly, and the boat was urged on in pursuit.

"Nay, that's no perch," cried Dave, who for the first time looked interested. "It's a pike, and a good one."

"Think it's that monster that took down the duck?" cried Dick.

"Nay, lad, I d'know," said the decoy-man; "all I say is that it be a girt lungeing pike o' some kind."

Dave plied his pole, and the boys, in their excitement, turned each a hand into an oar, and swept it through the water as the pursuit was kept up, for the bladder went sailing away, then stopped, and as soon as the punt drew near was off again. Sometimes it kept to the surface, but now and then, when in places where Dave's pole would not touch the bottom, no sooner did the punt glide up, than there was an eddying swirl, and the bladder was taken down out of sight.

Once or twice Dick made a dash at it with the hook, but each time to miss, and they were led a pretty dance.

"He's a girt big un, lads, a very girt big un," said Dave, as he rested for a moment or two with the end of the pole in the water, waiting for the bladder to reappear, and then rowed the punt softly in the direction in which it was gliding. "Says, shall a give 'em up?"

"No, no," cried Dick. "Here, lend me the pole. I'll soon catch him."

Dave smiled, but did not give up the pole.

"Nay, lad, I'll ketch up to un. Wait a bit; fish'll be tired 'fore Dave Gittans."

The pursuit continued in the most exasperating way, and to an onlooker it would have been exceedingly absurd, since it seemed as if the man and his companions were off oh the great mere with its open spaces of water and islands of reeds, and lanes through them like so many little crooked canals, in pursuit of a white pig's-bladder tied round the middle to make it double. There it would lie till the boat neared, and then off it went with a skim that took it twenty, thirty, or forty yards. Next time the boat neared, instead of the skim it would begin to dance as if in mockery, bobbing down whenever Dick reached over with his hook, and always keeping out of his reach, just as if a mocking spirit directed all its movements and delighted in tantalising them. Again, after a long run over the deep water, it would be quite still, and the punt would be sent forward so cautiously that the capture seemed to be a moral certainty; but so sure as Dick crept to the extreme end of the punt and reached out, there was a tremor for an instant visible on the water and the bladder disappeared.

"He must be a monster!" cried Dick, whose face was scarlet. "Oh, Dave, do go more quietly this time!"

"Let me try!" cried Tom, making a snatch at the hook.

"No! I'll have him," said Dick. "I wouldn't miss this chance for the world!"

"Ay, I'll goo up quiet-like," said Dave, pausing to give himself an opium pill before resuming his task. "Yow be quicker this time, lad—a bold dash and you'll get him!"

The double-looking bladder seemed now to be quite divided in two, for the string had grown tighter in being drawn through the water, and as it lay quite still, about forty yards from them, it looked a task that a child might have done, to go up to it softly and hook the string.

"Now!" said Dave as he propelled the boat stern foremost by working the pole behind as a fish does its tail.

"Oh! do get it this time, Dick!" panted Tom as he knelt in the boat.

"One quick dash, Mester Dick, and you hev it!"

Dick did not answer, but lay prone upon his chest well out over the stern of the boat, holding on with one hand, the hook stretched out over the water, ready, his heart beating and his eyes glittering with excitement.

As the punt glided on Dick's face was reflected in the dark amber-tinted water—for there was not a ripple made—but he saw nothing of the glassy surface; his eyes were riveted upon the gleaming white bladder, into which the string had cut so deeply.

Another moment or two and he would be within striking distance, but a glance at his hook showed that, perhaps from looseness in its socket, the point was turned too much away.

He had barely time to turn it, as the moment arrived to strike, and strike he did, just as the bladder was plunging down.

A yell came from behind him from Dave!

A groan from Tom!

Dick rose up in the boat with a feeling of misery and disappointment, such as he had never before experienced, for he was perfectly conscious of what he had done. The bladder had been snatched under so quickly, that when he struck, instead of the hook going beneath and catching the string, the point had entered the bladder. He had even felt the check, and knew that he had torn a hole in the side.

"Hey, but yow've done it now, Mester Dick!" said Dave, laying the pole across the boat and sitting down.

"I couldn't help it, Dave. I did try so hard!" pleaded the lad.

"And you wouldn't let me try—obstinate!" grumbled Tom.

"Deal better you'd have done it, wouldn't you!" cried Dick in an exasperated tone.

"Done it better than that!" cried Tom hotly.

"Nay, yow wouldn't, lad," said Dave coolly. "It's a girt big un, and he's too sharp for us. Well, it's getting on and we may as well go home. He's gone! Blether wean't come to the top no more!"

"But will he take a bait again, Dave?" said Dick; "I mean, if we come another time."

"Will yow want any dinner to-morrow, lad?" said Dave, laughing. "Ay, he'll tek a bait again, sure enough, and we'll hev him some day! Theer, it's getting late; look at the starnels sattling down on the reeds!"

He pointed to the great clouds of birds curving round in the distance as he stooped and picked up the pole, ready to send the punt homewards, for the evening was closing in, and it would be dark before they reached the shore.

"What's that?" cried Tom suddenly, as he swept the surface of the water, and he pointed to a faint white speck about twenty yards away.

"Hey? Why, it is!" cried Dave. "Tek the hook again, Mester Dick, lad; there's a little wind left yet in th' blether, and it's coom oop!"

"Let me!" cried Tom.

"Shall I do it, lad?" said Dave.

"No, let me try this once!" cried Dick. "Or, no; you try, Tom!"

Tom snatched at the staff of the hook, but offered it back to his companion.

"No, Dick," he said; "you missed, and you've a right to try again!"

"No, you try!" said Dick hurriedly, as he thrust his hands in his pockets to be out of temptation.

"Nay, let Mester Dick hev one more try!" cried Dave; and the lad took the staff, went through all his former manoeuvres, struck more deeply with the staff, and this time, as he felt a check, he twisted the hook round and round in the string, and felt as if it would be jerked out of his hand.

"Twist un again, mun! Get well twissen!" cried Dave; and as the lad obeyed, the punt, already in motion, was for a short distance literally drawn by the strong fish in its desperate efforts to escape.

"Let me come this time, young Tom Tallington!" cried Dave.

"No, no; I'll help!" cried Tom.

"But I shouldn't like you to lose this un, lads. Theer, go on and charnsh it. You get well howd o' the band while young squire untwisses the hook. He's 'bout bet out now and wean't mak' much of a fight!"

Tom obeyed, and Dick, who was trembling with excitement, set the hook at liberty.

Meanwhile the fish was struggling furiously at the end of some fifteen feet of stout line; but the fight had been going on some time now, and at the end of a few minutes, as Dave manoeuvred the punt so as to ease the strain on the line, Tom found that he could draw the captive slowly to the surface.

"Tak' care, Mester Dick, throost hook reight in his gills, and in wi' un at onced."

Dick did not reply, but stood ready, and it was well that he did so, for as Tom drew the fish right up, such a savage, great, teeth-armed pair of jaws came gaping at him out of the water, that he started and stumbled back, dragging the hook from its hold.

But before he could utter a cry of dismay there was a tremendous sputter and splash, for Dick had been in time, and, as the fish-hook was breaking out, had securely caught the pike with the gaff.

The next moment, all ablaze in the evening light with green, and gold, and silver, and cream, the monster was flopping on the floor of the punt, trying frantically to leap out, and snapping with its jaws in a way that would have been decidedly unpleasant for any hand that was near.

The monster's career was at an end, though. A heavy blow on the head stunned it, and a couple more put it beyond feeling, while the occupants of the boat stood gazing down at their prize, as grand a pike as is often seen, for it was nearly four feet long, and well-fed and thick.

"Look at his teeth!" cried Tom excitedly; "why, there's great fangs full half an inch long."

"Yes, and sharp as knives!" cried Dick.

"Ay, he've hed nice games in his time here, lads!" said Dave, grinning with pleasure. "I'm straänge and glad you've caught him. Many's the time I've sin him chase the fish and tak' down the water-rats. One day he hed howd of a big duck. He got it by its legs as I was going along, and the poor thing quacked and tried to fly, but down it went d'reckly. Big pike like this un'll yeat owt."

"And if he got hold of them with these hooked teeth, Dave, they wouldn't get away."

"Nay, lad, that they wouldn't. He'd take a pike half as big as hissen, if he got the charnsh."

"Well, he won't kill any more," cried Dick triumphantly. "Oh, Tom, if we had lost him after all!"

"I'd reyther hev lost a whole tak' o' duck, lads," said Dave, shaking each of his companions' hands warmly. "There'll be straänge games among all the fishes and birds here, because he's ketched. Look at him! Theer's a pike, and they're a trying to dree-ern all the watter off from the fens and turn 'em into fields. Hey, lads, it'll be a straänge bad time for us when it's done."

"But do you think it will take off all the water, and spoil the fen, Dave?" said Tom.

"Nay, lad, I don't," said Dave with sudden emphasis. "It's agen nature, and it wean't be done. Hey and we must be getting back."

He plunged the pole into the water as he spoke, and it seemed to grow blacker and blacker, as they talked pike over their capture, till the shore was reached, and the prize borne to Hickathrift's workshop, where a pair of big rough scales showed that within a few ounces the pike weighed just what Dave guessed, to wit two stone and a half old Lincolnshire weight of fourteen pounds to the stone, or thirty-five pounds.

Chapter Eleven.

Mr Marston's Narrow Escape.

The wintry weather passed away with its storms and continuous rains and floods, which hindered the progress of the great lode or drain, and then came the spring sunshine, with the lads waking up to the fact that here and there the arums were thrusting up their glossy-green spathes, that the celandines were out like yellow stars, and that the rustling reeds left uncut had been snapped off and beaten down, and had rotted in the water, and that from among them the young shoots of the fresh crop were beginning to peep.

Bold brisk winds swept over the fen and raised foamy waves in the meres, and the nights were clear and cold, though there had been little frost that year, never enough to well coat the lakes and pools with ice, so that the pattens could be cleaned from their rust and sharpened at Hickathrift's grindstone ready for the lads at the old Priory and Grimsey to skate in and out for miles. But, in spite of the cold, there was a feeling of spring in the air. The great grey-backed crows were getting scarce, and the short-eared owls, which, a couple of months before, could be flushed from the tufts in the fen, to fly off looking like chubby hawks, were gone, and the flights of ducks and peewits had broken up. The golden plovers were gone; but the green peewits were busy nesting, or rather laying eggs without nests—pear-shaped eggs, small at one end, large at the other, thickly blotched and splashed with dark green, and over which the birds watched, ready to fall as if with broken wing before the intruder, and try to lure him away.

Many a tramp over the sodden ground did the lads have with Dave, who generally waited for their coming, leaping-pole in hand, and then took them to the peewits' haunts to gather a basketful of their eggs.

"I don't know how you do it, Dave," said Dick. "We go and hunt for hours, and only get a few pie-wipes' eggs; you always get a basketful."

"It's a man's natur," said Dave.

"Well, show us how you know," said Dick, shouldering his leaping-pole, and pretending to hit his companion's head.

"Nay, lad, theer's no showing a thing like that," said Dave mysteriously. "It comes to a man."

"Gammon!" cried Dick. "It's a dodge you've learned."

Dave chuckled and tramped on beside the lads, having enough to do to avoid sinking in.

"She's reyther juicy this spring, eh? They haven't dree-ernt her yet," said Dave with a malicious grin. "See there, now, young Tom Tallington," he cried, stepping past the lad, and, picking up a couple of eggs in spite of the wailing of their owners, as they came napping close by, the cock bird in his glossy-green spring feathers, and a long pendent tuft hanging down from the back of his head.

"How stupid!" cried Tom. "I didn't see them."

"Nay, you wouldn't," said Dave, stepping across Dick, who was on his left; "and yow, young squire Dick, didn't see they two."

"Yes, I did, Dave, I did," cried Dick. "I was just going to pick them up."

"Pick' em up then," cried Dave quietly; "where are they then?" Dick looked sharply round him; but there was not an egg to be seen, and he realised that Dave had cheated him, and drawn him into a declaration that was not true.

He was very silent under the laughter of his companions, and felt it all the more.

They went on, the lads sometimes finding an egg or two, but nearly all falling to Dave, who, as if by unerring instinct, went straight to the spots where the nests lay, and secured the spoil.

Now and then a heron flew up, one with a small eel twining about its bill; and more than once a hare went bounding off from its form among the dry last year's grass.

"We want Hickathrift's dog here," cried Dick.

"What for, lad? what for?" said Dave, laughing.

"To catch the hares."

"Nay, yow want no dog," said Dave. "Easy enough to catch hares."

"Easy! How?" cried Tom.

"Go up to 'em and catch 'em," said Dave coolly.

"Ha, ha, ha!" laughed Dick, and his companion joined in. "I should like to see you catch a hare, Dave."

"Shouldst ta, lad? Very well, wait a bit."

They tramped on, with Dave picking up an egg here, a couple there, in a way that was most exasperating to the boys, whose luck was very bad.

"I never saw such eyes," said Tom. "I can't see the eggs like he can."

Dave chuckled as if he had a rattlesnake in his throat, and they went on for a while till Dick stopped suddenly, and pointed to the side of one of the fen ponds.

"That isn't a heron," he said.

"No. One o' them long-legged ones—a crane," said Dave. "Getting straänge and scarce now. Used to be lots of 'em breed here when my grandfather was a boy. Nay, nay, don't scar' him," he cried, checking Dick, who was about to wave his hands. "Niver disturb the birds wi'out you want 'em to eat or sell. Now, then: yonder's a hare."

"Where?" cried Tom. "I can't see it."

"Over yonder among that dry grass."

"There isn't," said Dick. "I can't see any hare."

"Like me to go and catch him, young Tom?"

"Here, I'll soon see if there's a hare," cried Dick; but Dave caught him by the shoulder with a grip of iron, and thrust the pole he carried into the soft bog.

"I didn't say I was going to run a hare down," he said. "Theer's a hare yonder in her form. Shall I go and catch her?"

"Yes," said Dick, grinning. "Shall I say, 'Sh!'"

"Nay, if thou'rt going to play tricks, lad, I shall howd my hand. I thowt yow wanted to see me ketch a hare."

"Go on, then," said Dick, laughing; "we won't move."

Dave chuckled, swung his basket behind him as if hung by a strip of cow-hide over his shoulder, and walked quietly on, in and out among the tufts of heather and moss, for some five-and-twenty yards.

"He's laughing at us," said Dick.

"No, he isn't. I've heard Hickathrift say he can catch hares," replied Tom. "Look!"

For just then they saw Dave go straight up to a tuft of dry grass, stoop down and pick up a hare by its ears, and place it on his left arm.

The boys ran up excitedly.

"Why, Dave, I didn't think you could do it!" cried Dick.

"Dessay not," replied the decoy-man, uttering his unpleasant laugh. "Theer, she's a beauty, isn't she?"

The hare struggled for a moment or two, and then crouched down in the man's arm, with its heart throbbing and great eyes staring round at its captors.

"Kill it, Dave, kill it," cried Tom.

"Kill it! What for? Pretty creatur'," said Dave, stroking the hare's brown speckled fur, and laying its long black-tipped sensitive ears smoothly down over its back.

"To take home."

"Nay, who kills hares at the end of March, lad? Hares is mad in March."

"Is that why it let you catch it, Dave?"

"Mebbe, lad, mebbe, Mester Dick. Theer, hev you done stroking her?"

"No. Why?"

"Going to let her run?"

"Wait a bit," cried Dick.

"Tek her by the ears, lad, and putt thy hand beneath her. That's the ways."

Dick took the hare in his arms, and the trembling beast submitted without a struggle.

"How did you know it was there?" said Tom.

"How did I know she was theer! Why, she had her ears cocked-up listening, plain enough to see. Theer, let her go now. She's got a wife somewheers about."

"*She's* got a wife! Why don't you say *He*?" cried Dick. "Now, Tom, I'm going to let him go; but he won't run, he's a sick one. You'll see. Anyone could catch a hare like this."

He carefully placed the hare upon the ground, holding tightly by its ears.

"There," he cried; "I told you so! Look how stupid and—Oh!"

The hare made one great leap, and then hardly seemed to touch the ground again with its muscular hind-legs; but went off at a tremendous rate, bounding over heath and tuft, till it disappeared in the distance.

"There's a sleepy sick one for you, Mester Dick!" cried Dave. "Now, then, goo and ketch her, lad."

"Well, I never!" cried Dick. "I say, Dave, how do you manage it? Could you catch another?"

"Ay, lad, many as I like."

"And rabbits too?"

"Nay, I don't say that. I hev ketched rabbuds that ways, but not often. Rabbud always makes for his hole."

As he spoke he walked back to where he had left his pole standing in the bog earth, and they trudged on again to where a lane of water impeded their further progress.

"Too wide for you, lads?" said Dave.

"No," replied Dick, "if it's good bottom."

"Good bottom a little higher up here," said Dave, bearing off to the left. "Now, then, over you go!"

Dick, pole in hand, took a run without the slightest hesitation, for Dave's word was law. He said there was good bottom to the lane of water, and he was sure to know, for he had the knowledge of his father and grandfather joined to his own. If it had been bad bottom Dick's feat would have been impossible, for his pole would have gone down perhaps to its full length in the soft bog; as it was, the end of the pole rested upon gravel in about three feet of water, and the lad went over easily and describing a curve through the air.

"Look out!" shouted Tom, following suit, and landing easily upon the other side; while Dave took off his basket of plovers' eggs by slipping the hide band over his head, then, hanging it to the end of his pole, he held it over the water to the boys, who reached across and took it together on their poles, landing it safely without breaking an egg.

The next minute, with the ease of one long practised in such leaps, Dave flew over and resumed his load.

Several more long lanes of water were cleared in this way, Dave leading the boys a good round, and taking them at last to his house, pretty well laden with eggs, where he set before them a loaf and butter, and lit a fire.

"Theer, you can boil your eggs," he said, "and mak' a meal. Mebbe you're hungry now."

There was no maybe in the matter, judging from the number of slices of bread and butter and hard-boiled plovers' eggs the lads consumed.

Over the meal the question of the draining was discussed sympathetically.

"No fish," said Dick.

"No decoy," said Tom.

"No plovers' eggs," said Dave.

"No rabbiting," said Dick.

"No eeling," said Tom.

"No nothing," said Dave. "Hey bud it'll be a sad job when it's done. But it arn't done yet, lads, eh?"

"No, it isn't done yet," said Dick. "I say, where's John Warren? I haven't seen him for months."

"I hev," said Dave. "He's a breaking his heart, lads, about big drain. Comes over to see me and smoke his pipe. It'll 'bout kill him if his rabbud-warren is took away. Bud dree-ern ar'n't done yet, lads, eh?"

Squire Winthorpe was of a different opinion that night when Dick reached home after seeing Tom well on his way.

"They're going on famously now," he said to Mrs Winthorpe, who was repairing the damage in one of Dick's garments.

"And was the meeting satisfied?"

"Yes, quite," said the squire. "We had a big meeting with the gentlemen from London who are interested in the business, and they praised young Mr Marston, the engineer, wonderfully fine young fellow too."

Dick pricked up his ears.

"I thought Mr Marston was coming to see us a deal, father!" he said.

"He's been away during the bad weather when the men couldn't work—up in town making plans and things. He's coming over to-night."

"And do the people about seem as dissatisfied as ever about the work?" said Mrs Winthorpe.

"I don't hear much about it," said the squire. "They'll soon settle down to it when they find how things are improved. Well, Dick, plenty of sport to-day?"

"Dave got plenty of pie-wipes' eggs, father. I didn't find many."

"Got enough to give Mr Marston a few?"

"Oh, yes, plenty for that! What time's he coming?"

"About eight, I should think. He's coming along the river bank after his men have done."

"And going back, father?"

"Oh no! he'll sleep here to-night."

The squire went out to have his customary look round the farmstead before settling down for the night, and Dick followed him. The thrushes were piping; sounds of ducks feeding out in the fen came off the water, and here and there a great shadowy-looking bird could be seen flapping its way over the desolate waste, but everywhere there was the feeling of returning spring in the air, and the light was lingering well in the west, making the planet in the east look pale and wan.

Everything seemed to be all right. There was a loud muttering among the fowls at roost. Solomon laid back his ears and twitched the skin of his back as if he meant to kick when Dick went near the lean-to shed supported on posts, thatched with reeds and built up against an old stone wall in which there were the remains of a groined arch.

Everything about the Toft was at peace, and down toward the wheelwright's the labourers' cottages were so still that it was evident that some of the people had gone to bed.

The squire went on down the gravel slope, past the clump of firs, and by the old ivied wall which marked the boundary of the ancient priory, when, after crossing a field or two, they came to the raised bank which kept the sluggish river within bounds.

"Looks cold and muddy, father," said Dick.

"Yes, not tempting for a bathe, Dick; but some day I hope to see a river nearly as big as that draining our great fen."

"But don't you think it will be a pity, father?"

"Yes, for idle boys who want to pass their lives fishing, and for men like Dave and John Warren. Depend upon it, Dick, it's the duty of every man to try and improve what he sees about."

"But natural things look so beautiful, father!"

"In moderation, boy. Don't see any sign of Mr Marston yet, do you?"

"No, father," replied Dick after taking a long look over the desolate level where the river wound between its raised banks toward the sea.

"Can't very well miss his way," said the squire, half to himself.

"Unless he came through the fen," said Dick.

"Oh, he wouldn't do that! He'd come along by the river wall, my boy; it's longer, but better walking."

The squire walked back toward the house, turning off so as to approach it by the back, where his men were digging for a great rain-water tank to be made.

The men had not progressed far, for their way was through stones and cement, which showed how, at one time, there must have been either a boundary-wall or a building there; and as they stood by the opening the latter was proved to be the case, for Dick stooped down and picked up a piece of ancient roofing lead.

"Yes, Dick, this must have been a fine old place at one time," said the squire. "Let's get back. Be a bit of a frost to-night, I think."

"I hope not, father."

"And I hope it will, my boy! I like to get the cold now, not when the young trees are budding and blossoming."

They went in, to find the ample supper spread upon its snowy cloth and the empty jug standing ready for the ale to be drawn to flank the pinky ham, yellow butter, and well-browned young fowl.

"No, wife, no! Can't see any sign of him yet," said the squire. "Dick, get me my pipe. I'll have just one while we're waiting. Hope he has not taken the wrong road!"

"Do you think he has?" said Mrs Winthorpe anxiously. "It would be very dangerous for him now it is growing dark."

"No, no; nonsense!" said the squire, filling his pipe from the stone tobacco-jar Dick had taken from the high chimney-piece of the cosy, low, oak-panelled room.

It was a curious receptacle, having been originally a corbel from the bottom of a groin of the old building, and represented an evil-looking grotesque head. This the squire had had hollowed out and fitted with a leaden lid.

"Think we ought to go and meet him, father?" said Dick, after watching the supper-table with the longing eyes of a young boy, and then taking them away to stare at his mother's glistening needle and the soft grey clouds from his father's pipe.

"No, Dick, we don't know which way to go. If we knew we would. Perhaps he will not come at all, and I'm too tired to go far to-night."

Dick bent down and stroked Tibb, the great black cat, which began to purr.

"Put on a few more turves, Dick, and a bit or two of wood," said his mother. "Mr Marston may be cold."

Dick laid a few pieces of the resinous pine-root from the fen upon the fire, and built up round it several black squares of well-dried peat where the rest glowed and fell away in a delicate creamy ash. Then the fir-wood began to blaze, and he returned to his seat.

"'Tatoes is done!" said a voice at the door, and the red-armed maid stood waiting for orders to bring them in.

"Put them in a dish, Sarah, and keep them in the oven with the door open. When Mr Marston comes you can put them in the best wooden bowl, and cover them with a clean napkin before you bring them in," said Mrs Winthorpe.

"Oh, I say, mother, I am so hungry! Mayn't I have one baked potato?"

"Surely you can wait, my boy, till our visitor comes," said Mrs Winthorpe quietly.

Dick stared across at the maid as she was closing the door, and a look of intelligence passed between them, one which asked a question and answered it; and Dick knew that if he went into the great kitchen there would be a mealy potato ready for him by the big open fireplace, with butter *ad libitum*, and pepper and salt.

Dick sat stroking the cat for a few minutes and then rose, to go to the long low casement bay-window, draw aside the curtain, and look out over the black fen.

"Can't see him," he said with a sigh; and then, as no notice was taken of his remark, he went slowly out and across the square stone-paved hall to the kitchen, where, just as he expected, a great potato was waiting for him by the peat-fire, and hot plate, butter, pepper, and salt were ready.

"Oh, I say, Sarah, you are a good one!" cried Dick.

"I thought you'd come, Mester Dick," said the maid; and then, with a start, "Gracious! what's that?"

"Sea-bird," said Dick shortly, and then he dropped the knife and ran back to the parlour, for another cry came from off the fen.

"Hear that, father!" cried Dick.

"Hear it! yes, my lad. Quick! get your cap. My staff, mother," he added. "Poor fellow's got in, p'r'aps."

The squire hurried out after Dick, who had taken the lead, and as they passed out of the great stone porch the lad uttered a hail, which was answered evidently from about a couple of hundred yards away.

"He has been coming across the fen path," said the squire. "Ahoy! don't stir till we come."

"Shall we want the lantern, father?" cried Dick.

"No, no, my lad; we can see. Seems darker first coming out of the light."

A fresh cry came from off the fen, and it was so unmistakably the word "Help!" that the squire and his son increased their pace.

"Ahoy, there!" cried a big gruff voice.

"Hickathrift?"

"Ay, mester! Hear that! some un's in trouble over yonder."

The wheelwright's big figure loomed up out of the darkness and joined them as they hurried on.

"Yes, I heard it. I think it must be Mr Marston missed his way."

"What! the young gent at the dreeaning! Hey, bud he'd no call to be out theer."

58

"Where are you?" shouted Dick, who was ahead now and hurrying along the track that struck off to the big reed-beds and then away over the fen to the sea-bank.

"Here! help!" came faintly.

"Tak' care, Mester Dick!" cried Hickathrift as he and the squire followed. "Why, he is reight off the path!"

"I'll take care!" shouted Dick. "Come on! All right; it isn't very soft here!"

Long usage had made him so familiar with the place that he was able to leave the track in the darkness and pick his way to where, guided by the voice, he found their expected visitor, not, as he expected, up to his middle in the soft peat, but lying prone.

"Why, Mr Marston, you're all right!" cried Dick. "You wouldn't have hurt if you had come across here."

"Help!" came faintly from the prostrate traveller, and Dick caught his arm, but only to elicit a groan.

"Well, he is a coward!" thought Dick. "Here, father! Hicky!"

"Rather soft, my boy!" said the squire.

"Ay, not meant for men o' our weight, mester," said the wheelwright; and they had to flounder in the soft bog a little before they reached the spot where Dick stood holding the young man's cold hand.

"He has fainted with fright, father," said Dick, who felt amused at anyone being so alarmed out there in the darkness.

"Let me tackle him, mester," said the wheelwright.

"No; each take a hand, my lad," said the squire, "and then let's move together for the path as quickly as possible."

"Reight!" cried Hickathrift, laconically; and, stooping down, they each took a hand, and half ran half waded through the black boggy mud, till they reached the path from which the young man had strayed.

"Poor chap! he were a bit scar'd to find himself in bog."

"Pity he ventured that way," said the squire.

"Here, Mr Marston, you're all right now," said Dick. "Can you get up and walk?"

There was no answer, but the young man tried to struggle up, and would have sunk down again had not the squire caught him round the waist.

"Poor lad! he's bet out. Not used to our parts," said Hickathrift. "Here, howd hard, sir. Help me get him o' my back like a sack, and I'll run him up to the house i' no time."

It seemed the best plan; and as the young man uttered a low moan he was half lifted on to Hickathrift's broad back, and carried toward the house.

"Run on, Dick, and tell your mother to mix a good glass of hollands and water," said the squire.

Dick obeyed, and the steaming glass of hot spirits was ready as the wheelwright bore in his load, and the young man was placed in a chair before the glowing kitchen fire.

"My arm!" he said faintly.

"You wrenched his arm, Hicky," said Dick, "when you dragged him out."

"Very sorry, Mester Dick."

"Ugh!" cried the lad, who had laid his hand tenderly on their visitor's shoulder.

"What is it?" cried Mrs Winthorpe.

"Blood. He has been hurt," said Dick.

"Shot! Here," said the young man in a whisper; and then his head sank down sidewise, and he fainted dead away.

Mr Marston's faintly-uttered words sent a thrill through all present, but no time was wasted. People who live in out-of-the-way places, far from medical help, learn to be self-reliant, and as soon as Squire Winthorpe realised what was wrong he gave orders for the injured man to be carried to the couch in the dining parlour, where his wet jacket was taken off by the simple process of ripping up the back seam.

"Now, mother, the scissors," said the squire, "and have some bandages ready. You, Dick, if it's too much for you, go away. If it isn't, stop. You may want to bind up a wound some day."

Dick felt a peculiar sensation of giddy sickness, but he tried to master it, and stood looking on as the shirt sleeve was cut open, and the young man's white arm laid bare to the shoulder, displaying an ugly wound in the fleshy part.

"Why, it's gone right through, mother," whispered the squire, shaking his head as he applied sponge and cold water to the bleeding wounds.

"And doctor says there's veins and artrys, mester," said Hickathrift, huskily. "One's bad and t'other's worse. Which is it, mester?"

"I hope and believe there is no artery touched," said the squire; "but we must run no risk. Hickathrift, my man, the doctor must be fetched. Go and send one of the men."

"Nay, squire, I'll go mysen," replied the big wheelwright. "Did'st see his goon, Mester Dick?"

"No, I saw no gun."

"Strange pity a man can't carry a gun like a Chrishtun," said the wheelwright, "and not go shutin hissen that way."

The wheelwright went off, and the squire busied himself binding up the wounds, padding and tightening, and proving beyond doubt that no artery had been touched, for the blood was soon nearly staunched, while, just as he was finishing, and Mrs Winthorpe was drawing the sleeve on one side so as to secure a bandage with some stitches, something rolled on to the floor, and Dick picked it up.

"What's that, Dick—money?"

"No, father; leaden bullet."

"Ha! that's it; nice thing to go through a man's arm," said the squire as he examined the roughly-cast ragged piece of lead. "We must look for his gun to-morrow. What did he expect to get with a bullet at a time like this? Eh? What were you trying to shoot, Marston?" said the squire, as he found that the young man's eyes were open and staring at him.

"I—trying to shoot!"

"Yes; of course you didn't mean to bring yourself down," said the squire, smiling; "but what in the world, man, were you trying to shoot with bullets out here?"

The young engineer did not reply, but looked round from one to the other, and gave Mrs Winthorpe a grateful smile.

"Do you recollect where you left your gun?" said Dick eagerly, for the thought of the rust and mischief that would result from a night in the bog troubled him.

"Left my gun!" he said.

"Never mind now, Mr Marston," said the squire kindly. "Your things are wet, and we'll get you to bed. It's a nasty wound, but it will soon get right again. I'm not a doctor, but I know the bone is not broken."

"I did not understand you at first," said the young engineer then. "You think I have been carrying a gun, and shot myself?"

"Yes, but never mind now," said Mrs Winthorpe, kindly. "I don't think you ought to talk."

"No," was the reply; "I will not say much; but I think Mr Winthorpe ought to know. Some one shot me as I was coming across the fen."

"What!" cried Dick.

"Shot you!" said the squire.

"Yes. It was quite dark, and I was carefully picking my way, when there was a puff of smoke from a bed of reeds, a loud report, and I seemed to feel a tremendous blow; and I remember no more till I came to, feeling sick and faint, and managed to crawl along till I saw the lights of the farm here, and cried for help."

"Great heavens!" cried the squire.

"Didn't you see any one?" cried Mrs Winthorpe.

"No, nothing but the smoke from the reeds. I feel rather faint now—if you will let me rest."

With the help of Dick and his father the young engineer was assisted to his bed, where he seemed to drop at once into a heavy sleep; and, satisfied that there was nothing to fear for some time, the squire returned to the parlour looking very serious, while Dick watched him intently to see what he would say.

"This is very dreadful, my dear," whispered Mrs Winthorpe at last. "Have we some strange robber in the fen?"

"Don't know," said the squire shortly. "Perhaps some one has a spite against him."

"How dreadful!" said Mrs Winthorpe.

"One of his men perhaps."

"Or a robber," cried Dick excitedly. "Why, father, we might get Dave and John Warren and Hicky and some more, and hunt him down."

"Robbers rob," said the squire laconically.

"Of course, my dear," said Mrs Winthorpe; "and it would be dreadful to think of. Why, we could never go to our beds in peace."

"But Mr Marston's watch and money are all right, my dear. Depend upon it he has offended one of the rough drain diggers, and it is an act of revenge."

"But the man ought to be punished."

"Of course, my dear, and we'll have the constables over from town, and he shall be found. It won't be very hard to do."

"Why not, father?"

"Because many of the men have no guns."

"But they might borrow, father?"

"The easier to find out then," said the squire. "Well, one must eat whether a man's shot or no. History does not say that everybody went without his supper because King Charles's head was cut off. Mother, draw the ale. Dick, tell Sarah to bring in those hot potatoes. I'm hungry, and I've got to sit up all night."

There proved to be no real need, for the squire's patient slept soundly, and there was nothing to disturb the silence at the Toft. But morning found the squire still watching, with Mrs Winthorpe busy with her needle in the dining parlour, and Dick lying down on the hearth-rug, and sleeping soundly by the glowing fire. For about four o'clock, after strenuously refusing to go to bed, he had thought he would lie down and rest for a bit, with the result that he was in an instant fast asleep, and breathing heavily.

By breakfast-time Farmer Tallington had heard the news, and was over with Tom, each ready to listen to the squire's and Dick's account; and before nine o'clock Dave and John Warren, who had come over to Hickathrift's, to find him from home, came on to the Toft to talk with Dick and Tom, and stare and gape.

"Why, theer heven't been such a thing happen since the big fight wi' the smugglers and the king's men," said Dave.

To which John Warren assented, and said it was "amaäzin'."

"And who do you think it weer?" said Dave, as he stood scratching his ear; and upon being told the squire's opinion, he shook his head, and said there was no knowing.

"It's a bad thing, Mester Dick, bringing straängers into a plaäce. Yow nivver know what characters they've got. Why, I do believe—it's a turruble thing to say—that some of they lads at work at big dree-ern hevven't got no characters at all."

"Here be Hickathrift a-coming wi' doctor," said John Warren.

And sure enough there was the doctor on his old cob coming along the fen road, with Hickathrift striding by his side, the man of powder and draught having been from home with a patient miles away when Hickathrift reached the town, and not returning till five o'clock.

"He'll do right enough, squire," said the doctor. "Young man like he is soon mends a hole in his flesh. You did quite right; but I suppose the bandaging was young Dick's doing, for of all the clumsy bungling I ever saw it was about the worst."

Dick gave his eye a peculiar twist in the direction of his father, who was giving him a droll look, and then they both laughed.

"Very delicately done, doctor," said the squire. "There, Dick, as he has put it on your shoulders you may as well bear it."

"Ah, let him!" said the doctor. "Now, what are you going to do?" he said aloud; "catch the scoundrel who shot Mr Marston, and get him transported for life?"

"That's what ought to be done to him," said John Warren solemnly, as he looked straight away over the fen.

"Ay," said Dave. "How do we know but what it may be our turn or Hickathrift's next? It's a straänge, bad thing."

"I must talk it over with Mr Marston," said the squire, "when he gets better, and then we shall see."

Chapter Twelve.

The Patient's Friends.

Mr Marston declared that he had not the most remote idea of having given any of his men offence, and then looked very serious about the question of bringing over the constables from the town to investigate the matter.

"It may have been an accident, Mr Winthorpe," he said; "and if so, I should be sorry to get any poor fellow into trouble."

"Yes, but it may not have been an accident," said the doctor.

This was in the evening, the doctor having ridden over again to see how his patient was getting on.

"Heaven forbid, sir," said Marston warmly, "that I should suspect any man of such a cowardly cruel deed! Impossible, sir! I cannot recall having done any man wrong since I have been here. My lads like me."

"How do you know that?" said the squire dryly. "Men somehow are not *very* fond of the master who is over them, and makes them fairly earn their wages."

"Well, sir, I don't know how to prove it," said Marston, who was lying on a dimity-covered couch, "but—"

"Hallo!" cried the squire, leaping up and going to the window, as a loud and excited buzzing arose, mingled with the trampling of feet, which sounded plainly in the clear cold spring evening.

"Anything wrong?" said the doctor.

"Why, here's a crowd of a hundred fellows armed with sticks!" cried the squire. "I believe they've got the rascal who fired the shot."

"No!" said the doctor.

"Father! Mr Marston!" cried Dick, rushing up stairs and into the visitor's bed-room; "here are all the drain-men—hundreds of them—Mr Marston's men."

"Not hundreds, young fellow," said Marston smiling, "only one, if they are all here. What do they want? Have they caught anyone?"

"No, sir. They want to see you. I told them you were too bad; but they say they will see you."

"I'll go and speak to them and see what they want," said the squire. "Is it anything about paying their wages?"

"Oh dear, no!" said Marston. "They have been paid as usual. Shall I go down to them, doctor?"

"If you do I'll throw up your case," cried the doctor fiercely. "Bless my soul, no! Do you think I want you in a state of high fever. Stop where you are, sir. Stop where you are."

"I'll go," said the squire, "before they pull the house down."

For the men were getting clamorous, and shouting loudly for Mr Marston.

The squire descended, and Dick with him, to find the front garden of the old farm-house full of great swarthy black-bearded fellows, everyone armed with a cudgel or a pick-axe handle, some having only the parts of broken shovels.

"Well, my lads, what is it?" said the squire, facing them.

A tremendous yell broke out, every man seeming to speak at once, and nothing could be understood.

"Hullo, Hickathrift! You're there, are you?" said the squire. "What do they want?"

"Well, you see, squire," began the wheelwright; but his voice was drowned by another furious yell.

"Don't all speak at once!" cried Dick, who had planted himself upon a rough block of stone that had been dug out of the ruins and placed in the front of the house.

There was something so droll to the great band of workmen in a mere stripling shouting to them in so commanding a way, that they all burst into a hearty laugh.

"Here, let Hicky speak!" cried Dick.

"Yes!—Ay!—Ah!—Let big Hickathrift speak!" was shouted out.

"Keep quiet, then," said the wheelwright, "or how can I! You see, squire," he continued, "the lads came along by my place, and they said some one had put it about that one of them had fired a shot at the young engyneer, and they're all popped about it, and want to see Mr Marston and tell him it isn't true."

"You can't see Mr Marston, my lads," said the squire.

Here there was a fierce yell.

"The doctor says it would do him harm," continued the squire, "and you don't want to do that."

"Nay, nay, we wean't do that," shouted one of the men.

"But I may tell you that Mr Marston says that he does not believe there's a man among you who would do him any harm."

"Hooray!" shouted one of the men, and this was followed by a roar. "We wouldn't hurt the ganger, and we're going to pay out him as did."

There was a tremendous yell at this, and the men nourished their weapons in a way that looked serious for the culprit if he should be discovered.

"Ay, but yow've got to find out first who it was," said Hickathrift.

"Yes, and we're going to find out too," cried one rough-looking fellow standing forward. "How do we know as it warn't you?"

"Me!" cried Hickathrift, staring blankly.

"Ay, yow," roared the great rough-looking fellow, a man not far short of the wheelwright's size. "We've heered all on you a going on and pecking about the dree-ern being made. We know yow all hates our being here, so how do we know it warn't yow?"

The man's fierce address was received with an angry outburst by the men, who had come out on purpose to inflict punishment upon some one, and in their excitement, one object failing, they were ready to snatch at another.

It was perhaps an insensate trick; but there was so much of the frank manly British boy in Dick Winthorpe that he forgot everything in the fact that big Hickathrift, the man he had known from a child—the great bluff fellow who had carried him in his arms and hundreds of times made him welcome in that wonderland, his workshop, where he was always ready to leave off lucrative work to fashion him eel-spear or leaping-pole, or to satisfy any other whim that was on the surface—that this old friend was being menaced by a great savage of a stranger nearly as big as himself, and backed by a roaring excited crowd who seemed ready for any outrage.

Dick did not hesitate a moment, but with eyes flashing, teeth clenched, and fists doubled, he leaped down from the stone, rushed into the midst of the crowd, closing round the wheelwright, and darting between the great fellow and the man who had raised a pick-handle to strike, seized hold of the stout piece of ash and tried to drag it away.

"You great coward!" he roared—"a hundred to one!"

It was as if the whole gang had been turned to stone, their self-constituted leader being the most rigid of the crowd, and he stared at Dick Winthorpe as a giant might stare at the pigmy who tried to snatch his weapon away.

But the silence and inert state lasted only a few seconds, before the black-bearded fellow's angry face began to pucker up, his eyes half closed, and, bending down, he burst into a hearty roar of laughter.

"See this, lads!" he cried. "See this! Don't hurt me, mester! Say, lads, I never felt so scared in my life."

The leader's laugh was contagious, and the crowd took it up in chorus; but the more they laughed, the more angry grew Dick. He could not see the ridiculous side of the matter; for, small as was his body in comparison with that of the man he had assailed, his spirit had swollen out as big as that of anyone present.

"I don't care," he cried; "I'll say it again—You're a set of great cowards; and as for you," he cried to the fellow whose weapon he had tried to wrest away, "you're the biggest of the lot."

"Well done, young un—so he is!" cried the nearest man. "Hooray for young ganger!"

The men were ready to fight or cheer, and as ready to change their mood as crowds always are. They answered the call with a stentorian roar; and if Dick Winthorpe had imitated Richard the Second just then, and called upon the crowd to accept him as their leader, they would have followed him to the attempt of any mad prank he could have designed.

"Thank ye, Mester Dick!" said Hickathrift, placing his great hand upon the lad's shoulder, as the squire forced his way to their side. "I always knowed we was mates; but we're bigger mates now than ever we was before."

"Ay, and so 'm I," said the big drain delver. "Shake hands, young un. You're English, you are. So 'm I. He's English, lads; that's what he is!" he roared as he seized Dick's hand and pumped it up and down. "So 'm I."

"Hooray!" shouted the crowd; and, seeing how the mood of all was changed, the squire refrained from speaking till the cheering was dying out, when, making signs to the men to hear him, he was about to utter a few words of a peacemaking character, but there was another burst of cheering, which was taken up again and again, the men waving their caps and flourishing their cudgels, and pressing nearer to the house.

For the moment Dick was puzzled, but he realised what it all meant directly, for, looking in the same direction as the men, it was to see that the young engineer had disregarded the doctor's orders, and was standing at the open window, with his face very pale and his arm in a sling.

He waved his uninjured arm to command silence, and this being obtained, his voice rang out firm and clear.

"My lads," he cried, "I know why you've come, and I thank you; but these people here are my very good friends, and as for the squire's son and the wheelwright there, they saved my life last night."

"Hooray!" roared the leader of the gang frantically; and as his companions cheered, he caught hold of Hickathrift's hand, and shook it as earnestly as if they were sworn brothers.

"As to my wound," continued the engineer, "I believe it was an accident; so now I ask you to go back home quietly, and good-night!"

"Well said, sir; good-night to you!" roared the leader as the window was closed. "Good-night to everybody! Come on, lads! Good-night, young un! We're good mates, eh?"

"Yes," said Dick, shortly.

"Then shake hands again. We don't bear no malice, do us? See, lads. We're mates. I wean't laugh at you. You're a good un, that's what you are, and you'll grow into a man."

The great fellow gave Dick's hand another shake that was very vigorous, but by no means pleasant; and then, after three roaring cheers, the whole party went off, striking up a chorus that went rolling over the fen and kept on dying out and rising again as the great sturdy fellows tramped away.

"I'm not an inhospitable man, doctor," said the squire, as the former shook hands to go, after giving orders for his patient to be kept quiet, and assuring the squire that the young fellow would be none the worse for the adventures of the night—"I'm not an inhospitable man, but one has to think twice before asking a hundred such to have a mug of ale. I should have liked to do it, and it was on my lips, but the barrel would have said no, I'm sure. Good-night!"

"Now, sir," said the squire as soon as he was alone with his son, "what have you got to say for yourself?"

"Say, father!" replied Dick, staring.

"Yes, sir. Don't you think you did about as mad and absurd a thing as the man who put his head into the lion's jaws?"

"I—I didn't know, father," replied Dick, who, after the exultation caused by the cheering, felt quite crestfallen.

"No, of course you did not, but it was a very reckless thing to do, and—er—don't—well, I hope you will never have cause to do it again."

Dick went away, feeling as if his comb had been cut, and of course he did not hear his father's words that night when he went to bed.

"Really, mother, I don't know whether I felt proud of the boy or vexed when he faced that great human ox."

"I do," said Mrs Winthorpe smiling, but with the tears in her eyes—"proud."

"Yes, I think I did," said the squire. "Good-night!"

"Don't you think some one ought to sit up with Mr Marston?"

"No: he is sleeping like a top; and after our bad time with him yesternight, I mean to have some sleep."

Five minutes after, the squire's nose proclaimed that it was the hour of rest, and Dick heard it as he stole from his bed-room, to see how the wounded man was; and this act he repeated at about hourly intervals all through the night, for he could not sleep soundly, his mind was so busy with trouble about the injury to their visitor's arm, and the wonder which kept working in his brain. Who was it fired that shot?

The doctor was right; the wounded man's arm soon began to mend; but naturally there was a period when he was unable to attend to his duties, and that period was a pleasant one for Dick Winthorpe, inasmuch as it was the commencement of a long friendship.

John Marston was for going back to his lodgings near the outfall or *gowt* as it was termed; but the squire and Mrs Winthorpe would not hear of it, and to the boys' great delight, he stayed.

He was an invalid, but the right kind of invalid to make a pleasant companion, for he loved the open air, and was never happier than when he was out with the boys and Dave or John Warren, somewhere in the fen.

"It's all gammon to call him ill, and for the doctor to keep coming," said Tom Tallington.

"Oh, he is ill!" said Dick; "but you see he's only ill in one arm."

Dick had only to propose a run out, and John Marston immediately seemed to forget that he was a man, became a boy for the time being, and entered into the spirit of their pursuits.

One day it was pike-fishing, with Dave to punt them about here and there among the pools. At another time ordinary tackle would be rigged up, and Dave would take them to some dark hole where fish were known to swarm, and for hours the decoy-man would sit and watch patiently while the three companions pulled up the various denizens of the mere.

One bright April morning Dave was seen coming out of the mist, looking gigantic as he stood up in his boat; and his visit was hailed with delight, for the trio had been wondering how they should pass that day.

"Morning, Dave!" said Marston as the fen-man landed slowly from his boat, and handed Dick a basket of fresh ducks' eggs.

"Morn', mester! Tak them up to the missus, Mester Dick. They be all noo-laid uns. Straänge thick haar this morn," he continued, wiping the condensed mist from his eyelashes. "Re'glar sea-haar." (sea-fog—mist from the German Ocean.)

"Take those eggs up to mother, Tom," said Dick imperatively.

"Sha'n't. I know! You want to be off without me."

"Hallo, young fellow!" said the squire cheerily. "What have you got there—eggs?"

"Yes, mester, fresh uns for the missus."

"I'm going in, and I'll take them," said the squire, thus disposing of the difficulty about a messenger. "There's a canister of powder for you, Dave, when you want some more."

"Thanky kindly, mester. I'll come and get it when I'm up at house."

The squire nodded and went on, but turned back to ask when Mr Marston was going over to the works, and upon hearing that it was in the afternoon, he said he would accompany him.

"And how's your lame arm, mester?" said Dave as soon as the squire had gone.

"Getting better fast, Dave, my man."

63

"And with two holes in it, mester?"

"Yes, with two holes in it."

"But are they both getting better?"

"Why, you've been told a dozen times over that they are!" cried Dick.

"Nay, Mester Dick, I know'd as one hole was getting reight, but Mester Marston here nivver said as both weer. I'm straänge and glad. Heered aught yet 'bout him as did it?"

"No, my man, and don't want to."

"Hark at that, Mester Dick! Why, if any one had shot at me, and hot me as they did him, I'd have found him out somehow afore now. Mebbe I shall find this out mysen."

"Why, you're not trying, Dave."

"Not trying, lad! Nay, but I am, and I shall find him yet some day. Look here, boys. If you want to find out anything like that, you mustn't go splashing about among the reeds, or tug-slugging through the bog-holes, or he hears you coming, and goos and hides. You must sit down among the bushes, and wait and wait quiet, like a man does when he wants to get the ducks, and by-and-by him as did it comes along. Dessay I shall catch him one of these days, and if I do, and I've got my pole with me, I'll throost him under water and half-drownd him."

"Never mind about all that, Dave. What are you going to do to-day?" cried Dick.

"Me, lad! Oh, nowt! I've brote a few eggs for the missus, and I shall tak' that can o' powder back wi' me, and then set down and go on makkin soom new coy-nets."

"That's his gammon, Mr Marston," cried Dick.

"Nay, nay, mester, it's solemn truth."

"'Tisn't; it's gammon. Isn't it, Tom?"

"Every bit of it. He's come on purpose to ask us to go out with him."

"Nay, nay, nay, lads," said Dave in an ill-used tone. "I did think o' asking if Mester Marston here would like to try for some eels up in the long shallows by Popley Watter, for they be theer as thick as herrin', bubblin' up and slithering in the mud."

"Let's go, then, Mr Marston. Eel-spearing," cried Dick.

"But I could not use an eel-spear," said the young engineer, smiling.

"But Tom and I could do the spearing, and you could put the eels in the basket."

"When you caught them," said Marston, laughing.

"Oh, we should be sure to catch some! Shouldn't we, Dave?"

"Ay, theer's plenty of 'em, mester."

"Let's go, then," cried Dick excitedly; "and if we get a whole lot, we'll take them over to your men, Mr Marston. Come on!"

"Nay, but yow weant," said Dave, with a dry chuckle.

"Why not?"

"Mester Hickathrift has got the stong-gad to mend. One of the tines is off, and it wants a noo ash pole."

"Here, stop a moment," said Marston, laughingly interrupting a groan of disgust uttered by the boys; "what, pray, is a stong-gad?"

"Ha—ha—ha!" laughed Tom. "Don't know what a stong-gad is!"

"Hold your tongue, stupid!" cried Dick indignantly, taking the part of his father's guest. "You don't know everything. What's a dumpy leveller? There, you don't know, and Mr Marston does."

"But what is a stong-gad?" said Marston.

"Eel-spear," said Dick. "How long would it take Hicky to mend it?"

"'Bout two hours—mebbe only one. I could mak' a new pole while he forged the tine."

"Come along, then. Hicky will leave anything to do it for me."

"Nay, he's gone to market," said Dave.

"Yes; I saw him pass our house," said Tom.

"What a shame!" cried Dick. "Here, I say, what's that basket for in the punt?" he added eagerly.

"Why, he's got a net, too, and some poles," cried Tom. "Yah! he meant to do something."

"Why, of course he did," cried Dick, running down to the boat. "Now, then, Dave, what's it to be?"

"Oh, nowt, Mester Dick! I thought to put a net in, and a pole or two, and ask if you'd care to go and get a few fish, but Mester Marston's too fine a gentleman to care for ought o' the sort."

"Oh, no, I'm not!" said Marston. "I should enjoy it, boys, above all things."

"There, Dave, now then! What is it—a drag-net?"

"Nay, Mester Dick, on'y a bit of a new."

"But where are you going?"

"I thowt o' the strip 'tween Long Patch and Bootherboomp's Roostens."

"Here, stop a moment," cried the engineer. "I've heard that name before. Who was Mr Bootherboomp?"

"Hi—hi—hi! hecker—hecker—hecker. Heigh!"

That does not express the sounds uttered by Dave, for they were more like an accident in a wooden clock, when the wheels run down and finish with a jerk which breaks the cogs. But that was Dave's way of laughing, and it ended with a horrible distortion of his features.

"I say: don't, Dave. What an old nut-cracker you are! You laugh like the old watchman's rattle in the garret. Be quiet, Tom!"

"But Mr Bootherboomp!" roared Tom, bursting into a second fit of laughter.

"It's butterbump, Mr Marston. It's what they call those tall brown birds something like herons. What do you call them in London?" said Dick.

"Oh, bitterns!"

"Yes, that's it. Come on!"

"Nay," said Dave; "I don't think you gentlemen would care for such poor sport. On'y a few fish'."

"You never mind about that! Jump in, Mr Marston. Who's going to pole?"

"Nay, I'll pole," said Dave. "If yow mean to go we may as well get theer i' good time; but I don't think it's worth the trouble."

"Get out! It's rare good fun, Mr Marston; sometimes we get lots of fish."

"I'm all expectation," said Marston as Dave smiled the tight smile, which made his mouth look like a healed-up cut; and, taking the pole, began to send the punt over the clear dark water. "Shall we find any of those curious fish my men caught in the river the other day?"

"What curious fish were they?" asked Dick.

"Well, to me they seemed as if so many young eels had grown ashamed of being so long and thin, and they had been feeding themselves up and squeezing themselves short, so as to look as like tench as possible."

"Oh, I know what you mean!" cried Tom. "Eel-pouts! they're just about half-way between eels and tench."

"Nay, yow wean't catch them here," said Dave oracularly. "They lives in muddy watter in rivers. Our watter here's clean and clear."

It was a bright pleasant journey over the mere, in and out of the lanes of water to pool after pool, till Dave suddenly halted at a canal-like spot, where the water ran in between two great beds of tender-growing reeds, which waved and undulated in the soft breeze. Here he thrust down his pole and steadied the punt, while he shook out his light net with its even meshes, securing one end to a pole and then letting the leaden sinkers carry it to the bottom before thrusting the punt over to the other side of the natural canal, to which he made fast the second end of the net in a similar way, so that the water was sealed with a light fence of network, whose lower edge was close to the black ooze of the bottom, held there by the leaden sinkers of the foot line, the top line being kept to the surface by a series of tightly-bound little bundles of dry rushes.

"Theer," said Dave as soon as he had done, his proceedings having been carefully watched; "that un do!"

"Will the fish go into that net?" said Marston.

"Nay, not unless we mak 'em, mester," said Dave, smiling. "Will they, Mester Dick?"

"Not they," cried Dick. "Wait a minute, Mr Marston; you'll see."

Dave took his pole and, leaving the net behind, coasted along by the shore of the little island formed by the canal or strait, which ran in, zigzagging about like a vein in a piece of marble; and after about a quarter of an hour's hard work he forced the punt round to the other side of the island, and abreast of a similar opening to that which they had left, in fact the other end of the natural canal or lane, here about twelve or fourteen feet broad.

"Oh, I see!" said the engineer. "You mean to go in here, and drive the fish to the net at the other end."

"That's the way, Mr Marston," said Tom Tallington. "Wait a bit, and you'll see such a haul."

"Perhaps of an empty net, Mr Marston," said Dick with a grin. "Perhaps there are none here."

"You set astarn, mester," said Dave. "I'll put her along, and you tak' one side, Mester Dick; and you t'other, young Tom Tallington."

The boys had already taken up two long light poles that lay in the boat, and standing up as Dave sent the boat along slowly and making a great deal of disturbance with his pole, they beat and splashed and stabbed the water on both sides of the boat, so as to scare any fish which might happen to be there, and send them flying along the lane toward the net.

This was a comparatively easy task, for the coming of the boat was sufficient as a rule to startle the timid fish, which in turn scared those in front, the beating with the poles at either side sending forward any which might be disposed to slip back.

There was more labour than excitement in the task; but the course along the lane of water was not entirely uneventful, for a moor-hen was startled from her nest in a half-liquid patch of bog, above which rose quite a tuft of coarse herbage; and farther on, just as Dick thrust in his pole to give it a good wriggle and splash, there was a tremendous swirl, and a huge pike literally shot out of the water, describing an arc, and after rising fully four feet from the surface dropped head-first among the tangled water-weeds and reedy growth, through which it could be seen to wriggle and force its way farther and farther, the waving reeds and bubbling water between showing the direction in which it had gone.

"Hooray, Dave! a forty-pounder!" cried Dick. "Push the punt in and we can easily catch him."

"Not you," said Dave stolidly; "he'll get through that faster than we could."

"But, look, look! I can see where he is."

"Nay, he'll go all through theer and get deeper and deeper, and it's more wattery farther on. He'll go right through theer, and come out the other side."

"But he was such a big one, Dave—wasn't he, Mr Marston?—quite forty pounds!"

"Nay, not half, lad," said Dave stolidly, as he thrust the boat on. "Beat away. We'll come and set a bait for him some day. That's the way to catch him."

Dick uttered an angry ejaculation as he looked back towards where he could still see the water plants waving; and in his vexation he raised his pole, and went on with the splashing so vigorously, and, as legal folks say, with so much *malice prepense*, that he sent the water flying over Dave as he stood up in the bows of the punt.

Tom chuckled and followed suit, sending another shower over the puntsman. Then Dick began again, the amber water flying and sparkling in the sunshine; but Dave took no notice till the splashing became too pronounced, when he stopped short, gave his head a shake, and turned slowly round.

"Want to turn back and give up?" he said slowly.

Dick knew the man too well to continue, and in penitent tones exclaimed:

"No, no, go on, Dave, we won't splash any more."

"Because if there's any more of it—"

"I won't splash any more, Dave," cried Dick, laughing, "It was Tom."

"Oh, what a shame!"

"So you did splash. Didn't he, Mr Marston?"

"I don't want to hear no more about it, Mester Dick. I know," growled Dave. "I only says, Is it to be fishing or games?"

"Fishing, Dave. It's all right; go on, Tom; splash away gently."

"Because if—"

"No, no, go on, Dave. There, we won't send any more over you."

Dave uttered a grunt, and forced the boat along once more, while Marston sat in the stern an amused spectator of the boys' antics.

Everything now went on orderly enough, till they had proceeded a long way on, in and out, for a quarter of a mile, when at a word from Dave the splashing and stabbing of the water grew more vigorous, the punt being now pretty close to the net, the irregular row of bundles of rushes showing plainly.

And now Dave executed a fresh evolution, changing the position of the punt, for instead of its approaching end on, he turned it abreast, so that it pretty well touched the reedy sides of the canal, and with the poles now being plied on one side, the boat was made to approach more slowly.

"Now, mester, you'd better stand up," said Dave.

"Yes, Mr Marston, stand up," cried Dick. "Look!"

Marston rose to his feet, and as he looked toward the entrance where the net was spread there was a wave-like swell upon the surface, which might have been caused by the movement of the boat or by fish.

There was no doubt about its being caused by fish, for all at once, close by the row of rush bundles, there was a splash. Then, as they approached, another and another.

"They're feeling the net," cried Dick excitedly.

"Ay, keep it oop, lads, or they'll come back," cried Dave, making the water swirl with his pole, which he worked about vigorously.

Even as he spoke there came another splash, and this time the sun flashed upon the glittering sides of the fish which darted out and fell over the other side of the top line of the net.

"There goes one," shouted Tom.

"Ay, and theer goes another," said Dave with a chuckle as he forced the boat along slowly.

And now, as Marston watched, he saw that the irregular line of rush bundles which stretched across the mouth of the canal was changing its shape, and he needed no telling that the regular semicircular form it assumed was caused by the pressure of a shoal of fish seeking to escape into the open mere, but of course checked by the fragile wall of net.

"There must be a lot, Tom," cried Dick excitedly. "Look, Mr Marston! There goes another. Oh, Dave, we shall lose them all!"

This was consequent upon another good-sized fish flying out of the water, falling heavily upon one of the rush floats, and then darting away.

"Nay, we sha'n't lose 'em all," said Dave coolly. "Some on 'em's safe to go. Now, then, splash away. Reach over your end, young Tom Tallington, or some on 'em 'll go round that way."

Tom changed his place a little, to stand now on what had been the front of their advance, and thrusting in his pole he splashed and beat the narrow space between him and the dense boggy side, where the sphagnum came down into the water.

Dick followed suit at the other end, and Dave swept his pole sidewise as if he were mowing weeds below the surface.

"Oh!" cried Dick, as he overbalanced himself, and nearly went in from the stern. He would have gone headlong had not Mr Marston made a bound, and caught him as he vainly strove to recover his balance.

The effort was well timed, and saved him, but of course the consequences of jumping about in a boat are well-known. The punt gave such a lurch that Dave almost went out, while, as for Tom, he was literally jerked up as from a spring-board, and, dropping his pole, he seemed to be taking a voluntary dive, describing a semicircle, and going down head-first, not into the narrow slit between him and the boggy shore, but right into the semi-fluid mass of sphagnum, water, and ooze, where he disappeared to his knees.

Tom's dive sent the boat, as he impelled it with his feet, a couple of yards away; and for a moment or two those who were in it seemed half paralysed, till a roar of laughter from Dick, who did not realise the danger, roused Dave to action.

For the dense mass, while fluid enough to allow Tom to dive in, was not sufficiently loose to let him rise; and there he stuck, head downwards, and with his legs kicking furiously.

"Now if we was to leave him," said Dave sententiously, "he wouldn't never be no more trouble to his father; but I suppose we must pull him out."

"Pull him out, man? Quick, use your pole!"

"Ay, I'm going to, mester," said Dave coolly. "Theer we are," he continued, as he sent the end of the punt back to where poor Tom's legs went on performing a series of kicks which were sometimes like those made by a swimming frog, and at others as if he were trying to walk upside down along an imaginary flight of aerial stairs.

The time seemed long, but probably it was not half a minute from the time Tom dived into the bog till the young engineer seized him by the legs and dragged him into the boat, to sit upon the bottom, gasping, spitting, and rubbing the ooze from his eyes. But it was a good two minutes before he was sufficiently recovered to look round angrily, and in a highly-pitched quavering voice exclaimed:

"Look here: who was it did that?"

"Nobody," roared Dick. "Oh, I say, Tom, what a game! Are your feet wet?"

Tom turned upon him savagely, but everyone in the boat was laughing, and his countenance relaxed, and he rose up and leaned over the side of the boat to wash his face, which a splash or two relieved from the pieces of bog and dead vegetation which adhered.

"I don't mind," he said. "Only you wouldn't have found it a game if you'd been there."

"Let's get back quickly," said Mr Marston, "or the boy will catch cold."

"Oh, it won't hurt me!" cried Tom. "Let's catch the fish first. They never get cold."

"Yes: let's haul the net out first," said Dick. "Tom won't mind a ducking."

"Ay, we're going to hev out the net," said Dave. "Splash away, my lad. That'll keep away the cold."

Poor Tom's feet had not been wet, but as he stood up with the water trickling from him, a couple of streams soon made their way down the legs of his trousers into his boots. This was, however, soon forgotten in the excitement of the hauling.

For, after a fresh amount of splashing, though Dave declared the fish had all come back, the punt was run pretty close up to one side, the lines and pole taken on board, and the punt thrust toward the other side.

Before they reached it the bobbing of the rush floats and the semicircular shape of the top line showed plainly enough that there were a good many fish there; and when Dave had secured the lines at the other end, removed the poles, and by ingenious manipulation drawn on the bottom line so as to raise the cord, it was not long before the net began to assume the shape of a huge bag, and one that was pretty heavy.

Every now and then a swirl in the water and a splash showed where some large fish was trying to escape, while sometimes one did leap out and get away. Then the surface would be necked with silvery arrows as swarms of small-fry appeared flashing into sight and disappearing, these little bits of excitement growing less frequent as the small fish found their way over the top of the net, or discovered that the meshes were wide enough to allow them to pass through.

"How is it, Dave, that all the little fish like to keep to the top of the water, and the big ones out of sight down at the bottom?" said Dick.

Dave chuckled, or rather made a noise something like a bray.

"S'pose you was a fish, young mester, wouldn't you, if you was a little one, keep nigh the top if you found going down to the bottom among the big uns meant being swallowed up?"

"Oh, of course!" cried Dick. "I forgot that they eat one another. Look, Mr Marston, that was a pike."

He pointed excitedly to a large fish which rose to the surface, just showing its dark olive-green back as it curved over and disappeared again, making the water eddy.

"They do not seem to have all gone, Dave," said Mr Marston.

"Nay, theer's a few on 'em left, mester," replied Dave. "Now, my lads, all together. That's the way."

The lines were drawn, and the weight of the great bag of meshes proved that after all a good fair haul had been made, the net being drawn close to the boat and the bag seeming to shrink in size till there was a mass of struggling, splashing fish alongside, apparently enough to far more than fill a bushel basket.

"What are you going to do?" asked Mr Marston, who was as excited now as the boys, while Dave worked away stolidly, as if it was all one of the most commonplace matters for him.

"Haul the net into the boat," cried Tom.

"Nay, my net would break," said Dave. "There's a lot of owd rushes and roots, and rotten weeds in it."

"I don't believe there are, Dave," said Dick. "It's all solid fish."

"Nay, lad, but net'll break. Let's hev out some of the big uns first."

"Look! there's a fine one," cried Dick, making a dash at a large fish which rose out of the writhing mass, but it glided through his hands.

"Howd hard!" said Dave. "You lads go th'other side o' the punt or we shall capsize. Let me and the London gentleman get them in."

"Oh!" groaned Tom.

"No, I've only one hand to work with," said Marston, who saw the reasonableness of the old fen-man's remark, for the side of the boat had gone down very low once or twice, and the effect of dragging a portion of the laden net on board might have been sufficient to admit the water. "I'll give way, and act as ballast."

"No, no!" cried Dick. "You help, Mr Marston."

But the young engineer remained steadfast to his proposal, and seated himself on the other side.

"Better let me lade out a few o' the big uns, Mester Dick," said Dave, "while you lads hold on."

The boys hardly approved of the proposal, but they gave way; and each taking a good grip of the wet net, they separated toward the head and stern, while Dave stayed in the middle, and taking off his jacket, rolled up his sleeves close to the shoulder, and then plunging his arms in among the swarm of fish he brought out a good-sized pike of six or seven pounds.

This was thrown into the basket, to flap furiously and nearly leap out, renewing its efforts as another of its kind was thrown in to keep it company.

"Is there a very big one, Dave?" cried Dick.

"Nay; nought very big," was the reply. "Draw her up, my lads. That's reight."

As Dave spoke he kept on plunging his hands into the splashing and struggling mass of fish, and sometimes brought out one, sometimes missed. But he kept on vigorously till, feeling satisfied that the net would bear the rest, he drew the loaded line well over into the boat, and, giving the boys a hint to tighten the line, he plunged in his arms once more, got well hold, and the next minute, by a dexterous lift, raised the bag, so that its contents came pouring over the edge of the punt in a silvery, glittering cataract of fish, leaping, gliding, and flapping all over the bottom about his feet.

Then a few fish, which were hanging by their gills, their heads being thrust through the meshes, were shaken out, the net bundled up together and thrown into the fore part of the boat, and the little party came together to gloat over their capture.

"Theer, lads," said Dave, coolly resuming his jacket, "you can pitch 'em all into the baskets, all the sizable ones, and put all the little ones back into the watter. I'll throost the punt back, so as young Tom Tallington can get some dry clothes."

These latter were the last things in Tom's mind, for just then, as Dave resumed the pole, and began sending the boat quickly through the water, the boy was trying to grasp an eel, which had found the meshes one size too small for his well-fed body, and was now in regular serpentine fashion trying to discover a retreat into which he could plunge, and so escape the inevitable frying-pan or pot.

Irrespective of the fact that a large eel can bite sharply, it is, as everyone knows, one of the most awkward things to hold, for the moment a good grip of its slimy body is made, the result seems to be that it helps the elongated fish to go forward or slip back. And this Tom found as he grasped the eel again and again, only for it to make a few muscular contortions and escape.

Then Dick tried, with no better effect, the pursuit lasting till the active fish made its way in among the meshes of the net, when its capture became easy, and it was swept into the great basket, to set the pike flapping and leaping once more.

Then the sorting commenced, all the small fish being thrown back to increase in size, while the rest of the slimy captives went into the basket.

There was no larger pike than the one first taken out of the net by Dave, but plenty of small ones, all extremely dark in colour, as if affected by living in the amber-tinted water, and nearly all these were thrown back, in company with dozens of silvery roach and orange-finned, brightly gilded rudd, all thicker and broader than their relatives the roach.

Many scores of fish were thrown overboard, some to turn up and float for a few minutes before they recovered their breath, as Tom called it, but for the most part they dived down at once, uninjured by what they had gone through, while their largeness fortunate friends were tossed into the basket—gilded side-striped perch, with now and then a fat-looking, small-eyed, small-scaled tench, brightly brazen at the sides, and looking as if cast in a soft kind of bronze. Then there were a couple of large-scaled brilliantly golden carp; but the majority of the fish were good-sized, broad, dingy-looking bream, whose slimy emanations made the bottom of the punt literally ask for a cleansing when the basket was nearly filled.

By that time the party were well on their way to the Toft, and as they neared the shore, it was to find the squire waiting to speak to the engineer, while John Warren was close behind with his dog, ready to join Dave, in whose company he went off after the latter had been up to the house and had a good feast of bread and cheese and ale.

That evening the squire and Mr Marston went over to the works to see how matters were progressing, to find all satisfactory, and the night passed quietly enough; but at breakfast the next morning, when some of the best of the tench appeared fried in butter, a messenger came over to see the engineer on his way to the town for the doctor, to announce that Hez Bargle, the big delver, who had been leader of the party who came over so fiercely about the attack upon Mr Marston, had been found that morning lying in the rough hovel where he slept alone, nearly dead.

The man was sharply examined by the engineer, a fresh messenger in the shape of Hickathrift being found to carry on the demand for the doctor. But there was very little to learn. Bargle had not come up to his work, and the foreman of the next gang went to see why his fellow-ganger had not joined him, and found him lying on the floor of the peat-built hut quite insensible, with the marks of savage blows about the head, as if he had been suddenly attacked and beaten with a club, for there was no sign of any struggle.

Mr Marston went over at once with the squire, Dick obtaining permission to accompany them; and upon their arrival it was to find all the work at a stand-still, the men being grouped about with their sleeves rolled-up, and smoking, and staring silently at the rough peat hovel where their fellow-worker lay.

The engineer entered the shelter—it did not deserve the title of cottage—and the squire and Dick followed, to find the man nearly insensible, and quite unable to give any account of how the affair had happened.

The men were questioned, but knew nothing beyond the fact that they had parted from him as usual to go to their own quarters, Bargle being the only one who lodged alone. There had been no quarrel as far as Mr Marston could make out, everyone he spoke to declaring that the work had gone on the previous day in the smoothest way possible; and at last there seemed to be nothing to do but wait until the great, rough fellow could give an account of the case for himself.

The doctor came at last, and formed his opinion.

"He is such a great, strong fellow that unless he was attacked by two or three together, I should say someone came upon him as he lay asleep and stunned him with a blow on the head."

"The result of some quarrel or offence given to one of the men under him, I'm afraid," said the engineer with a look of intense vexation in his eyes. "These men are very brutal sometimes to their fellows, especially when they are placed in authority. Will he be long before he is better?"

"No," replied the doctor. "The blows would have killed an ordinary man, but he has a skull like an ox. He'll be at work again in a fortnight if he'll behave sensibly, and carry out my instructions."

A couple of days later Bargle was sitting up smoking, when the engineer entered the reed-thatched hut, in company with Dick.

"Hallo, youngster!" growled the great fellow, with a smile slowly spreading over his rugged face, and growing into a grin, which accorded ill with his bandaged head; "shak' hands!"

Dick obeyed heartily enough, the great fellow retaining the lad's hand in his, and slowly pumping it up and down.

"We're mates, that's what we two are," he growled. "You ar'n't half a bad un, you ar'n't. Ah, mester, how are you? Arm better?"

"Mending fast, my lad; and how are you?"

"Tidy, mester, tidy! Going to handle a spade again to-morrow."

"Nonsense, man! you're too weak yet."

"Weak! Who says so? I don't, and the doctor had better not."

"Never mind that. I want you to tell me how all this happened."

"He ar'n't half a bad un, mester," said the injured man, ignoring the remark, as he held on to the boy's hand. "We're mates, that's what we are. See him stand up again me that day? It were fine."

"Yes; but you must tell me how this occurred. I want to take some steps about it."

"Hey! and you needn't take no steps again it, mester. I shall lay hold on him some day, and when I do—Hah!"

He stretched out a huge fist in a menacing way that promised ill to his assailant.

"But do you know who it was?" said the engineer.

"It warn't him," growled Bargle, smiling at Dick. "He wouldn't come and hit a man when he's asleep. Would you, mate?"

"I wouldn't be such a coward," cried Dick.

"Theer! Hear that, mester! I knowed he wouldn't. He'd hev come up to me and hit me a doubler right in the chest fair and square, and said, 'now, then, come on!'"

"Then someone did strike you when you were asleep, Bargle, eh?"

"Dunno, mester; I s'pose so. Looks like it, don't it?"

"Yes, my man, very much so. Then you were woke out of your sleep by a blow, eh?"

"Weer I? I don't know."

"Tell me who have you had a quarrel with lately?"

"Quarrel?"

"Well, row, then."

"Wi' him," said the big fellow, pointing at Dick.

"Oh, but he would not have come to you in the night!"

"Who said he would, mester?" growled Bargle menacingly. "Not he. He'd come up square and give a man a doubler in the chest and—"

"Yes, yes," said the engineer impatiently; "but I want to know who it was made this attack upon you—this cowardly attack. You say it was while you slept."

"Yes, I s'pose so; but don't you trouble about that, mester. I'm big enough to fight my bit. I shall drop on to him one of these days, and when I do—why, he'll find it okkard."

Mr Marston questioned and cross-questioned the man, but there was no more to be got from him. He s'posed some un come in at that theer door and give it him; but he was so much taken up with Dick's visit that he could hardly think of self, and when they came away Mr Marston had learned comparatively nothing, the big fellow shouting after Dick:

"I've got a tush for you, lad, when I get down to the dreern again—one I digged out, and you shall hev it."

Dick said, "Thank you," for the promised "tush," and walked away.

"I don't like it," said Mr Marston. "Someone shooting at me; someone striking down this man. I'm afraid it's due to ill-will towards me, Dick. But," he added, laughing, "I will not suspect you, as Bargle lets you off."

Chapter Thirteen.

The Shakes.

The time glided on. Bargle grew better; Mr Marston's wound healed; and these troubles were forgotten in the busy season which the fine weather brought. For the great drain progressed rapidly in the bright spring and early summer-time. There were stoppages when heavy rains fell; but on the whole nature seemed to be of opinion that the fen had lain uncultivated for long enough, and that it was time there was a change.

The old people scattered here and there about the edge shook their heads, especially when they came over to Hickathrift's, and said it would all be swept away one of these fine nights—*it* being the new river stretching week by week farther into the morass; but the flood did not seem to have that effect when it did come. On the contrary, short as was the distance which the great drain had penetrated, its effect was wonderful, for it carried off water in a few days which would otherwise have stayed for weeks.

Dick said it was a good job that Mr Marston had been shot.

Asked why by his crony Tom, he replied that it had made them such good friends, and it was nice to have a chap who knew such a lot over at the Toft.

For the intimacy had grown; and whenever work was done, reports written out and sent off, and no duties raised their little reproving heads to say, "You are neglecting us!" the engineer made his way to the Toft, ready to join the two boys on some expedition—egg-collecting, fishing, fowling, or hunting for some of the botanical treasures of the bog.

"I wish he wouldn't be so fond of moss and weeds!" said Tom. "It seems so stupid to make a collection of things like that, and to dry them. Why, you could go to one of our haystacks any day and pull out a better lot than he has got."

Dick said nothing, for he thought those summer evenings delightful. He and Tom, too, had been ready enough to laugh at their new friend whenever he displayed ignorance of some term common to the district; but now this laughter was lost in admiration as they found how he could point out objects in their various excursions which they had never seen before, book-lore having prepared him to find treasures in the neighbourhood of the Toft of whose existence its occupants knew naught.

"Don't you find it very dull out there, Mr Marston," said Mrs Winthorpe one day, "always watching your men cut—cut—cut—through that wet black bog?"

"Dull, madam!" he said, smiling; "why, it is one continual time of excitement. I watch every spadeful that is taken out, expecting to come upon some relic of the past, historical or natural. By the way, Dick, did that man Bargle ever give you the big tusk he said he had found?"

"No, he has never said any more about it, and I don't like to ask."

"Then I will. Perhaps it is the tooth of some strange beast which used to roam these parts hundreds of years ago."

"I say, Marston," said the squire, "you'd like to see your great band of ruffians at work excavating here, eh?"

"Mr Winthorpe," said the young man, "I'd give anything to be allowed to search the ruins."

"Yes, and turn my place upside down, and disturb the home of the poor old monks who used to live here! No, no; I'm not going to have my place ragged to pieces. But when we do dig down, we come upon some curious old stones."

"Like your tobacco-jar?" the engineer said, pointing to the old carven corbel.

The squire nodded.

"You've got plenty of digging to do, my lad," he said, laughing. "Finish that, and then perhaps I may let you have a turn my way. Who's going over to see John Warren?"

"Ah, I wish you would go," said Mrs Winthorpe, "and take the poor fellow over some things I have ready, in a basket!"

"I'll go," said Dick. "Hicky will take us in his punt. There'll be plenty of time, and it's moonlight at nine."

"I'll go with you, Dick," said Marston. "What's the matter with the man?"

"Our own particular complaint, which the people don't want you to kill, my lad," said the squire. "Marsh fever—ague. Years to come when it's swept away by the drainage, the people will talk of it as one of the good things destroyed by our work. They are rare ones to grumble, and stick to their old notions."

"But the people seem to be getting used to us now."

"Oh yes! we shall live it down."

Dick sat and listened, but said nothing. Still he could not help recalling how one old labourer's wife had shaken her head and spit upon the ground as his father went by, and wondered in his mind whether this was some form of curse.

"Tak' you over to the Warren, my lad?" said Hickathrift, as they reached the wheelwright's shed, where the big fellow was just taking down a hoe to go gardening.

"Why, of course I will. Straänge niced evening, Mr Marston! Come along. I'll put on my coat though, for the mist'll be thick to-night."

Hickathrift took his coat from behind the door, led the way to the place where his punt was floating, fastened to an old willow-stump; and as soon as his visitors were aboard he began to unfasten the rope.

"Like to tak' a goon, sir, or a fishing-pole?"

"No: I think we'll be content with what we can see to-night."

Hickathrift nodded, and Dick thought the engineer very stupid, for a gun had a peculiar fascination for him; but he said nothing, only seated himself, and trailed his hand in the dark water as the lusty wheelwright sent the punt surging along.

"Why, Hickathrift," cried Mr Marston, "I thought our friend Dave a wonder at managing a punt; but you beat him. What muscles you have!"

"Muscles, mester? Ay, they be tidy; but I'm nowt to Dave. I can shove stronger, but he'd ding (beat) me at it. He's cunning like. Always at it, you see. Straänge and badly though."

"What, Dave is?" cried Dick.

"Ay, lad; he's got the shakes, same as John Warren. They two lay out together one night after a couple o' wild swans they seen, and it give 'em both ager."

It was a glorious evening, without a breath of air stirring, and the broad mere glistened and glowed with the wonderful reflection from the sky. The great patches of reeds waved, and every now and then the weird cry of the moor-hen came over the water. Here and there perfect clouds of gnats were dancing with their peculiar flight; swallows were still busy darting about, and now and then a leather-winged bat fluttered over them seeking its insect food.

"What a lovely place this looks in a summer evening!" said Mr Marston thoughtfully.

"Ay, mester, and I suppose you are going to spoil it all with your big drain," said the wheelwright, and he ceased poling for a few moments, as the punt entered a natural canal through a reed-bed.

"Spoil it, my man! No. Only change its aspect. It will be as beautiful in its way when corn is growing upon it, and far more useful."

"Ay, bud that's what our people don't think. Look, Mester Dick!"

Dick was already looking at a shoal of fish ahead flying out of the water, falling back, and rising again, somewhat after the fashion of flying-fish in the Red Sea.

"Know what that means?" said the wheelwright.

"Perch," said Dick, shortly. "A big chap too, and he has got one," he added excitedly, as a large fish rose, made a tremendous splash, and then seemed to be working its way among the bending reeds. "Might have got him perhaps if we had had a line."

Mr Marston made no reply, for he was watching the slow heavy flap-flap of a heron as it rose from before them with something indistinctly seen in its beak.

"What has it got?" he said.

Dick turned sharply, and made out that there seemed to be a round knob about the great bird's bill, giving it the appearance of having thrust it through a turnip or a ball.

"Why, it's an eel," he cried, "twisting itself into a knot. Yes: look!"

The evening light gleamed upon the glistening skin of the fish, as it suddenly untwisted itself, and writhed into another form. Then the heron changed its direction, and nothing but the great, grey beating pinions of the bird were visible, the long legs outstretched like a tail, the bent back neck, and projecting beak being merged in the body as it flew straight away.

Hickathrift worked hard at the pole, and soon after rounding one great bed of reeds they came in sight of the rough gravelly patch with a somewhat rounded outline, which formed the Warren, and upon which was the hut inhabited by John o' the Warren, out of whose name "o'-the" was generally dropped.

The moment they came in sight there was a loud burst of barking, and Snig, John Warren's little rabbit-dog, came tearing down to the shore, with the effect of rendering visible scores of rabbits, until then unseen; for the dog's barking sent them scurrying off to their holes, each displaying its clear, white, downy tuft of a tail, which showed clearly in the evening light.

The dog's bark was at first an angry challenge, but as he came nearer his tone changed to a whine of welcome; and as soon as he reached the water's edge he began to perform a series of the most absurd antics, springing round, dancing upon his hind-legs, and leaping up at each in turn, as the visitors to the sandy island landed, and began to walk up to the sick man's hut.

There were no rabbits visible now, but the ground was honey-combed with their holes, many of which were quite close to the home of their tyrant master, who lived as a sort of king among them, and slew as many as he thought fit.

John Warren's home was not an attractive one, being merely a hut built up of bricks of peat cut from the fen, furnished with a small window, a narrow door, and thickly thatched with reeds.

He heard them coming, and, as they approached, came and stood at the door, looking yellow, hollow of cheek, and shivering visibly.

"Here, John Warren, we've brought you a basket!" cried Dick. "How are you? I say, don't you want the doctor?"

"Yah! what should I do with a doctor?" growled the man, scowling at all in turn.

"To do you good," said Dick, laughing good-humouredly.

"He couldn't tell me nothing I dunno. I've got the ager."

"Well, aren't you going to ask us in?"

"Nay, lad. What do you want?"

"That basket," said Dick briskly. "Here, how is Dave?"

"Badly! Got the ager!"

"But is he no better?"

"Don't I tell you he's got the ager!" growled the man; and without more ado he took the basket from the extended hand, opened the lid, and turned it upside down, so that its contents rolled upon the sand, and displayed the kind-heartedness of Mrs Winthorpe.

Dick glanced at Marston and laughed.

"Theer's your basket," growled John Warren. "Want any rabbuds?"

"No; they're out of season, John!" cried Dick. "You don't want us here, then?"

"Nay; what should I want you here for?" growled the man. "Can't you see I've got the ager?"

"Yes, I see!" cried Dick; "but you needn't be so precious cross. Good-night!"

John Warren stared at Dick, and then at his two companions, and, turning upon his heel, walked back into the hut, while Snig, his dog, seated himself beside the contents of the basket, and kept a self-constituted guard over them, from which he could not be coaxed.

"Might have showed us something about the Warren," said Dick in an ill-used tone; "but never mind, there isn't much to see."

He turned to go back to the boat.

71

"I say, Hicky," he said; "let's go and see Dave. You won't mind poling?"

"He says I won't mind poling, Mester Marston," said Hickathrift with a chuckle. "Here, come along."

John Warren had disappeared into the cottage, but as they walked away some of the rabbits came to the mouths of their holes and watched their departure, while Snig, who could not leave his master's property, uttered a valedictory bark from time to time.

"I say, Mr Marston," cried Dick, pausing, "isn't he a little beauty, to have such a master! Look at him watching that food, and not touching it. Wait a minute!"

Dick ran back to the dog and stooped down to open a cloth, when the faithful guard began to snarl at him and show his teeth.

"Why, you ungrateful beggar!" cried Dick; "I was going to give you a bit of the chicken. Lie down, sir!"

But Snig would not lie down. He only barked the more furiously.

"Do you want me to kick you?" cried Dick.

Snig evidently did, for not only did he bark, but he began to make charges at the visitor's legs so fiercely that Dick deemed it prudent to stand still for a few moments.

"Now, then," he said, as the dog seemed to grow more calm; "just see if you can't understand plain English!"

The dog looked up at him and uttered a low whine, accompanying it by a wag of the tail.

"That's better!" cried Dick. "I'm going to pull you off a leg of that chicken for yourself. Do you understand?"

Snig gave a short, friendly bark.

"Ah, now you're a sensible dog," said Dick, stooping down to pick up the cloth in which the chicken was wrapped; but Snig made such a furious onslaught upon him that the boy started back, half in alarm, half in anger, and turned away.

"Won't he let you touch it, Mester Dick?" chuckled Hickathrift.

"No; and he may go without," said Dick. "Come along!"

They returned to the boat, Snig giving them a friendly bark or two as they got on board; and directly after, with lusty thrusts, the wheelwright sent the punt along in the direction of Dave's home.

The evening was still beautiful, but here and there little patches of mist hung over the water, and the rich glow in the west was fast fading out.

"I say, Mr Marston," said Dick, "you'll stay at our place to-night?"

"No; I must go home, thank you," was the reply.

"But it will be so late!"

"Can't help that, Dick. I want to be out early with the men. They came upon a great tree trunk this afternoon, and I want to examine it when it is dug out. Is that Decoy Dave's place?"

"That's it, and there's Chip!" cried Dick, as the boat neared the shore. "You see how different he'll be!"

Dick was right in calling attention to the dog's welcome, for Chip's bark was one of delight from the very first, and dashing down to the water, he rushed in and began swimming rapidly to meet them.

"Why, Chip, old doggie!" cried Dick, as, snorting and panting with the water he splashed into his nostrils, the dog came aside, and after being lifted into the boat gave himself a shake, and then thrust his nose into every hand in turn. "This is something like a dog, Mr Marston!" continued Dick.

"Yes; but he would behave just the same as the other," said the engineer.

"Here's Dave," said Dick. "Hoy, Dave!"

The decoy-man came slowly down toward the shore to meet them, and waved his hand in answer to Dick's call.

"Oh, I am sorry!" cried the latter. "I wish I'd brought him something too. I daresay he's as bad as John Warren."

Dave's appearance proved the truth of Dick's assertion. The decoy-man never looked healthy, but now he seemed ghastly of aspect and exceedingly weak, as he leaned upon the tall staff he held in his hand.

"We've come to see how you are, Dave," cried Dick as the boat bumped up against the boggy edge of the landing-place.

"That's kindly, Mester Dick. Servant, mester. How do, neighbour?"

Dave's head went up and down as if he had a hinge at the back; and as the party landed, he too shivered and looked exceedingly feverish and ill.

"Why, Dave, my man, you ought to see a doctor!" said Mr Marston, kindly.

"Nay, sir, no good to do ought but bear it. Soon be gone. Only a shivering fit."

"Well, I'm trying to doctor you," said the engineer, laughing. "Once we get the fen drained, ague will begin to die out."

"Think so, mester?"

"I am sure so."

"Hear that, neighbour?" said Dave, looking at Hickathrift. "Think o' the fen wi'out the shakes."

"We can't stop, Dave," cried Dick; "because we've got to get home, for Mr Marston to walk over to the sea-bank to-night; but I'll come over and see you to-morrow and bring you something. What would you like?"

"What you haven't got, Mester Dick," said the fen-man, showing his yellow teeth. "Bit of opium or a drop o' lodulum. Nay, I don't want you to send me owt. Neighbour Hick'thrift here'll get me some when he goes over to market."

Hickathrift nodded, and after a little more conversation the party returned toward the boat.

"Straänge and thick to-night, Mester Dick," said Dave. "Be thicker soon. Yow couldn't pole the boat across wi'out losing your way."

"Couldn't I?" cried Dick. "Oh, yes, I could! Good-night! I want you to show Mr Marston some sport with the ducks some day."

"Ay; you bring him over, Mester Dick, and we'll hev' a good turn at the 'coy. Good-night!"

They pushed off, and before they were fifty yards from the shore the boat seemed to enter a bank of mist, so thick that the wheelwright, as he poled, was almost invisible from where Mr Marston and Dick were seated.

"I say, Hicky, turn back and let's go along the edge of the fog," cried Dick.

"Nay, it's driftin' ower us," replied the wheelwright. "Best keep on and go reight through."

"Go on, then," cried Dick. "Feel how cold and damp it is."

"Feel it, Dick? Yes; and right in my wounded arm."

"Does it hurt much?"

"No; only aches. Why, how dense it is!"

"Can you find your way?"

"Dunno, mester. Best keep straight on, I think. Dessay it'll soon pass over."

But it did not soon pass over; and as the wheelwright pushed on it seemed to be into a denser mist than ever.

For a long time they were going over perfectly clear water; but soon the rustling of reeds against the prow of the boat told that they must be going wrong, and Hickathrift bore off to the right till the reeds warned him to bear to the left. And so it went on, with the night falling, and the thick mist seeming to shut them in, and so confusing him that at last the wheelwright said:

"Best wait a bit, Mester Dick. I dunno which way I'm going, and it's like being blind."

"Here, let me have the pole!" cried Dick. And going to the front of the boat, the wheelwright good-humouredly gave way for him, with the result that the lad vigorously

MR. MARSTON AND HIS COMPANIONS FIRED AT BY AN UNSEEN FOE

Page 210

propelled the craft for the space of about ten minutes, ending by driving it right into a reed-bed and stopping short.

"Oh, I say, here's a muddle!" he cried. "You can't see where you are going in the least."

"Shall I try?" said Mr Marston.

"Yes, do, please," cried Dick, eager to get out of his difficulty. "Take the pole."

"No, thank you," was the laughing reply. "I cannot handle a pole, and as to finding my way through this fog I could as soon fly."

Bang!

A heavy dull report of a gun from close by, and Hickathrift started aside and nearly went overboard, but recovered himself, and sat down panting.

"Here! hi! Mind where you're shooting!" cried Dick. "Who's that?"

He stared in the direction from which the sound had come, but nothing but mist was visible, and no answer came.

"Do you hear? Who's that?" shouted Dick with both his hands to his mouth.

No answer came, and Hickathrift now shouted.

Still no reply. His great sonorous voice seemed to return upon him, as if he were enveloped in a tremendous tent of wet flannel; and though he shouted again and again it was without result.

"Why, what's the matter with your hand, man?" cried Mr Marston, as the wheelwright took his cotton kerchief from his neck, and began to bind it round his bleeding palm.

"Nowt much, sir," said the man smiling.

"Why, Hickathrift, were you hit?"

"S'pose I weer, sir. Something came with a whuzz and knocked my hand aside."

"Oh!" ejaculated Dick; while Mr Marston sat with his heart beating, since in spite of his efforts to be cool he could not help recalling the evening when he was shot, and he glanced round, expecting to see a flash and hear another report.

Dick seized the pole which he had laid down, and, thrusting it down, forced the punt back from the reeds, and then, as soon as they were in open water, began to toil as hard as he could for a few minutes till the wheelwright relieved him. Declaring his injury to be a trifle, he in turn worked hard with the pole till, after running into the reeds several times, and more than once striking against patches of bog and rush, they must have got at least a mile from where the shot was fired, by accident or purposely, when the great fellow sat down very suddenly in the bottom of the boat.

As he seated himself he laid the pole across, and then without warning fell back fainting dead away.

A few minutes, however, only elapsed before he sat up again and looked round.

"Bit sick," he said. "That's all. Heven't felt like that since one o' squire's horses kicked me and broke my ribs. Better now."

"My poor fellow, your hand must be badly hurt!" said Mr Marston; while Dick looked wildly on, scared by what was taking place.

"Nay, it's nowt much, mester," said the great fellow rather huskily, "and we'd best wait till the mist goes. It's no use to pole. We may be going farther away, like as not."

Dick said nothing, but stood listening, fancying he heard the splash of a pole in water; but there was no sound save the throbbing of his own heart to break the silence, and he quite started as Mr Marston spoke.

"How long is this mist likely to last?"

"Mebbe an hour, mebbe a week," was the unsatisfactory reply. "Bud when the moon rises theer may come a breeze, and then it'll go directly."

Hickathrift rested his chin upon his uninjured hand, and Dick sat down in silence, for by one consent, and influenced by the feeling that some stealthy foe might be near at hand keen-eyed enough to see them through the fog, or at all events cunning enough to trace them by sound, they sat and waited for the rising of the moon.

The time seemed to be drawn out to a terrible extent before there was a perceptible lightening on their left; and as soon as he saw that, though the mist was as thick as ever, Hickathrift rose and began to work with the pole, for he knew his bearings now by the position of the rising moon, and working away, in half an hour the little party emerged from the mist as suddenly as they had dived in, but they were far wide of their destination, and quite another hour elapsed before they reached the old willow-stump, where the wheelwright made fast his boat, and assuring his companions that there was nothing much wrong he went to his cottage, while Mr Marston gladly accompanied Dick to the Toft, feeling after the shock they had had that even if it had not been so late, a walk down to the sea-beach that night would neither be pleasant nor one to undertake.

Dick was boiling over with impatience, and told his father the news the moment they entered the room where supper was waiting.

"A shot from close by!" cried the squire, excitedly.

"Yes, Mr Winthorpe," said the engineer; "and I'm afraid, greatly afraid, it was meant for me."

Chapter Fourteen.

Hicky's Opinions.

"Nay, lads, I don't say as it weer the will-o'-the-wisps, only as it might have been."

"Now, Hicky," cried Dick, "who ever heard of a will-o'-the-wisp with a gun?"

"Can't say as ever I did," said the wheelwright; "but I don't see why not."

"What stuff! Do you hear what he says, Tom? He says it may have been one of the will-o'-the-wisps that shot and broke his finger."

"A will-o'-the-wisp with a gun!" cried Tom. "Ha! ha! ha!"

"Why shouldn't a will hev a goon as well as a lanthorn?" said Hickathrift, stolidly.

"Why, where would he get his powder and shot?" said Dick.

"Same place as he gets his candle for his lanthorn."

"Oh, but what nonsense! The will-o'-the-wisp is a light that moves about," cried Dick. "It is not anybody."

"I don't know so much about that," said the wheelwright, lifting up his bandaged hand. "All I know is that something shot at me, and broke my finger just the same as something shot at Mester Marston. They don't like it, lads. Mark my words, they don't like it."

"Who don't like what?" said Tom.

"Will-o'-the-wisps don't like people cootting big drains acrost the fen, my lads. They don't mind you fishing or going after the eels with the stong-gad; but they don't like the draining, and you see if it don't come to harm!"

"Nonsense!" cried Dick. "But I say, Hicky, you are so quiet about it all, did you see who it was shot at you?"

The big wheelwright looked cautiously round, as if in fear of being overheard, and then said in a husky whisper:

"Ay, lads, I seen him."

"What was he like, Hicky?" said Tom, who suffered a peculiar kind of thrill as the wheelwright spoke.

"Somethin' between a big cloud, shape of a man, and a flash of lightning with a bit o' thunder."

"Get out!" roared Dick. "Why, he's laughing at us, Tom."

"Nay, lads, I'm not laughing. It's just what I seemed to see, and it 'most knocked me over."

"It's very queer," said Dick thoughtfully. "But I say, Hicky, what did the doctor say to your hand? Will it soon get well?"

"Didn't go to the doctor, lad."

"Why, what did you do then?"

"Went to old Mikey Dodbrooke, the bone-setter."

"What did you go to him for?"

"Because it's his trade. He knows how to mend bones better than any doctor."

"Father says he's an old sham, and doesn't understand anything about it," said Dick. "You ought to have gone to the doctor, or had him, same as Mr Marston did."

"Tchah!" ejaculated Hickathrift. "Why, he had no bones broken. Doctors don't understand bone-setting."

"Who says so?"

"The bone-setter."

"Well, is it getting better, Hicky?"

"Oh yes! It ar'n't very bad. Going down to the drain?"

"Yes. Mr Marston's found a curious great piece of wood, and the men are digging it out."

"Don't stop late, my lads," said the wheelwright, anxiously. "I wouldn't be coming back after dark when the will-o'-the-wisps is out."

"I don't believe all that stuff, Hicky," said Dick. "Father says—"

"Eh! What does he say?" cried the wheelwright, excitedly.

"That he thinks it's one of Mr Marston's men who has a spite against him, and that when there was that shot the other night, it was meant for the engineer."

"Hah! Yes! Maybe," said the wheelwright, drawing a long breath and looking relieved. "But I wouldn't stop late, my lads."

"We shall stop just as long as we like, sha'n't we, Tom?"

"Yes."

"Then I shall come and meet you, my lads. I sha'n't be happy till I see you back safe."

"I say, Hicky, you've got a gun, haven't you?" said Tom.

"Eh! A goon!" cried the wheelwright, starting.

"Yes; you've got one?"

"An old one. She's roosty, and put awaya. I heven't hed her out for years."

"Clean it up, and bring it, Hicky," said Dick. "We may get a shot at something. I say, you'd lend me that gun if I wanted it, wouldn't you?"

"Nay, nay; thou'rt not big enew to handle a goon, lad. Wait a bit for that."

"Come along, Tom!" cried Dick. "And I say, Hicky, bring the forge-bellows with you, so as we can blow out the will's light if he comes after us."

"Haw—haw—haw—haw!" rang out like the bray of a donkey with a bad cold; and Jacob, Hickathrift's lad, threw back his head, and roared till his master gave him a sounding slap on the back, and made him close his mouth with a snap, look serious, and go on with his work.

"Jacob laughs just like our old Solemn-un, sometimes," said Dick merrily. "Come along!"

The morning was hot, but there was a fine brisk breeze from off the sea, and the lads trudged on, talking of the progress of the drain, and the way in which people grumbled.

"Father says that if he had known he wouldn't have joined the adventure," said Tom.

"And my father says, the more opposition there is, the more he shall go on, for if people don't know what's good for them they've got to be taught. There's a beauty!"

Dick went off in chase of a swallow-tail butterfly—one of the beautiful insects whose home was in the fens; but after letting him come very close two or three times, the brightly-marked creature fluttered off over the treacherous bog, a place of danger for followers, of safety for the insect.

"That's the way they always serve you," said Dick.

"Well, you don't want it."

"No, I don't want it. Yes I do. Mr Marston said he should like a few more to put in his case. I say, they are getting on with the drain," Dick continued, as he shaded his eyes and gazed at where, a mile away, the engineer's men were wheeling peat up planks, and forming a long embankment on either side of the cutting through the fen.

"Can you see Mr Marston from here?"

"Why, of course not! Come along! I say, Tom, you didn't think what old Hicky said was true, did you?"

"N–n–no. Of course not."

"Why, you did. Ha—ha—ha! That's what father and Mr Marston call superstition. I shall tell Mr Marston that you believe in will-o'-the-wisps."

"Well, so do you. Who can help believing in them, when you see them going along over the fen on the soft dark nights!"

"Oh, I believe in the lights," said Dick, "but that's all I don't believe they shot Mr Marston and old Hicky; that's all stuff!"

"Well, somebody shot them, and my father says it ought to be found out and stopped."

"So does mine; but how are you going to find it out? He thinks sometimes it's one and sometimes another; and if we wait long enough, my gentleman is sure to be caught."

"Ah, but is it a man?"

"Why, you don't think it's a woman, do you?"

"No, of course not; but mightn't it be something—I mean one of the—well, you know what I mean."

"Yes, I know what you mean," cried Dick—"a ghost—a big tall white ghost, who goes out every night shooting, and has a will-o'-the-wisp on each side with a lantern to show him a light."

"Ah, it's all very well for you to laugh now out in the sunshine; but if it was quite dark you wouldn't talk like that."

"Oh yes, I should!"

"I don't believe it," said Tom; "and I'll be bound you were awfully frightened when Hicky was shot. Come, tell the truth now—weren't you?"

"There goes a big hawk, Tom. Look!" cried Dick, suddenly becoming interested in a broad-winged bird skimming along just over the surface of the fen; and this bird sufficed to change the conversation, which was getting unpleasant for Dick, till they came to the place where the men were hard at work on the huge ditch, the boggy earth from which, piled up as it was, serving to consolidate the sides and keep them from flooding the fen when the drain was full, and the high-tide prevented the water from coming out by the flood-gates at the end.

Mr Marston welcomed the lads warmly.

"I've got a surprise for you," he said.

"What is it—anything good?" cried Dick.

"That depends on taste, my boy. Come and see."

He led the way along the black ridge of juicy peat, to where, in an oblique cutting running out from the main drain, a dozen men were at work, with their sharp spades cutting out great square bricks of peat, and clearing away the accumulations of hundreds of years from the sides of what at first appeared to be an enormous trunk of a tree, but which, upon closer inspection, drew forth from Dick a loud ejaculation.

"Why, it's an old boat!" cried Tom.

"That it is, my lad."

"But how did it come there?" cried Dick, gazing wonderingly at the black timber of the ancient craft.

"Who can tell, Dick? Perhaps it floated out of the river at some time when there was a flood, and it was too big to move back again, and the people in the days when it was used did not care to dig a canal from here to the river."

"Half a mile," said Dick.

"No, no. Not more than a quarter."

"But it doesn't look like a fishing-boat," said Dick.

"No, my lad. As far as I can make out, it is the remains of an old war galley."

"Then it must have belonged to the Danes."

"Danes or Saxons, Dick."

"But the wood's sound," cried Tom. "It can't be so old as that."

"Why not, Tom? Your people dig out pine-roots, don't they, perfectly sound, and full of turpentine? This is pine wood, and full of turpentine too."

"But it's such a while since the Danes and Saxons were here, Mr Marston," said Tom.

"A mere yesterday, my lad, compared to the time when the country about here was a great pine and birch forest, before this peat began to form."

"Before the peat began to form!"

"To be sure! Pine and birch don't grow in peaty swamps, but in sandy ground with plenty of gravel. Look all about you at the scores of great pine-roots my men have dug out. They are all pine, and there must have been quite a large forest here once."

"And was that farther back?"

"Perhaps thousands of years before the Danes first landed. The peat preserves the wood, Tom. Bog is not rotten mud, but the decayed masses that have grown in the watery expanse. Well, Dick, what do you think of it?"

"I wish we could get it home to our place to keep as a curiosity?"

"But it would want a shed over it, my lad, for the rain, wind, and sun would soon make an end of it."

"Then, what are you going to do?"

"Get it out and up that slope they are cutting, along some planks if we can, and then fill up the trench."

The lads inspected the curious-looking old hull, whose aspect seemed to bring up recollections of the history of early England, when fierce-looking men, half sailors, half warriors, came over from the Norland in boats like this, propelled by great oars, and carrying a short thick mast and one sail. All the upper portions had rotted away, but enough of the hull remained to show pretty well what its shape must have been, and that it had had a curiously-projecting place that must have curved out like the neck of a bird, the whole vessel having borne a rough resemblance to an elongated duck or swan.

The boys were, however, by no means so enthusiastic as the engineer; and as a great figure came looming up behind them, Dick was ready enough to welcome the incident of the man's reminder about the disturbance at the Toft.

"We're mates, we are," cried the great fellow, holding out his broad hairy hand to take Dick's in his grasp, and shake it steadily up and down. "I heven't forgot, I heven't forgot."

"Are you all right again, Bargle?" said Dick, trying in vain to extricate his hand.

"Yeees. Knock o' the yead don't hot me. See here."

He slowly drew out of his pocket a great piece of dark-yellow ivory, evidently the point, and about a foot in length, of the tusk of some animal, probably an elephant.

"Theer's what I promised you, lad. That's a tush, that is. What yer think o' that?"

Dick did not seem to know what to think of it, but he expressed his gratitude as well as he could, and had to shake hands again and again with the great fellow, who seemed to take intense delight in smiling at Dick and shaking his head at him.

How long this scene would have lasted it is impossible to say; but at last, as it was growing irksome, there came a shout from the end of the drain.

"They've found something else," said Mr Marston; and the lads needed no telling to hasten their steps, for the finding of *something* buried in the peat could not fail to prove interesting; but in this case the discovery was startling to the strongest nerves.

As they neared the end of the drain where the men were slowly delving out the peat, and a section of the bog was before them showing about twelve feet of, the wet black soil, Mr Marston stepped eagerly forward, and the group of men who were standing together opened out to let him and his companions pass through.

Dick shuddered at the object before him: the figure of a man clothed apparently in some kind of leather garb, and partly uncovered from the position it had occupied in the peat.

"Some un been murdered and berrid," growled Bargle, who was close behind.

"No, my man," said Mr Marston, taking a spade and cutting down some more of the turf, so as to lay bare the figure from the middle of the thigh to the feet.

"Lemme come," growled Bargle, striding forward and almost snatching the sharp spade from his leader's hand.

"Don't hurt it," cried Mr Marston, giving way.

"Nay, no fear o' hotting him," growled Bargle, grinning, and, bending to his work, he deftly cut away the black peat till the figure stood before them upright in the bog as if fitted exactly in the face of the section like some brownish-black fossil of a human being.

It was the figure of a man in a leather garb, and wearing a kind of gaiters bound to the legs by strips of hide which went across and across from the instep to far above the knee. There was a leathern girdle about the waist, and one hand was slightly raised, as if it had held a staff or spear, but no remains of these were to be seen. Probably the head had once been covered, but it was bare now, and a quantity of long shaggy hair still clung to the dark-brown skin, the face being half covered by a beard; and, in spite of the brown-black leathery aspect of the face, and the contracted skin, it did not seem half so horrible as might have been supposed.

"Why, boys," said Mr Marston after a long examination, "this might be the body of someone who lived as long back as the date when that old galley was in use."

"So long back as that!" cried Dick, looking curiously at the strange figure, whose head was fully six feet below the surface of the bog.

"Got a-walking across in the dark, and sinked in," said Bargle gruffly.

That might or might not have been the case. At any rate there was the body of a man in a wonderful state of preservation, kept from decay by the action of the peat; and, judging from the clothing, the body must have been in its position there for many hundred years.

"What's got to be done now?" said Bargle. "We want to get on."

Mr Marston gave prompt orders, which resulted in a shallow grave being dug in the peat about fifty yards from where the drain was being cut, and in this the strange figure was carefully laid, ready for exhumation by any naturalist who should wish to investigate farther; and after this was done, and a careful search made for remains of weapons or coins, the cutting of the drain progressed; till, after an enjoyable day with the engineer, the boys said good-bye, and tried to escape without having to shake hands with Bargle.

But this was not to be. The big fellow waylaid them, smiling and holding out his hand to Dick for a farewell grip, and a declaration that they were mates.

About half-way back, and just as it was growing toward sundown, they were met by Hickathrift, who came up smiling, and looking like a Bargle carefully smoothed down.

"Thought I'd see you safe back," said Hickathrift so seriously that a feeling of nervousness which had not before existed made the boys glance round and look suspiciously at a reed-bed on one side and a patch of alders on the other.

"What are you talking like that for?" cried Dick angrily; "just as if we couldn't walk along here and be quite safe! What is there to mind?"

The wheelwright shook his head and looked round uneasily, as if he too felt the influence of coming danger; but no puff of smoke came from clump of bushes or patch of reeds; no sharp report rose from the alders that fringed part of the walk, and they reached the wheelwright's cottage without adventure.

Here Hickathrift began to smile in a peculiar way, and, having only one hand at liberty, he made use of it to grip Dick by the arm, and use him as if he were an instrument or tool for entrapping Tom, with the result that he packed them both into his cottage, and into the presence of his wife, who was also smiling, as she stood behind a cleanly-scrubbed table, upon which was spread a tempting-looking supper.

"Here, Hicky, don't! What do you mean?" cried Dick, whom the great fellow's grip punished.

"Wittles," said the wheelwright, indulging in a broad grin.

"Oh, nonsense! We're off home. Tom Tallington's going to have supper with me."

"Nay, he's going to hev his supper here along o' uz," said Hickathrift. "Didn't I say, missus, I'd bring 'em home?"

"Yes, Mester Dick," cried Mrs Hickathrift; "and thank ye kindly, do stop."

"Oh, but we must get back!" cried Dick, who shrank from partaking of the wheelwright's kindly hospitality.

"Theer, I towd you so," cried Mrs Hickathrift to her husband, and speaking in an ill-used tone. "They're used to table-cloths, and squire's wife's got silver spoons."

"Nay, nay, never mind the cloths and spoons, Mester Dick; stop and have a bite."

"But, Hicky—"

"Nay, now," cried the wheelwright interrupting; "don't thee say thou'rt not hungry."

"I wasn't going to," said Dick, laughing, "because I am horribly hungry. Aren't you, Tom?"

Tom showed his teeth. It was meant for a smile, but bore a wonderful resemblance to a declaration of war against the food upon the table.

"Don't be proud, then, lad. Stop. Why, you nivver knew me say I wouldn't when I've been at your place."

That appeal removed the last objection, and the boys took off their caps, sat down with the wheelwright, and Mrs Hickathrift, according to the custom, waited upon them.

It is unnecessary to state what there was for supper, and how many times Dick and Tom had their plates replenished with—never mind what—and—it does not signify. Suffice it to say that for the space of half an hour the wheelwright's wife was exceedingly busy; and when at the end of an hour the trio rose from the table, and Hickathrift filled his pipe, both of his visitors seemed as if they had gone through a process of taming. For though a boy—a hearty boy in his teens—living say anywhere, can, as a rule, eat, in the exception of boys of the old fen-land, where the eastern breezes blow right off the German Ocean, they were troubled with an appetite which was startling, and might have been condemned but for the fact that it resulted in their growing into magnificent specimens of humanity, six feet high not being considered particularly tall.

It was quite late when the boys reached the Toft, to find the squire standing outside smoking his pipe and waiting for them.

"Where have you been, lads?" he said; and on being told, he uttered a good-humoured grunt, and laying his hand upon Tom's shoulder, "Here," he said, "you'd better stop with Dick to-night. They won't be uneasy at home?"

"No, sir," said Tom naïvely; "I told father perhaps I should stay."

"Oh, you did, eh!" said the squire. "Well, you're welcome. If you don't want any supper, you'd better be off to bed."

Both lads declared that they did not want any supper, but Mrs Winthorpe had made certain preparations for them which they could not resist, and something very like a second meal was eaten before they retired for the night.

As a rule, when one boy has a visitor for bed-fellow, it is some time before there is peace in that room. Set aside unruly demonstrations whose effects are broken pillowcase strings, ruptured bolsters, and loose feathers about the carpet, if nothing worse has happened in the way of broken jugs and basins, there is always something else to say at the end of the long conversation upon the past day's occurrences or the morrow's plans.

But in this instance it was doubtful whether Dick fell asleep in the act of getting into bed, or whether Tom was nodding as he undressed; suffice it that the moment their heads touched pillows they were fast asleep, and the big beetle which flew in at the open window and circled about the room had it all to himself. Now he ground his head against the ceiling, then he rasped his wings against the wall, then he buzzed in one corner, burred in another, and banged himself up against the white dimity curtains, till, seeing what appeared to be a gleam of light in the looking-glass, he swept by the open window, out of which he could easily have passed, and struck himself so heavily against the mirror that he fell on the floor with a pat, and probably a dint in his steely blue armour.

Then came a huge moth, and almost simultaneously a bat, to whirr round and round over the bed and along the ceiling, while from off the dark waters of the fen came from time to time strange splashings and uncouth cries, which would have startled a wakeful stranger to these parts. Now and then a peculiar moan would be heard, then what sounded like a dismal, distant roaring, followed by the cackling of ducks, and plaintive whistlings of ox-birds, oyster-catchers, and sandpipers, all of which seemed to be very busy hunting food in the soft stillness of the dewy night.

But neither splash nor cry awakened the sleepers, who were, like Barney O'Reardon, after keeping awake for a week; when they went to sleep they paid "attintion to it," and the night wore on till it must have been one o'clock.

The bat and the moth had managed to find their way out of the open window at last, and perhaps out of malice had told another bat and another moth that it was a delightful place in there. At all events another couple were careering about, the moth noisily brushing its wings against wall and ceiling, the bat silently on its fine soft leather wings, but uttering a fine squeak now and then, so thin, and sharp, and shrill that, compared to other squeaks, it was as the point of a fine needle is to that of a tenpenny nail.

The beetle had got over the stunning blow it had received, to some extent, and had carefully folded up and put away its gauzy wings beneath their hard horny cases, deeming that he would be better off and safer if he walked for the rest of the night, and after a good deal of awkward progression he came to the side of the bed.

It was a hot night, and some of the clothes had been kicked off, so that the counterpane on Tom's side touched the floor. In contact with this piece of drapery the beetle came, and began to crawl up, taking his time pretty well, and finally reaching the bed.

Here he turned to the left and progressed slowly till he reached the pillow, which he climbed, and in a few more moments found himself in front of a cavern in a forest—a curiously designed cavern, with a cosy hole in connection with certain labyrinths.

This hole seemed just of a size to suit the beetle's purpose, and he proceeded to enter for the purpose of snuggling up and taking a good long nap to ease the dull aching he probably felt in his bruised head.

But, soundly as Tom Tallington slept, the scriggly legs of a beetle were rather too much when they began to work in his ear, and he started up and brushed the creature away, the investigating insect falling on the floor with a sharp rap.

Tom sat listening to the sounds which came through the window and heard the splashing of water in the distance, and the pipings and quackings of the wild-fowl; but as he leaned forward intently and looked through the open window at the starry sky, there were other noises he heard which made him think of sundry occasions at home when he had been awakened by similar sounds.

After a few moments he lay down again, but started up directly, got out of bed, and went to the window to listen.

The next minute he was back at the bed-side.

"Dick," he whispered, shaking him; "Dick!"

"What is it?"

"There's something wrong with the horses."

"Nonsense!"

"There is, I tell you. Sit up and listen."

"Oh, I say, what a nuisance you are! I was having such a dream!"

Dick sat up and listened, and certainly a sound came from the yard.

He jumped out of bed and went with Tom to the open window, but all was perfectly still round the house, and he was about to return to bed when a dim shadowy-looking creature flew silently across the yard.

Dick uttered a peculiar squeak which was so exactly like that of a mouse that the bird curved round in its flight, came rapidly up toward the window, and hovered there with extended claws, and its great eyes staring from its full round face.

The next moment it was flying silently away, but another shrill squeak brought it back to hover before them, staring in wonder, till, apparently divining that it was being imposed upon, it swooped away.

"What a big owl!" said Tom in a whisper. "There! Hear that?"

Dick did hear *that*! A low whinnying noise, and the blow given by a horse's hoof, as if it had stamped impatiently while in pain.

Directly after there was a mournful lowing from the direction of the cow-house, followed by an angry bellow.

"That's old Billy," said Dick. "What's the matter with the things! It's a hot night, and some kind of flies are worrying them. Here, let's get to bed."

He was moving in the direction of the bed; but just then there was another louder whinnying from the lodge where the cart-horses were kept, and a series of angry stamps, followed by a bellow from the bull.

"There is something wrong with the beasts," said Dick. "I'll call father. No, I won't. Perhaps it's nothing. Let's go down and see."

"But we should have to dress."

"No; only slip on our trousers and boots. You'll go with me, won't you?"

"Yes, I'll go," said Tom; "but I don't want to."

"What! after waking me up to listen!"

"Oh, I'll go!" said Tom, following his companion's lead and beginning to dress.

"Tell you what," said Dick; "we'll get out of the window and drop down."

"And how are we to get back?"

"Short ladder," said Dick laconically. "Come along. Ready?"

"Yes, I'm ready."

The boys moved to the window, and, setting the example, Dick placed one leg out, and was seated astride the sill, when the bed-room door was suddenly thrown open, and the squire appeared.

"Now, then! What does this mean?" he cried angrily.

"We heard something wrong with the beasts, father, and we were going to see," cried Dick.

"Heard something wrong with the beasts, indeed! Yes, and I heard something wrong with them. Now, then, both of you jump into bed, and if I hear another sound, I'll—"

The squire stopped short, for there was a piteous whinny from the stable again.

79

"There, father! and old Billy's got something the matter with him too," cried Dick eagerly, the bull endorsing his statement with a melancholy bellow.

"Why, there is something wrong, then, my boys!" said the squire, angry now with himself for suspecting them of playing some prank. "Here, let's go down."

He led the way directly, and lit a lantern in the kitchen before throwing back the bolts and going out, armed with a big stick, the boys following close behind, and feeling somewhat awe-stricken at the strangeness of the proceedings.

"Hullo, my lads, what is it then?" cried the squire, entering the rough stable, where three horses were fastened up, and all half lying in the straw.

One of them turned to him with a piteous whinny, and then the great soft eyes of all three of the patient beasts were turned toward them, the light gleaming upon their eyes strangely.

"Why, what's this?" cried the squire, holding down the lantern, whose light fell upon the hocks of the poor beasts. "Oh, it's too cruel! what savage has done this!"

As he held down the light the boys hardly realised what had happened. All they could make out was that the light gleamed horribly on the horses' hind-legs, and Dick exclaimed:

"Why, they must have been kicking, father, terribly!"

"Kicking, my boy!" groaned the squire. "I wish they had kicked the monster to death who has done this."

"Done this! Has anybody done this?" faltered Dick, while Tom turned quite white.

"Yes; don't you understand?"

"No, father," cried Dick, looking at him vacantly.

"The poor beasts have been houghed—hamstrung by some cruel wretch. Here, quick!"

He hurried across to the lodge where a favourite cow and the bull were tethered, and as he saw that these poor beasts had been treated in the same barbarous way—

"Did you hear or see anyone, Dick?" he cried, turning sharply on his son.

"No, father. I was asleep till Tom woke me, and told me that the beasts were uneasy."

"It is too cruel, too cruel," groaned the squire huskily. "What is to happen next? Here, go and call up the men. You, Tom Tallington, go and rouse up Hickathrift. We may be in time to catch the wretches who have done this. Quick, boys! quick! And if I do—"

He did not finish his sentence; but as the boys ran off he walked into the house, to return with his gun, and thus armed he made a hasty survey of the place.

By the time he had done, Dick was back with the men, and soon after, Hickathrift came panting up, with Tom; but though a hot search was carried on for hours, nothing more was found, and by breakfast-time five reports had rung out on the bright morning air, as Squire Winthorpe loaded his old flint-lock gun with a leaden bullet five times, and put the poor helpless suffering brutes out of their misery.

"Three good useful horses, and the best-bred bull and cow in the marsh, squire," said Farmer Tallington, who had come over as soon as he heard the news. "Any idea who it could be?"

"No," said the squire; "thank goodness, no. I don't want to find out the wretch's name, Tallington, for I'm a hot-tempered, passionate man."

"It's the drain, neighbour, the drain," said the farmer, shaking his head. "Let's be content with the money we've lost, and try to put a stop to proceedings before we suffer more and worse. There's them about as hev sworn the drain sha'n't be made, and it's the same hands that fired my stacks and those shots, neighbour."

"I daresay it is, farmer," said the squire sternly; "but do you know what it says in the Book about the man who puts his hand to the plough?"

"Ay, I think I know what you mean."

"And so do you, Dick?" said the squire.

"Yes, father."

"Well, my boy, I've put my hand to the plough to do a good, honest, sensible work, and, knowing as I do, that it's a man's duty to go on with it, I shall stand fast, come what may."

"And not leave me in the lurch, Mr Winthorpe?" said a voice.

"No, Marston, not if they hamstring me in turn," cried the squire, holding out his hand to the young engineer, who had hurried over. "I suppose I shall get a bullet in me one of these days; but never mind, we've begun the drain. And do you hear, all of you?" he shouted; "spread it about that the fen will be drained, and that if they killed me, and a hundred more who took my place, it would still be done."

Chapter Fifteen.

The Man of Suspicion.

There was a good deal of inquiry made about the houghing of Squire Winthorpe's horses, and there was a great deal of excitement before the poor beasts were skinned, for their hides to go to town to the tanyard and their carcasses were carted away.

People came from miles in all directions, including all the men who were at work for Mr Marston—every one to stand and stare at the poor dead beasts and say nothing.

Small farmers, fen-men, people from the town, folk from the shore where the cockle-beds lay, and the fisher-people who were supposed to live upon very little fish and a great deal of smuggling.

Even Dave and John Warren punted themselves over, both looking yellow and thin, and so weak that they could hardly manage their poles; and they too stared, the former frowning at the bull and shaking his head at the horses, but wiping away a weak tear as he stood by the cow.

"Many's the drop of good fresh milk the missus has given me from her, Mester Dick," he said with a sigh; "and now theer's no cow, no milk, no nothing for a poor sick man. Hey, bud the ager's a sad thing when you hev it bad as this."

There was a visit from a couple of magistrates, who asked a great many questions, and left behind them a squinting constable, who took very bad snuff, and annoyed Dick by looking at him suspiciously, as if he believed him to be the cause of all the mischief. This man stopped in the village at a cottage next to Hickathrift's, from which place he made little journeys in all directions, evidently full of the belief that he was going to discover the people who did all this mischief in the neighbourhood.

This constable's name was Thorpeley, and he did a great deal of business with a brass box and a short black clay-pipe, in which he smoked short black tobacco.

"I don't know," said Dick one day as he stood with his arms folded, leaning upon Solomon, talking to Tom Tallington and staring at Thorpeley the constable, who was leaning against a post smoking and staring with one eye at the fen, while with the other he watched the group of three in the Toft farm-yard.

"Well, I'm sure I don't," said Tom. "He never goes over to the town to buy any."

"And Hicky says nobody fetches any for him, but he always seems to have plenty though he hasn't any luggage or box or anything."

"No; I saw him come," said Tom. "He only had a small bundle in a red handkerchief!"

"And he keeps on smoking from morning till night."

"And watching you!"

"Yes. He's always watching me," cried Dick in an aggrieved tone. "Stand still, will you? Yes, you'd better! You kick, and I'll kick you!"

This was to Solomon, who had hitched up his back in an arch, laid down his ears, thrust his head between his fore-legs and his tail between his hind, giving himself the aspect of being about to reach under and bite the tip of the said tail. But that was not the case, and Dick knew by experience that all this was preparatory to a display of kicking.

Solomon may have understood plain English or he may not. This is a matter which cannot be decided. At all events he slowly raised his head and twisted his tail in a peculiar manner, stretched out his neck, and cocking his ears he sighed loudly a sigh like the fag-end of a long bray, all of which seemed to point to the fact that he felt himself to be a slave in leathern chains, gagged with a rusty bit, and at the mercy of his master.

"Flies tease him," said Tom apologetically. "Poor old Sol!"

"Don't touch him!" cried Dick, "or he'll kick you."

"Poor old Sol!" said Tom again, and this time he approached the donkey's head.

"Don't touch him, I tell you! He'll bite if you do! He's in a nasty temper because I would put on his bridle, and I was obliged to persuade him to be quiet with a pitchfork handle."

"What a shame!" said Tom.

"Shame, eh! Just you look here," cried Dick, and down one of his coarse worsted stockings, he displayed a great bruise on his white leg. "He did that three days ago, and he tried to do it again this morning, only I was too quick for him."

"Haugh! haugh–h–haugh!" sighed Solomon in a most dismal tone.

"Says he's sorry for it!" cried Tom, grinning.

"Oh, very well then, I'm sorry I hit him with the pitchfork handle. I say, Tom, I gave him such a whop!"

"Where did you hit him?"

"Where I could. You can't pick your place when you try to hit Solomon. You must look sharp or you'll get it first."

"But he wouldn't be so disagreeable if you were kind to him," said Tom. "Poor old Sol, then!"

There was a sharp twist of the donkey's neck, and, quick as lightning, the fierce little animal made a grab at Tom. Fortunately he missed his shoulder, but he got tightly hold of the sleeve of his coat, and held on till Dick gave him a furious kick, when he let go.

"Kick him again, Dick!" cried Tom, who looked very pale. "Ugh! the treacherous beast!"

"It's his nature," said Dick coolly, as he resumed his position and leaned over the donkey's back. "He always was so from a foal! Father's always kind to dumb beasts, and feeds them well, and nurses them when they're ill; but he often gives Solomon a crack. I say, look at old Thorpeley; he's watching you now."

"He isn't; he's looking all round. I say, Dick, you can't tell where he is looking. I wonder what makes any one squint like that!"

"Had one of his eyes knocked out and put in again upside down," said Dick.

"Get out!" cried Tom.

"Haugh, haugh, haugh, haugh, haugh, haugh!" cried Solomon.

"There, he's laughing at you. I say, Dick, do you think he really does watch us?"

"Sure of it. He thinks I houghed the poor horses. I know he does, and he expects to find out that I did it by following me about."

"How do you know he suspects you?"

"Because he is always asking questions about our window being open that night, and about how I found out there was something the matter with the poor beasts. I say, Tom, I hate that fellow."

"So do I," said Tom in tones which indicated his loyalty to his friend. "Let's serve him out!"

"Oh, but you mustn't! A constable is sworn in."

"What difference does that make?"

"I don't know, but he is; and he has a little staff in his pocket with a brass crown upon it, and he says, 'In the king's name!'"

"Well, let him if he likes. The king in London can't know what we do down here in the fen. I say, let's serve him out!"

"No," said Dick, "it might get father into trouble. I say, I know what I'll do if you like."

"What, take him out in a boat and upset it?"

"No, lend him Solomon to ride!"

As he spoke Dick looked at Tom and Tom looked at Dick before they both burst into a hearty fit of laughter.

"Here, let's get away. He's coming!"

Dick turned to go, but Solomon objected. Possibly he understood what had been said. At all events he stood fast, and refused to move till, in obedience to a call from his friend, Tom took hold of the bridle and dragged, while Dick made a sudden rush behind, as if to deliver a tremendous kick.

Solomon sighed and consented to move, and, evidently considering himself mastered, he became amiable, made a playful attempt to bite, and then started off at a canter.

"Jump on, Tom!" cried Dick.

The lad wanted no second invitation, but scuffled on to the donkey's back as it went on, and the trio trotted along for about a hundred yards.

"Where shall we go?" cried Tom.

"Straight on. Let's see how Mr Marston's getting along. Here, you ride on to the alders' corner and tie up Sol, and then go on."

"I say: here's the constable coming." Dick looked back and frowned.

"There, I told you so!" he cried. "It doesn't matter what I do, that man watches me."

"He's only going for a walk."

"Going for a walk!" cried Dick fiercely; "he's following me. You'll see he'll keep to me all the time. I should like to serve him out."

Tom was going to say something else, but his words were jerked out at random, and the next died away, for, as if he approved of the smell of the salt-sea air, Solomon suddenly whisked his tail, uttered a squeak, and after a bound went off at a tremendous gallop, stretching out like a greyhound, and showing what speed he possessed whenever he liked to put it forth.

The sudden spring he made produced such comical effects that Dick Winthorpe stopped short in the rough track along the edge of the fen, to laugh. For Tom Tallington had been seated carelessly on the donkey's back right behind, and turned half round to talk to his companion. The consequence was that he was jerked up in the air, and came down again as if bound to slip off. But Tom and Dick had practised the art of riding almost ever since they could run alone, and in their early lessons one had ridden astride the top bar of a gate hundreds of times, while the other swung it open and then threw it back, the great feat being to give the gate a tremendous bang against the post, so as to nearly shake the rider from his seat.

The jerk was unpleasant, at times even painful; but it taught the lads to hold on with their legs, and made them better able to display their prowess in other mounts which were tested from time to time.

They were not particular as to what they turned into a steed. Sometimes it was Farmer Tallington's Hips, the brindled cow, when she was fetched from the end of the home close to be milked. This would have been one of the calmest of rides, and afforded plenty of room for both boys to ride Knight-Templar fashion, after old Sam had helped them on, but it was not a ride much sought for, because Hips was not a mollusc. Quite the contrary: she was a vertebrate animal, very vertebrate indeed, and a ride on her back represented a journey upon the edge of a Brobdingnagian blunt saw, set up along a kind of broad lattice covered with a skin.

There was a favourite old sow at the Toft which was often put in requisition, but she only carried one. Still it was a comfortable seat, only in the early days of the boys' life that pig's back was wont to tickle; and then too she had a very bad habit.

Of course these rides were not had in the sty, nor yet in the farm-yard, but out along by the edge of the fen, and the enjoyment was nearly perfect till it was brought to an end, always in the same way, as soon as a nice convenient shallow pool was encountered, for here Lady Winthorpe, as she was called, always lay down for a comfortable wallow, when it was no use to wait for another ride, for the seat became too wet.

Tallington's ram was splendid when he could be caught, which was not often; but upon the rare occasions when he did fall captive to the boys' prowess, he had rather a trying time, considering how big he was, and how thin his legs. But his back was beautiful. The wool formed a magnificent cushion, and a couple of locks could be grasped for security by the rider, while the attendant, who waited his turn drove with a branch of furze or heather.

A pole across a stone wall was another splendid aid to horsemanship, see-saw fashion, or turned into a steed for one, by wedging the thick end into a hole and riding the thin end, spring fashion; while, as the years rolled by and the boys were back from school, an occasional mount was had upon Saxon, Tallington's old grey horse, falsely said to be nearly two hundred. But if he was not, he looked it.

Of course it was pleasant to be seated on high upon his back, but the ride was not exhilarating, for whether he was bound for the ploughed fields, or to harrow, or to fetch home a load, it seemed to make no difference to Saxon, who always seemed to be examining the ground before him with his big dull eyes before he lifted a foot to set it down in advance. He was a cautious beast, and this may have arisen from his having been often bogged. These rides were, then, not much sought after, and when Solomon was placed at Dick's disposal he was voted by far the best, and the donkey was not long in finding that his young master had learned how to ride; as, with his long head he debated how he might best rid himself of such incubi as Dick and his friend.

All this is explanatory of the reason why Tom Tallington did not slip off at Solomon's first bout, but kept on when he came down by hooking himself, as it were, with his leg and gripping a piece of the donkey's skin with his hand.

By these means he regained his perpendicular, but only for a moment, Solomon having at command a perfect battery of ruses for ridding himself of a rider. No sooner was Tom upright than the donkey gave the whole of his skin and muscles a wrench sidewise, which felt as if the seat was being dragged away.

The consequence was that Tom nearly went off to the right. He was too good an assman, though, and by a dexterous gymnastic feat he dragged himself once more upright, when Solemn-un's back suddenly grew round and began to treat Tom as if he were a ball. Now he was jerked up; now he was jerked forward; now he was jerked back—bob—bob—bob—bob—till he nearly went off over the tail. There was another bout of kicking, and away went Tom again forward till he was a long way on toward the donkey's neck, but only to shuffle himself back to the normal seat upon the animal, after which, in token of defeat, Solomon went on out of sight at a rapid canter, leaving Dick laughing till he had to wipe his eyes.

"He will be so sore and so cross!" cried Dick, as he walked swiftly on; when, involuntarily turning his head, he saw that the constable was following him.

"The idiot!" cried the lad angrily. "Well, he shall have a run for it."

Setting his teeth and doubling his fists, he bent his head, and started off running as hard as he could go, with the result that as he was going somewhat after the fashion of a hare making use of his eyes to watch his pursuer, and not looking ahead, he suddenly went round a curve, right into Hickathrift's chest, and was caught and held by the big wheelwright.

"Why, Mester Dick, what now?"

"Don't stop me, Hicky. I was running because that stupid constable fellow is after me."

"Hey, and what should make you run away from constable, lad?" said Hickathrift severely. "You've done nowt to be 'shamed on?"

"No, of course not!" cried Dick, shaking himself free. "Did you meet Tom Tallington?"

"Ay, iver so far-off, trying to stop old Solomon, and he wouldn't stay."

Dick nodded and glanced at him; and then, as he ran on again, the lad ground his teeth.

"It's a shame!" he cried. "Why, old Hicky thinks now that there's something wrong. I'll serve that old stupid out for all this; see if I don't!"

He ran on, getting very hot, and beginning now to abuse Tom Tallington for going so far before he tied up; and at last saw the donkey browsing by the side of a tree, while Tom was well on along the track to the drain, walking as fast as he could go.

Solomon pointed one ear at Dick, as he came up, but took no further notice, being engaged in picking nutriment out of some scraps of as unlikely looking vegetation as could be found in the fen. Perhaps it was the thistly food he ate which had an effect upon his temper and made him the awkward creature he had grown.

"My turn now," cried Dick, unfastening the rein, which was tightly tied with string to the stout stem of an alder.

Solomon had cocked one ear at his master as he came up. The animal now laid both ears down and began to back so rapidly along the road, keeping the reins at their full stretch, that it was impossible to mount him, and it was evident that a long battle was beginning, in which the ass might win.

Dick, however, found an ally in the shape of Grip, Hickathrift's lurcher, who had been evidently off on some expedition upon his own account, and was now hastening to overtake his master.

Solomon's attention was taken up by Dick, and he did not perceive Grip coming up at full speed till, with a rush, the dog made a bound at him, and sent him towards Dick, who was dragging at the reins.

Grip seemed to enjoy the donkey's astonishment as it backed from him and then wheeled sharply round to deliver a goodly kick; but before this could be planted satisfactorily, Dick had mounted and began tugging at the reins and drumming with his heels in a way there was no resisting, so Solomon went off at a gallop and Grip followed his master.

At the end of a mile Tom had been passed, and Dick drew up by the first scrubby willow he reached, to tie up the donkey and leave it for his friend; but a glance back showed him the constable returning toward the Toft, so the boy stood leaning over Solomon's back, waiting.

"I don't want to ride," he said to himself. "Tom can have the donkey, and I'll walk."

"Why didn't you go on?" cried Tom, as he came up with a very red face.

"Don't want to be alone," replied Dick lazily, as he gazed away over the wide-stretching fen-land with the moist air quivering in the glorious sunshine. "I say, Tom, what a shame it seems!"

"What seems a shame?"

"Corn-fields and pastures and orchards are all very well, but the old fen does look so lovely now!"

"Yes, it does," said Tom; "and father's horribly sorry he joined in the draining scheme. He says it's going to cost heaps of money, and then be no good. But come along."

"Where?" said Dick.

"I don't know. Where we're going."

"We're not going anywhere, are we?"

"Well, you are a fellow! Come galloping off here into the fen, and then say you don't know where we're going!"

"I did it to get away from that Thorpeley. What shall we do?"

"Pst! Look there! What's that?"

"Snake!"

"No; it's an adder. Look!"

"'Tisn't," said Dick; "it's a snake. Adders aren't so long as that. No, no; don't throw at it. Let's see what it's going to do."

The reptile was crossing the track from a tuft of alders, and seemed to be about three feet long and unusually thick, while, as it reached the dense heath and rushes, interspersed with grey coral moss on that side, it disappeared for a few moments, and they thought it had gone; but directly after it reappeared, gliding over a rounded tuft of bog-moss, and continued its way.

"Why, it's going to that pool!" cried Dick.

"To drink," said Tom. "No wonder. Oh, I am hot and thirsty! Here, I could knock him over with a stone easily."

"Let him alone," said Dick, who had become interested in the snake's movements. "How would you like to be knocked over with a stone?"

"I'm not a snake," said Tom, grinning.

"Look!" cried Dick, as the reptile reached the edge of one of the many deep fen pools, whose amber-coloured water was so clear that the vegetation at the bottom could be seen plainly, and, lit up by the sunshine, seemed to be of a deep-golden hue across which every now and then some armoured beetle or tiny fish darted.

To the surprise of both, instead of the snake beginning to drink, it went right into the water, and, swimming easily and well, somewhat after the fashion of an eel, sent the water rippling and gleaming toward the sides.

"Look!" cried Tom. "Oh, what a bait for a pike!" For just then one of these fishes about a foot long rose slowly from where it had lain concealed at the side, and so clear was the water that they could make out its every movement.

"Pooh! a pike could not swallow a snake," said Dick, as the reptile swam on, and the pike slowly followed as if in doubt.

"Oh, yes, he could!" said Tom, "a bit at a time."

"Nonsense! Don't make a noise; let's watch. The snake's a yard long, and the pike only a foot. I say, can't the snake swim!"

It could unmistakably, and as easily as if it were quite at home, gliding along over the surface and sending the water rippling away in rings, while the little pike followed its movements a few inches from the top so quietly that the movements of its fins could hardly be made out.

"Now he'll have him!" said Tom, as the snake reached the far side of the pool, raised its head, darted out its tongue, and then turned and swam back toward the middle, glistening in the sun and seeming to enjoy its bath.

But Tom was wrong; the pike followed closely, evidently watching its strange visitor, but making no effort to seize it, and at last, quite out of patience, the lads made a dash forward.

The result was a swirl in the water, and the fish had gone to some lurking-place among the water plants, while the snake made a dive, and they traced its course right to the bottom, where it lay perfectly still.

They sat down to wait till it came up, but after a time, during which Tom had lamented sorely that he had not killed the snake, which seemed comfortable enough in its prolonged dive, they both grew tired, and returned to where Solomon stood making good use of his time and browsing upon everything which seemed to him good to eat.

"Here, let's go and see how they're getting on with the drain," said Dick.

"But we're always going to see how they're getting on with the drain," grumbled Tom.

"Never mind! Mr Marston may have had something else dug up."

"I don't want to see any more old boats; and as for that other thing—Ugh!"

"Never mind! Come along! Perhaps they've found something else."

"Don't believe it. Are you going to ride?"

"No; you can ride," said Dick. "I'll walk."

The heat of the day seemed to make the boys silent as they walked and rode in turn, gazing longingly the while over the spreading pools glistening in the sunshine, with the dragon-flies glancing here and there upon their gauzy wings which rustled and thrilled as they darted and turned in their wonderful flight, chasing their unfortunate winged prey. Every now and then a beautiful swallow-tail butterfly, plentiful once in these regions, flitted by, inviting pursuit where pursuit was impossible; while from the waving beds of giant grass which rose from the water and now began to show their empurpled heads, came the chattering of the reed-birds, as if in answer to the chirping of the crickets in the crisp dark heath.

"Look at the bulrushes, Tom!" said Dick lazily. And he nodded in the direction of a patch of the tall, brown, poker-like flowers and leaves of the reed-mace.

"Oh, yes, look at them!" said Tom sourly. "What a shame it is that we weren't born with wings! Everything grows where you can't get at it. If there's a good nest, it's surrounded by water."

"Like an island," assented Dick.

"The best butterflies are where you can't get them without you go in a boat."

"You can't catch butterflies out of a boat," said Dick contemptuously.

"You could, if you poled it along fast enough. Here, you jump on now. What a hot back old Solomon has got!"

"I daresay he thinks you've got horribly hot legs," said Dick, laughing. "Here, come along quick!"

"What for?"

"Can't you see!" cried Dick, starting off in the direction of where the men were at work; "there's something the matter."

Certainly something did seem to be wrong, for the men were hurrying along the black embankment of the great drain in the direction of the sea; and as the boys reached the spot where the digging had been going on, the explanation was plain.

The last time they were there, the men were at work in the bottom of the oozy dike, where a little water lay, soaked out of the sides; but now, right away to the flood-gates, there was a glistening lane of water, the open ditch resembling a long canal in which a barge could have been sailed.

"There isn't anything the matter," said Tom. "They've let the water in to try how it goes."

But when at last they reached the sea end, it was to find Mr Marston very busy with his men closing the great gates to keep out the tide, which had risen high and threatened to flood a good deal of low-lying ground. For probably by carelessness the sluice-gate down by the sea had been left open, and the tide had come up and drowned the works.

The two lads stood looking on for some time, until the gates were closed, and then, as the men sauntered away to their lodgings, Mr Marston joined them.

"What did you fill the dike for, Mr Marston?" said Dick.

"Yes: wasn't it to try how it would go?"

"No," said the young engineer. "I did not want it filled. The gates were left open."

"And what are you going to do now?"

"Wait till the tide's down, so that we can open them and let the water run off."

"You can't do anything till then?"

"We could begin digging farther on," said Mr Marston; "but as the tide will soon be going down I shall wait. It is a great nuisance, but I suppose I must have some accidents."

The lads stayed with him all the afternoon, waiting till the tide had turned, and getting a good insight at last into how the drain would act.

It was very simple, for as soon as the tide was low enough the water ran rapidly from the drain; and that evening the gates were closed tightly to keep out the next rise, the great dike being quite empty.

The engineer walked back with the boys, for there was no riding. They had left Solomon tethered where he could get a good feed of grass and tender shoots; but upon reaching the spot when they were ready to return there was the tethering line gnawed completely through, and the donkey was out of sight.

"Not taken away?" said Mr Marston.

"No: he has gone home," said Dick. "That rope wasn't thick enough to hold him. I thought he would get away."

"Then why not have asked me for a thicker rope, Dick?"

"What's the good! If I had tied him there with a thicker rope, he'd have bitten through the bridle. He wanted to go back home, and when he does, he will go somehow."

"He seems a wonderful beast," said Mr Marston, smiling.

"I don't know about being wonderful. He's a rum one, and as cunning as a fox. Why, he'll unfasten any gate to get into a field, and he'll get out too. He unhooks the doors and lifts the gates off the hinges, and one day he was shut up in the big barn, and what do you think he did?"

"I know," said Tom; "jumped out of the window."

"Yes, that he did," said Dick. "He climbed up the straw till he got to the window, and then squeezed himself through."

That evening, after tea, the squire was seated in the orchard where the stone table had been built up under the big gnarled apple-tree, and the engineer was talking to him earnestly as Dick came up from going part of the way home with his companion.

"Shall I go away, father?" asked the lad, as he saw how serious his father looked.

"No, my boy, no. You are getting old enough now to think seriously; and this draining business will be more for you than for myself—better for your children than for you. Mr Marston has some more ugly news about the work."

"Ugly news, father?"

"Yes, Dick," said Mr Marston; "that was no accident this afternoon, but a wilful attempt made by some miserably prejudiced person to destroy our work."

"But it did no harm, Mr Marston."

"No, my boy; but the ignorant person who thrust open that gate hoped it would. If it had been a high-tide and a storm, instead of stopping our work for a few hours he might have stopped it for a few weeks."

"And who do you think it was?" asked Dick.

"Someone who hates the idea of the drain being made. I have seen the constable, Mr Winthorpe," continued Marston.

"Well, and what does he say?"

"That he thinks he knows who is at the bottom of all these attacks."

"And whom does he suspect?" cried Dick excitedly.

"He will not say," replied the engineer. "He only wants time, and then he is going to lay his hand upon the offender."

"Or offenders," said the squire drily.

85

"Yes, of course," said the engineer; "but the mischief is doubtless started by one brain; those who carry it out are only the tools."

Mr Marston had come with the intention of staying for the night at the Toft; and after a ramble round the old orchard and garden, and some talk of a fishing expedition into the wilder parts of the fen "some day when he was not so busy," supper was eaten, and in due time Dick went to bed, to stand at his window listening to the sounds which floated off the mere, and at last to throw himself upon his bed feeling hot and feverish with his thoughts.

"I wish Tom was here to talk to," he said to himself. "But if I did talk to him about it he'd only laugh. That constable thinks I'm at the bottom of it all, and that I set the people to do these things, and he's trying to make Mr Marston believe it, and it's too bad!"

He turned over upon one side, but it was no more comfortable than the other; so he tried his back, but the bed, stuffed as it was with the softest feathers from the geese grown at the farm, felt hard and thorny; there was a singing and humming noise made by the gnats, and the animals about the place were so uneasy that they suggested the idea of something wrong once more.

Then at last a drowsy sensation full of restfulness began to come over the weary lad, and he was fast dropping off to sleep, when—*Cock-a-doodle-doo*!

A shrill and sonorous challenge came from one of the lodges, which made Dick start and throw one leg out of bed, sit up, and throw himself down again.

"Ugh! you stupid!" he cried angrily. "I don't believe I've been asleep yet."

He seized his pillow, gave it a few savage punches, and lay down again, but only to find himself more wakeful than ever, with the unpleasant feeling that he was suspected of fighting against his father's plans; and after turning the matter over and over, and asking himself whether he should go straight to his father in the morning and tell him, or whether he should make Mr Marston his confidant, he came to the conclusion that he should not like to, for it might make them suspicious, and think that he really was concerned in the case.

Then he resolved to tell Hickathrift and ask his advice, or Dave, or John Warren.

Lastly, he resolved to tell his mother; and as he thought of how she would take his hand and listen to him attentively, and give him the best of counsel, he asked himself why he had not thought of her before.

But he grew more hot and uncomfortable, thinking till his troubled brain seemed to get everything in a knot, and he had just come to the conclusion that he would say nothing to anybody, for the constable's suspicions were not worth notice, when there was a sharp rap on the floor as if something had fallen, and he lay listening with every sense on the strain.

He had not long to wait, for from beneath his window came a low familiar whistle.

"Why, it's Tom!" he thought, starting up in bed; and as he was in the act of gliding out, a second thought troubled him—Tom there in the middle of the night! And if the squire heard him he would believe they were engaged in some scheme.

"Tom!" he whispered, as he leaned out of the open window.

"Yes. May I come up?"

"No, don't. What do you want? Why have you come over?"

"Nobody knows I've come. I got out of the bed-room window and ran across."

"What for?"

"I can't tell you down here, Dick; I must come up."

He ran away softly over the grass, and came back in a few minutes with one of the short ladders, of whose whereabouts he knew as well as Dick, and planting it against the window-sill, he ran up and thrust in his head.

"I say, Dick," he whispered, "I couldn't sleep to-night, and I went to the window and looked out."

"So did I. Well, what of that? Here, be quick and go, or father will hear you, and we shall get into trouble."

"There's going to be something done to-night."

"What! the horses again, or a fire?"

"I don't know, only I'm sure I saw two men creep along on their hands and knees down to the water."

"Pigs," said Dick, contemptuously.

"They weren't. Think I can't tell a man from a pig!"

"Not in the dark."

"I tell you they were men."

"Pigs!"

"Men! and they went down to the water."

"To drink, stupid! They were pigs! They look just like men crawling in the dark!"

"Pigs don't get in punts and pole themselves along the mere!"

"You didn't see two men get in a punt and pole themselves along!"

"No, but I heard them quite plain."

"Well, and suppose you did, what then?"

"I don't know. Only I couldn't sleep, and I was obliged to come over to you."

"And wake me out of a beautiful sleep! What was that you threw in?"

"Stone!"

"Then now go back, and don't come here in the night to get me into trouble! What's the good of going and dreaming such stuff and then coming along the dark road to tell me? What's that?"

Tom was going to say *lightning* as a brilliant flash made their faces quite plain for a moment, but before he could give the word utterance there was a heavy dull report as of a cannon, which seemed to run over the surface of the mere, and murmur among the reeds and trees.

"Why, it's out at sea," said Tom in a whisper. "It can't be a wreck!"

"I know!" cried Dick excitedly. "Smugglers and a king's ship!"

Just then a window was heard being opened, and the squire's voice speaking to Mrs Winthorpe.

"I don't know," he said; "sounded like a gun. That you, Marston?" he cried aloud as another window was thrown open.

"Yes. Did you hear a report?"

"Yes. Like a gun out at sea."

"I heard a slight noise a little while ago, and I was listening when I saw a flash and heard the report. Mr Winthorpe, I'm afraid there's something wrong again."

"No, no, man!"

"I'm afraid I must say, Yes, sir. That sound was not off the sea, but much nearer the house. Who's that?"

"Hallo! who's on that ladder?" cried the squire, turning sharply round at the engineer's query. "Tom Tallington?"

"Yes, sir," faltered Tom.

"What are you doing here, sir? Is Dick there?"

"Yes, father."

"What's the meaning of this, sir?"

"We saw a flash, father, and heard a report!"

"Where?" cried Mr Marston.

"I think it must have been close to the outfall of the big drain, father."

"There! you hear," said Mr Marston in a low voice. "There is something wrong!"

"Stop a moment," said the squire sternly. "You, Tom Tallington, why are you there?"

"Tell him, Tom," said Dick in a low voice.

"Speak out, sir," cried the squire. "What are you whispering there, Dick?"

"I was asking him to tell you, father," faltered Dick; for their being caught like this a second time, and the feeling that he was suspected, troubled the lad sorely at that moment.

"Once more, then, my lad," said the squire. "Why are you here?"

"I came to tell Dick, sir, that I had seen two men come from the town way past our place, and that I heard them get into a boat and go away across the mere."

"You saw that?"

"Yes, sir."

"Well, what of it? Why did you come and tell Dick that?"

"Because I thought there was something wrong, sir."

"You hear?" said Mr Marston again.

"Yes, I hear," muttered the squire, "but I don't like it. These boys know more than they care to say."

The squire's window was heard to shut, and his heavy footstep sounded loudly on the floor in the silence of the night, while the two lads stood listening.

"What shall we do, Dick?"

"I'm going to dress," was the reply; and the speaker began to hurry on his things. "You had better go home."

"No," said Tom sturdily; "if I've got you into a hobble I'll stand by you. But I didn't mean any harm."

Five minutes later all were standing down in the great stone porch, the squire with a stout staff and Mr Marston similarly armed.

The squire looked very hard at the two lads, but he did not speak. Still there was something in his glance, dimly seen though it was in the star-light, which made Dick wince. It was as if something had risen up between father and son; and, rightly or wrongly the lad felt that his father was looking upon him with doubt.

At the end of a few moments Dick mastered his awkwardness, and spoke to his father as the latter came down from saying a few parting words to Mrs Winthorpe.

"Shall I come with you, father—I mean, shall we?"

"If you like," said the squire coldly. "Come, Marston."

Dick made a movement to speak to the latter, but he was staring straight out across the fen in the direction of the draining works, and fretting with impatience at the delay.

The next minute a start was made, and the boys were left behind.

"Mr Marston might have said come," said Tom in a low sulky voice.

"They both think we've been at some mischief," said Dick sadly.

"Then don't let's go with them. I should have liked to go though."

"And so we will," cried Dick angrily. "We'll go and show them that we're not afraid to face anybody. I wish people wouldn't be so suspicious."

"So do I," cried Tom. "But I say, Dick, it does look suspicious when you're found getting into anybody's house in the middle of the night with a ladder."

"Well, I suppose it does," replied Dick thoughtfully.

"Why, my father would have shot at anybody he saw climbing in. I say, are we going?"

"Yes, come along," cried Dick; and the two lads started off at a rapid pace, following in the tracks of the squire and the engineer, whose voices could be heard in a low murmur now some way ahead.

The night was glorious, and the stars were reflected in the face of the mere, whose black smooth waters seemed to form an inverted curve to complete the arch of spangled glory overhead. From far and near came the many sounds peculiar to the wild fen, while every now and then there was a solitary splash, or perhaps a loud flapping and beating of the water following closely upon the whistling and whirring of wings.

The lads had an hour's walk before them, and if they wished to keep up with those in front, an arduous and sharp walk, for it soon became evident that they were hurrying on at a great rate.

"We shall have to run directly," said Dick, after they had been going on for about twenty minutes. "Hist! what did Mr Marston say?"

"That he must have been mad to stop away from his lodgings to-night," whispered Tom, who had been a little in advance on the narrow path. "Here, what's that?"

"Somebody on the mere," cried Dick excitedly. "Hi! ho!"

"Hi! ho!" came from out of the darkness where the splashing of water had been heard, accompanied by the peculiar sliding sound made by drawing a pole over the edge of a boat.

"That you, Dave?"

"Yes, Mester Dick. Hear a noise?"

"Yes. Did you?"

"Something like thunder, and it wakkened me. I think it weer a fireball."

These words were shouted as the man forced the punt along rapidly, till it was abreast of the rough road track which ran along by the edge of the mere.

"Wheer are you going?" cried Dave as soon as he came close up.

"Down to the drain-works," said Tom.

"Think it fell theer?" asked Dave.

"Yes: there was a flash of light went up."

"Hey, bud I'll come wi' you," said Dave earnestly. "I'd best land here, for I can't get much farther."

For thereabouts the track went wide of the edge of the mere, and Dave was just landing, talking volubly the while, as the squire and Mr Marston pressed on, leaving them behind, when there came another hail off the water.

"Why, it's John Warren!" cried Tom.

"What's matter?"

"We dunno, lad," shouted back Dave. "Fireball come down, I think."

"That all?" said the rabbit-catcher. "Any mischief? Don't see no fire."

"Nay, bud we don't know," replied Dave. "Squire and engineer chap's on ahead, and we're going to see. Coming?"

"Nay, I'm going back to bed again. Busy day wi' me to-morrow. I thowt someone was killed."

There was a faint glimpse of the man and his boat seen for a moment, and the water flashed in the rays of the stars as he turned; then his voice was heard muttering, and the splash of his pole came more faintly, while Dave secured and stepped out of the boat, to burst out suddenly in his grating unmusical laugh.

"He, he, he! His, hec, hac! Seems straänge and disappointed, lads. Talks as if he wanted someone killed. Now, then, come on."

By this time the squire and Mr Marston were a long way ahead, and Tom proposed a run to overtake them.

"Ay, run, lads. Keep up a trot. Dessay I shall be clost behind."

"Come along!" cried Dick; and they started off along the track, with Dave increasing his stride and seeming to skim without effort over the ground, his long wiry legs and great strength enabling him to keep up with the boys, who, whenever they looked back, found him close behind.

"You needn't mind about me, lads," he said with a chuckle; "I sha'n't be far."

They were rapidly gaining upon those in front; knowing this fact from the murmur of their voices as they kept up an animated discussion, when, all at once, it seemed as if the squire had begun to talk much more rapidly, and that Mr Marston was replying to him at a terrible rate, their voices becoming blurred and confused, as it were, when Dick realised what it meant.

"There's a party of the drain-men coming. Let's run!"

Dick was right, and five minutes after, he and his companions had joined a group gathered round Mr Marston, while Bargle, the big labourer, was talking.

"Ay, mester, we *all* tumbled out, and went away down to the gaäts as soon as we'd tumbled out, and they're all knocked down and the water in."

"Knocked down!" cried the squire.

"Ay," cried another of the men, "far as we could see; one's smashed to bits, and brickwork's all ploughed up."

"Come along!" said the engineer. "Two of you run on first and get lanthorns."

The big labourer and another went off back with a heavy trot, and the party were advancing again when a heavy step was heard behind.

"Who's that?" said Tom.

"Me, lad, me," came back in the thick hearty voice of the wheelwright. "What's amiss?"

They told him.

"I was straänge and fast asleep," he said, "and didn't hear nowt; but my missus wakkened me, and I come on."

"Ay, bud it wakkened me, neighbour," said Dave, who was busy administering to himself a pill. "I've slep' badly since I had that last touch of ager, and I thowt some un was broosting in the wall, and as soon as I jumped up and looked out, the plaäce seemed alive, for all the birds in the fen were flying round and round, and you could hear their wings whistling as they flew away. I was scarred."

Half an hour later they were picking their way along the embankment at the side of the great drain, now once more filled with salt water, while when they reached the mouth, where a peculiar dank saline odour was perceptible, the two men who had been flitting before them with lanthorns like a couple of will-o'-the-wisps, went cautiously down the crumbling bank, followed by the engineer, and the mischief done was at once plain to see.

Apparently a powerful blast of powder had been placed in the hollow of the stone-work, where the mechanism for opening and closing the great sluice-gates was fixed, and the result of the explosion was a huge chasm in the stone, and one of the gates blown right off, leaving the way for the water free.

A dead silence fell upon the group as the engineer took one of the lanthorns and carefully examined the damage, the squire holding the other light, and peering forward in the darkness till the engineer climbed back to his side.

"They've managed it well," he said bitterly.

"Well!" cried the squire angrily. "I'm not a harsh man, but I'd give a hundred pounds down to see the wretch who did this lying dead in the ruins."

"Ay, mester," said Hickathrift in a low hoarse voice; "it be a shaäme. Will it spoil the dreern, and stop all the work?"

"Ay," said Dave, as he stood leaning upon his pole, which he had brought over his shoulder; "will it stop dreern?"

The two lads leaned forward to hear the answer, and there was a peculiar solemnity in the scene out there in the wild place in the darkness, merely illumined by the two lanthorns.

"Stop the drain!" exclaimed the squire hoarsely, and in a voice full of rage.

"No, my men," said the engineer coolly. "It will make a job for the carpenters and the masons; but if the madman, or the man with the brains of a mischievous monkey, thinks he is going to stop our great enterprise by such an act as this, he is greatly mistaken. You, Bargle, be here to meet me at daylight with a double gang. Get the piles up here at once, and if we work hard we can have the piles in and an embankment up before the next tide. A few days' hindrance, Mr Winthorpe, that's all."

The men broke into a cheer, in which Dave and Hickathrift joined; and as nothing more could be done, the little crowd separated, the men going slowly back to their huts, while the squire and Marston made for the track so as to return, talking earnestly the while.

"You talked as if the thing were a trifle," said the squire angrily. "It will cost us hundreds!"

"Yes, but it might cost us thousands if we let the scoundrels know how big a breach they have made in our works, and they would renew the attack at once."

"Hah, there's something in that!" said the squire, drawing his breath in angrily through his teeth. "If I only knew who was at the bottom of it! Marston, it must be the work of a gang among your men."

"Think so?" said the engineer quietly.

"I do."

"But why should my men do such a dastardly act?"

"To make the job last longer."

"Nonsense, my dear sir! We have work before us that will last us for years, for this drain is only the first of many."

"Then who is it—who can it be?"

"I think I've got an insight to-night," said Marston. "Tom Tallington saw a couple of men coming along the road and creep to the edge of the mere."

"True! I had forgotten that," said the squire sharply.

"And that shows us that our enemies belong to a party somewhere at a distance, and that we should be wasting time in searching here. Hallo! who's this?"

The exclamation was caused by the appearance of a dark figure coming towards them from the direction of the Toft.

"Why, it's Thorpeley, the constable!" said Dick in a whisper to his companion.

"Oh, it's you!" said the squire gruffly. "Pity you weren't down here sooner."

"Has it been an explosion, sir?" said the constable in a smooth unctuous voice.

"Yes," said the squire abruptly, and he walked on with the engineer.

"Ah, I was going on to see!" said the constable; "but as you're all going back, I'll go back too."

No one spoke, but all walked on in silence, for the man's coming seemed to have damped the conversation; but the opportunity for making himself heard and showing his importance was not to be ignored.

"They're very clever," he said in a high voice, so that the squire and Mr Marston, who were in front, could hear; "but I've got my hye upon them."

"Why didn't you ketch 'em, then, 'fore they did this here?" said Dave with a little laugh.

"Ay, why didst thou not stop this?" growled Hickathrift.

"Because the thing was not quite ripe. I shall tak' 'em yet red-handed, and then—"

He paused and rubbed his hands.

"What then?" asked Dave.

"Transportation or hanging—one of them," said the constable with a chuckle.

"Ay, but you heven't found 'em yet," said Dave, shaking his head.

"Nay, bud I can put my hand on 'em pretty well when I like."

"Wheer are they, then?" said Hickathrift excitedly.

"Ay, wheer are they?" said the constable. "Going about stealthily of a night, creeping behind hedges, and carrying messages one to the other. I know! They think no one suspects them, and that they're going to be passed over, but I'm set here to find them out, and I've nearly got things ready."

"Look here, my man," said the engineer, stopping short; "can you say for certain who's at the bottom of this mischief?"

"Mebbe I can, sir."

"Then who was it?"

"Nay," said the constable with a little laugh; "if theer's going to be any credit for takkin of 'em, I mean to hev it, and not give it over to someone else."

"Pish!" ejaculated the squire angrily; "come along! The man knows nothing."

"Mebbe not," said the constable with a sneer. "Mebbe if people treated people proper, and asked them to their house, and gave 'em a lodging and a bit of food, things might hev been found out sooner; but some people thinks they know best."

The squire understood the hint, but he scorned to notice it, and went on talking sternly to the engineer; but Thorpeley was not to be put down like that, for he continued:

"Mebbe theer's people in it—old people and young people—as wouldn't like to be exposed, but who hev got to be exposed, and—"

"Look here," said Dick boldly, "if my father won't speak, I will. Do you mean to say you believe Tom Tallington and I know anything about these cowardly tricks?"

"Nay, I'm not going to show my hand," said the man. "Wait a bit, and you'll see."

"No; you speak out now," cried Dick. "I won't be suspected by any man. Do you mean to say Tom Tallington and I know?"

"Nay, I shall na speak till proper time comes. I know what I know, and I know what I've seen, and when time comes mebbe I shall speak, and not before."

"He don't know anything," cried Tom, laughing. "He's a regular sham."

"Nay, I don't know as boys steals out o' windows at nights, and goes creeping along in the dark, and playing their games as other people gets the credit on. I don't know nothing. Oh, no!"

"Why, you cowardly—"

Dick did not finish his speech, for at that moment Hickathrift stretched out one of his great arms, and his big hand closed with a mighty grip on the constable's shoulder, making the man utter a sharp ejaculation.

"That'll do," he growled. "Yow shoot thee neb. Man as says owt again Mester Dick here's saying things agen me."

"What do you mean?" cried the constable. "Are you going to resist the law?"

"Nay, not I," said Hickathrift. "I am a good subject o' the king's. God bless him! But if yow says owt more again Mester Dick, I'll take thee by the scruff and pitch thee right out yonder into the bog."

"Ay," snarled Dave, spitting in his hands and giving his staff a twist; "and I'll howd him down till he says he's sorry."

How the constable was to beg Dick's pardon when held down under the black ooze and water of the mere was not very evident; but the threat had a good effect, for the man stared from one of the speakers to the other, and held his peace till they reached the Toft.

The explosion proved to have done more mischief than was at first supposed, and necessitated the taking down of all one side of the gowt and the making of a new sluice door. It was all plain enough, as the engineer had surmised upon the first inspection: a heavy charge of powder had been lowered down by the miscreants who were fighting against the project, and they had probably used a long fuse sufficient to enable them to get far enough away before the explosion.

What followed was, however, quite enough to daunt the most determined foe, for in place of disheartening the engineer, the mishap seemed to spur him on to renewed exertions. He was on the spot by daybreak, and before long a strong dam was made across, to prevent the entrance of the sea-water; the drain was emptied, and while one gang was engaged in taking down the ruined side of the gowt, the rest of the men went on with the delving, as if nothing had happened, and the dike increased.

Dick and Tom were down at the works directly after breakfast, but Mr Marston took very little notice of them, and it seemed to Dick that the engineer shared the squire's doubts.

The consequence was, that, being a very natural boy, who, save when at school, had led rather a solitary life, finding companionship in Tom Tallington and the grown-up denizens of the fen, Dick, who was by no means a model, turned sulky, and shrank within his metaphorical shell.

"I sha'n't go begging him to talk to me if he doesn't like," he said to Tom; "and if my father likes to believe I would do such things I shall go."

"Go where?" said Tom, looking at him wonderingly.

"I don't know—anywhere. I say, let's find an island and build a hut, and go there whenever we like."

"But where?—out in the sea somewhere?"

"No, no, I mean such a place as Dave's and John Warren's. You and I could retreat there whenever we liked."

Tom stared, and did not seem to grasp the idea for a few minutes; then his eyes brightened.

"Why, Dick," he cried, "that would be glorious! We could catch and shoot birds, and have our own fire, and no one could get to us."

"Without a boat," said Dick slowly.

"I'd forgotten that," said Tom thoughtfully. "How could we get there, then?"

"We'd borrow Hicky's punt till we had built one for ourselves."

"But could we build one?"

"Of course we could, or make one of skins, or a raft of reeds. There are lots of ways."

"But what will your father say?"

"I don't know," said Dick dolefully; "he thinks I'm fighting against him, so I suppose he'll be glad I've gone."

"But how about your mother?"

Dick paused a few moments before answering.

"I should tell her as a secret, and she'd help me, and lend me things we should want. I don't care to be at home now, with everybody looking at one as if there was something wrong."

"I don't think my father would let me go," said Tom thoughtfully, "and I'm sure my mother wouldn't; and I say, Dick, isn't it all nonsense?"

"I don't think it's nonsense," said Dick, who was taking a very morbid view of matters, consequent upon a mistaken notion of his father's ideas and thoughts at that time, and matters were not improved by a conversation which ensued in the course of the next day.

Dick was in the garden with Tom, paying court to the gooseberry trees, for though fruit by no means abounded there, the garden always supplied a fair amount of the commoner kinds, consequent upon the shelter afforded from the north and bitter easterly sea-winds by the old buildings which intervened.

"Here, I want to talk to you two," said the squire; and he led the way into the house, where Mrs Winthorpe was seated at work, and, probably by a preconcerted arrangement, to Dick's great disgust she rose and left the room.

"Now," said the squire, "I don't like for there to be anything between us, Dick; and as for you, Tom Tallington, I should be sorry to think anything about you but that you were a frank, straightforward companion for my son."

"I'm sure, sir—" blundered out Tom.

"Wait a minute, my lad. I have not done. Now, I'm going to ask you a plain question, both of you, and I want a frank, manly answer. But before I ask it, I'm going to say a few words."

He drew his tobacco-jar towards him, and took down his pipe, carefully filled it, and laid it down again.

"Now, look here," he said. "I'm a great believer in keeping faith and being true to one another, and looking down with contempt upon a tale-bearer, or one who betrays a secret. Do you understand?"

"Yes, sir," said Tom, for Dick felt that he could not speak. "You mean, sir, that you don't like a sneak."

"That's it," said the squire; "but I should have liked to hear you say that, Dick. However, that is what I mean. There are times, though, when lads have been led into connections where things are done of which they are heartily ashamed. They have joined in them from the idea that it was a good bit of fun, or that there was some injustice being perpetrated, and they have, as they think, joined the weaker side. But I want you both to see that in such cases as we have had lately it would be weak and criminal to keep silence from the mistaken notion that it would be cowardly to speak, and betraying friends."

Dick's face was scarlet, and his bosom swelled with emotion as he felt choked with indignation at his father suspecting him, while he changed countenance the more as he saw his father watching him keenly. In fact the more innocent Dick strove to look the worse he succeeded, and the squire seemed troubled as he went on.

"Now, my lads, as you are well aware, there are some cowardly outrages being perpetrated from time to time; and I want you to answer me at once—do you either of you know anything whatever about the persons who have done these things?"

"No," said Tom at once; and the squire turned to Dick.

"Now, my boy," he said, "why don't you speak?"

Dick felt as if he would choke, and with his morbid feeling increasing, he said in a husky voice:

"No, father, I do not know anything either."

"On your honour, Dick?" said his father, gazing at him searchingly.

"On my honour, father."

"That will do," said the squire in a short decisive tone. "I must own that I thought you two knew something of the matter. I suspected you before that meddling, chattering idiot shared my ideas. But now there's an end to it, and I shall go to work to find out who is fighting against us, since I am sure that you two boys are quite innocent. That will do."

"Father doesn't believe me," said Dick bitterly as soon as they were alone.

"Nonsense!" cried Tom. "Why, he said he did."

"Yes, but I could see it in his eyes that he did not I know his looks so well, and it does seem so hard."

As if to endorse Dick's fancy, the squire passed them an hour afterwards in the garden and there was a heavy frown upon his countenance as he glanced for a moment at his son, who was, of course, perfectly ignorant of the fact that his father was so intent upon the troubles connected with the drain, and the heavy loss which would ensue if the scheme failed, that he did not even realise the presence of his boy.

It was enough, though, for Dick; and he turned to his companion.

"There," he said, "what did I tell you? Father doesn't believe me. But I know what I'll do."

"What will you do—run away from home?" said Tom.

"Like a coward, and make him feel sure that I knew all this and told a lie. No, I won't. I'll just show him."

"Show him what?"

"That I'm innocent."

"Yes, that's all very well; but how are you going to do it?"

"Find out the people and let him see."

"Yes, but how?" cried Tom eagerly, as he knocked an apple off one of the trees and tried to take a bite, but it was so hard and green that he jerked it away.

"I don't know yet; but someone does all these cowardly things, and I mean to find it out before I've done."

"Oh, I am disappointed!" said Tom dolefully.

"Disappointed! Why? Won't you help me?"

"Yes, I will. But I thought we were going to find an island of our own somewhere out in the mere, where no one ever goes, and have no end of fun."

"And so we will," said Dick eagerly. "We could keep it secret, and there would be the sort of place to be and watch."

"What, out there?"

"To be sure! Whoever does all this mischief comes in a boat, I'm sure of that, and he wouldn't suspect us of watching, and so we could catch him."

Tom screwed up his face in doubt, but the idea of starting a sort of home out there in the middle of the wild fen-land had its fascinations, and the plan was discussed for long enough before they parted that day.

Chapter Sixteen.

Another Trip.

The two lads had left the grammar-school in the county town about a year before in consequence of a terrible outbreak of fever; and, Mrs Winthorpe declaring against their going back, they had been kept at home. But though several plans had been proposed of sending them for another year's education somewhere, the time had glided by, the business of the draining had cropped up, and as the lads proved useful at times, the school business kept on being deferred, to the delight of both, the elongated holiday growing greatly to their taste. Even though they were backward from a more modern point of view, they were not losing much, for they were acquiring knowledge which would be useful to them in their future careers, and in addition growing bone and muscle such as would make them strong men.

Hence it was that the time glided pleasantly on, with the two lads finding plenty of opportunities for the various amusements which gratified them when not occupied in some way about the farms.

It was a few days after the conversation with the squire that Tom proposed a turn after the fish in Hickathrift's boat.

"We could pole ourselves without Dave; and let's ask Mr Marston to come. It's a long time since he has had a holiday."

Dick's brow was overcast, and he wore generally the aspect of a boy who had partaken of baking pears for a week, but his face cleared at this, and he eagerly joined in the plan.

"We'll get Hicky to lend us his boat, and pole down as far as we can, and then run across to Mr Marston."

Their preparations did not take long, and though they were made before they knew whether they could have the punt, they did not anticipate any objections, and they were right.

Hickathrift was busy sawing, but he looked up with a broad grin, and leaving his work went down with them to the water side.

"Course I'll lend it to you, lads," he said. "Wish I could come wi' you."

"Do, then, Hicky. It's a long time since we've had a fish."

"Nay; don't ask me," was the reply. "I wean't leave the work. Ay, bud it's nice to be a boy," he added, with a smile.

"Couldn't you do your work afterward?" cried Tom.

"Nay, nay, don't tempt a poor weak fellow," he cried. "I'm going to do that bit o' sawing 'fore I leave it. Now, theer, in wi' you!"

The boys made another appeal to the great fellow to come; but he was staunch. Still he uttered a sigh of relief as he gave the punt a tremendous thrust from the bank into deep water, where it went rustling by the willow boughs and over the wild growth where the pink-blossomed persicaria sent up its pretty heads.

"If we had pressed Hicky a little more, I believe he would have come," said Dick.

"No, he wouldn't. He never will when he says he won't."

Just at that moment Hickathrift was muttering to himself on the bank, as he watched the boat.

"Straänge thing," he said, "that a girt big man like I am should allus feel like a boy. I wanted to go wi' they two straänge and badly. I will go next time."

Taking it in turns, the boys sent the punt quickly over the amber water, the exercise in the bright sunshine chasing the clouds from Dick's countenance, so that before they reached their intended landing-place on the edge of the mere, as near as they could go to the spot where Mr Marston's men were at work, he was once more his old self, laughing, reckoning on the fish they would catch with the trimmers that lay ready, and forgetting for the time all about the plots to injure the drain and its projectors.

There was a low patch of alders at the spot where they intended to land, and Dick was just about to run the punt close in, when he suddenly ceased poling and stood motionless staring before him.

"What's the matter?" cried Tom.

There was no answer, in fact none was needed, for at that moment Tom's eyes fell upon the object which had arrested his companion's action, to wit, the flabby, unpleasant-looking face of Thorpeley, the constable, that individual being seated by the low bushes smoking his pipe in a position where he must have been watching the lads ever since they started.

Dick's teeth gave forth a peculiar gritting sound, and then, thrusting down the pole, he ran in the punt, leaped on to the quivering shore with the rope, fastened it to a bush, and signed to Tom to follow.

The man said nothing, but there was a curiously aggravating leering grin upon his countenance as he sat taking in every movement on the part of the boys, who walked away rapidly with the full knowledge that they were followed.

"Don't look back, Tom," said Dick between his teeth. "Oh, how I should have liked to give him a topper with the pole!"

"I wish old Dave was here to pitch him in the water," growled Tom.

"Did you ever see anything so aggravating? He's following us. I can hear his boots. Don't take any notice. Let's go on fast as if he wasn't there."

"I don't know that I can," grumbled Tom. "I feel alloverish like."

"Feel how?"

"As if I couldn't do as I liked. My head wants to turn round and look at him, my tongue wants to call him names, and my toes itch, and my fists want to feel as if it would be like punching a sack of corn to hit him in the nose."

"Come along!" cried Dick, who was too angry to laugh at his companion's remarks. "Let's make haste to Mr Marston."

As they reached the works the first man they encountered was big Bargle, who stuck his spade into the soft peat and came slowly up the embankment, to stand wiping his fist on his side, before opening it and holding it out, smiling broadly the while.

He shook hands with both lads, and then went back to his work smiling; and as they walked on they could hear him say confidentially to all around him:

"We're mates, we are, lads; we're mates."

The engineer was coming towards them; and as they met, Dick unfolded his plan, but before he had half-finished his words trailed off, and he stopped short. For the severe countenance before him checked his utterance.

"No," said Mr Marston, shortly. "I am too busy. Good day!"

He went on to speak to his men, and Dick looked at Tom with a dismal expression of countenance which spoke volumes.

"Come along back!" he said.

Tom obeyed without a word, and glancing neither to the right nor left, the two boys walked heavily back over the dry surface of the quaking bog, so as to reach their boat.

Before they had travelled half-way they met Thorpeley, who leered at them in a sinister way, and, as they passed on, turned and followed at a distance.

"Look here, Dick," whispered Tom, "let's give him something to think about. Come along!"

Tom started running as if in a great state of excitement, and Dick followed involuntarily, while after a momentary hesitation the constable also began to run.

"I say, don't go that way," said Dick, as his companion struck off to the left. "Bog's soft there."

"I know: come along! Keep on the tufts."

Dick understood Tom's low chuckling laugh, which was just like that of a cuckoo in a bush, and divining that the object was to reach the boat by a détour, he did not slacken his speed.

Long familiarity with the worst parts of the fen enabled the lads to pick their way exactly, and they went on bounding from tuft to tuft, finding fairly firm ground for their feet as if by instinct, though very often they were going gingerly over patches of bog which undulated and sprang beneath their tread, while now and then they only saved themselves from going through the dry coat of moss by making a tremendous leap.

They had pretty well half a mile to run to reach the boat by the alder bush, and the constable soon began to go heavily; but he was so satisfied that the boys had some sinister design in view, and were trying to throw him off their scent, that he put forth all his energies, and as Dick glanced back once, it was to see him, hat in hand, toiling along in the hot sun right in their wake.

"You'd better not go round there, Tom," said Dick as they approached a patch of rushes. "It's very soft."

"I don't care if I go in; do you?" was the reply.

"No, I don't mind," said Dick sadly. "I don't seem to mind anything now."

"Come along then," cried Tom; "and as we get round let's both look back and then try to keep out of sight—pretend, you know."

They reached the patch of tall rushes and reeds, which was high enough to hide them, and giving a frightened look back at their pursuer, plunged out of sight.

"Oh, I say, isn't it soft?" cried Dick.

"Never mind: some people like it soft," said Tom. "Follow me."

He had arranged his plan so deftly that while keeping the patch of reeds between them and their pursuer, Tom managed, with no little risk of going through, to reach a second patch of the marsh growth, behind which he dodged, and threw himself down, Dick following closely; and they were well hidden and lay panting as the constable came round the first patch, glanced round, and then made for a third patch still more to the left, and beyond which was quite a copse of scrubby firs.

"Ho—ho—ho!" laughed Tom in a low voice, as he nearly choked with mirth, for all at once there was a splash, a shout, a strange wallowing noise, and as the lads parted and peered through the rushes they could see that the constable was down and floundering in the bog.

"Oh, Tom," cried Dick, struggling up, "he'll be smothered!"

"Sit down; he won't. It'll be a lesson to him."

"But suppose—"

"No, don't suppose anything. He'll get out right enough."

The constable had a hard struggle for a few minutes, and doubtless would have got out sooner if he had worked a little more with his brains; but finally he crawled to firmer ground, just as a scuffle began between Dick and Tom, the former being determined to go to his enemy's help, the latter clinging to him with all his might to keep him back.

"Now, come along down to the boat. We can get nearly there before he sees us," whispered Tom.

"But do you think he will get back safe?"

"Of course he will. He won't try to run any more."

Dick took a long look at the constable to see that he was really out of danger, and feeling satisfied at last that there was nothing to mind, he followed Tom once more, the two managing so well that after losing sight of them altogether for some time, their inquisitive pursuer had the mortification of seeing them enter the punt and push off, leaving him to make a long and tedious circuit, crawling part of the way, and when he stood erect, wanting as he was in the boys' experience, making very slow progress to the regular track.

As soon as the excitement was over, and the boat reached once more, Dick's gloomy feelings came back, and but for his companion's efforts he would have relapsed into a mournfully depressed condition, which would have done little towards making their trip agreeable.

Tom, however, worked hard, and using the pole with vigour he drove the punt along, till Dick roused up from a fit of musing on his father's severe looks and Mr Marston's distant manner, to find that they were close to Dave's home.

"Why have you come here?" he cried.

"To see how he is," replied Tom; and, thrusting down his pole, he soon had the punt ashore.

"Why, he isn't at home!" said Dick.

His words proved correct, for the punt was missing, and unless it lay on the other side of an alder patch or was drawn out to be repaired, the master must have it far away somewhere on the mere.

It need not be supposed that the two lads were troubled with more curiosity than is the property of most boys of their age, because they landed and looked round, ending by going up to the fen-man's hut and entering.

It was not a particularly cleanly place, but everything there, dealing as it did with Dave's pursuits, had its attraction, from the gun hanging upon a couple of wooden pegs to the nets and lines above the rough bed-place, with its sheep-skins and dingy-looking blanket.

"I should like to take the gun and have a turn by ourselves," said Dick, gazing at the long rusty piece longingly.

But it remained untouched, and, returning to the boat, the boys pushed off and made for the more remote portion of the fen, passing from one open lake to another as they followed the long meandering lanes of water, in and out among reed-beds and alder patches, islands of bog-plants, islets of sedge, and others where the gravel and sand enabled the purple heather and lavender ling to blow profusely, in company with here and there a little gorgeous orange-yellow furze.

The hours went by, and the sun was declining fast as they neared at length a spot which had attracted them for some time past. It was either a little promontory or an isthmus, where the ground was strong enough for fir-trees to flourish, and this promised dry ground, wood, and a good site for a little hut if they set one up.

Dick brightened at the sight, for there was a cheering notion in his mind that he was going to find rest, peace, and happiness here in a little home of his own making, to which he could retire from the world to fish, shoot, and eat the fruits he would be able to gather in the season.

In short, Dick Winthorpe, being in a marsh, was suffering from a sharp fit of goose, such as attacks many boys who, because matters do not go exactly as they like at home, consider that they are ill-used, and long for what they call their freedom—a freedom which is really slavery, inasmuch as they make themselves the bond-servants of their silly fancies, and it takes some time to win them back.

The clump of firs here, which they had before seen at a distance, surpassed their expectations, for it was a good-sized island, far from the shore, and promised fishing, fowling, and security from interruption, for it was not likely that any one would venture there.

But the evening was rapidly coming on, and the punt's head was turned homewards, the distance they had come proving startling, as they began now to feel that they were very hungry, and that they had hours of work before them before they could reach the Toft.

"Not many fish to land," said Dick rather dismally.

"Why, you wouldn't fish!" replied Tom. "Never mind, we've found the island. Shall we build a place?"

Dick's reply was in the affirmative, and for the next two hours they debated on the subject of what they should take over, and how soon, and so passed the time away till after dark, when, being still quite a mile from home, there came the sharp report of a gun, and then they fancied that they heard a cry.

"Why, who can be shooting now?" said Dick in an awe-stricken whisper. "Is anything wrong?"

"I don't know. Look! look!"

Tom whispered these words, and pointed in the opposite direction, to a lambent light which seemed to be moving slowly over the marshy edge of the mere.

The light was in a portion of the shore where the mere narrowed; and the two lads let the boat drift as they sat and watched, each thinking of the place in the light of experience.

"Why, Tom, that can't be a boat," whispered Dick.

"Boat! No, it's land there."

"Land! It's soft bog that nobody could walk on!"

"Then it couldn't be a boat. Why, it's a will-o'-the-wisp."

"Yes," said Dick, after a sceptical pause, during which he watched the lambent light as it played about in a slow fantastic way, just as if it were a softly-glowing lantern carried by a short-winged moth, which used it to inspect the flowering plants as it sought for a meal. "Let's go over and look at it."

"No, no! no, no!" whispered Tom excitedly.

"Why not? Are you afraid?"

"No, not a bit; but I don't want to go. I'm tired and hungry. I don't believe you want to go either."

"Yes, I do," said Dick eagerly. "I feel as if I wanted to go, but my body didn't."

"Ha, ha, ha!" laughed Tom, but very softly, as he kept his eyes fixed on the distant light. "That's a nice way of backing out of it. Why, you're as much afraid as I am, only I'm honest and you're not."

"Yes, I am," whispered Dick. "I'm as honest as you are, and I'll show you that I am. There, I should feel afraid to go by myself."

"Will you go if I go with you?"

Before Dick could answer there was a long, low, piteous cry from the other direction, that from whence they had heard the shot.

"I say, what's that?" whispered Tom in an awe-stricken tone.

"I don't know. It sounds very queer. There it is again."

"Is it a bird?" whispered Tom.

"No. I never heard a bird cry like that."

"What is it then—a fox trapped?"

"Nobody would trap the foxes, and it can't be a rabbit, because that would be a squeal."

The cry came again over the dark water of the mere, and sounded so strange and weird that Dick shivered.

"It's something queer," said Tom huskily. "Take the pole and let's get away. Don't make a noise."

"But—"

"No, no; don't stop. We don't know what it is. Perhaps it's one of those things Hicky talks about that he has heard sometimes."

"Father says it's all nonsense, and there are no such things in the fens."

"He'd better say there are no will-o'-the-wisps to lead people astray," whispered Tom.

"He doesn't say that. He says there are jack-o'-lanterns, but they don't lead people astray—people go astray to try and catch them."

"Hist! there it is again!" said Tom, gripping his companion's arm, as the long piteous cry came faintly over the water. "It is something horrible!"

"It isn't," said Dick. "It's someone in distress."

"People in distress never cry out like that."

"Why, Tom, it's that Thorpeley stuck in the mud somewhere; and it's our doing."

"It's his own if he is stuck there. But I don't believe it is. Why, it's two miles nearer home than where we left him."

"Then it's somebody else in trouble," said Dick excitedly.

"It isn't. Let's go home."

Tom was, as a rule, no coward; but he was faint and tired, and the very fact of being seated out on the dark waters with the gloom so thick that they could see but a short distance, and with an unnatural-looking light on one side and a strange marrow-thrilling cry coming on the other, was enough to startle stouter-hearted lads than he, and he held more tightly to his companion as Dick seized the pole.

"Let's get back home," he said again.

"You said I was afraid to go to the will o' the wisp," said Dick stoutly. "You're afraid to go now and see what it is makes that noise."

"Well, I can't help it," said Tom appealingly; "but if you go I shall go with you. There, listen! Isn't it horrible!"

He spoke as the cry came again faintly but piteous in the extreme.

Dick drove the pole down into the soft bottom of the mere and sent the punt surging through the water, determined now to go straight to the spot whence the cry seemed to come; and, guided by the sound, he toiled away for about ten minutes before giving way to Tom, who worked hard to reach the place.

For, once the two lads had taken action, they seemed to forget their nervous dread, while what was more encouraging to them to proceed was the fact that as they reduced the distance the cries gradually seemed to be more human, and were evidently those of some person in peril or great distress.

It was a weird strange journey over the water now, the excitement lent by their mission seeming to change the aspect of all around. The reeds whispered, the patches of growth looked black, and every now and then they disturbed some water-fowl, whose hurried flight seemed suddenly to have become mysterious and awe-inspiring, as if it were a creature of the darkness which had been watching their coming and had risen to hover round.

But there was the cry again and again, sometimes faint and distant, sometimes sounding as if close at hand, and, as is often the case, apparently varying in position to right or left as it was borne by the soft night wind.

"We cannot go any farther," cried Dick at last as he drove the boat in amongst the broad belt of reeds which fringed the edge of the mere.

"Yes, we can. There's a way here," cried Tom excitedly, pointing through the gloom to his left where there was an opening. "Coming!" he yelled as the cry rose once more.

Dick backed the boat out, with the reeds whistling and rustling strangely, and the next minute he had it right in the gloomy opening, which proved to be quite a little bay, where, at the end of a few good thrusts of the pole, the prow of the punt bumped up against the quivering moss.

The two boys got out cautiously; the pole was driven down into the peat, and the boat made fast; and then they paused and listened for the next cry.

Everything now was perfectly silent, not so much as the whisper of a reed or the whir of the wing of a nightbird fell upon their ears; and at last, in an awe-stricken whisper, Tom said:

"Hicky is right. It was something strange from out of the marsh. Let's get away."

Dick was stouter-hearted than his companion, and lifting his voice he shouted, and then stood silent.

"Help! help!" came faintly in reply.

"There!" cried Dick turning sharply. "It's a man."

"Think so?"

"Why, of course! Come along! Here, I can see where we are now."

"Yes, I think I know where we are," whispered Tom. "But is it safe to go after it?"

"You mean after *him*," said Dick. "Yes, it's pretty firm here—yes, it's all right. We're amongst heath and bilberry as soon as we get by this bit of bog. Hoy! shout again," he cried as he plodded on cautiously, with his feet sometimes sinking in the bog, sometimes finding it pretty firm.

But there was no answer; and though as far as was possible Dick walked in the direction of the sound, the guidance was of the most unsatisfactory nature, and at the end of a minute or two they listened again.

"It must be that Thorpeley regularly bogged," said Dick at last, and a curious shiver ran through him. "I hope he hasn't sunk in."

"He couldn't," said Tom. "I know this part. It's all firm ground between the water and the track to the sea."

"I can't quite make out where we are," said Dick, staring about him.

"I can. There's the big alder clump, and beyond it there's the river wall." (Mud embankment.)

"So it is. Yes, I know now. Why, it is all firm about here, and nobody could be bogged unless he got into a hole. Ahoy!"

He shouted once more, but there was no answer; and when he raised his voice again it was only for the sound to seem to come back, just as if they were shut up in some large room.

"He must be hereabout," said Dick.

"Shall we find our way back to the boat?" said Tom in a doubting tone.

"I don't know, but if we don't we could walk home in half an hour. Come along. Ahoy!"

Still no answer; and in spite of his companion's suggestions and strange doubts Dick kept on hunting about in the darkness among the patches of alders and the heath that here grew freely. For, save in places, the ground was sandy and firm, and, dark as it was, they had no difficulty in making out the watery spots by their faint gleam or the different character of the growth.

They shouted in turns and together, listening, going in different directions, and all to no purpose. Not a sound could they get in reply; and at last, with a curious feeling of horror stealing over him, compounded of equal parts of superstition and dread lest the person whose cry they had heard had sunk in the mire of some hole, Dick reluctantly gave way to Tom's suggestion that they should go back to the boat.

"I knew it was something queer," whispered Tom. "If we had gone on, we should have been led into some dangerous hole and lost."

"Don't believe it," said Dick, as they trudged slowly back, utterly worn-out and hoarse with shouting.

"You're such a doubting fellow!" grumbled Tom. "If it had been anybody in distress we should have found him."

"Perhaps," said Dick sadly. "It's so dark, though, that we might have passed him over."

"Nonsense!" cried Tom; "we were sure to find him. There wasn't anybody. It was a marsh cry, and—oh!"

Tom uttered a yell and went headlong down, with the effect of so startling his companion that he ran a few steps before he could recover his nerve, when he returned to extend his hand to Tom, who rose trembling, while Dick stood staring aghast at the dark figure lying extended among the heath, and over which his friend had stumbled.

"Why, Tom, it's Thorpeley!" cried Dick, as he went down on one knee and peered into the upturned face. "Mr Thorpeley, Mr Thorpeley!" he cried; "what's the matter?"

There was no reply.

"It must have been him," whispered Dick. "He had lost his way."

"Then let him find it again," grumbled Tom, "instead of watching us."

"But perhaps there is something the matter. Mr Thorpeley, Mr Thorpeley!"

Dick laid his hand upon the man's shoulder and shook him, but there was no response.

"Is he dead?" said Tom in an awe-stricken whisper.

"Dead!" cried Dick, leaping up and shrinking away at the suggestion. "No, he can't be. He's quite warm," he added, going down on his knee again to shake the recumbent man, who now uttered a low groan.

"What shall we do, Dick?" said Tom huskily. "I hate him, but we can't leave him here."

"Well," said Dick, "I'm not very fond of him, but it would be like leaving anybody to die to go away now. We must carry him down to the boat."

"Come on then, quick!"

Dick placed his hands beneath the constable's arms and locked his fingers across his breast, while Tom turned his back as he got between the man's legs, stooped in turn, and proceeded to lift them as if they were the handles of a wheel-barrow.

"Ready?"

"Yes."

"Then both together."

The two lads lifted the constable, staggered along a few yards, and set him down again.

"Oh, I say!" groaned Tom. "Isn't he heavy?"

"Come and try this end," retorted Dick. "He's an awful weight. We must go a few yards at a time, and we shall do it yet. Now then."

"Stop a minute," said Tom, who had picked up a handful of moss, and was rubbing one hand. "I—it's warm and sticky, and—oh, Dick, he's bleeding."

Dick lowered the insensible man down again, and, shuddering with horror, stepped to his companion's side.

Then kneeling down he tried to examine the spot pointed out by Tom, to find out as well as was possible in the dim light that the constable was bleeding freely from one leg.

"Dick, what shall we do?" cried Tom piteously.

"Why, what would anybody do if he had cut his finger?" cried Dick manfully, as he undid his neckcloth and doubled it afresh.

"I don't know," cried Tom, who was sadly scared.

"You don't know! Suppose you had cut your finger, wouldn't you tie it up?"

"Yes, I suppose so," faltered Tom, whom the situation had completely unnerved.

"Take off his neckerchief while I tie this on," said Dick, whom the emergency had rendered more helpful. "How can he have hurt himself like this?"

As he spoke he busied himself in tightly bandaging the man's leg, and added to the bandage the cotton cloth that Tom handed to him.

"I think that has stopped it," said Dick. "Now then, we must carry him down."

"But we shall sink into the bog with him," faltered Tom.

"No, we sha'n't if we are careful. Now, then, are you ready?"

"I don't like to try and lift him now," said Tom. "It's so horrible. The man's bleeding to death."

"More shame for you to stand still and not try to help him," said Dick hotly. "Here, you come and carry this end."

Tom hastened to obey, heedless of the fact that the task would be the harder; and setting to with a will, the lads carried their load a few yards before setting it down again to rest.

This time, in spite of Tom's appeal not to be left alone, Dick went on for a bit so as to explore and make sure of the best way to get back to the boat, and not without avail, for he was able, in spite of the darkness, to pick out the firmest ground, his knowledge of the growth of the fen and its choice of soil helping him.

But it was a long and painful task. The lads were faint and terribly hungry. They had been working hard for several hours propelling the punt, and the load they were carrying would not have been an easy one for a couple of stout men. Still, by means of that wonderful aid to success, perseverance, they at last got past bog and water-pool, patch of sphagnum, bed of reed, and slimy hollow, where the cotton rushes nourished, and reached the belt of waving reeds which separated them from the water.

It was not done without tremendous effort and a constant succession of rests; but they stood there at last bathed in perspiration, and waiting for a few minutes before lifting the sufferer into the boat.

Up to this time they had been so busy and excited that they had not paused to ask the question: How was it that the man had been wounded? but as they lifted him carefully into the boat, Tom being in and Dick ashore, they both burst out with the query, as if moved by the same spring.

"I know," said Dick, as the truth seemed to flash upon him. "Some one must have shot him."

Tom had taken up the pole and was just about to force the boat along when this announcement seemed to paralyse him, and he stood there thinking of what had taken place before.

"Why, Dick," he whispered, "isn't it very horrible?"

"Don't talk," cried his companion, entering the boat; "let's get home."

The pole plashed in the water, which rippled against the bows, and once more they glided over the surface, just as the injured man uttered a low groan.

"We sha'n't be very long," said Dick, kneeling down and carefully feeling whether the kerchiefs he had bound round the leg were fulfilling their purpose. "Are you in much pain?"

"Pain!" groaned the man. "Hah! Give me some water."

There was no vessel of any kind in the punt, and Dick had to scoop up some water in the hollow of his hand, and pour it between the injured man's lips, with the result that he became sufficiently refreshed to sit up a little and begin muttering.

Dick now took the pole, and it was Tom's turn to try and administer a little comfort in the shape of words as to the time that would elapse before they could reach the Toft; but the only result was to produce an angry snarl from their patient.

"How does he seem?" Dick asked, as Tom went to his relief.

"Better not ask him."

"Why not?"

"Perhaps he'll bite you. He nearly did me. I say, how much farther is it?"

"Take another quarter of an hour. Oh, I shall be glad, Tom! Work hard."

Tom looked in his companion's face, and uttered a low laugh, as he toiled away at the poling, and that laugh seemed to say more than a dozen long speeches. Then there was nothing heard for some time but the regular plash and ripple of the water, as it was disturbed by pole and punt, while the darkness seemed to increase. At the same time, though, the hopes of the two lads rose high, for, standing as it were alone in the midst of the black darkness, there was a soft yellow light. At first it was so dull and lambent that it suggested thoughts of the will-o'-the-wisp. But this was no dancing flame, being a steady glow in one fixed spot, and Tom expressed his companion's thoughts exactly as he exclaimed:

"There's Hicky's old horn lanthorn!"

A few minutes more and the big bluff voice of the wheelwright was heard in a loud hail.

This was answered, and the sounds roused the wounded man.

"Nearly there?" he said hoarsely.

"Very close now," replied Dick; and snatching the pole from Tom he drove it down vigorously, making a tremendous spurt to reach the patch of old pollard willows by the landing-place, on one of whose old posts the lanthorn had been hung, and beyond which could now be seen the light in the Hickathrifts' cot.

"Why, I was a-coming swimming after you, lads," shouted Hickathrift. "You scarred me. Squire's been down twiced to see if you'd got back, and the missus is in a fine way."

"Don't talk, Hicky," shouted back Dick. "Is Jacob there?"

"Ay, lad. Why?"

"You'll want help. Look here, send for the doctor."

"Doctor, lad?"

"Yes; I know. Let Jacob go and tell my father, and he'll send down the old cob. Thorpeley's hurt badly."

They heard a low whistle, then the wheelwright's orders given sharply to his apprentice, followed by the dull *thud, thud* of his boots as he ran off; and directly after the punt glided in and its bow was seized by the big strong hand upon which the soft glowing light of the horn lanthorn shone.

"Hey, but what's the matter with the man?" cried Hickathrift. "We've been wondering why he didn't come back."

"I don't know, only we heard a shot," said Dick excitedly; "and then we heard someone calling for help, and found him lying ashore."

"Let me get a good howd on him," said the wheelwright; and with one foot in the boat he passed his great arm under the constable and lifted him out as tenderly as if he had been a child.

But, gentle as was the wheelwright's act, it roused the injured man, who seemed to be driven into a fit of fury by the pain he suffered, and he burst into a torrent of bad language against Hickathrift and the two boys, which he kept up till he had been carried into his lodging and laid upon his bed.

"Hey, lads," said the wheelwright with a low chuckle, as he walked down with the boys to where the lanthorn still hung upon the willow-stump, the care of the constable having been left to the women; "he don't seem to hev lost his tongue."

"But he's very bad, isn't he?" said Dick anxiously.

"I should say no," replied Hickathrift. "Man who's very badly don't call people."

"But his leg?"

"Ay, that's badly. I give the hankycher a good tighten up, and that hot him, so that he had to howd his tongue."

"That made him hold his tongue, Hicky?"

"Ay, lad. I med him feel that if he didn't shoot his neb, I'd pull tighter, and so he quieted down. Now, tell us all about it."

"Give us some bread and butter first, Hicky; we're nearly starved."

"Hey, lads," cried the wheelwright. "Here, coom in to missus and—"

Hickathrift's speech was cut short by the coming of the squire, who hurried up.

"Here, boys," he cried; "what's all this?"

Dick told all he knew, and the squire drew a long breath and turned by the light of the lanthorn to gaze first in the lads' faces, and then to speak to the wheelwright.

"This is bad, Hickathrift," he said hoarsely.

As he spoke he gazed searchingly at the great workman.

"Ay, squire; it is a straänge awkard thing."

Mr Winthorpe gazed in his great frank face again; and then, with his lips compressed, he went to the bed-side of the injured man.

"Bad business," said Hickathrift; "but lads mustn't starve because a constable's shot. Coom along. Here, missus, let's hev bit o'— Nay, she's gone to see the neighbours, and hev a bit o' ruckatongue." (A gossip.)

That did not much matter, for Hickathrift knew the ways of his own house; and in a very short time had placed a loaf and a piece of cold bacon before the hungry boys.

This they attacked furiously, for now that they were relieved of the responsibility of the injured man, their hunger had asserted itself. But they had not partaken of many mouthfuls before they heard the squire's voice outside, in hurried conversation with Hickathrift.

"Yes, I sent him off directly on the cob," the squire said; "but it must be some hours before the doctor can get here."

"Think he's very badly, squire?" came next, in Hickathrift's deep bass.

"No, not very bad as to his wound, my lad; but this is a terrible business."

"Ay, mester, it is trubble. Straänge thing to hev first one man shot and then another. Say, squire, hope it wean't be our turn next."

"Go on eating, Tom," whispered Dick, setting the example, and cutting a slice for his companion, while Tom hacked the bread.

"I'm hard at work," said Tom thickly. "I shall eat as much as ever I can, and make mother give Hicky a piece o' chine."

"So will I," said Dick; "and a couple o' chickens."

The hungry lad had taken a piece of pink-fleshed bacon upon his fork, and was about to transfer it to his mouth, when he stopped short with his lips apart and eyes staring, while Tom let fall his knife and thrust his chair back over the stone floor.

They had been eating and listening to the conversation outside, till it reached its climax in the following words:

"What, man? You don't know what he says."

"What he says!" chuckled the wheelwright. "Ay, I heerd what he said; a whole heap o' bad words till I checked him, and let him feel he'd best howd his tongue."

"But you know what he says about who shot at him?"

"Nay, but if he says as it were me, I'll go and pitch him into the watter."

"You did not hear, then?" cried the squire, huskily. "Hickathrift, he says it was done by those boys!"

"What!" roared the wheelwright.

"It's a lie, father!" shouted Dick, recovering himself and running out. "Here, ask Tom."

"Why, of course it's a lie," cried Tom.

"But that man says—" cried the squire.

"Yah!" shouted Hickathrift angrily, "they never shot him; they heven't got no goon."

Chapter Seventeen.

Under Clouds.

Thorpeley was not badly hurt, so the doctor said when he came; but, as usual, he added, "If it had been an inch or two more to the right an important vessel would have been divided, and he would have bled to death."

But if the constable was not badly wounded, though the injury caused by a bullet passing through his leg was an ugly one, the reputations of Dick Winthorpe and Tom Tallington had received such ugly wounds that their fathers found it difficult to get them cured.

For Thorpeley stuck to his first story, that he suspected the two boys to be engaged in some nefarious trick, and he had watched them from the time they borrowed the wheelwright's punt. He went on to describe how he had offended them by keeping his eye upon their movements, and told how they had tried to smother him by leading him into a dangerous morass, while just at dusk, as he was watching their boat, he saw them start towards him, and evidently believing that they were unseen from where they had tied their punt, they had deliberately taken aim at him and shot him.

The squire questioned him very sharply, but he adhered to everything. He swore that he saw them thrust the punt away, and go into the misty darkness; and then when they had heard his cries, they came back and landed, evidently repentant and frightened, and then helped him down to the boat.

"But," said the squire, "it might have been two other people in a punt who shot at you."

"Two others!" shouted the man; "it weer they, and I heered 'em laughing and bragging about it as I lay theer in the bottom o' the boat nearly in a swownd, bud I could hear what they said."

This charge was so serious that, as a matter of course, there was a magisterial inquiry, which was repeated as soon as the constable was sufficiently well to limp into the justice-room in the little town where he had been removed as soon as the doctor gave permission, the neighbourhood of the Toft and Hickathrift having grown uncomfortably warm.

At that last examination the magistrates shook their heads, and, after hearing a great deal of speaking, decided that Thorpeley must have been deceived in the darkness, and the charge was dismissed.

In those days the law had two qualities in an out-of-the-way place that have pretty well died out now. These qualities were laxity and severity—the disposition to go to extremes; and in this case some idea of the way in which the work of petty sessions was carried on will be grasped when it is told that after the examination the chairman of the bench of magistrates, an old landholder of the neighbourhood, shook hands with the squire, and then less freely with Farmer Tallington.

"Look here, you two," he said; "we've let off these two young scamps; but you had better send them to sea, or at all events away from here."

"I don't understand you, sir," said the squire hotly.

"I can't help that," was the gruff reply. "You take my advice. Send 'em away before there's more mischief done. I sha'n't let 'em off next time."

Hickathrift, who had watched all the proceedings, heard these words; and as the two lads trudged home beside him, with the squire and Farmer Tallington in front, he told them all that had been said.

Dick said nothing, but Tom fired up and exclaimed angrily, while the wheelwright kept on talking quietly to the former.

"Niver yow mind, lad; we don't think you shot at him. It's some o' they lads t'other side o' the fen. They comes acrost and waits their chance, and then goes back, and nobody's none the wiser. Niver you mind what owd magistrit said. Magistrit indeed! Why, I'd mak' a better magistrit out of owd Solomon any day o' the week."

It was kindly spoken; but if there is a difficult thing to do it is to "never mind" when the heart is sore through some accusation that rankles from its injustice.

"Yes, Tom," said Dick, when they were about half-way home; "they'd better send us away."

He looked longingly across the fen with its gleaming waters, waving reeds, and many-tinted flowers; and as he gazed in the bright afternoon sunshine it seemed as if it had never looked so beautiful before. To an agricultural-minded man it was a watery waste; but to a boy who had passed his life there, and found it the home of bird, insect, fish, and flower, and an ever-changing scene of pleasure, it was all that could be called attractive and bright.

"I'm ready to go," said Tom sturdily; "only I don't know which to do."

"Which to do!" cried Dick, with his face growing red, and his eyes flashing. "Why, what do you mean?"

"Whether to go for a soldier or a sailor."

"Haw! haw!"

Hickathrift's was a curious laugh. At a distance it might have been taken for a hail; but a fine heron standing heel-deep in the shallow water took it to be a cry to scare him, so spreading his great flap wings, and stooping so as to get a spring, he flew slowly off with outstretched legs, while the squire and Farmer Tallington looked back to see if they had been called.

"What are you laughing at?" said Tom angrily.

"Yow, lad, yow. Why, you arn't big enew to carry a goon; and as for sailing, do you think a ship's like a punt, and shoved along wi' a pole!"

"Never mind," grumbled Tom. "I'm not going to stop here and be suspected for nothing."

"Nay, nay, don't you lads talk nonsense."

"It's no nonsense, Hicky," said Dick bitterly. "I've made up my mind to go."

"Nay, nay, I tell thee. Thou wean't goo, lads."

"Indeed but we will," cried Dick energetically.

"What, goo?"

"Yes."

"Height awayer?"

"Yes, right away."

"Then what's to become of me?" cried the wheelwright excitedly.

"Become of you! Why, what's it got to do with you?" cried Tom surlily.

"Do wi' me! Why, iverything. What's the good o' my punt? what's the good o' me laying up a couple o' good ash-poles for you, and putting a bit o' wood up chimney to season, so as to hev it ready for new soles for your pattens (skates) next winter. Good, indeed! What call hev you to talk that clat?"

"You're a good old chap, Hicky," said Dick, smiling up at the big fellow; "but you can't understand what I feel over this."

"Hey, bud I can," cried the wheelwright quickly; "you feel just the same as I did when Farmer Tallington—Tom's father here—said I'd sent him in his bill after he'd sattled it; and as I did when my missus said I'd took half a guinea outer money-box to spend i' town. I know, lads. Yes, I know."

"Well, I suppose it is something like that, Hicky," said Dick sadly.

"Ay, joost the same; bud I didn't tell Farmer Tallington as I should go for a soldier, and I didn't turn on my wife and tell her I should go to sea."

Dick was silent the rest of the way home, but he shook hands very solemnly with Tom, and Tom pressed his hand hard as they parted at the farm. Then Dick went on beside the wheelwright, while the squire walked swiftly ahead, evidently thinking deeply.

There was a meaning in that grip of the hand which Hickathrift did not understand; but he kept on talking cheerily to the lad till they were close up to the Toft, when, just as the squire turned in and stopped for Dick to join him, the wheelwright shook hands with the lad.

"Good day, Mester Dick!" he said aloud; and then in a whisper:

"Don't you go away, lad, for if you do they'll be sure to say it was yow as fired the shot."

Chapter Eighteen.

Preparations for Flight.

The squire was very quiet over the evening meal, but he looked across at Dick very sternly two or three times, and the lad did not meet his eye.

For certain plans which he had been concerting with Tom wore so strange an aspect in his eyes that he felt quite guilty, and the old frank light in his face seemed to have died out as he bent down over his supper, and listened to his father's answers to his mother about the proceedings of the past day.

Bed-time at last, and for the first time since he had returned Dick was alone with his mother, the squire having gone to take his customary look round the house.

"Good-night, mother!" said Dick in a low sombre manner, very different to his usual way.

Mrs Winthorpe did not answer for a moment or two, but gazed full at her son.

"And so the magistrate thought you guilty, Dick?" she said.

"Yes, mother," he flashed out, "and—"

"Ah!" exclaimed Mrs Winthorpe, flinging her arms about his neck. "That's my boy who spoke out then. Dick, if you had spoken out like that to your father and everyone they would not have suspected you for a moment. There, good-night! It will all come right at last."

Dick said "good-night" to his father, who gave him a short nod, and then the lad went slowly up to his room, to sit on the edge of the bed and think of the possibility of building a hut out there in the island they had found in the fen, and then of how it would be if he and Tom did so, and went there to live; and when he had debated it well, he asked himself what would be the use, and confessed that it would be all nonsense, and that he had been thinking like a child.

"No," he said; "I'm no baby now. All this has made a man of me, and Tom Tallington is right; we must go and begin life somewhere else—where the world will not be so hard."

"He will not be here for an hour yet," he thought; so he employed himself very busily in putting together the few things he meant to take on his journey into that little-known place beyond the fen, where there were big towns, and people different to themselves; and as Dick packed his bundle he tried to keep back a weak tear or two which would gather as if to drop on the lavender-scented linen, that reminded him of her who had that night called him her boy.

But there was a stubborn feeling upon him which made him viciously knot together the handkerchief ends of his bundle, and then go and stand at the window and watch and listen for the coming of Tom.

For he had made up his mind to go with Tom if he came, without him if he failed, for he told himself the world elsewhere would not be so hard.

One hour—two hours passed. He heard them strike on the old eight-day clock below. But no Tom.

Could he have repented and made up his mind not to keep faith, or was there some reason?

Never mind, he would go alone and fight the world, and some day people would be sorry for having suspected him as they did now.

He laughed bitterly, and stepped to the open window bundle in hand. He had but to swing himself out and drop to the ground, and trudge away into that romantic land—the unknown. Yes, he would go. "Good-bye, dear mother; father, good-bye!" he whispered softly; and the next moment one foot was over the window-sill, and he was about to drop, when a miserably absurd sound rose on the midnight air, a sound which made him dart back into his room like some guilty creature, as there rang out the strange cry:

"He—haw, he—haw!" as dismal a bray as Solomon had ever uttered in his life; and for no reason whatever, as it seemed, Dick Winthorpe went back and sat upon his bed thinking of the wheelwright's words:

That if he went away people would declare he fired the shot.

"I can't help it," cried Dick at last, after an hour's bitter struggle there in the darkness of the night; and once more he ran to the window, meaning to drop out, when, as if he saw what was about to take place, Solomon roused the echoes about the old buildings with another dismal bray.

"Who can run away with a donkey crying out at him like that!" said Dick to himself; and in spite of his misery, he once more seated himself upon the bed-side and laughed.

It was more a hysterical than a natural laugh; but it relieved Dick Winthorpe's feelings, and just then the clock struck two.

Dick sat on the bed-side and thought. He was not afraid to go—far from it. A reckless spirit of determination had come over him, and he was ready to do anything, dare anything; but all the same the wheelwright's words troubled him, and he could not master the feeling that it would be painful for the constant repetition to come to his mother's knowledge, till even she began to think that there must be some truth in the matter, and he would not be there to defend himself.

That was a painful thought, one which made Dick Winthorpe rise and go and seat himself on the window-sill and gaze out over the fen.

From where he was seated his eyes ranged over the portion where the drain was being cut; and as he looked, it seemed to him that all his troubles had dated from the commencement of the venture by his father, and those who had joined in the experiment.

Then he thought of the evening when Mr Marston had been brought in wounded, and the other cases which had evidently been the work of those opposed to the draining—the fire at Tallington's, the houghing of the horses, the shots fired, the blowing up of the sluice-gate.

"And they think I did it all," he said to himself with a bitter laugh; "a boy like me!"

Then he began considering as to who possibly could be the culprit, and thought and thought till his head ached, and he rose sadly and replaced the articles in his bundle in the drawer.

"I can't go," he said softly. "I'll face it out like a man, and they may say what they like."

He stood looking at his bed, with its white pillow just showing in the faint light which came through the open window, but it did not tempt him to undress.

"I can't sleep," he said; "and perhaps, if I lie down, I may not hear Tom coming, if he comes. Why is one so miserable? What have I done?"

There was no mental answer to his question, and he once more went softly across the room, and sat in the window-sill to gaze out across the fen.

How long he had been watching he could not tell, for his brain felt dazed, and he was in a half-dreamy state, when all of a sudden he grew wakeful and alert, for right away out over the mere he saw a faint gleam of light which flashed upon the water and then expired.

For a moment he thought that it might have been the reflection of a star, but it flashed out again, and then was gone.

The marsh lights always had a strange fascination for him, and this appearance completely changed the current of his thoughts. A few moments before and they were dull and sluggish, now they were all excitement; and he sat there longing for the next appearance when, as of old, he expected to see the faint light go dancing along, as a moth dances over the moist herbage, disappearing from time to time.

He strained his eyes, but there was no light, and he was beginning to think that it was fancy, when he heard a faint rustling apparently outside his door; and as he listened, he felt that someone must be going down stairs.

Then there was complete silence for a few minutes, and he was ready to think that both the light and the sound were fancy, when all doubts were set at rest, for the door below opened and someone passed out.

It was still very dark, in spite of a faint sign of dawn in the north-east; but the watcher had no difficulty in making out the figure which passed silently along in the shadow of the house, and close beneath him, to be that of his father.

What did it mean? Dick asked himself as he sat there holding his breath, while he watched intently, and saw his father steal from place to place in the most secretive manner, taking advantage of bush, wall, and outbuilding, and every now and then pausing as if gazing out across the fen.

"I know," thought Dick, as a flash of comprehension came across his brain. "He saw that light, and he is watching too."

The thought was quite exciting.

The reaction as depressing, for directly after he very naturally said to himself: "My father would not get out of bed to watch a will-o'-the-wisp."

But suppose it was not a will-o'-the-wisp, but a light!

He sat thinking and trying to trace which way his father had gone; and as far as he could make out, he had gone right down to the nearest spot to the water, where, about a hundred yards away, there was fair landing, by one of the many clumps of alder.

Dick had just come to the conclusion that he ought not to watch his father, who was angry enough with him as it was, and who would be more suspicious still if he again caught him at the window dressed, and he was about to close it, after wondering whether anyone would be on the water with a light—Dave, for instance—and if so, what form of fowling or netting it would be, when there was a low hiss—such a sound as is made by a snake—just beneath his window.

"Dick!"

"Hallo!"

"Couldn't come before. Ready?"

"No," said Dick shortly, for the plan to run away seemed now to belong to some project of the past.

"I couldn't come before," whispered Tom. "I was all ready, but father did not go to bed for ever so long; and when at last I thought it was all right, and was ready to start, I heard him go down and open the back-door."

"And go out?" whispered Dick.

"Yes. How did you know?"

"I didn't know, but my father has done just the same."

"Oh!"

"Did yours come back?"

"No," said Tom; "and I daren't start for ever so long. But I've come now, so let's start off quick."

"Which way did your father go?"

"I don't know, but we're wasting time."

"Did he take the boat?"

"How should I know? I didn't see him go. I only heard. Come, are you ready?"

"No," said Dick hoarsely, and not prepared to tell his companion that he had repented. "How can we go now with them both somewhere about? They would be sure to catch us and bring us back."

It was a subterfuge, and Dick's face turned scarlet, as he knew by the burning sensation. The next instant he had felt so ashamed of his paltry excuse that he blurted out:

"I sha'n't go. I'm sorry I said I would. It's cowardly, but I don't mean to go—there!"

The hot tears of vexation and misery stood in his eyes as he made this confession, and rose up prepared to resent his companion's reproaches with angry words; but he was disarmed, for Tom whispered hastily:

"Oh, Dick, I am so glad! I wouldn't show the white feather and play sneak, but I didn't want to go. It seemed too bad to mother and father. But you mean it?"

"Yes, I mean it!" said Dick, with a load off his breast. "I felt that it would be like running away because we were afraid to face a charge."

"Hooray!" cried Tom in a whisper. "I say, Dick, don't think me a coward, but I am so glad! I say, shall I go back now?"

"No; stop a bit," whispered Dick, with his heart beating, and a strange suspicion making its way into his breast. For in an incoherent vague manner he found himself thinking of Farmer Tallington stealing out of his house in the middle of the night. He had a boat, as most of the fen farmers had, for gunning, fishing, and

DICK AND HICKATHRIFT FIND THE WOUNDED SQUIRE

Page 64

cutting reeds. What was he doing on the water at night? For it must have been he with a light.

Then a terrible suspicion flashed across him, and the vague ideas began to shape themselves and grow solid. Suppose it was Farmer Tallington who had been guilty of—

Dick made a strong effort at this point to master his wandering imagination, and forced himself to think only of what he really knew to be the fact, namely, that Farmer Tallington was out somewhere, and that the squire was out too.

"My father must have come to meet yours, Dick," whispered Tom at that point. "I know they suspect there's something wrong, and they have gone down to watch the drain, or to meet Mr Marston."

"Yes," said Dick, in a tone which did not carry conviction with it. "That must be it."

"What shall we do? Go back to bed?"

"Ye–es, we had better," said Dick thoughtfully. "I say, Tom, we have done quite right. We couldn't have gone away."

"Hist! did you hear that?"

For answer Dick strained out of the window. He had heard that—a sudden splashing in the water, a shout—and the next moment there was a flash which cut the darkness apparently a couple of hundred yards away, and then came a dull report, and silence.

The boys remained listening for some moments, but they could not hear a sound. The signs of the coming morning were growing plainer; there was a faint twittering in some bushes at a distance, followed by the sharp metallic *chink chink* of a blackbird; and then all at once, loud and clear from the farm-yard, rang out the morning challenge of a cock.

Then once more all was still. There was no footstep, no splash of pole in the water.

For a few minutes neither spoke, but listened intently with every nerve upon the strain; and then with a catching of the breath as he realised what had gone before, and that he had seen his father steal carefully down in the direction of the mere, Dick sprang from the window and gripped his companion by the arm.

"Tom," he gasped, "quick! come on! Some one else has been—"

He would have said *shot*, but his voice failed, and with a cold chill of horror stealing over him he remained for a few moments as if paralysed.

Then, with Tom Tallington close behind, he ran swiftly down towards the mere.

Chapter Nineteen.

The New Horror.

They did not know exactly where to go, for the guidance afforded by a sound is very deceptive, but there had been the splash of water, so that the shot must have been from somewhere at the foot of the Toft, down where the meadow land gave place to rough marsh, bog, and reedy water.

Dick listened as he ran; but there was no splash now—no sound of footstep.

As the lads advanced the dawning light increased, and a startled bird flew out from the bushes, another from a tuft of dry grass; and once more there was the *chink—chink* of a blackbird. The day was awakening, and Dick Winthorpe asked himself what the dawn was to show.

It was still dark enough to necessitate care, and over the mere as they neared it a low mist hung, completely screening its waters as they vainly attempted to pierce the gloom.

Plash, plash through the boggy parts of the mere fringe, for Dick had not paused to follow any track, stumbling among tufts of grass and marsh growth, they hurried on with eager eyes, longing to shout, but afraid, for there was a growing horror upon both the lads of having to be shortly in presence of some terrible scene.

They neither of them spoke, but mutually clung together for support, though all the time there was a strange repugnance in Dick's breast as he now began to realise the strength of the suspicion he entertained.

But if they dared not shout, there was some one near at hand ready to utter a lusty cry, which startled them as it rang out of the gloom from away down by the labourers' cottages and the wheelwright's.

"Ahoy! Hillo!" rang out.

"Hillo, Hicky!" yelled Tom. "Here!"

"Where away, lads?" came back; and then there was the dull low beat of feet, and they heard the wheelwright shout to his apprentice to follow him.

The two little parties joined directly, to stand in the mist all panting and excited, the wheelwright half-dressed, and his bare head rough from contact with the pillow.

"Hey, lads," he cried, "was that you two shouting?"

Dick tried to speak, but he could not frame a word.

"No; we heard it from somewhere down here," panted Tom.

"I heered it too," cried Jacob, "and wackened the mester."

"Ay, that's a true word," cried Hickathrift. "What does it mean?"

"Hicky," panted Dick in piteous tones, "I don't know—I'm afraid I—my father's out here somewhere."

"Hey! The squire?" cried Hickathrift with a curious stare at first one and then the other. "Yow don't think—"

He paused, and Dick replied in a whisper:

"Yes, Hicky, I do."

"Here, let's search about; it's getting light fast. Now, then," cried the wheelwright, "yow go that way, Jacob; I'll go this; and you two lads—"

"No, no," said Dick. "It must be somewhere close by here, near the water. Let's keep together, please."

"Aw reight!" muttered the wheelwright; and following Dick they went as close to the water's edge as they could go, and crept along, with the bushes and trees growing more plain to view, and the sky showing one dull orange fleck as the advance guard of the coming glory of the morn.

They went along for a couple of hundred yards in one direction, but there was nothing to be seen; then a couple of hundred yards in the other direction, but there was nothing visible there. And as the light grew stronger they sought about them, seeing clearly now that the ghastly figure Dick dreaded to find was nowhere as far as they could make out inshore.

"Hillo!" shouted Hickathrift again and again; "squire!"

There was no reply, and the chill of horror increased as the feeling that they were searching in vain out and in pressed itself upon all, and they knew that the man they sought must be in the water.

"Here, howd hard," cried Hickathrift. "What a moodle head I am! You, Jacob, run back and let loose owd Grip."

The apprentice ran back as hard as he could, and the group remained in silence till they saw him disappear behind the shed. Then there was a loud burst of barking.

Hickathrift whistled, and the great long-legged lurcher came bounding over the rough boggy land, to leap at his master and then stand panting, open-mouthed, eager, and ready to dart anywhere his owner bade.

"Here, Grip, lad, find him, then—find him, boy!"

The dog uttered one low, growling bark, and then bounded off, hurrying here and there in the wildest way, while the boys watched intently.

"Will he find him, Hicky?" said Dick huskily.

"Ay, or anyone else," said the wheelwright, who alternately watched the dog, and swept the surface of the mere wherever the mist allowed.

"There! Look at that!" he cried, as, after a minute, the dog settled down to a steady hunt, with his nose close to the ground, and rapidly followed the track lately taken by someone who had passed.

"But perhaps he is following our steps!" said Dick excitedly.

"Nay, not he. Theer, what did I tell you?" cried Hickathrift as the dog suddenly stopped by the water, opposite to a thick bed of reeds a dozen yards or so from the bank.

Dick turned pale; the wheelwright ran down to the edge of the mere; and as the dog stood by the water barking loudly, Hickathrift waded in without hesitation, the boys following, with Grip swimming and snorting at their side, and taking up the chase again as soon as he reached the reeds.

It was only a matter of minutes now before the dog had rushed on before them, disappeared in the long growth, and then they heard him barking furiously.

"Let me go first, Mester Dick," said Hickathrift hoarsely. "Nay, don't, lad."

There was a kindly tone of sympathy in the great fellow's voice, but Dick did not give way. He splashed on through the reeds, his position having placed him in advance of his companions, and parting the tall growth he uttered a cry of pain.

The others joined him directly, and stood for a moment gazing down at where, standing on the very edge of the mere, Dick was holding up his father's head from where he lay insensible among the reeds, his face white and drawn, his eyes nearly closed, and his hands clenched and stretched out before him.

Hickathrift said not a word, but, as in similar cases before, he raised the inanimate form, hung it over his shoulder, and waded back to firm ground.

"Hey, Mester Dick," he said huskily, as he hurried towards his cottage, "I nivver thowt to hev seen a sight like this."

"No, no," cried Dick; "not there."

"Yes, I'll tak' him home to my place," whispered Hickathrift. "You'd scare your mother to dead. Here, Jacob, lad, don't stop to knock or ask questions, but go and tak' squire's cob, and ride him hard to town for doctor."

"Tell my father as you go by, Jacob," cried Tom excitedly; and as the apprentice dashed off, Tom's eyes met those of Dick.

"Don't look so wild and strange, Dick, old chap," whispered the lad kindly; and he laid a hand upon Dick's shoulder, but the boy shrank from him with a shudder which the other could not comprehend.

Hickathrift shouted to his wife, who had risen and dressed in his absence, and in a short time the squire was lying upon a mattress with Hickathrift eagerly searching for the injury which had laid him low; but when he found it, the wound seemed so small and trifling that he looked wondering up at Dick.

"That couldn't have done it," he said in a whisper.

The wheelwright was wrong. That tiny blue wound in the strong man's chest had been sufficient to lay him there helpless, and so near death that a feeling of awe fell upon those who watched and waited, and tried to revive the victim of this last outrage.

It was a terrible feeling of helplessness that which pervaded the place. There was nothing to do save bathe the wounded man's brow and moisten his lips with a little of the smuggled spirit with which most of the coast cottages were provided in those distant days. There was no blood to staunch, nothing to excite, nothing to do but wait, wait for the doctor's coming.

Before very long Farmer Tallington arrived, and as he encountered Dick's eyes fixed upon him he turned very pale, and directly after, when he bent over the squire's couch and took his hand, the lad saw that he trembled violently.

"It's straänge and horrible—it's straänge and horrible," he said: "only yesterday he was like I am: as strong and well as a man can be; while now—Hickathrift, my lad, do you think he'll die?"

The wheelwright shook his head—he could not trust himself to speak; and Dick stood with a sensation of rage gathering in his breast, which made him feel ready to spring at Farmer Tallington's throat, and accuse him of being his father's murderer.

"The hypocrite—the cowardly hypocrite!" he said to himself; "but we know now, and he shall be punished."

The boy's anger was fast growing so ungovernable that he was about to fly out and denounce his school-fellow's father, but just then a hasty step was heard outside, and a familiar voice exclaimed:

"Where is my husband?"

The next minute Mrs Winthorpe was in the room, wild-eyed and pale, but perfectly collected in her manner and acts.

"How long will it be before the doctor can get here?" she said hoarsely, as she passed her arm under the injured man's neck, and pressed her lips to his white brow.

"Hickathrift's lad went off at a hard gallop," said Farmer Tallington in a voice full of sympathy. "Please God, Mrs Winthorpe, we'll save him yet."

Dick uttered a hoarse cry and staggered out of the room, for the man's hypocrisy maddened him, and he knew that if he stayed he should speak out and say all he knew.

As he reached the little garden there was a step behind him, a hand was laid upon his shoulder, another grasped his arm.

"I can't talk and say things, Dicky," said Tom in a low half-choking voice; "but I want to comfort you. Don't break down, old fellow. The doctor will save his life."

This from the son of the man whom he believed to have shot his father! and the rage Dick felt against the one seemed to be ready to fall upon the other. But as his eyes met those of his old school-fellow and companion full of sorrowful sympathy, Dick could only grasp Tom's hands, feeling that he was a true friend, and in no wise answerable for his father's sins.

"Ay, that's right," said a low, rough voice. "Nowt like sticking together and helping each other in trouble. Bud don't you fret, Mester Dick. Squire's a fine stark man, and the missus has happed him up waärm, and you see the doctor will set him right."

"Thank you, Hicky," said Dick, calming down; and then he stood thinking and asking himself how he could denounce the father of his old friend and companion as the man who, for some hidden reason of his own, was the plotter and executor of all these outrages.

At one moment he felt that he could not do this. At another there was the blank suffering face of his father before his eyes, seeming to ask him to revenge his injuries and to bring a scoundrel to justice.

For a time Dick was quite determined; but directly after there came before him the face of poor, kind-hearted Mrs Tallington, who had always treated him with the greatest hospitality, while, as he seemed to look at her eyes pleading upon her husband's behalf, Tom took his hand and wrung it.

"I'm going to stick by you, Dick," he said; "and you and I are going to find out who did this, and when we do we'll show him what it is to shoot at people, and burn people's homesteads, and hough their beasts."

Dick gazed at him wildly. Tom going to help him run his own father down and condemn him by giving evidence when it was all found out! Impossible! Those words of his old companion completely disarmed him for the moment, and to finish his discomfiture, just then Farmer Tallington came out of the cottage looking whiter and more haggard than before.

He came to where the wheelwright was standing, and spoke huskily.

"I can't bear it," he said. "It is too horrible. Might hev been me, and what would my poor lass do? Hickathrift, mun, the villain who does all this must be found out."

"Ay, farmer, but how?"

"I don't know how," said the farmer, gazing from one to the other. "I on'y know it must be done. If I'd gone on this morning I might have found out something, but I went back."

Dick gazed at him searchingly, but the farmer did not meet his eyes.

"I've been straänge and fidgety ever since my fire," continued the farmer; "and it's med me get out o' bed o' nights and look round for fear of another. I was out o' bed towards morning last night, and as I looked I could see yonder on the mere what seemed to be a lanthorn."

"You saw that?" said Dick involuntarily.

"Ay, lad, I saw that," said the farmer, rubbing his hands together softly; "and first of all I thowt it was a will-o'-the-wisp, but it didn't go about like one o' they, and as it went out directly and came again, I thought it was some one wi' a light."

"What, out on the watter?" said Hickathrift.

"Yes, my lad; out on the watter," said the farmer; "and that med me say to mysen: What's any one doing wi' a light out on the watter at this time? and I could on'y think as they wanted it to set fire to some one's plaäce, and I couldn't stop abed and think that. So I got up, and went down to the shore, got into my owd punt, and loosed her, and went out torst wheer I'd seen the light."

"And did you see it, mester?" said Hickathrift.

"Nay, my lad. I went on and on as quietly as I could go, and round the reed-bed, but all was as quiet as could be."

"Didn't you see the poont?" said the wheelwright.

"What punt?" said Tom sharply.

Hickathrift looked confused.

"Poont o' him as hed the light, I meant," he said hurriedly.

"Nay, not a sign of it," said Farmer Tallington; "and at last I turned back and poled gently home, keeping a sharp look-out and listening all the way, but I niver see nowt nor heered nowt. But if I'd kept out on the waiter I should p'raps have seen and saved my poor owd neighbour."

"You might, mebbe," said the wheelwright thoughtfully; while, after gazing in the faces of the two men and trying to read the truth, Dick turned away with his suspicions somewhat blunted, to go to his mother's side, and watch with her till the sound of hoofs on the rough track told that the messenger had returned.

Chapter Twenty.

The Doctor's Dictum.

Dick leaped up and came to the window as soon as he heard the beating of the horse's hoofs; and to his great joy, as the mounted man turned the corner he saw that it was the doctor, whom he ran down to meet.

"Hah, my lad! here is a bad business!" exclaimed the doctor as he dismounted. "Well, come, they cannot say this was your doing. You wouldn't shoot your own father, eh?"

"Oh, pray, come up, sir, and don't talk," cried Dick excitedly. "Poor father is dying!"

"Oh, no," said the doctor; "we must not let him die."

"But be quick, sir! You are so long!" cried Dick.

"Don't be impatient, my lad," said the doctor smiling. "We folks have to be calm and quiet in all we do. Now show me the way."

Dick led him to the room, the doctor beckoning Hickathrift to follow; and as soon as he reached the injured man's side he quietly sent Mrs Winthorpe and Dick to wait in the next room, retaining the great wheelwright to help him move his patient.

The time seemed interminable, and as mother and son sat waiting, every word spoken in the next room sounded like a moan from the injured man. Mrs Winthorpe's face appeared to be that of a woman ten years older, and her agony was supreme; but like a true wife and tender mother—ah, how little we think of what a mother's patience and self-denial are when we are young!—she devoted her whole energies to administering comfort to her sorely-tried son.

A dozen times over Dick felt that he could not keep the secret that troubled him—that he must tell his mother his suspicions and ask her advice; but so sure as he made up his mind to speak, the fear that he might be wrong troubled him, and he forebore.

Then began the whole struggle again, and at last he was nearer than ever to confiding his horrible belief in their neighbour's treachery, when the doctor suddenly appeared.

Dick rose from where he had been kneeling by his mother's side, and she started from her seat to grasp the doctor's hand.

She did not speak, but her eyes asked the one great question of her heart, and then, as the doctor's hard sour face softened and he smiled, Mrs Winthorpe uttered a piteous sigh and clasped her hands together in thankfulness to Heaven.

"Then he is not very bad, doctor?" cried Dick joyfully.

"Yes, my boy, he is very bad indeed, and dangerously wounded," replied the doctor; "but, please God, I think I can pull him through."

"Tell me—tell me!" faltered Mrs Winthorpe piteously.

"It is a painful thing to tell a lady," said the doctor kindly; "but I will explain. Mrs Winthorpe, he has a terrible wound. The bullet has passed obliquely through his chest; it was just within the skin at the back, and I have successfully extracted it. As far as I can tell there is no important organ injured, but at present I am not quite sure. Still I think I may say he is in no immediate danger."

Mrs Winthorpe could not trust herself to speak, but she looked her thanks and glided toward the other room.

"Do not speak to him and do not let him speak," whispered the doctor. "Everything depends upon keeping him perfectly still, so that nature may not be interrupted in doing her portion of the work."

Mrs Winthorpe bowed her head in acquiescence, and with a promise that he would return later in the day the doctor departed.

Dick found, a short time after, that the news had been carried to the works at the drain, where Mr Marston was busy; and no sooner did that gentleman hear of the state of affairs than he hurried over to offer his sympathy to Mrs Winthorpe and Dick.

"I little thought that your father was to be a victim," he said to the latter as soon as they were alone. "I have been trying my hand to fix the guilt upon somebody, but so far I have failed. Come, Dick, you and I have not been very good friends lately, and I must confess that I have been disposed to think you knew something about these outrages."

"Yes, I knew you suspected me, Mr Marston."

"Not suspected you, but that you knew something about them; but I beg your pardon: I am sorry I ever thought such things; and I am sure you will forgive me, for indeed I do not think you know anything of the kind now."

Dick quite started as he gazed in Mr Marston's face, so strangely that the engineer wondered, and then felt chilled once more and stood without speaking.

Mr Marston took a step up and down for a few moments and then turned to Dick again.

"Look here, my lad," he said. "I don't like for there to be anything between us. I want to be friends with you, for I like you, Richard Winthorpe; but you keep on making yourself appear so guilty that you repel me. Speak to me, Dick, and say out downright, like a man, that you know nothing about this last affair."

Dick looked at him wildly, but remained silent.

"Come!" said Mr Marston sternly, and he fixed the lad with his eye; "there has been a dastardly outrage committed and your father nearly murdered. Tell me plainly whether you know whose hand fired the shot."

No answer.

"Dick, my good lad, I tell you once more that I do not suspect you—only that you know who was the guilty party."

Still no answer.

"It is your duty to speak, boy," cried Mr Marston angrily. "You are not afraid to speak out?"

"I—I don't know," said Dick.

"Then you confess that you do know who fired at your father?"

"I did not confess," said Dick slowly. "I cannot say. I only think I know."

"Then who was it?"

No answer.

"Dick, I command you to speak," cried Mr Marston, catching his arm and holding him tightly.

"I don't know," said Dick.

"You do know, cried Mr Marston angrily, and I will have an answer. No man's life is safe, and these proceedings must be stopped."

For answer Dick wrested himself free.

"I don't know for certain," he said determinedly, "and I'm not going to say who it is I suspect, when I may be wrong."

"But if the person suspected is innocent, he can very well prove it. Ah, here is Tom Tallington! Come, Tom, my lad, you can help me here with your old companion."

"No," cried Dick angrily, "don't ask him."

"I shall ask him," said Mr Marston firmly. "Look here, Tom; our friend Dick here either knows or suspects who it was that fired that shot; and if he knows that, he can tell who fired the other shots, and perhaps did all the other mischief."

"Do you know, Dick?" cried Tom excitedly.

"I don't know for certain, I only suspect," said Dick sadly.

"And I want him to speak out, my lad, while he persists in trying to hide it."

"He won't," said Tom. "He thinks it is being a bit of a coward to tell tales; but he knows it is right to tell, don't you, Dick?"

"No," said the latter sternly.

"You do, now," said Tom. "Come, I say, let's know who it was. Here, shall I call father?"

"No, no," cried Dick excitedly, "and I won't say a word. I cannot. It is impossible."

"You are a strange lad, Dick Winthorpe," said the engineer, looking at them curiously.

"Oh, but he will speak, Mr Marston! I can get him to," cried Tom. "Come, Dick, say who it was."

Dick stared at him wildly, for there was something so horrible to him in this boy trying now to make him state what would result in his father's imprisonment and death, that Tom seemed for the moment in his eyes quite an unnatural young monster at whose presence he was ready to shudder.

"How can you be so obstinate!" cried Tom. "You shall tell. Who was it?"

Dick turned from him in horror, and would have hurried away, but Mr Marston caught his arm.

"Stop a moment, Dick Winthorpe," he said. "I must have a few words with you before we part. It is plain enough that all these outrages are directed against the persons who are connected with the drainage scheme, and that their lives are in danger. Now I am one of these persons, and to gratify the petty revenge of a set of ignorant prejudiced people who cannot see the good of the work upon which we are engaged, I decline to have myself made a target. I ask you, then, who this was. Will you speak?"

Dick shook his head.

"Well, then, I am afraid you will be forced to speak. I consider it to be my duty to have these outrages investigated, and to do this I shall write up to town. The man or men who will be sent down will be of a different class to the unfortunate constable who was watching here. Now, come, why not speak?"

"Mr Marston!" cried Dick hoarsely.

"Yes! Ah, that is better! Now, come, Dick; we began by being friends. Let us be greater friends than ever, as we shall be, I am sure."

"No, no," cried Dick passionately. "I want to be good friends, but I cannot speak to you. I don't know anything for certain, I only suspect."

"Then whom do you suspect?"

"Yes; who is it?" cried Tom angrily.

"Hold your tongue!" said Dick so fiercely that Tom shrank away.

"I say you shall speak out," retorted the lad, recovering himself.

"For your father's sake speak out, my lad," said Mr Marston.

Dick shook his head and turned away, to go back into the wheelwright's cottage, where, suffering from a pain and anguish of mind to which he had before been a stranger, he sought refuge at his mother's side, and shared her toil of watching his father as he lay there between life and death.

Chapter Twenty One.

Trouble Grows.

The next fortnight was passed in a state of misery, which made Dick Winthorpe feel as if he had ceased to be a boy, and had suddenly become a grown-up man.

He wanted to do what was right. He wished for the man who had shot his father in this cowardly way to be brought to justice; but he was not sure that Farmer Tallington was the guilty man, and he shrank from denouncing the parent of his companion from childhood, and his father's old friend.

Mr Marston came over again and tried him sorely. But the more Dick Winthorpe thought, the more he grew determined that he would not speak unless he felt quite sure.

It was one day at the end of the fortnight that Mr Marston tried him again, and Dick told him that his father would soon be able to speak for himself, and till then he would not say a word.

Mr Marston left him angrily, feeling bitterly annoyed with the lad, but, in spite of himself, admiring his firmness.

Dick stood in the road gazing after him sadly, and was about to retrace his steps to the old house, to which his father had been carefully borne, when, happening to glance in the direction of the track leading to the town, he caught sight of Tom coming along slowly.

Dick turned sullenly away, but Tom ran before him.

"Stop a minute," he cried; "let you and me have a talk. I don't want to be bad friends, Dick."

"Neither do I," said the latter sadly.

"But you keep trying to be."

"No, I do not. You try to make me angry with you every time we meet."

"That's not true. I want to have you do your duty and tell all you know. Father says you ought, as you know who it was."

"Have you told your father, then?"

"Yes, I told him to-day, and he said you ought to do your duty and speak."

"Your father said that?"

"Yes: and why don't you—like a man."

Dick's brow grew all corrugated as if Black Care were sitting upon the roof of his head and squeezing the skin down into wrinkles.

"Come, speak out, and don't be such a miserable coward. Father says you don't speak because you are afraid that whoever did it may shoot you."

Dick's brow grew more puckered than ever.

"Now, then, let you and me go over and see Mr Marston and tell him everything at once."

Dick looked at the speaker with a feeling of anger against him for his obstinate perseverance that was almost vicious.

"Now, are you coming?"

"No, I am not."

"Then I've done with you," cried Tom angrily. "Father says that a lad who knows who attacked his parent in that way, and will not speak out, is a coward and a cur, and that's what you are, Dick Winthorpe."

"Tom Tallington," cried Dick, with his eyes flashing, "you are a fool."

"Say that again," said Tom menacingly.

"You are a fool and an idiot, and not worth speaking to again."

Whack!

That is the nearest way of spelling the back-handed blow which Tom Tallington delivered in his old school-fellow's face, while the straightforward blow which was the result of Dick Winthorpe's fist darting out to the full stretch of his arm sounded like an echo; and the next moment Tom was lying upon the ground.

There was no cowardice in Tom Tallington's nature. Springing up he made at Dick, and the former friends were directly after engaged in delivering furious blows, whose result must have been rather serious for both; but before they had had time to do much mischief, each of the lads was gripped on the shoulder by a giant hand, and they were forced apart, and held beyond striking distance quivering with rage, and each seeing nothing but the adversary at whom he longed to get.

"Hey, lads, and I thowt you two was such friends!" cried the herald of peace, who had sung truce in so forcible and convincing a way.

"Let go, Hicky! He struck me."

"Yes; let me get at him," cried Tom. "He knocked me down."

"And I'll do it again a dozen times," panted Dick. "Let go, Hicky, I tell you!"

"Nay, nay, nay, lads, I wean't let go, and you sha'n't neither of you fight any more. I'm ashamed of you, Mester Dick, with your poor father lying theer 'most dead, and the missus a-nigh wherritted to death wi' trouble."

"But he struck me," panted Dick.

"And I'll do it again," cried Tom.

"If you do, young Tom Tallington, I'll just pick you up by the scruff and the breeches and pitch you into the mere, to get out as you may; so now then."

Tom uttered a low growl which was more like that of a dog than a human being; and after an ineffectual attempt to get at Dick, he dragged himself away to kneel down at the first clear pool to bathe his bleeding nose.

"Theer, now, I'll let you go," said Hickathrift, "and I'm straänge and glad I was i' time to stop you. Think o' you two mates falling out and fighting like a couple o' dogs! Why, I should as soon hev expected to see me and my missus fight. Mester Dick, I'm 'bout 'shamed o' yow."

"I'm ashamed of myself, Hicky, and I feel as if I was never going to be happy again," cried Dick.

"Nay, nay, lad, don't talk like that," said the big wheelwright. "Why, doctor says he's sewer that he can bring squire reight again, and what more do you want?"

"To see the man punished who shot him, Hicky," cried Dick passionately.

"Ay, I'd like to see that, or hev the punishing of him," said Hickathrift, stretching out a great fist. "It's one o' they big shacks (idle scoundrels, from Irish *shaughraun*) yonder up at the dree-ern. I'm going to find him out yet, and when I do— Theer, go and wesh thy faäce."

Dick was going sadly away when a word from Hickathrift arrested him; and turning, it was to see that the big fellow was looking at him reproachfully, and holding out a hand for him to grasp.

"Ay, that's better, lad," said the wheelwright smiling. "Good-bye, lad, and don't feight again!"

The result of this encounter was that Dick found himself without a companion, and he went day by day bitterly about thinking how hard it was that he should be suspected and ill-treated for trying to spare Tom the agony of having his father denounced and dragged off to jail.

Constables came and made investigations in the loose way of the time; but they discovered nothing, and after a while they departed to do duty elsewhere; but only to come back at the end of a week to re-investigate the state of affairs, for a large low building occupied by about twenty of the drainers was, one windy night, set on fire, and its drowsy occupants had a narrow escape from death.

But there was no discovery made, the constables setting it down to accident, saying that the men must have been smoking; and once more the fen was left to its own resources.

Mr Winthorpe grew rapidly better after the first fortnight, and Dick watched his convalescence with no little anxiety, for he expected to hear him accuse Farmer Tallington of being his attempted murderer. But Dick had no cause for fear. The squire told Mr Marston that he had seen a light on the mere, and dreading that it might mean an attempt to burn down some barn, he had gone out to watch, and he had just made out the shape of a punt on the water when he saw a flash, felt the shock, and fell helpless and insensible among the reeds.

This was as near an account as he could give of the affair, for the injury seemed to have confused him, and he knew little of what had taken place before, nothing of what has since occurred.

"But your life has been spared, Mr Winthorpe," said Marston; "and some day I hope we shall know that your assailant and mine has received his due."

"Ay," said the squire; "we must find him out, for fear he should spoil our plans, for we are not beaten yet."

"Beaten! no, squire," said the engineer; "we are getting on faster than ever, and the success of the project is assured."

Chapter Twenty Two.

After a Space.

The time rolled on. The drain-making progressed, and for a while there was no further trouble. Mr Winthorpe improved in health, but always seemed to avoid any allusion to the outrage; and after the constables had been a few times and found out nothing, and the magistrates of the neighbourhood had held consultation, the trouble once more dropped.

Dick Winthorpe always lived in apprehension of being examined, and pressed to tell all he knew, but his father never said a word, to his great relief, and the matter died out.

"I can't take any steps about it," Dick said to himself, "if my father doesn't;" and there were times when he longed to speak, others when he wished that he could forget everything about the past.

"Yow two med it up yet?" Hickathrift used to ask every time he saw Dick; but the answer was always the same— "No."

"Ah, well, you will some day, my lad. It arn't good for boys to make quarrels last."

There was no more warm friendship with Mr Marston, who, whenever he came over to the Toft, was studiously polite to Dick, treating him as if he were not one whose friendship was worth cultivating, to the lad's great disgust, though he was too proud to show it; and the result was that Dick's life at the Toft grew very lonely, and he was driven to seek the companionship of John Warren and his rabbits, and of Dave with his boat, gun, and fishing-tackle.

Then all at once there was a change. The outrages, which had ceased for a time, broke out again furiously; and all through the winter there were fires here and there, the very fact of a person, whether farmer or labourer, seeming to favour the making of the drain, being enough to make him receive an unwelcome visit from the party or parties who opposed the scheme.

So bad did matters grow that at last people armed and prepared themselves for the struggle which was daily growing more desperate; and at the same time a feeling of suspicion increased so strongly that throughout the fen every man looked upon his neighbour as an enemy.

But still the drain grew steadily in spite of the fact that Mr Marston had been shot at twice again, and never went anywhere now without a brace of pistols in his pocket.

One bright wintry morning John Warren came in with a long tale of woe, and his arm in a sling.

It was the old story. He had been out with his gun to try and get a wild-goose which he had marked down, when, just in the dusk, about half-past four, he was suddenly startled by a shot, and received the contents of a gun in his arm.

"But you'd got a gun," said Hickathrift, who was listening with Dick, while Tom Tallington, who had business at the wheelwright's that morning, stood hearing all. "Why didst na let him hev it again?"

"What's the use o' shuting at a sperrit?" grumbled John Warren. "'Sides, I couldn't see him."

"Tchah! it warn't a sperrit," said Hickathrift contemptuously.

"Well, I don't know so much about that," grumbled John Warren. "If it weern't a sperrit what was to mak my little dog, Snig, creep down in the bottom of the boat and howl? Yow mark my words: it's sperrits, that's what it is; and it's because o' that theer dreern; but they needn't shute at me, for I don't want dreern made."

"Going over to town to see the doctor, John?" said Dick.

"Nay, lad, not I. It's only a hole in my arm. There arn't nowt the matter wi' me. I've tied it oop wi' some wet 'bacco, and it'll all grow oop again, same as a cooten finger do."

"But someone ought to see it."

"Well, someun has sin it. I showed it to owd Dave, and he said it weer all right. Tchah! what's the good o' doctors? Did they cure my ager?"

"Well, go up and ask mother to give you some clean linen rag for it."

"Ay," said the rabbit-trapper with a grim smile, "I'll do that."

So John Warren went to the Toft, obtained the clean linen rag, but refused to have his wound dressed, and went off again; while the squire knit his brow when he returned soon after, and, taking Dick with him, poled across in the punt to see Dave and make him promise to keep a sharp look-out.

A week passed away, and the frost had come in so keenly that the ice promised to bear, and consequent upon this Dick was at the wheelwright's one evening superintending the finishing up of his pattens, as they called their skates. Hickathrift had ground the blades until they were perfectly sharp at the edges, and had made a new pair of ashen soles for them, into which he had just finished fitting the steel.

"There, Mester Dick," said the bluff fellow with a grin; "that's a pair o' pattens as you ought 'most to fly in. Going out in the morning?"

"Yes, Hicky, I shall go directly after breakfast."

"Ay, she'll bear splendid to-morrow, and the ice is as hard and black as it can be. Hello, who's this? Haw-haw! I thowt you'd want yours done," he added, as he heard steps coming over the frozen ground, and the jingle of skates knocking together. "It's young Tom Tallington, Mester Dick. Come, you two ought to mak friends now, and go and hev a good skate to-morrow."

"I'm never going to be friends with Tom Tallington again," said Dick sternly; but he sighed as he said it.

Just then Tom rushed into the workshop. "Here," he cried, "Dick Winthorpe, come along. I've been to the house."

"What do you want?" said Dick coldly.

"What do I want! Why, they don't know!" cried Tom. "Look here!"

He caught Dick by the collar, dragged him to the door, and pointed.

"Fire!" he cried.

"Hey!" cried the wheelwright. "Fire! So it is. But there's no house or stack out theer."

"Only old Dave's. Father said he thought it must be his place. Come on, Dick."

"But how are we to get there?" cried Dick, forgetting the feud in the excitement.

"How are we to get there! Why, skate."

"Will it be strong enough, Hicky?"

"Mebbe for you, lads; but it wouldn't bear me, and I couldn't get along the boat nor yet a sled."

Tom had already seated himself, and was putting on his skates, while Dick immediately began to follow suit, with the result that in five minutes both were ready and all past troubles forgotten. The memory of the terrible night when his father was shot did come for a moment to Dick, but the trouble had grown dull, and the excitement of Dave's place being on fire carried everything before it.

"Poor owd Dave!" said Hickathrift, as he gazed over the mere at the glow in the black frosty night. "He's got off so far. Mebbe it'll be my turn next. Come back and tell me, lads."

"Yes, yes," they shouted, as they walked clumsily to the ice edge, Dick first, and as he glided on there was an ominous ringing crack which seemed to run right out with a continuous splitting noise.

"Will it bear, Hicky?"

"Ay, she'll bear you, lad, only keep well out, and away from the reeds."

Tom dashed on, and as the wheelwright stood with the group of labourers, who were just beginning to comprehend the new alarm, the two lads went off stroke for stroke over the ringing ice, which cracked now and again but did not yield, save to undulate beneath them, as they kept gathering speed and glided away.

Far ahead there was the ruddy glow, showing like a golden patch upon the dark sky, which overhead was almost black, and glittering with the brilliant stars. The ice gleamed, little puffs of white powder rose at every stroke of the skates, and on and on they went, gathering speed till they were gliding over the ringing metallic surface like arrows from a bow, while as soon as the first timidity had passed away they began to feel their feet, and in a few minutes were skating nearly as well as when the ice broke up last.

The feud was forgotten, and it had lasted long enough. With a buoyant feeling of excitement, and a sensation of joy increased by the brisk beat of the freezing wind upon their cheeks, the two lads joined hands in a firm grip, kept time together, and sped on as Lincoln and Cambridge boys alone can speed over the ice.

Not that they are more clever with their legs than the boys of other counties; but from the fact that skating has always been a favourite pastime with them, and that when others were longing for a bit of bearing ice, and getting it sometimes in a crowded place, the marsh and fen lads had miles of clear bright surface, over which they could career as a swallow flies.

Away and away over the open ice, unmarked before by skate-iron and looking black as hardened unpolished steel, stroke for stroke, stroke for stroke, the wind whistling by them, and the ominous cracking forgotten as they dashed on past reed-bed and bog-clump, keeping to the open water where they had so often been by punt.

"His reed-stack must be on fire," panted Dick as they dashed on.

"Ay, and his peat-stack and cottage too," shouted Tom so as to be heard above the ringing of their skates. "Oh, Dick, if I only knew who it was did these things I think I could kill him!"

Dick was silent for a minute, for his companion's words jarred upon him.

"How much farther is it?" he said at last.

"Good mile and a half," said Tom; "but it's fine going. I say, look at the golden smoke. It must be at Dave's, eh?"

"Yes, it's there, sure enough. Oh, Tom, suppose some one were to burn down the duck 'coy!"

"It wouldn't burn so as to do much harm. Look, there goes a flock of plovers."

They could just catch the gleam of the wings in the dark night, as the great flock, evidently startled by the strange glare, swept by.

"I say!" cried Dick, as they dashed on as rapidly as the birds themselves.

"What is it?"

"Suppose poor Dave—"

"Oh, don't think things like that!" cried Tom with a shudder. "He'd be clever enough to get out. Come along. Look at the sparks."

What Tom called sparks were glowing flakes of fire which floated on, glittering against the black sky, and so furiously was the fire burning that it seemed as if something far more than the hut and stacks of the decoy-man must be ablaze.

And now they had to curve off some distance to the right, for they came upon an embayment of the mere, so well sheltered from the icy blast that to have persevered in skating over the very thin ice must have meant serious accident to one, probably to both.

For a long time past the ice had been blushing, as it were, with the warm glow from the sky; but now, as they drew nearer and passed a little copse of willows, they glided full into the view of the burning hut and stacks, and found that a bed of dry reeds was burning too. At this point of their journey the cold black ice was lit up, and as they advanced it seemed as if they were about to skim over red-hot glowing steel.

"Now, then," cried Dick excitedly, "a rush—as fast as we can go!"

But they could get on at no greater speed, and rather slackened than increased as they drew near to the fire; while a feeling of thankfulness came over both as all at once they were aware of the fact that a tall thin figure was standing apparently with its back to them staring at the glowing fire, against which it stood out like a black silhouette.

"Dave, ho!" shouted Dick.

The figure turned slowly, and one hand was raised as if to shade the eyes.

"Dave, ho!" shouted Tom.

"Ay, ay!" shouted back the man; and the next minute the boys glided up to the firm earth and leaped ashore, as their old fishing and trapping friend came slowly to meet them.

"How was it, Dave?" cried Dick.

"Was it an accident?" cried Tom.

"Accident! Just such an accident as folks hev as shoves a burning candle in a corn stack. Just you two slither out yonder straight away, and see if you can see anyone."

"But there can't be anyone," said Dick, looking in the direction indicated.

"Ice wouldn't bear, and they couldn't come in a punt."

"Nay, they coom i' pattens," said Dave sharply. "I joost caught a blink of 'em as they went off, and I let 'em hev the whole charge o' my goon."

"A bullet?" said Tom huskily.

"Nay, lad; swan-shot. I'd been out after the wild-geese at the end of the bit o' reed-bed here, when I see a light wheer there couldn't be no light, and I roon back and see what they'd done, and let fly at 'em."

"And hit them, Dave?" said Dick.

"Nay, lad, I can't say. I fired and I heered a squeal. Ice wouldn't bear for me to go and see."

"Come along, Tom," cried Dick; and they skated away once more, to curve here and there in all directions, till a hail from the island took them back.

"Can't you find 'em?"

"No."

"Then they must have got away; but they've took some swan-shot wi' 'em, whoever they be."

"But, Dave, were there two?"

"Don't know, lad. I only see one, and fired sharp. Look ye here," he continued, pointing to the glowing remains of his hut, "I nivver made no dreerns. They might have left me alone. Now they'll come back some day and pay me back for that shot. All comes o' your father makkin dreerns, Mester Dick, just as if we weren't reight before."

"It's very, very sad, Dave."

"Ay, bairn, and I feel sadly. Theer's a whole pound o' powder gone, and if I'd happened to be happed up i' my bed instead of out after they geese, I should hev gone wi' it, or been bont to dead. Why did they want to go meddling wi' me?"

"They've been meddling with every one, Dave," said Tom.

"'Cept you two," grumbled Dave. "Theer was my sheepskin coat and a pair o' leggin's and my new boots."

"Were the nets there, Dave?" asked Dick.

"Course they weer. Look, dessay that's them burning now. All my shot too melted down, and my tatoes, and everything I have."

"Where was the dog?"

"Over at John Warren's. Wasn't well. Nice sort o' neighbour he is to stop away!"

"But he couldn't come, Dave," said Tom in remonstrant tones. "The ice wouldn't bear anyone but us boys."

"Why, I'd ha' swimmed to him," growled Dave, "if his place had been afire."

"No you wouldn't, Dave. You couldn't when it's frozen. I say, couldn't we put anything out?"

"Nay, lads. It must bon right away, and then there'll be a clear place to build again."

"But," cried Dick, "a bucket or two, and we could do a good deal."

"Boocket's bont," said Dave sadly, "and everything else. They might hev left me alone, for I hates the dreerns."

The trio stood watching the fire, which was rapidly going down now for want of something to burn; but as they stood near, their faces scorched, while the cold wind drawn by the rising heat cut by their ears and threatened to stiffen their backs. The reeds and young trees which had been burning were now smoking feebly, and the only place which made any show was the peat-stack, which glowed warmly and kept crumbling down in cream-coloured ash. But when a fire begins to sink it ceases to be exciting, and as the two lads stood there upon their skates, with their faces burning, the tightness of their straps stopped the circulation, and their feet grew cold.

"I say, Dave," said Dick just then, "what's to be done?"

"Build 'em up again. I builded this, and I can build another, lad."

"Yes, but I mean about you. What's to be done? The ice won't bear you, and you've got no shelter."

The rough fellow shook his head.

"Nay, but it wean't rain, and I can sit close to the fire and keep mysen warm."

"But you ought to have some cover."

"Ay, I ought to hev some cover, and I'll get my punt ashore, and turn her up, and sit under her."

"And no wraps! Look here, I shall be warm enough skating back. I'll lend you my coat."

"Nay, nay, lad," said Dave, with his eyes twinkling, and his face looking less grim. "Keep on thy coat, lad, I wean't hev it. Thankye, though, all the same, and thou shalt hev a good bit o' sport for that, Mester Dick. But, theer, you two had best go back."

"But we don't like leaving you," said Tom.

"Thankye, lads, thankye. Bud nivver yow mind about me. Look at the times I've wetched all night in my poont for the wild-geese, and wi'out a fire, eh? Yow both get back home. Wouldn't bear me to walk wi' ye to sleep in one of the barns at the Toft, would it?"

"I don't think it would, Dave."

"Nay, it wouldn't, lad; and I don't want to get wet, so off with you."

The boys hesitated; but Dave was determined.

"Here, give me a hand wi' my poont," he said; and going to where it was moored, he took hold of the boat, drew it close in, and then, he on one side, the two lads on the other, they ran it right up ashore, and close to the glowing peat-stack, where, with a good deal of laughter at their clumsiness in skates ashore, the punt was turned over, and Dave propped one side up with a couple of short pieces of wood.

"Theer," he said. "Looks like setting a trap to ketch a big bird. I'm the big bird, and I shall be warm enew faäcing the fire. When it goes out I can tak' away the sticks and let the poont down and go to sleep. Come and see me again, lads, and bring me a moothful o' something. Mebbe the ice'll bear to-morrow."

"We'll come, Dave, never fear," said Dick, taking out his knife as he reached the ice, and cleaning the mud off his skates, for the ground was soft near the fire, though hard as iron everywhere else.

"I don't fear, lads," said Dave smiling, and letting off his watchman-rattle laugh. "It's a bad job, but not so bad as Farmer Tallington's stables burning, or squire's beasts heving theer legs cooten. I'll soon get oop another house when I've been and seen neighbour Hickathrift for some wood. Now, then, off you go, and see who's best man over the ice."

"One moment, Dave," cried Dick, checking himself in the act of starting. "It was easy enough to come here with the fire to guide us, but we must know which way to go back."

"Ay, to be sure, lad," cried Dave eagerly. "You mak' straight for yon star and yow'll be right. That star's reight over the Toft. Now, then—off!"

There was a momentary hesitation, and then the boys struck the ice almost at the same time. There was a ringing hissing sound, mingled with a peculiar splitting as if the ice were parting from where they started across the mere to the Toft, and then they were going at a rapidly increasing speed straight for home.

Chapter Twenty Three.

The Question.

There are many pleasures in life, and plenty of people to sing the praises of the sport most to their taste; but it is doubtful whether there is any manly pursuit which gives so much satisfaction to an adept in the art as skating.

I don't mean skating upon the ornamental water of a park, elbowed here, run against there, crowded into a narrow limit, and abortively trying to cut figures upon a few square feet of dirty, trampled ice, full of holes, dotted with stones thrown on by mischievous urchins to try whether it will bear, and being so much unlike ice that it is hardly to be distinguished from the trampled banks; but skating over miles of clear black crystal, on open water, with the stars twinkling above like diamonds, the air perfectly still around, but roaring far on high, as Jack Frost and his satellites go hurrying on to mow down vegetation and fetter streams; when there is so much vitality in the air you breathe that fatigue is hardly felt, and when, though the glass registers so many degrees of frost, your pulses beat, your cheeks glow, and a faint dew upon your forehead beneath your cap tells you that you are thoroughly warm. How the blood dances through the veins! How the eyes sparkle! How tense is every nerve! How strong each muscle! The ice looks like steel. Your skates are steel, and your legs feel the same as stroke, *whish*! stroke, *whish*! stroke! stroke! stroke! stroke! away you go, gathering power, velocity, confidence, delight, at the unwonted exercise, till you feel as if you could go on for ever, and begin wishing that the whole world was ice, and human beings had been born with skates to their toes instead of nails.

Some such feelings as these pervaded the breasts of Dick Winthorpe and Tom Tallington as they glided along homeward on that night. Every now and then there was a sharp report, and a hissing splitting sound. Then another and another, for the ice was really too thin to bear them properly, and it undulated beneath their weight like the soft swell of the Atlantic in a calm.

"Sha'n't go through, shall we?" said Tom, as there was a crack as loud as a pistol-shot.

"We should if we stopped," said Dick. "Keep on and we shall be on fresh ice before it breaks."

And so it seemed. Crack! crack! crack! But at every report and its following splitting the lads redoubled their exertions, and skimmed at a tremendous rate over the treacherous surface.

At times it was quite startling; but they were growing so inured to the peril that they laughed loudly—a joyous hearty laugh—which rang out to the music made by their skates.

They were in the highest of glee, for though they did not revert to it in words, each boy kept thinking of the past quarrel, and rejoicing at its end, while he looked forward to days of enjoyment in companionship such as had gone before.

The star—one of those in the Great Bear—did them good stead, for it was easy to follow; and saving that they were always within an ace of going through, they skimmed on in safety.

From time to time they glanced back to see the glare of the fire dying out to such an extent that when they were well in sight of the light at the landing-place which they felt convinced Hickathrift was showing, the last sign had died out, and just then a loud crack made them forget it.

"Don't seem to be freezing so hard, does it?" said Tom.

"Oh, yes, I think so; only we must be going over ice we cracked before. Now, then, let's put on all the speed we can, and go right in to where the light is with a rush."

Tom answered to his companion's call by taking stroke for stroke, and away they went quicker than ever. The ice bent and swayed and cracked, and literally hissed as they sped on, with the white powder flying as it was struck off. The metallic ring sounded louder, and the splitting more intense; but still they passed on in safety till they were within one hundred yards of where the wheelwright was waiting, when there was a sharp report as loud as that of a gun, a crack, and there were no skaters on the surface, only a quantity of broken ice in so much black water, and directly after a loud yell rose from the shore.

"Now, Jacob, out with it!" came in stentorian tones; and then there was a cracking sound, a great deal of splashing, and the punt was partly slid along the ice, partly used to break it up, by the two men who waded by its side, and finally got it right upon the ice and thrust along till it was close to the place where the lads had broken in.

"Now, then, where are you?" shouted Hickathrift as he peered around.

"Here we are, all right, only so precious cold!" cried Dick. "It isn't very deep here; only up to your chest."

"It's up to my chin," cried Tom with a shiver, "and I'm holding on by the ice."

Hickathrift did not hesitate, but waded towards him, breaking opposing sheets of ice with a thump of his fist, and at last, with some little difficulty, all got ashore.

"Theer, both of you, run for it to the Toft and get to bed. The missus knows what to do better than I can tell her. Nivver mind your pattens."

If they had stopped to get them off it would have been a terribly long job with their rapidly-numbing hands, so they did not pause, but scuffled over the ground in the best way they could to the house, where hot beds and a peculiar decoction Mrs Winthorpe prepared had a double property, for it sent them into a perspiration and off to sleep, one of the labourers bearing the news to Grimsey that the heir to the house of Tallington would not return that night, consequent upon having become "straänge and wet."

The next morning the boys came down to breakfast none the worse for their wetting, to find that Mr Marston was already there looking very serious.

He had been told of the burning-out of poor Dave, and he had other news of his own, that three of the cottages had been fired during the past night.

"And the peculiar part of the business is," said Mr Marston, "that big Bargle saw the person who fired the last of the houses."

The engineer looked at Dick as he spoke.

"Why didn't he catch him then?" said Dick sharply, for Mr Marston's look annoyed him; "he is big enough."

"Don't speak pertly, Dick!" said his father sternly.

"It was because he is so big that he did not catch him, Richard Winthorpe," said the engineer coldly. "The ice bore the person who fired the places, because he was skating."

"Skating!" cried Dick, flushing up.

"Yes, skating!" said Mr Marston. "Bargle says that the man hobbled over the ground in his skates, but as soon as he reached the ice he went off like a bird. The ice cracked and splintered, but it seemed to bear him, and in less than a minute he was out of sight, but Bargle could hear him for a long time."

"Well, it wasn't me, Mr Marston," said Tom, laughing. "I was skating along with Dick, but it was neither of us. We went to another fire."

"Breakfast is getting cold," said Mrs Winthorpe, who looked troubled, for the squire was frowning, and Dick turning pale and red by turns.

"Look here," said the squire suddenly; "I cannot, and I will not, have unpleasantness of this kind in my house. I must speak plainly, Marston. You suspect my boy of firing your men's huts last night?"

"I am very sorry, Mr Winthorpe, and I do it unwillingly, but appearances are very much against him."

"They are," said the squire gravely.

"I like Dick; I always did like Dick," said the engineer; "and it seems to me horrible to have to suspect such a lad as he is; but put yourself in my place, Mr Winthorpe. Can you be surprised?"

"I am not surprised, Mr Marston," said Mrs Winthorpe, rising and going to her son's side. "Dick was out last night skating with Tom here over the thin ice, and of course it must have been a very light person to cross last night in skates; but you are mistaken. My boy would not commit such a cowardly crime."

The moment before, Dick, who was half-stunned by the accusation, and ready to give up in despair, leaped to his feet and flung his arms about his mother's waist. His eyes flashed and the colour flushed right up into his brows as he kissed her passionately again and again.

"You are right," said the squire. "But speak out, Dick. You did not do this dastardly thing?"

"No, father," said Dick, meeting his eyes boldly. "I couldn't."

"There, Marston," said the squire; "and I will not insult Tom Tallington by accusing him."

"Oh, no, father! we were together all the time."

"But I say," cried Tom, "old Dave said it was a chap in skates who set fire to his place, and he couldn't follow him over the ice."

"Yes; I'd forgotten," cried Dick, "and he shot at him."

"Then I am wrong once more, Dick," said Mr Marston. "I beg your pardon. Will you forgive me?"

"Of course I will, Mr Marston," said Dick huskily, as he took the extended hand; "but I don't think you ought to be so ready to think ill of me."

"And I say the same, Mr Marston," said Mrs Winthorpe. "My boy is wilful, and he may have been a bit mischievous, but he could not be guilty of such cowardly tricks as these."

"No," said Tom, with his mouth full of pork-pie; "of course he could not. Dick isn't a coward!"

"I humbly apologise, Mrs Winthorpe," said Marston, smiling, "and you must forgive me. A man who has been shot at has his temper spoiled."

"Say no more, Marston, my lad," said the squire warmly; "we all forgive you, and—breakfast waits."

The subject was hurriedly changed, Dick being after all able to make a good meal, during which he thought of the past, and of how glad he was to be friends with Tom Tallington again; and then, as he had his second help of pie to Tom's third, it seemed to him that the same person must be guilty of all these outrages, and if so it could not by any possibility be Farmer Tallington, for he never skated, and even if he could, he weighed at least sixteen stone, and the ice had broken under the weight of Tom's seven or eight.

"We shall find him yet, Marston; never fear," said the squire; "and when we do—well, I shall be sorry for the man."

"Why?" said Mrs Winthorpe.

"Because," said the squire gravely, "I have been so near death myself that—there, this is not a pleasant subject to talk about. We will wait."

Chapter Twenty Four.

Preparing for Action.

Hickathrift shook his head; Mrs Hickathrift screwed up her lips, shut her eyes, and shuddered; and the former doubled up his hard fist and shook it in the air, as if he were going to hit nothing, as he gave out his opinion—this being also the opinion of all the labouring people near.

"Ay, yow may laugh, Mester Dick, but they'll nivver find out nowt. It's sperrits, that's what it is—sperrits of the owd fen, them as makes the ager, and sends will-o'-the-wisps to lead folkses into the bog. They don't like the drain being med, and they shutes and bons, and does all they can to stop it."

115

"You're a great goose, Hicky," said Dick sharply. "Who ever heard of a ghost—"

"I didn't say ghost, my lad. I said sperrits!"

"Well, they're all the same."

"Nay, nay, ghosts is ghosts, and sperrits is sperrits."

"Well, then, who ever heard of a spirit going out skating with a lantern, or poling about with a punt, or shooting people, or blowing up sluice-gates, or cutting beasts' legs, or setting fire to their houses? Did you?"

"I nivver did till now, Mester Dick."

"It's all nonsense about spirits; isn't it, Tom?"

"Of course it is," was the reply. "We're going to catch the spirit some day, and we'll bring him here."

"Ay, do," said Hickathrift, nodding his head softly. "Well, I'm glad you two hev made it up."

"Never mind about that. Has Dave been over?"

"Ay, lad. Soon as the ice went away and he could get his punt along he come to me and asked me to get him some wood sawn out; and we done it already. Ice is gone and to-morrow I'm going to pole across and help him knock up a frame, and he'll do the rest hissen."

The damage was far more severe at the drainage works; but even here the traces of the fire soon disappeared, and fresh huts were run up nearer to where the men were at work.

One thing, however, was noticeable, and that was the action of the squire, the engineer, and Farmer Tallington—the engineer, after hanging away for a time, becoming again more friendly, though Dick never seemed at ease in his presence now.

These three leaders on the north side of the fen held a meeting with dwellers on the west and south, and after long consultation the results were seen in a quiet way which must have been rather startling to wrong-doer? and those who were secretly fighting to maintain the fen undrained.

Tom was the first to begin talking about these precautions as he and Dick started to go down to the drain one morning early in spring, after a long spell of bitter miserable weather, succeeded by a continuance of fierce squalls off the sea.

"I say," he said, "father's got such a splendid new pair of pistols."

"Has he? So has my father," said Dick staring. "Are yours mounted with brass and with brass pans?"

"Yes, and got lions' heads on the handles just at the end."

"Ours are just the same," said Dick. "I say, Tom, it won't be very pleasant for the spirits if they come now. Hullo, what does Hicky want?"

The big wheelwright was signalling to them to come, and they turned in to his work-shed.

"Thowt you lads 'd like to see," he said. "What d'yer think o' them?"

He pointed to a couple of muskets lying on the bench.

"Are these yours?" said Tom.

"Yes and no, lads. They're for me and Jacob, and we've got orders to be ready at any time to join in and help run down them as does all the mischief; but it's a sorry business, lads. Powther and shot's no use. Yow can't get shut of sperrits that ways. Good goons, aren't they?"

The pieces were inspected and the boys soon afterwards started.

"I don't see much use in our going down here," said Tom, "for if there is anything stupid it's the cutting of a drain. It's all alike, just the same as the first bit they cut."

"Only we don't have to go so far to see the men at work. I suppose one of these days we shall have Mr Marston setting up huts for the men about the Toft. Hist! look out! What's that?"

"Whittrick!" said Tom, running in pursuit of the little animal which crossed their path. "There must be rabbits about here."

"Yes. Do you know what they call whittricks down south?"

"No."

"Stoats."

"How stupid!" said Tom after a vain chase after the snaky-looking little creature. "They must be very silly people down south. Do they call them stoats in London?"

"Haven't got any in London—only rats."

The engineer greeted the lads warmly and went up to the temporary hut he occupied to fetch his gun, when, in the corner of the room Dick saw something which made him glance at Tom.

"Yes," said the engineer, who saw the glance; "we're going to show your fen-men, Master Dick, that we do not mean to be trifled with. I've got muskets; and as the law does not help us, we shall help ourselves. So if anyone intends to come shooting us, blowing up our works, or setting fire to our huts, he had better look out for bullets."

"But you wouldn't shoot anyone, Mr Marston?" said Tom.

"Indeed but we would, or any two, sir. It's a case of self-defence. There, Dick, don't look at me as if I were a bloodthirsty savage. I have got all these muskets down and shown my men how to use them, and I am letting it be known that we are prepared."

"Seems rather horrible," said Dick.

"More horrible for your father to be shot, Dick, and for people to be burned in their beds, eh!"

"Ever so much," cried Tom. "You shoot 'em all, Mr Marston."

"Precaution is better than cure, Tom," said the engineer smiling. "Now that we are prepared, you will see that we shall not be interfered with, and my arming the men will save bloodshed instead of causing it."

"Think so, sir?"

"I am sure of it, my lad. Besides, if I had not done something, my men would not have stayed. Even Bargle said it was getting too warm. He said he was not afraid, but he would not stay. So here we are ready for the worst: self-defence, my lads. And now let's go and get a few ducks for dinner. They are pretty plentiful, and my men like them as well as I."

The result was a long walk round the edge of the fen and the bringing back of a fairly miscellaneous bag of wild-fowl, the engineer having become a skilful gunner during his stay in the wild coast land.

Mr Marston was right; the preparations made by him and all the farmers round who had an interest in the draining of the fen had the effect of putting a stop to the outrages. The work went on as the weeks glided by, and spring passed, and summer came to beautify the wild expanse of bog and water. There had been storm and flood, but people had slept in peace, and the troubles of the past were beginning to be forgotten.

There were plenty of fishing and fowling expeditions, visits to the decoy with good results, and journeys to John Warren's home for the hunting out of rabbits; but life was beginning seriously for the two lads, who found occupation with Mr Marston and began to acquire the rudiments of knowledge necessary for learning to be draining engineers. Sometimes they were making drawings, sometimes overlooking, and at others studying works under their teacher's guidance.

But it was a pleasant time, for Marston readily broke off work to join them in some expedition.

One day, as they were poling along, Tom gave Dick a queer look, and nodded in the direction of a fir-crowned gravelly island lying about a mile away.

"When's the Robinson Crusoe business going to begin, Dick?" he said.

Dick laughed, but it was not a merry laugh, for the memory was a painful one, and mingled with recollections of times when everyone was suspicious of him, or seemed to be; and he was fast relapsing into an unhappy morbid state.

"What was the Robinson Crusoe business?" said Marston; and on being told, he laughingly proposed going on.

"Let's have a look at the place, boys," he said. "Why shouldn't we have a summer-house out here to come and stay at sometimes, shooting, fishing, or collecting. We cannot always work."

The pole was vigorously plied, and at the end of half an hour they had landed, to find the place just as they remembered it to have been the year before. There were the bushes, the heath, and heather in the gravelly soil, and the fir-trees flourishing.

"A capital place!" said the engineer. "I tell you what, boys, we'll bring Big Bargle over, and a couple of men; the wheelwright shall cut us some posts, rafters, and a door, and we'll make a great hut, and—"

He stopped short at that point and stared, as they all stood in the depths of the little fir-wood, with the water and reed-beds hidden from sight. For there, just before them, as if raised by magic, was the very building Mr Marston had described, and upon examination they found it very dry and warm, with a bed of heath in one corner.

"Some sportsman has forestalled us," said the engineer. "One of the farmers, I suppose, from the other side of the fen."

They came away, with the lads sharing the same feeling of disappointment, for the little island was robbed of all its romance. It was no longer uninhabited, and the temptation to have a hut there was gone.

"Plenty more such places, boys," said Mr Marston, "so never mind. We'll hunt one out and make much of it before my drain turns all this waste into fertile fields. Now let's get back, for I have a lot to chat over with the wheelwright."

The next morning Hickathrift was beaming, and he came up to the Toft to catch Dick, who was feeding Solomon and avoiding his friendly kicks, while he waited for Tom to go over with him to the works.

"Say, Mester Dick, on'y think of it! Leave that owd ass alone, lad, and listen to me."

"What is it, Hicky?"

"Why, lad, I'm a man full o'—what do you call that when a chap wants to get on in the world?"

"Ambition, Hicky."

"That's it, Mester Dick. I'm full on it, bud I've nivver hed a chance. You see I've had to mend gates, and owd carts, and put up fences. I did nearly get the job to build a new barn, bud I lost it, and all my life's been jobs."

"And what now?" said Dick warmly.

"What now, lad! Why, Mester Marston's set me to mak three sets o' small watter gates for sides o' the dreern, and I'm to hev money in advance for the wood and iron work, and my fortune's about made."

"Hooray, Hicky! I am glad," cried Dick; and Tom, coming up, was initiated into the great new step in advance, and added his congratulations.

"Why, you're carpenter and joiner to the works now, Hicky!" said Dick, laughing.

"Ay, lad, that's it, and I don't fear for nowt."

It was less than a fortnight after, that Dick lay asleep one night and dreaming of being in a boat on the mere, or one of its many additional pools, when he started into wakefulness with the impression that the house was coming down.

"Eh? What is it?" he cried, as there was a heavy thumping on the wall close to his bed's head.

"Get up—fire!" came in muffled tones; and bounding out of bed he saw that there was a lurid light on the water, evidently reflected from something burning pretty near at hand, while there was the distant hum of voices, mingled with shrieks and the barking of a dog.

117

Dick began hurriedly dressing, and threw open the window, to find that the dog was Grip, who was out in the yard barking frantically, as if to alarm the house.

"What is it, father? Where?" cried Dick.

"Don't know; not here. Labourers' cottages, I think," replied the squire, who was still dressing. Then, as a burst of flame seemed to rush up skyward, and a cloud of brilliant sparks floated away, he added, "Dick, my lad, it is poor Hickathrift's turn now."

He was quite right, for as they ran the few hundred yards which separated them from the burning place, it was to find that the poor fellow's house, work-shed, stock of wood, peat-stack, and out-buildings were in a blaze; even his punt, which had been brought up for its annual repair and pitching, blazing furiously.

Hickathrift, Jacob, Mrs Hickathrift, and the farm people were all at work with buckets, which they handed along from the dipping place by the old willows; but at the first glance the squire saw that it was in vain, and that the fire had taken such hold that nothing could be saved. Both he and Dick, however, joined in the efforts, saying nothing but working with all their might, the squire taking Jacob's place and dipping the water, while the apprentice and Dick helped to pass the full buckets along and the empty back, for they were not enough to form a double line.

For about a quarter of an hour this was kept up, the wheelwright throwing the water where he thought it would do most good; but the flames only roared the louder, and, fanned by a pleasant breeze, fluttered and sent up sparks of orange and gold, till a cask of pitch got well alight, and then the smoke arose in one dense cloud.

It was a glorious sight in spite of its horror, for the wood in the shed and the pile without burned brilliantly, lighting up the mere, gilding the reeds, and spreading a glow around that was at times dazzling.

"Pass it along quick! pass it along!" Jacob kept saying, probably to incite people to work harder; but it was not necessary, for everyone was doing his or her best, when, just as they were toiling their hardest, the wheelwright took a bucket of water, hurled it as far as he could, and then dashed on the empty vessel and turned away.

"No good," he said bitterly, as he wiped his face. "Fire joost spits at me when I throw in the watter. It must bon down, squire, eh?"

"Yes, my man, nothing could save the place now."

"And all my same (lard) in a jar—ten pounds good," murmured Mrs Hickathrift.

"Ay, moother, and my Sunday clothes," said the wheelwright with a bitter laugh.

"And my best frock."

"Ay, and my tools, and a bit o' mooney I'd saved, and all my stoof. Eh, but I'm about ruined, moother, and just when I was going to get on and do the bit o' work for the dreern folk."

The fire seemed to leap up suddenly with a great flash as if to enlighten the great fellow's understanding, but he did not grasp the situation for a few moments, till his wife, as she bemoaned the loss of a paste-board and a flour-tub, suddenly exclaimed:

"It's them sperrits of the fen as has done it all."

"Ay, so it be!" roared Hickathrift. "Ay! Hey, bud if I could git one of 'em joost now by scruff of his neck and the seat of his breeches, I'd—I'd—I'd roast him."

"Then it was no accident, Hickathrift?"

"Yes, squire," said the man bitterly; "same sort o' axden as bont Farmer Tallington's stable and shed. Hah, here he is!" he added, as the farmer came panting up with Tom. "Come to waärm theesen, farmer? It's my turn now."

"My lad! My lad!" panted the farmer, "I am sorry."

"Thanky, farmer; but fine words butter no parsneps. Theer, bairn," he cried, putting his arm round his wife's waist; "don't cry that away. We aren't owd folks, and I'm going to begin again. Be a good dry plaäce after fire's done, and theer'll be some niced bits left for yow to heat the oven when fire's out."

"And no oven, no roof, no fireside."

"Hush! hush! bairn!" said the big fellow thickly. "Don't I tell thee I'm going to begin again! What say, Mester Dick? Nay, nay, lad, nay."

"What did Dick say?" said the squire sharply.

"Hush, Hicky!" whispered Dick quickly.

"Nay, lad, I wean't hoosh! Said, squire, as he's got thretty shillings saved up, and he'd give it to me to start wi'."

"And so he shall, my man, and other neighbours will help you too. I'll make Dick's thirty shillings a hundred guineas."

"Well, I can't do that, Hickathrift," said Farmer Tallington; "but if ever you want to borrow twenty guineas come to me; and there's my horse and sled to lead wood wheniver you like, and a willing hand or two to help."

Hickathrift turned sharply to say something; but he could only utter a great gulp, and, turning away, he went a few yards, and leaned his head upon his arm against a willow tree, and in the bright glow of the burning building, whose gilded smoke rose up like some vast plume, they could see his shoulders heave, while his wife turned to the squire, and in a simple, homely fashion, kissed his hand.

The squire turned to stop Dick, but it was too late, for the lad had reached the wheelwright and laid his hand upon his shoulder.

"Hicky," he said softly; "be a man!"

"Ay, lad, I will," said the great fellow, starting up with his eyes wet with tears. "It isn't the bont plaäce made me soft like that, but what's been said."

He had hardly spoken before there was a peculiar noise heard in the distance, as if a drove of cattle had escaped and were coming along the hard road of the fen; but it soon explained itself, for there were shouts and cries, and five minutes later Mr Marston and his men, nearly a hundred strong, came running up, ready to assist, and then utter the fiercest of denunciations against those who had done this thing.

Then there was an ominous silence, as all stood and watched the burning building till there was nothing but a heap of smouldering wood, which was scattered and the last sparks quenched.

Chapter Twenty Five.

The Troubles culminate.

The fire at the wheelwright's lasted people nearly a month for gossip, but Hickathrift would not believe it was the work of spirits now.

Then came the news of a fresh outrage. The horses employed in bringing stones for certain piers to water-gates were shot dead one night.

Next, a fresh attempt was made to blow up the sluice, but failed.

Last of all, the man who was put on to watch was shot dead, and his body found in the drain.

After this there was a pause, and the work was carried on with sullen watchfulness and bitter hate. The denunciations against the workers of the evil were fierce and long.

But in spite of all, the drain progressed slowly and steadily. The engineer was carrying his advances right into the stronghold of the fen-men, who bore it all in silence, but struck sharply again and again.

"I wonder who is to get the next taste!" said Tom Tallington one day as he and Dick were talking.

"No one," said Dick; "so don't talk about it. The people are getting used to the draining, and father thinks they'll all settle down quietly now."

"How long is it since that poor fellow was shot?"

"Don't talk about it, I tell you," said Dick angrily. "Three months."

"No."

"Nearly."

Dick was right; nearly three months had gone by since the poor fellow set to keep watch by Mr Marston had been shot dead, and this culmination of the horrors of the opposition had apparently startled his murderers from making farther attempts.

"I tell you what it is," said Tom, "the man who fired that shot and did all the other mischief has left the country. He dare not stay any longer for fear of being caught."

"Then it was no one over our side of the fen," said Dick thoughtfully. "Perhaps you are right. Well, I'm going to have a good long day in the bog to-morrow. It's wonderfully dry now, and I mean to have a good wander. What time shall you be ready?"

"Can't go," said Tom. "I've promised to ride with father over to the town."

"What a pity! Well, never mind; we'll go again the next day and have a good long day then."

"Will Mr Marston go with us?"

"No. I asked him, and he said he should be too busy at present, but he would go in a fortnight's time. He said he should not want either of us for a week, so we can go twice if we like."

Tom smiled as if, in spite of his many wanderings, the idea of a ramble in the fen would be agreeable.

"Shall you fish?" he said.

"N–no, I don't think I shall. I mean to have a long wander through the flats away west of the fir island."

"You can't," said Tom; "it's too boggy."

"Not it. Only got to pick your way. Do you think I don't know what I'm about?"

"Better take old Solomon with you, and ride him till he sinks in, and then you can walk along his back into a safe place."

"Then I'd better take another donkey too, and get him to lie down when I come to another soft place."

"Ah, I would!" said Tom.

"I shall," said Dick. "Will you come?"

"Do you mean by that to say that I am a donkey?" cried Tom half angrily.

"Yes, when you talk such stupid nonsense. Just as if I couldn't get through any bog out here in the fen. Anyone would think I was a child."

"Well, don't get lost," said Tom; "but I must go now."

The boys parted, with the promise that Tom was to come over from Grimsey to breakfast the next morning but one, well provided with lunch; that in the interim Dick was to arrange with Hickathrift about his punt, and that then they were to have a thoroughly good long exploring day, right into some of the mysterious parts of the fen, Dick's first journey being so much scouting ready for the following day's advance.

As soon as Dick was left alone he strolled down to the wheelwright's, having certain plans of his own to exploit.

"Well, Hicky, nearly got all right?" he said.

"Nay, nay, lad, and sha'n't be for a twelvemonth," replied the great bluff fellow, staring at his newly-erected cottage. "Taks a deal o' doing to get that streight. How is it you're not over at the works?"

"Not wanted for a bit. I say, Hicky, may I have the punt to-morrow?"

"Sewerly, Mester Dick, sewerly. I'll set Jacob to clear her oot a bit for you. Going fishing?"

"Well—no," said Dick, hesitating. "I was—er—thinking of doing a little shooting."

"What at fend o' June! Nay, nay, theer's no shooting now."

"Not regular shooting, but I thought I might get something curious, perhaps, right away yonder."

"Ay, ay, perhaps so."

"Might see a big pike basking, and shoot that."

"Like enough, my lad, like enough. Squire going to lend you a goon?"

Dick shook his head, but the wheelwright was busy taking a shaving off a piece of wood, so did not see it, and repeated his question.

"No, Hicky, I want you to lend me one of those new ones."

"What, as squire and Mr Marston left for me and Jacob! Nay, nay, lad, that wean't do."

"Oh, yes, it will, Hicky. I'll take great care of it, and clean it when I've done. Lend me the gun, there's a good fellow."

"Nay, nay. That would never do, my lad. Couldn't do it."

"Why not, Hicky?"

"Not mine. What would squire say?"

"He wouldn't know, Hicky. I shouldn't tell him."

"Bud I should, lad. Suppose thou wast to shoot thee sen, or blow off a leg or a hand? Nay, nay. Yow can hev the boat, bud don't come to me for a gun."

Hickathrift was inexorable, and what was more, he watched his applicant narrowly, to make sure that Dick did not corrupt Jacob.

His visitor noticed it, and charged him with the fact.

"Ay," he said, laughing, "that's a true word. I know what Jacob is. He'd do anything for sixpence."

"I hope he wouldn't set fire to the house for that," said Dick angrily.

Hickathrift started as if stung, and stared at his visitor.

"Nay," he said, recovering himself, "our Jacob nivver did that. He were fast asleep that night, and his bed were afire when I wackened him. Don't say such a word as that."

"I didn't mean it, Hicky; but do lend me the gun."

"Nay, my, lad, I wean't. There's the poont and welcome, but no gun."

Dick knew the wheelwright too well to persevere; and in his heart he could not help admiring the man's stern sense of honesty; so making up his mind to be content with some fishing and a good wander in the untrodden parts of the fen, he asked Hickathrift to get him some baits with his cast-net.

"Ay, I'll soon get them for you, my lad," said Hickathrift. "Get a boocket, Jacob, lad."

The next minute he was getting the newly-made circular net with its pipe-leads from where it hung over the rafters of his shed, and striding down to a suitable shallow where a shoal of small fish could be seen, he ranged the net upon his arm, holding the cord tightly, and, giving himself a spin round, threw the net so that it spread out flat, with the pipe-leads flying out centrifugally, and covering a good deal of space, the leads driving the fish into the centre. When it was drawn a couple of dozen young roach and rudd were made captives, and transferred to the bucket of water Jacob brought.

"Fetch that little bit o' net and a piece o' band, lad," said the wheelwright; and as soon as Jacob reappeared, Hickathrift bound the fine net over the top of the pail, and lowered it by the cord into a deep cold pool close by the punt.

"Theer they'll be all ready and lively for you in the morning, and you'll hev better sport than you would wi' a gun."

Opinions are various, and Dick's were very different to the wheelwright's; but he accepted his rebuff with as good a grace as he could, and went home.

The next morning was delicious. One of those lovely summer-times when the sky is blue, and the earth is just in its most beautiful robe of green.

"Going on the mere, Dick?" said his father. "Well, don't get drowned or bogged."

"Dick will take care," said Mrs Winthorpe, who was busy cutting provender.

"Tom Tallington going with you?" said the squire.

"No, father; I'm going alone."

"I wish you could have come with me, Hicky!" said Dick, as, laden with his basket of fishing-tackle and provender, he took his place in the punt.

"Ay, and I wish so too," said the wheelwright, smiling, as he drew up and uncovered the pail of bait to set it in the boat. "Bud too busy. Theer you are! Now, go along, and don't stop tempting a man who ought to be at work. Be off!"

To secure himself against further temptation he gave the punt a push which sent it several yards away; so, picking up the pole, Dick thrust it down and soon left the Toft behind, while the water glistened, the marsh-marigolds glowed, and the reeds looked quite purple in places, so dark was their green.

Dick poled himself along, watching the water-fowl and the rising herons disturbed in their fishing, while here and there he could see plenty of small fish playing about the surface of the mere; but he was not in an angling humour, and though the tempting baits played about in the bucket he did not select any to hook and set trimmers for the pike that were lurking here and there.

At last, though, he began to grow tired of poling, for the sun was hot; and, thinking it would be better to wait for Tom before he tried to explore the wild part of the fen, he thrust the punt along, to select a place and try for a pike.

This drew his attention to the baits, where one of the little roach had turned up nearly dead, a sure sign that the water required changing, so, setting down the pole, he took up the bucket, and, lowering it slowly over the side, he held one edge level with the water, so that the fresh could pour in and the stale and warm be displaced.

Trifles act as large levers sometimes. In this case for one, a few drops of water from the dripping pole made the bottom of the punt slippery; and as Dick leaned over the side his foot gave way, the weight of the bucket overbalanced him, and he had to seize the side of the punt to save himself. This he did, but as he leaned over, nearly touching the water, it was to gaze at the bucket descending rapidly, and the fish escaping, for he had let go.

"What a nuisance!" he cried, as he saw the great vessel seem to turn of a deeper golden hue as it descended and then disappeared, becoming invisible in the dark water, while the punt drifted away before he could take up the pole to thrust it back.

There was nothing to guide him, and the poling was difficult, for the water was here very deep, and though he tried several times to find the spot where the bucket had gone down, it was without success.

"Why, if I did find it," he muttered, "I shouldn't be able to get it up without a hook."

This ended the prospect of fishing, and as he stood there idly dipping down the pole he hesitated as to what he should do, ending by beginning to go vigorously in the direction of Dave Gittan's newly-built-up hut.

"I'll make him take me out shooting," he said; "and we'll go all over that rough part of the fen."

There were very few traces of the past winter's fire visible at Dave's home as Dick approached, ran his punt on to the soft bog-moss, and landed, securing his rope to a tree, and there were no signs of Dave.

He shouted, but there was no reply, and it seemed evident that the dog was away as well.

A walk across to Dave's own special landing-place put it beyond doubt, for the boat was absent.

"What a bother!" muttered Dick, walking back toward the hut, a stronger and better place than the one which had been burned. "Perhaps he has gone to see John Warren!"

Dick hesitated as to whether he should follow, and as he hesitated he reached the door of the hut and peeped in, to make sure that the dog was not there asleep.

The place was vacant, and as untidy already as the old hut. In one corner there was a heap of feathers plucked from the wild-geese he had shot; in another a few skins, two being those of foxes, the cunning animals making the fen, where hunters never came, their sanctuary. There were traces, too, of Dave's last meal.

But it was at none of these that Dick looked so earnestly, but at the 'coy-man's old well-rubbed gun hanging in a pair of slings cut from some old boot, and tempting the lad as, under the circumstances, a gun would tempt.

Hickathrift had refused to lend him one, badly as he wanted it; and here by accident was the very thing he wanted staring at him almost as if asking him to take it.

And Dave! where was he?

Dave might be anywhere, and not return perhaps for days. His comings and goings were very erratic, and Dick tried to think that if the man were there he would have lent him the gun.

But it was a failure.

"He wouldn't have lent it to me," said Dick sadly; and he turned to go. But as he glanced round, there was the old powder-horn upon a roughly-made shelf, and beside it, the leathern bag in which Dave kept his shot, with a little shell loose therein which he used for a measure.

It was tempting. There was the gun; there lay the ammunition. He could take the gun, use it, and bring it back, and give Dave twice as much powder and shot as he had fired away. He could even clean the gun if he liked; but he would not do that, but bring it back boldly, and own to having taken it Dave would not be very cross, and if he were it did not matter.

He would take the gun.

No, he would not. It was like stealing the man's piece.

No, it was not—only borrowing, and Dave would be the gainer.

Still he hesitated, thinking of his father, of Hickathrift's refusal, of its being a mean action to come and take a man's property in his absence; and in this spirit Dick flung out of the hut and walked straight down to the boat, seeing nothing but that gun tempting him as it were, and asking him to seize the opportunity and enjoy a day's shooting untrammelled by anyone.

"It wouldn't do," he said with a sigh as he got slowly into the boat and stooped to untie the rope, when, perhaps, the position sent the blood rushing to his head. At any rate his wilful thoughts mastered him, and in a spirit of reckless indifference to the consequences he leaped ashore, ran up to the hut, dashed in, caught up the powder-horn and shot-bag, thrust them into his pockets, and seizing the gun, he took it from its leather slings, his hands trembling, and a sensation upon him that Dave was looking in at the door.

"What an idiot I was!" he cried, with a feeling of bravado now upon the increase. "Dave won't mind, and I want to shoot all by myself."

He glanced round uneasily enough as he made for the punt, where he laid the gun carefully down, and, seizing his pole, soon sent the vessel to some distance from the hut, every stroke seeming to make him breathe more freely, while a keen sensation of joy pervaded him as he glanced from time to time at the old flint-lock piece, and longed to be where there would be a chance to shoot.

The day was hot as ever, but the heat was forgotten as the punt was sent rapidly along in the direction of the fir-clump island, for it was out there that the wilder part of the fen commenced, and the hope that he would there find the birds more tame consequent upon the absence of molestation made the laborious toil of poling seem light.

But all the same a couple of hours' hard work had been given to the task, and Dick was still far from his goal, when it occurred to him that a little of the bread and butter cut in slices, and with a good thick piece of ham between each pair, would not be amiss.

He laid the pole across the boat, then, and for a quarter of an hour devoted himself to the task of food conversion for bodily support.

This done, there was the gun lying there. It was not likely that he would have a chance at anything; but he thought it would be as well to be prepared, and in this spirit, with hands trembling from eagerness, he raised the piece and began the task of loading, so much powder, and so much paper to ram down upon it.

But he had no paper. It was forgotten, and Dick paused.

Necessity is the mother of invention. Dick took out his pocket-handkerchief and his knife, and in a few minutes the cotton square was cut up, a piece rammed in as a wad, and a measure of shot poured on the top.

Another piece of handkerchief succeeded, going down the barrel with that peculiar *whish whash* sound, to be thumped hard with the ramrod at the bottom till the rod was ready to leap out of the barrel again.

Then there was the pan to open and prove full of powder, and all ready for the first great wild bird he should see, or perhaps a hare or a fox, as soon as he should land.

For it was thought no sin to shoot the foxes there in that wild corner of England, where hounds had never been laid on, and the only chance of hunting would have been in boats. Foxes lived and bred there year after year, and died without ever hearing the music of the huntsman's horn.

Dick laid the gun down with a sigh, and took up the pole, which he used for nearly an hour before, with the fir island well to his left, he ran the punt into a narrow cove among the reeds which spread before him, and, taking the piece, stepped out upon what was a new land.

It must have been with something of the feelings of the old navigators who touched at some far western isle, that Dick Winthorpe landed from his boat, and secured it by knotting together some long rushes and tying the punt rope to them. For here he was in a place where the foot of man could have rarely if ever trod, and, revelling in his freedom and the beauty of the scene around, he shouldered the piece.

He would have acted more wisely if he had filled his pockets with provender from the basket; but he wanted those pockets for the powder and shot, and without intending to go very far from the punt he started, meaning to go in a straight line for some trees he could see at a great distance off, hoping to find something in the shape of game before he had gone far.

It is very easy to make a straight line on a map, but a difficult feat to go direct from one spot to another in a bog.

Dick did not find it out, for he knew it of old, and so troubled himself very little as he plodded on under the hot afternoon sun, now on firm ground, now making some wide deviation so as to avoid a pool of black water. Then there were treacherous morass-like pieces of dark mire thinly covered with a scum-like growth, here green, there bleached in the June sunshine.

It was always hot walking, and made the worse by the way in which, in spite of all his care, his feet sank in the soft soil. At times he plashed along, having to leap from place to place, and then when the way seemed so bad that he felt that he must return, it suddenly became better and lured him on.

He panted and perspired, and struggled on, with the gun always ready; but saving a moor-hen or two upon one or other of the pools, and a coot sailing proudly along at the edge of a reed-bed with her little dingy family, he saw nothing worthy of a shot.

Once there was a rustle among the reeds, but whatever made it was gone before he could see what it was. Once a great heron rose from a shallow place, offering himself as a mark; but it took Dick some time to get a good view of the grey bird, and when at last he brought the sight of the gun to bear upon it, the heron refused to remain still, and the muzzle of the piece described two or three peculiar circles. When at last it was brought steadily to bear upon the mark it was about a hundred yards away, and the trigger was not pulled.

How long Dick had tramped and struggled on through mire and water and over treacherous ground he did not know, but he did not get one chance; and at last, when he stopped short with a horrible sinking sensation in his inner boy, the only things which presented themselves as being ready to be shot were some beautiful swallow-tailed butterflies, while, save that the sun was right before him and going down, the lad had not the slightest idea of where he was.

But he could not stand still, for he was on a soft spot, so he struggled on to where the ground looked more dry, and fortunately for him it proved to be so, and he stood looking round and thinking of going back.

"I wish I had brought something to eat," he said, gazing wistfully in the direction in which he believed the punt lay.

But it was in vain to wish, so he determined to retrace his steps, fighting against the thought that it would be a difficult task, for to all intents and purposes he had lost all idea of the direction in which he had come. It was very hot, though, and the gun was very heavy. He was weary too with poling the boat and walking, and but for the romance of the expedition he would have declared himself fagged out.

As it was, he thought he would have ten minutes' rest before starting back, so picking out a good dry firm place, he laid the gun down, and then, seeing how comfortable the gun seemed, he lay at full length upon his back on the soft heather and gazed straight up at the blue sky.

Then his eyes wandered to a cloud of flies, long gnat-like creatures, which were beginning to dance over the reeds, and he lay watching them till he thought he would get up and be on the move.

Then he thought, as it was so refreshing to be still, he would wait another five minutes.

So he waited another five minutes, and then he did not get up, but lay, not looking at the cloud of gnats which were dancing now just over his face as if the tip of his nose were the point from which they streamed upward in the shape of a plume, for Dick Winthorpe was fast asleep.

How long it was Dick did not know, only that it was a great nuisance that that bull would keep on making such a tremendous noise, bellowing and roaring round and round his bed till it annoyed him so much that he started up wide awake and stared.

It was very dark, not a star to be seen; but the bull was bellowing away in the most peculiar manner, seeming as if he were now high up in the air, and now with his muzzle close to the ground practising ventriloquism.

"Where am I?" said Dick aloud; and then, as the peculiar bellowing noise came apparently nearer, "Why, it's the butterbump!"

Dick was right, it was the butterbump, as the fen people called the great brown bittern, which passed its days in the thickest parts of the bog, and during the darkness rose on high, to circle round and over the unfortunate frogs that were to form its supper, and utter its peculiar bellowing roar.

Dick had never heard it so closely before, and he was half startled by the weird cry. The fen, that had been so silent in the hot June sun, now seemed to be alive with peculiar whisperings and pipings. The frogs were whistling here, a low soft plaintive whistle, and croaking there, while from all around came splashings and quackings and strange cries that were startling in the extreme to one just awakened from the depths of sleep to find himself alone in the darkness, and puzzled by the question: How am I to get back?

No; return was impossible—quite impossible, and the knowledge was forced upon him more and more that he had to make up his mind to pass the night where he was, for to stir meant to go plunge into some bog, perhaps one so deep that his escape with life might be doubtful.

"How stupid I was!" mused Dick. "How hungry I am!" he said aloud. "What a tiresome job!"

He looked around, to see darkness closing him in, not a star visible; but the fen all alive with the sounds, which seemed to increase, for a bittern was answering the one overhead, and another at a greater distance forming himself into a second echo.

"I wonder how long it is since I lay down!" thought Dick.

It might have been four hours—it might have been six or eight. He could not tell, only that he was there, and that his mother would be in a horrible state of dread.

This impressed him so strongly that he was about to start off in a vain effort to find the boat, but his better sense prevailed, and he remained where he was, wondering whether it would be possible to pass the night like that, and, in spite of himself, feeling no little dread of the weird sounds which seemed to come nearer and nearer.

Then the feeling of dread increased, for, though he could see nothing, certain noises he heard suggested themselves as being caused by strange creatures—dwellers in the fen—coming nearer to watch him, and among them he fancied that there were huge eels fresh from the black slime, crawling out of the water, and winding themselves like serpents in and out among the rough grass and heath to get at him and fix their strong jaws upon his legs.

Then little four-footed, sharp-teethed creatures appeared to be creeping about in companies, rushing here and there, while whittricks and rats were waiting till he dropped asleep to leap upon him and bite him, tearing out little pieces of his flesh.

His imagination was so active that his face grew wet with horror, till, making an effort over himself, he started right up and angrily stamped his foot.

"I didn't think I was such a coward," he said half aloud; and then, "I hope poor mother will not be very much alarmed, and I wish Tom Tallington was here!"

The wish was so selfishly comic that he laughed and felt better, for now a new idea came to him.

It was very dark, but the nights were at their shortest now, and it would be daybreak before three—at least so light that he might venture to try and regain the boat.

He stood for a while listening to the noises in the fen; the whispering and chattering, piping and croaking, with the loud splashings and rustlings among the reeds, mingled with the quacking of ducks and the scuttering of the drakes, while every now and then the bittern uttered his hoarse wild roar.

Then, growing weary, he sat down again, and after a time he must have dropped asleep, for he rose feeling quite startled, and stood staring as a peculiarly soft lambent light shone here and there before him.

It was apparently about fifty yards away, and looked like nothing which he had ever seen, for when he had noticed this light before it had always been much farther away.

He knew it was the marsh light, but somehow it seemed more weird and strange now than ever, and as if all the tales he had heard of it were true.

For there it was coming and going and gliding up and down, as if inviting him to follow it, while, as he seemed to feel that this was an invitation, he shuddered and his brow grew cold and dank, for he believed that to follow such a light would be to go direct to his death.

All the old legendary stories crowded into his mind as that light came and went, and seemed to play here and there for what must have been half an hour, when it disappeared. But as it passed away he saw another away to his left, and he was watching this intently when he noticed that far beyond there was a faint light visible; and feeling that this was the first sign of the dawn, he turned to gaze at the will-o'-the-wisp again, and watched it, shuddering as it seemed to approach, growing bolder as it glided away.

"But that was not dawn—that," he said, "that faint light!" It was growing stronger and it was nearer, and more like the rising of the sun, or like—yes, it must be fire again.

Dick's heart leaped, and the chilly feeling of nervous dread and the coldness of the temperature passed away, to give place to a sense of excitement which made his blood dance in his veins and his cheeks flush.

He was not mistaken—he had had too much experience of late. It was fire, and he asked himself whose turn it was now, and why, after the long lapse from outrage, there should be another such a scene as that.

It was impossible to tell where the fire was, but it was a big conflagration evidently, for it was lighting up the sky far more than when he first observed it, but whether it was in the direction of his home or toward the far end of the fen he could not tell.

He thought once that he might be mistaken, and that it was the forerunner of the rising moon; but he was convinced directly that it was fire he saw from the way in which it rose and fell and flickered softly in the sky.

He must have been watching the glow for quite a couple of hours, and it was evidently paling, and he was hopefully looking for another light—that of day, when it seemed to him that he could hear the splashing of water and the rustling of reeds.

The sounds ceased and began again more loudly, and at last they seemed to be coming nearer, but passing him by—somewhere about a hundred yards away.

The sounds ceased—began again—ceased—then sounded more loudly; and at last, with palpitating heart, Dick began to move in the direction of the noise, for he realised that either there was open water or a canal-like passage across the bog, which someone was passing through in a boat.

Dick paused again to listen, but there could be no mistake, the sounds were too familiar, and with voice husky with excitement he put his hand to his mouth and uttered a loud hail.

Chapter Twenty Six.

A Startling Scene.

To Dick Winthorpe's great surprise there was no answer to his cry, and raising his voice again he shouted: "Who's that? Help!"

His voice sounded wild and strange to him out there in that waste, closed in as he was by the darkness, and as he listened he could not repress a shudder, for everything now had become so silent that it was terrible. Away to his left there was the faint glow of light—very faint now—but everywhere else darkness, and all around him now a dead silence. His cry had seemed to alarm every moving creature in the fen, and it had crouched down, or dived, or in some way hidden itself, so that there was neither rustle of body passing through the reeds, splash of foot in the mire, nor beat of pinion in the air. He looked around him half in awe for the strange lights which he had seen gliding here and there like moths of lambent fire, but they too had disappeared, and startling as had been the noise he had heard, the silence seemed now so terrible that he turned cold.

"What a coward I am!" he said to himself at last. "What is there to be afraid about?"

He shouted again, and felt more uneasy, for as his voice died away all seemed more silent than ever, and he drew in a long hissing breath as he gazed vainly in the direction from which the splashing had seemed to come.

For quite half an hour all was perfectly still, but he did not move, partly from an intense desire to be certain, partly, it must be confessed, from a feeling of dread which oppressed him.

Then there was a rustle and a splash from somewhere behind him, such a noise as a bird might make. Directly after there came from a distance the scuttering noise made by a duck dabbling its bill in the ooze, and this was followed by a low *quawk* uttered by some nocturnal bird, perhaps by one of the butterbumps whose hoarse booming cry had come so strangely in the earlier part of the night.

As if these were signals to indicate to the animal life of the fen that all was right, sound after sound arose such as he had heard before; but there was one so different that it filled Dick Winthorpe's ears, and as he listened he seemed to see a man in a punt, who had been crouching down among the reeds, rising up softly, and silently lowering a pole into the water to thrust the boat onward from where it had lain.

Even if it had been light the reeds and undergrowth would have hindered him from seeing anything, and in that darkness the impossibility was emphasised the more strongly; but all the same the faint splash, the light rubbing of wood against wood as the pole seemed to touch the side of the boat, the soft dripping of water, and the silky brushing rustle of the boat among the reeds and withes, joined in painting a mental picture upon the listener's brain till it seemed to Dick that he was seeing with his ears this man in his boat escaping furtively so as not to be heard.

Dick was about to shout again, but he felt that if he did there would be no answer, and his heart began to beat strangely.

It was not fear now, but from a sudden excitement consequent upon a line of thought which suggested itself.

"Why did not this man answer to his cry—this man who was so furtively stealing away? Was it from fear of him?"

Undoubtedly fear of being seen and known.

Dick absolutely panted now with excitement. All feeling of dread passed away, taking with it the chilly sensation of cold and damp. He listened.

Should he shout again and order him to stop? No; he knew that would be of no use, for, as if to make all more sure, there, as Dick listened, each and every nerve on the strain, was the increasing rapidity of the thrusts made with the pole, as the man evidently thought he was getting more and more out of hearing.

"Who is it?" thought Dick, as he realised that by his accident he had discovered what had been hidden from all who had patiently watched.

It was all plain enough to him now; and as he listened to the sounds dying away and growing lost among the splashings and rustlings made by the birds, which were recovering their confidence, the excitement quite took away the lad's breath.

For there it all was. This wretch—some fen-man from the other side—miles away—had stolen across in the darkness, wending his way along the mere channels and over the pools, to commit another dastardly outrage, firing another cottage or stack, and then stolen back, his evil work done.

Whose house had been burned?

It must be the huts of the drain-makers. Dick felt sure of that. He did not know why, but there was the proof lately painted in the sky. And this base wretch, who could it be? he asked himself. Oh, if he could but have seen!

Would this be the same man who had been guilty of all these crimes? thought Dick, as he listened and found that the sounds had died out; and now far away there was a soft faint opalescent light telling him of the coming morn, and sending a thrill of joy through his breast. For there would be light and warmth, and the power to find the boat once more, and with it food. Better still, if he could get to his boat he might follow the wretch who was escaping, and know who it was.

Dick felt directly that it was impossible, for the man would be beyond pursuit long before he could find his boat; and after listening again he began to creep cautiously back to where he had lain down and slept and left Dave Gittan's gun.

The dawn was spreading, and it showed the watcher which was the east, and hence taught him that the fire must have been somewhere in the direction of the Toft, for the glare in the sky was certainly north of where he now stood.

The dawn spread faster, and the reeds and alders about him began to be visible; and—yes, there was the gun, all cold to the touch and wet with dew.

"Not much shooting," thought Dick as he mentally planned getting back to the boat, and hurrying across to Dave's hut to replace the piece and suffer a good scolding.

"Never mind; I'll give him a pound of powder. What's that?"

Splashing—the rustling of reeds—voices.

There was no concealment here, and besides the sounds came in a contrary direction to that taken by the fleeing man.

"Hoi!" shouted Dick loudly.

"Hoi! hallo!" came back; and then a well-known voice cried: "Is that you, Dick?"

"Yes, father. Here! Ahoy!"

There was more splashing, more talking, and Dick's heart leaped as he felt that his father had come in search of him, and that he would have an easier task than he had expected in finding his boat.

As the sounds approached the light increased, and Dick had no difficulty in going to meet them, picking his way carefully through the bog till he found himself close to a broad channel of reedy water, and here he had to pause.

"Where are you?" came from about a hundred yards away. And as he shouted to guide the search party he soon saw through the dim light a crowded punt propelled by two polers, and that there was another behind.

The next minute the foremost punt was within reach, and Dick stepped from a clump of rushes on board.

"Got anything to eat?" cried Dick, obeying his dominant instinct, and his voice sounded wolfish and strange.

"To eat!—no, sir," cried his father sternly. "What are you doing here?"

"I lost myself, father, and went to sleep—woke up in the darkness, and couldn't stir. Morning, Hicky!"

"Wheer's my poont?" said the wheelwright.

"Close round here somewhere," said Dick. "Go on and we shall find it. But where was the fire?"

The squire drew a hissing breath between his teeth as if in pain, and yet as if in relief; for it seemed to him that once more he was suspecting wrongfully, and that if his son had been mixed up with the past night's outrage he would never have spoken so frankly.

"The fire, boy!" he said hoarsely; "at the Toft. The place is nearly burned down."

"Oh!" ejaculated Dick; and there was so much genuine pain and agony in his voice that the squire grasped his son's hand.

"Never mind, Dick; we'll build it up again."

"Ay, squire, we will," cried Hickathrift; "and afore long."

"And what is better, my boy, we saw the wretch who stole off the mere last night and fired the big reed-stack."

"Yes, father," cried Dick excitedly. "And I heard him come stealing by here."

"You did, Dick?"

"Yes, father—not an hour ago."

"Marston!" cried the squire, hailing the other boat.

"Yes."

"We're right. He came by here an hour ago. Dick heard him."

"You did, Dick?" cried Mr Marston.

"Yes, but it was all in the dark, and I couldn't see who it was."

"That does not matter, my lad," said the squire. "We know him now, and we only want to run him down."

"Know him, father?"

"Yes, boy. It was Dave Gittan."

"Nonsense!"

Dick burst into a laugh.

"Why, father, his place was burned too!"

"Yes, boy, to throw us off the scent—the scoundrel! but we shall have him now."

Dick sat down in the punt like one astounded, while Hickathrift poled along the channel till he came to open water, where, just as the sun rose above the horizon, they caught sight of the tied-up boat.

"We're too many in this," said Hickathrift, making for the other punt. "You pole this here, and I'll tak' mine. Will you come, squire?"

"Yes," said Dick's father; and the change being made, the three boats were now propelled over the sunlit water, where, as the lad gladly applied himself to the food he had left behind, he learned something of what had taken place during the night.

Hickathrift was his informant, for the squire was very stern and silent, and Mr Marston was in one of the other boats, which were manned by drain-men and farm-labourers, and had for leaders Farmer Tallington and the engineer, while many were armed with muskets.

"Is Tom there?" said Dick in a whisper.

"Ay, lad, he's theer," said the big wheelwright, "along o' Mr Marston."

And then in answer to questions he related that Mr Marston had been over at the Toft, and stopped up watching with the squire for Dick's return, dropping asleep at last, and then awakening suddenly to hear a strange noise among the fowls.

The squire went out, followed by Mr Marston, and the truth was before them.

"The big stack was afire!" whispered Hickathrift, "and burning so as they knew it would be impossible to put it out, and just as they realised the terrible state of affairs there was the sound of a shot, and then of another and another from somewhere down among the cottages, and directly after the beating of feet, and a party of the labourers hurried up, startled from their beds.

"'Your turn now, squire,' I says to him," whispered the wheelwright.

"'Ay,' he says, 'my turn now. Who fired that shot?'

"'Oh! some un here,' I says. 'We thought we seed him as did it going off in the poont, but it was so dark we couldn't be sure.'

"Squire didn't ask no more, for there was too much to do getting out your moother, lad, and trying to save the furnitur, 'sides throwing watter on the fire.

"Bud, theer, it warn't no use. Plaäce burned like a bit o' paäper, and we could do nowt bud save the best o' the things."

"Did you save the clock?" asked Dick.

"Ay, lad, I carried it out mysen, just as Mr Marston come oop wi' a lot of his lads, and Farmer Tallington come from t'other way; and we saved all we could, and got out the beasts and horses, but t'owd plaäce is bont out."

"And where is mother?"

"All reight along o' my missus, bless her; and when we see we could do no more, squire began about who done it."

"Yes: go on."

"Well, theer's nowt much to say, lad, only that soon as squire knowd who it weer he—"

"But how did he know who it was?" cried Dick.

"Some un towd him."

"Yes, but who told?"

"Him as fired his goon at him when he see'd him by the light o' the fire poling along in his poont."

"And who was that?"

"Nay, lad, I'm not going to tell thee. Some un as thowt he desarved a shot for setting fire to folks's houses and shooting honest men. Some folk don't stop to think. If they've got goons in their hands, and sees varmen running away, they oops wi' the goon and shutes, and that's what some un did. Thou'lt know who it weer one day."

"And he told my father?"

"It weer our Jacob towd squire. He sin his faäce quite plain, and that it weer Dave."

"Now, Marston, where for next?" shouted the squire, after taking a long look round over the open water, now illumined by the sun.

"Try that island yonder," was the reply. "There's a hut among the low fir-trees, and I fancy it is his making."

The boats were turned in the suggested direction, and Dick felt a curious sensation of nervous dread stealing over him as he thought of seeing that hut not long before, and of how likely it was that Mr Marston was right.

A strange sense of shock and horror came over Dick as he now seemed to realise, for the first time, that he was one of a party engaged in hunting down Dave Gittan, the man who had always been to him as a friend, the companion of endless excursions over the mere; and his heart sank within him as he glanced round in search of an opportunity to land and get away from the horrible pursuit.

But there was no escape, for he knew that the pursuers would not turn backward, and he glanced helplessly at where he could see Tom Tallington's face in the farther of the other boats, and responded to his wave of the hand.

There was a stern relentless look in every face he saw, and he thought of how his father and Mr Marston had been shot, how first one and then another had been nearly burned in his bed, while their property was destroyed, and he felt the justice of the severe looks. But all the same there was a lingering liking for Dave, and he felt disposed to stand up in his defence and say it was impossible that he could have done these things, though all the time, as he ran over the matters in his mind, he began to recall various suspicious incidents, and to think that, perhaps, they were right.

One thing buoyed him up though, and that was the thought that they were not going straight to the decoy-man's hut, and perhaps through this delay he might escape.

It was a vain hope, one which was swept away directly after, for Hickathrift whispered:

"We went straight to his plaäce to try and ketch him, but he slipped away in his poont, and dodged us about in the dark, till Mester Marston held out that he was makking for the far part of the fen, and we followed him theer, but lost all sound on him, and then you know, Mester Dick, we fun you."

With a stern effort to be firm Dick watched the progress of the punt toward the island that was to have been his abode when he felt huffed at home, and wondered whether Dave were there now.

"He isn't there," thought Dick; and he turned to telegraph a look at Tom Tallington, who he felt sure would be as anxious as himself about Dave's escape.

"Do you want Tom Tallington?" said his father, who, though apparently paying no attention, had noted every exchange of glances.

"Yes, father; there is more room here," said Dick boldly.

The squire made a sign to Hickathrift, who ceased poling, and the other two boats came up on either side.

"Come in here, Tom," said Dick eagerly.

Tom obeyed with alacrity and stepped on board, while in short decisive tones the squire spoke:

"We will divide now, and approach on three sides. You, Marston, and you, Tallington, get well over so as to command a view all round, for this man must not escape."

"Escape! No!" said Farmer Tallington fiercely.

"If he is there, I don't think he will escape," said Mr Marston sternly.

"Hah!" ejaculated the squire; "that is one reason why I waited for you both to come up. Now, gentlemen, and you, my good fellows, listen. There must be no violence."

"No violence, eh!" said Farmer Tallington. "Didn't he bon my place?"

"And shoot me?" said Mr Marston sternly.

"Yes, and his is evidently the hand which has committed a score of outrages, but all the same we must act as if we were the officers of the law: seize, bind, and hand him over to justice unhurt."

There was a low murmur from the drain-men in Mr Marston's boat.

"Yes, and that is why I speak," said the squire firmly. "I am leader here, and I insist upon this man being taken uninjured. Let the law deal with him. It is not our duty to punish him for the crimes."

There was another low murmur here, but the squire paid no heed and went on:

"In the first place, not a shot is to be fired."

"Not if he shutes at us?" cried Farmer Tallington.

"No: not even if he fires at any of us. If he should draw trigger, rush in and seize him before he has time to reload, and then, with no more violence than is necessary, let him be bound."

"Well," said Farmer Tallington, "perhaps you're reight neighbour; and as long as he is punished I don't know as I mind much how it's done."

"Then we all understand each other, and you, my men, I shall hold you answerable for any injury this man receives."

"What! Mayn't us knock him down, squire?" grumbled the big wheelwright.

"Of course you may, Hickathrift. Stun him if you like; he will be the easier to bind."

"Hey, that's better, lads," cried the wheelwright, brightening up. "Squire's talking sense now."

"But he'll shoot his sen oop in yon hut, squire, and fire at us and bring us down."

"There will only be time for one shot, Mr Tallington," said Marston quietly, "and we can fetch him out before he has a chance to reload. Mr Winthorpe is right."

"Oh well, I wean't stick out," said the farmer rather sulkily; "but Dave's a rare good shot and one of us will hev to go home flat on his back before we get up to yon wood."

"He will not dare to fire," said the squire firmly.

"I do not agree with you, Mr Winthorpe," said Marston. "The man is desperate, and he will do anything now to escape."

"And if he can't," cried Farmer Tallington, "he'll die like a rat in a corner, biting, so look out. He's got that long gun of his loaded and ready for the first man who goes up to yon hut, and that man arn't me."

"I will go up first," said the squire quietly; "and he will not dare to fire."

"Bud he hev dared to fire, mester," said the wheelwright.

"Yes, at those who did not see him lurking in some hiding-place, but he will not dare to fire now."

"He can't fire, father," cried Dick excitedly.

"Why?"

"Because I have his gun here in the boat."

"What?" cried the squire; and the matter was explained.

There was no further hesitation. The boats divided as if going to the attack upon some fort, and after giving the others time to get well on either side of the island, the squire gave Hickathrift orders to go on, and the punt glided swiftly toward the shore.

"You two boys lie down in the bottom of the boat," said the squire.

"Oh, father!" exclaimed Dick, as Tom slowly obeyed.

"What is it, Dick?"

"It seems so cowardly."

"It is more cowardly to risk life unnecessarily for the sake of bravado," said his father; and then, reading the look upon his son's face, the squire continued with a sad smile:

"I am captain of this little expedition, Dick, and the captain must lead."

Dick never felt half so much inclined to disobey his father before, as he slowly took his place in the bottom of the punt, while Hickathrift sent it forward so quickly that it was the first to touch the gravelly shore. When the squire sprang out Hickathrift followed him, after driving down the pole and securing the boat.

"I say, Tom," said Dick.

"I say, Dick," replied Tom.

"Do you think he would be very cross if we went after them? I do want to see."

Tom shook his head, and, landing, sat down on the edge of the boat, Dick following and seating himself beside his companion, to watch his father steadily approach the hut, of which not so much as a glimpse could be obtained, so closely was it hidden among the trees.

By this time the squire was half-way to the fir-wood, and Dick could bear it no longer.

"How could I meet mother," he cried angrily, "if I let him go alone like that?"

"But he can't be shot," said Tom.

"No, but he may be hurt," retorted Dick; and he ran eagerly after his father.

"And so may my father be hurt," said Tom as soon as he was left alone; and he looked in the direction by which Farmer Tallington must approach the wood, but no one was visible there, and he ran rapidly after his companion and rejoined him just as he was following his father into the wood.

The morning sun shone brilliantly without, but as soon as they were in the wood they seemed to have entered upon a dusky twilight, cut here and there by brilliant shafts and bands which struck the ground in places and made broad patches of golden hue.

No word was spoken, and in the dim wood with the rustling increasing, the scene in some way suggested to Dick the fen during the night when he was listening to the passing of the punt—evidently Dave's—and he fell a-wondering whether the decoy-man was now far away on the other side of the mere.

"That you, squire?" shouted Farmer Tallington from the trees beyond the hut, which now appeared before them, sombre and gloomy, half hidden by the growth.

"Yes, we are here," was the reply.

"He's in here some'ere's, for his poont's ashore."

"Where are you?" came from the other side, and, guided by the voices, Marston soon came up, with his men.

The squire gave a short sharp order, and the two parties separated, so as to surround the little hut. Tom whispered to Dick what he was already thinking.

"Why, Dick, old Dave's as cunning as a rat, and could slip through there easy."

The moment the place was surrounded the squire gave a sharp glance back at his son, stepped forward, stooped down, and entered the low hut.

Hickathrift was close behind him, and the next moment he, too, had disappeared.

"Is he there, Mr Winthorpe?" cried Marston excitedly; and he, too, stepped forward and entered the hut.

"Why, what's it all mean?" said Farmer Tallington impatiently; and he, too, stepped up to the low doorway and entered.

"They're tying his hands and feet, Tom," whispered Dick excitedly; and unable to control himself he ran up to the door, followed by his schoolmate, but as he did so it was to encounter the squire coming out with a peculiarly solemn look upon his countenance.

"Isn't he there, father?" cried Dick wonderingly.

"Yes, boy—no," said the squire solemnly, as the others came slowly out. "He managed to crawl here to die."

Chapter Twenty Seven.

Last Words.

It was a solemn party that returned to the Toft that day: three boats, with the last propelled by Hickathrift, towing another behind. That last punt was Dave Gittan's, and in it, later on, the man was taken to his last resting-place.

At the inquiry it was found that Dave had been mortally wounded by a bullet; and in this state he had managed to force his boat to his hut, and when pursued, to his lurking-place in the farther part of the fen, to lie down and die.

Who fired the shot which took his life? No one could say. Five bullets were sent winging to stop his career on the night of his last insane act, when pretty well everything which would burn upon the Toft was destroyed; but whose was the hand which pulled the trigger, and whose the eye which took the aim, was not divulged.

Dave had well kept his secret, and struggled hard to stay the advance of progress, but fought in vain, and with his fall almost the last opposition to the making of the great drain died out.

There were old fen-men who murmured and declared that the place was being destroyed, but for the most part they lived to see that great drain and others made, and the wild morass become dry land upon which the plough turned up the black soil and the harrow smoothed, and great waving crops of corn took the place of those of reed. Meadows, too, spread out around the Toft, and Farmer Tallington's home at Grimsey—meads upon which pastured fine cattle; while in that part of the wide fen-land ague nearly died away.

It was one evening twenty years later that a couple of stalwart well-dressed men, engineers engaged upon the cutting of another lode or drain many miles to the north, strolled down from the Toft farm to have a chat with the great grey-haired wheelwright, who carried on a large business now that a village had sprung up in the fen.

His delight was extreme to see the visitors, and they had hard work to extricate their ringers from his grip.

"Think of you two coming to see me now! It caps owt."

"Why, of course we've come to see you, Hicky," said the taller of the two. "How well you look!"

128

"Well! Hearty, Mester Dick, bless you! and the missus too. Hearty as the squire and his lady, bless 'em. But your father looks sadly, Mester Tom, sir. He don't wear as I should like to see un. He's wankle." (Sickly.)

"Rheumatism, Hicky; that's all. He'll be better soon. I say, what's that—a summer-house?" said Tom, pointing.

"That, Mester Tom! Why, you know?"

"Why, it's the old punt!" cried Dick.

"Ay, it's the owd poont, Mester Dick. What games yow did hev in her too, eh?"

"Yes, Hicky," said Dick with a sigh. "Ah! those were happy days."

"They weer, lad; they weer. Owd poont got dry and cracked, and of no use bud to go on the dreern, and who wanted to go on a dreern as had been used to the mere?"

"No one, of course," said Dick, gazing across the fields and meadows where he had once propelled the punt.

"Ay, no one, o' course, so Jacob sawed her i' two one day, and we set her oop theer i' the garden for a summer-hoose, and Jacob painted her green. I say, Mester Dick, ony think," added Hickathrift, laughing violently.

"Think what? Don't laugh like that, Hicky, or you'll shake your head off."

"Nay, not I, my lad; but it do mak' me laugh."

"What does?"

"Jacob's married!"

"No!"

"He is, Mester Dick, and theer's a babby."

"Never!" said Dick, laughing, to humour the great fellow, who wiped his eyes and became quite solemn now.

"Yes, that he hes, Mester Dick, and you'd nivver guess what he's ca'd him."

"Jacob, of course."

"Nay, Mester Dick; he's ca'd him Dave."

Dick and Tom went down to the wheelwright's again next day to chat over old times—fishing, shooting, the netting at the decoy, and the like; and heard how John Warren had lately died, a venerable old man, who confessed at last how he had helped Dave Gittan in some of the outrages when the drain was made, because he hated it, and said it would ruin honest men.

But it was not to see John Warren's nor Dave Gittan's grave that Hickathrift led the young men to the one bit of waste land left, and there pointed to a wooden tablet nailed against a willow tree.

"The squire give me leave, Mester Dick, and Jacob and me buried him theer when he died. Jacob painted his name on it, rather rough, but the best he could, and we'd hev put his age on it, as well as the date, if we'd ha' known."

"How old was he, do you think, Hicky?" said Dick.

"Don't know, sir, but straänge and old."

"But why did you take so much interest in him? You never liked the donkey."

"Nay, bud you did, lad, and that was enough for me."

"Poor old Solomon!" said Dick, smiling at the recollections the rough tablet evoked; "how he could kick!"

"And so you and young Tom—I beg pardon, sir," said Hicky, "Mester Tallington—are going to help Mester Marston wi the big dreerning out in Cambridgeshire, eh?"

"Yes, Hicky, ours is a busy life now; but we're beginning to find people more sensible about such matters. Mr Marston was laughing over it the other day, and saying that all the romance had gone out of our profession now there was no chance of getting shot."

"Weer he, now?" said Hickathrift wonderingly. "Think of a man liking to be shot at!"

"Oh, he does not like to be shot at, Hicky! By the way, though, who was it shot Dave Gittan? Come, now, you know."

"Owd Dave Gittan's been buried twenty year, Mester Dick, so let him rest."

"Rest! Of course; but come—you do know?"

"Yes, Mester Dick," said the wheelwright stolidly. "I do know, but I sweered as I'd nivver tell, and I'll keep my word."

"Ah, well, I will not press you, Hicky! It was a sad time."

"Ay, my lads, a sad time when a man maks war like that again his brothers wi' fire and sword, leastwise wi' goon. That theer fen was like a battlefield in them days, while now it's as pleasant a place to look upon as a man need wish to see."

"A lovely landscape, Hicky," said Dick, gazing across the verdant plain.

"Ay, lad, and once all bog and watter, and hardly a tree from end to end."

"A great change, Hicky, showing what man can do."

"Ay, a great change, Mester Dick, but somehow theer are times when I get longing for the black watter and the wild birds, and all as it used to be."

"Yes, Hicky," said Dick almost sadly as he saw in memory's mirror the days of his boyhood; "but this is a world of change, man; we must look forward and not back."

"Ay, Mester, Dick, 'cause all's for the best."

"Yes, Hicky, keep to that—all's for the best! Come, Tom; it's time we said good-bye to the old fen!"

The End.

Printed in Great Britain
by Amazon